# The
# Left-Handed
# God

# The Left-Handed God

## I. J. PARKER

2013

I · J · P

Copyright 2013 by I. J. Parker

Published 2013 by I.J.Parker and I·J·P Books, 428 Cedar Lane, Virginia Beach, VA. 23452.

http://www.ijparker.com

Cover design by I. J. Parker;
 *Cover image Jean-Etienne Liotard, portrait of Mlle Lavergne; 1746.*

The Left-Handed God / I. J. Parker – 1st Ed.
ISBN 978 1493782192

# Acknowledgments

I wrote this novel in 2007 and no longer have records of who read for me, but I thank them nevertheless. In addition, two extremely nice and generous gentlemen answered my questions and sent me material about the battle of Freiberg, the participants, and their uniforms. To Torstein Snorrason and Robert Hall my very special thanks.

This is a work of fiction, but the plot plays out in historical time (1762-1763), touches on historical events (the Seven Years' War in central Europe) and involves several historical characters and actual incidents.

The battle of Freiberg (1762) ended the war between the Imperial forces under Empress Maria Theresa of Austria and the armies of Frederick the Great of Prussia. One of the participating countries was the Kurpfalz (the Palatinate), a small principality in what later became Germany. By this time it had lost much of its ancient significance and was primarily still important because its sovereigns were among those who elected or were elected Holy Roman Emperors. The Kurfürst Karl Theodor and his wife Elisabeth Augusta in this novel are historical figures, and the stories about them are factual. Their palaces are still among the wonders of German Baroque architecture. Mozart really performed at Mannheim and Schwetzingen in 1763, and the famous Doktor Mesmer (who gave his name to "mesmerizing") really grew up on the shores of Lake Constance (Bodensee). Lindau was a free city then, subject only to the Holy Roman Emperor.

I have made slight changes to the names of the villains, but they, too, are based on real characters, and the punishment visited on one of them by Karl Theodor is exactly what happened in 1763. Their crimes are fictional, though believable, given the political climate of the day and their reputations. Karl Theodor seems to have been a forgiving husband who protected his wife's good name even after their separation.

# 1

## Freiberg, October 28, 1762

*God is always on the side of the strongest battalions.*

(Frederick the Great, King of Prussia)

awn was slow in coming on the day of the battle. This late in October the soldiers should
have been in their winter quarters instead of on
this cold hillside in Saxony. The infantrymen lying
about looked ghostly in the gloom, like bodies scattered
by some cataclysmic event. One or two snored. Those
who were awake said little and spoke in subdued voices.
Empty bellies and the knowledge that they might not
live through the coming day kept them quiet. On this
cold and dark night far from home, men's hearts were
full of tears. If they survived, they might be crippled for
life and forced to beg on the street.

Somewhere, horses snorted and scampered, harness metal clinking. A sudden burst of nervous laughter was stifled abruptly. The sun would rise whether those on the hillside wanted it to or not.

They wore the white and red uniforms of Austria, but their regiment was made up of troops from several principalities within the Holy Roman Empire. They had gathered here to defend one of its members, the duchy of Saxony, against the Prussian king. The Prussians were commanded by Prince Heinrich, brother to a king who had already become a legendary commander during the seven years of this war.

That morning only two men on that cold, wooded hillside were impatient for daylight.

The assassin crouched in a thicket to the side of the waiting regiment. His green uniform coat looked black in the darkness. He had borrowed it from one of the supply wagons and wore it because the "green coats" were the sharpshooters and skirmishers who would begin this battle. They were not confined to their companies but moved independently ahead of the rest of the army to take out enemy officers. Like them, he carried a rifle, though his weapon was a far better quality than those issued to ordinary sharpshooters. It rarely failed him.

He had planned carefully and informed himself about the order of battle for the initial engagement. He must not fail, and his success depended on perfect timing, but he had a feeling that his luck was with him.

It was early and still too dark to see details, but he knew that ahead lay the overlook and that at sunrise the plain below would become the battlefield. Somewhere to his left, the Regiment Salzburg would be readying soon, but he had time. He made himself comfortable and waited.


Franz Wilhelm von Langsdorff stood about fifty yards from the assassin. He was twenty years old, an ensign of the Salzburg regiment, and this was his first battle. He was too excited to rest with the men and leaned against a tree, looking northward across the wide plain to the points of light less than two miles away. The Prussian campfires shimmered like a necklace of red stars in the night. They stretched for miles in a wide sweep across the plain below.

Prince Heinrich had caught them unready, still frantically building defensive positions for their guns when night fell. With the coming daylight, the Prussians would seize their advantage and force a decision, perhaps the final decision of this long war.

Franz felt oddly suspended between his two worlds—that of his recent past as a student in Heidelberg and this one as a soldier. He was newly embarked on the military career and felt as naked as a newborn child.

A pastor's son, he had been raised to believe that the world was perfect because it was created by a perfect and benevolent God. So far neither his father's death, nor the sudden curtailment of his studies in Heidelberg, nor their sudden poverty had convinced him otherwise.

He still trusted explicitly in God and believed in His special good will toward him and all men.

M. Voltaire's *Candide* and other godless writings mocked the Deity, but Franz rejected such cynicism toward His creation.

His youth and religious upbringing had something to do with his optimism, but at the moment more pagan ideals buoyed his spirit. He was Hektor, bearing a hard duty heroically. He was Achilles, filled with a righteous anger against his enemies. He was Odysseus, the patient, clever one, who succeeded and survived against all odds. He would prove himself worthy today of carrying the regimental flag and leading his men into battle.

"Sir?"

Franz started and looked down at the regiment's drummer boy. His name was Carl and he was freckle-faced and slight at fourteen. He had attached himself to the new ensign, perhaps because they were close in age. Franz had been told to discourage familiarity with the men and now he frowned. "Aren't you a long way from your place?" he asked. "And where is your drum?"

The boy grinned, his face a pale shadow in the gloom. "Plenty o' time, sir. It won't start till daylight."

Franz glanced at the eastern horizon and thought he saw a slight brightening above the tree line. He felt a pang of envy. For all his youth, Carl had seen more battles than he. The boy had lived with the regiment for two years already. Proof was the grimy and ragged condition of his white uniform. The Salzburg regiment wore white coats with crimson cuffs and linings, white breeches, red vest, black tricornes, and black, buttoned gaiters. The Austrian colors were striking, but they did not stay presentable very long on a campaign, and most of the regiment had fought and marched for seven years now.

"Are you scared, sir?" the boy asked.

"No," Franz snapped, then was sorry he had spoken so harshly. It was all very well for grown men to fight battles, but Carl was a mere child. Boys his age belonged in school, not on the battlefield. He wanted to say so, but that would not do at all. He said instead, "And you mustn't be afraid either. We will win today."

"How do you know, sir?"

"What do you mean? Of course, we'll win. God is on our side. The Prussian invaders will be stopped and driven back where they belong."

The boy gave a snort. "The men don't think so, sir. Old Fritz is a stubborn bastard, and his brother's just like him. The men say it'll be a bloody day." He paused, then added with morbid gusto, "And we'll get slaughtered, being right in front like this."

What he meant was that Salzburg had been ordered early to this hillside within sight of the Prussian camp because they would be among the first to march into battle. Moreover, ensigns and drummers tended to walk in the first lines of an infantry regiment. Franz swallowed and pushed the thought away. "Nonsense! Just march forward and drum up a good measure to give the soldiers heart. They'll take care of the rest."

"Yeah. But I wish it were over." The boy fell silent. After a pause, he said, "They've got a lot of fires, don't they? They say more troops've come overnight.

There's talk of fifty thousand of 'em. They're devils in a fight. The men don't have much relish for it."

There it was again. The mood in the regiment was shocking, but Franz was not going to acknowledge this. He looked toward the Prussian camp. Were there fewer campfires than before? Were they putting them out already? He checked the east again. Yes, the sky was lightening to a charcoal gray that was not much more cheerful than the pitch black night that had preceded it. "You must go back," he said, his heart beating a little faster. "The sun will be up soon."

Carl snorted again. Franz tried to see his expression. He felt sorry for the youngster. Drummer boys were often the sons of common soldiers by the women who followed the army. The men made a pet out of Carl because he was small and had not yet lost his boyish looks. Franz wondered if he had lied about his age. He looked like an eleven-year old.

Carl's eyes met his defiantly. "Well, good luck then, sir," he said and scampered off.

"God's blessings on you, Carl," Franz called after him and heard a stifled guffaw from a soldier. He had caught their sneers and sniggers before when he had wished them "God's speed," and yet they were almost to a man superstitious, practicing all sorts of heathen rituals to protect themselves against death and injury. It did not matter to them that he had a good education and an officer's training, meager though the latter had been. They knew that this was his first battle and that he might blunder and take them into harm's way.

Only a month before, the recruiters in Heidelberg had paid him the princely sum of one hundred and forty *taler* to serve in this war. They made him an ensign because of his year at the university and the "von" in his name. Then they had deducted forty-five *taler* for his uniform. He had not minded that expense because the uniform brought him melting glances from pretty young women he was too shy to approach. The remainder of the money, along with a loving letter, he had posted to his mother and sister in Lindau. Then he had hopped a mail coach to the battle fields.

In Hof, he reported to General Luszinsky, and presented his orders.

The general had looked at him and frowned. "You're from the Kurpfalz? Are they so pressed for able-bodied men that they send us children?"

Aware of his new and still much too thin mustache, Franz blushed, but he stiffened his back and said, "I am twenty, sir."

The general had sighed and smiled a little. "Very well, Ensign. You will join the Seventh Company of the Infantry Regiment Salzburg. Regiment Salzburg is made up of different companies, the Seventh being from the Kurpfalz. Field Marshall Serbelloni has ordered Austrian uniforms for everyone."

So Franz's handsome light blue and white Kurpfalz regimentals were packed away. In theory, the Austrian uniform should have been quite as handsome, except that his was secondhand, taken off the wounded or dying, and of summer-weight cotton. But one of the women who followed every army had washed and mended it and made some alterations for a small amount of money, and he was quite content with his appearance. Though he shivered a little in the cold this morning, his spirits were high.

The same could not be said of the men of the Seventh Company, who were discouraged, tired, and sullen, their uniforms dirty and ragged, their shoes and gaiters muddy from marching on rain-drenched roads churned up by wagons, horses, and the heavy guns. They had fought Prussians and Russians all over Eastern Europe and spent the past three weeks crossing and recrossing Württemberg and Sachsen to no apparent purpose. Once or twice they had briefly engaged the enemy, but both sides had parted without decisive action.

Today would be different. Today, two large armies would clash in the open country outside Freiberg.


The assassin blew on his cold hands, then checked his pocket watch. Less than an hour until daylight. He was aware of the position of the seventh on the wooded hillside near him and knew their eyes would be glazed from lack of sleep and their mood bitter from lack of proper food. They would not be fed this morning either, and last night's ration had been a scant piece of rough dark bread. Provisions ran low in a war-ravaged country, and they would have had no time to steal or hunt so close to the enemy.

But neither their discomfort nor the outcome of the coming battle concerned him. He would take measures to stay alive as soon as he had done what he had come to do. His plan was brilliantly simple. All eyes would be on the enemy, the advance action would cover the sound of a single shot, and one more body would attract no interest once the battle had started.

Franz, too, was hungry, but his belly was warmed by the excitement of coming battle. He touched the grip of his sword. This day fate beckoned, and Franz wanted glory with every fiber of his body, knew it would be his, saw himself already victorious, carried on the shoulders of his men, congratulated by his commanding officer, promoted and decorated for his valor. He would return a hero, and Mama would shed tears of joy and his sister Augusta would look at her big brother with admiring eyes.

The men were coming awake now and getting to their feet. Some talked, a couple cursed, and someone hacked and spat. He could smell tobacco. The men smoked their clay pipes in lieu of breakfast.

Franz cast another look at the lightening sky, then took up the standard of his flag and went among them, counting every man, making sure they had loaded their muskets and fixed their bayonets. They tolerated this without the usual smirks and muttered comments, but he saw in their faces that they did not respect him. They held his youth and inexperience against him.

He worried briefly about this. But he was an officer, though the lowest ranking of the officers, and they would have to follow him, follow the flag he would carry. They probably feared that, in his inexperience, he would lead them into disaster. There had been the drummer boy's warning. If they decided to run today, where would be his glory? With God's help he hoped to prove to them—and to himself—that he was brave and a good officer.

When he had finished his inspection, he returned to his lookout. It was much lighter now, and things stirred. Several officers passed at a gallop. A cavalry regiment gathered on the next hillside, and at the unfinished gun placements, the gunners were building some last-minute reinforcements, moving another cannon into place, and carrying buckets of water.

Between the rolling hills and the enemy camp the ground sloped gently downward. The Prussian lines extended from the village Lang Hennersdorf southward. Two roads to Freiberg lay between the imperial position and the Prussian army. One led from Lang Hennersdorf, the other from the hamlet of Klein Schirma through the Spittal Woods. The fields lay fallow at this time of year, but a farm or two, a few stands of trees and some shacks dotted them here and there. Toward the west more hills rose, and toward the east, beyond the imperial positions, lay the small town of Freiberg.

Franz could see troops behind the Prussian lines, reserves, an indistinct roiling of dark bodies among the white tents. The Prussians had dark blue uniforms and were easy to tell apart from the Austrians' white but not so easily distinguishable from some of their allies—like the Bavarians and the dragoons and cuirassiers of the Kurpfalz, who also wore blue.

He had not yet learned to identify all the uniforms of troops gathered here under the command of Field Marshal, Prince von Stolberg. The colors were handsome but confusing. The dragoons from Pfalz-Zweibrücken wore red and yellow, but those from Württemberg blue and yellow. The Hungarian hussars had light blue breeches with dark green jackets, or red with dark blue, or with light green, and they had short, fur-trimmed jackets slung over their left shoulders. The hussars spoke hardly any German, drank like fish, and wore their dark hair in long curls or braids on either temple, like girls—a very strange sight with their large stiffened mustaches.

A number of mounted staff officers rode into Franz's field of vision and stopped on the small promontory to survey through their telescopes the terrain and the enemy's preparations. Franz recognized General Luszinsky. He commanded the infantry regiments "Salzburg," "Würzburg" and "Varell." With him were Generals Vecsey of the cavalry and Kleefeld of the Austrian advance guard, and their aides.

Sometimes Franz wished he were a dragoon or cuirassier. They looked very dashing on their fine horses. But at least he was not an artillery officer or sapper who could do nothing but point their guns and fire. Once in place they were immovable and, if overrun by the enemy, they had to abandon their positions and run for it. No, the infantry was the place to be. It was the fist that punched the enemy in the belly, forcing them back, separating their columns, and making them easy prey for cavalry swords.

He watched the generals, trying to guess from their gestures what they were planning. He knew the green-coated sharpshooters would begin the battle. They would try to kill the enemy's officers and thus disable their regiments early on. He had seen one of them pass through their own ranks during the night and wondered about it at the time, but the man would have found his place by now.

Strangely, he still felt no fear at all, not even when the long Prussian infantry columns formed in the distance. God was with the just cause.

It was time. The light was not perfect but quite good enough. The assassin crept up behind the fallen oak, gauged the distance once more, and found it still right. He knelt and raised his rifle, sighted, and nodded to himself. It was one of the new wheel lock rifles made by a master gunsmith in Switzerland. He drew a cartridge from his pocket—he carried only two and did not expect to need the second. Biting off the end of the paper cover, he took the bullet between his teeth, then poured a pinch of the powder into the priming pan, and closed the frisson. The rest of the powder went into the barrel, followed by the paper, and the whole thing was tamped down firmly. The bullet went in next—he spit it down the barrel—and was tamped down again. Then he rested the barrel on the fallen tree, pulled back the cock, and was ready.

Any moment now his man would appear. He slowed his breathing. It would be a tricky shot—a moving target was always difficult—but he was close enough and the angle was good. And while he was still in the shadows and hidden by the trunk and branches, his victim would be in the open. In a matter of minutes, perhaps seconds, he would move into his sights.

On the promontory, General Luszinsky separated from his colleagues and their aides, and turned his horse to gallop back. As he passed in front of Franz, the general's eye brushed over him and the soldiers of the Seventh. He swerved to an abrupt halt before Franz.

"You look familiar. What's your name?" he snapped, looking from the glum-faced, slouching figures of the men to Franz.

His heart beating faster, Franz saluted. "Ensign von Langsdorff, sir. We met in Hof a few weeks ago."

Luszinsky stared at him for a moment. "Are these men yours, Ensign?"

Franz thought of their disreputable appearance and reddened. "Some of them, sir."

"Some of them? Don't you know?"

"I do know, sir. All of us belong to the Infantry Regiment Salzburg, sir. I am with the company from Kurpfalz."

The bewhiskered face softened slightly. "Ah. Kurpfalz. Right. Some of your dragoons and cuirassiers are also here today. How old are you?"

"Twenty, sir."

"You look younger. And you have just started your service?"

"Yes, sir. Three weeks ago, sir." Franz felt a little resentful that he had been forgotten so soon, but then generals were busy people.

The general still stared down at him. "*Ils sont fou!*" he muttered. "*Des enfants!* Children to take men into battle. You have not seen any action, Ensign?"

Franz felt his ears burn. "Not yet, sir. But I completed my course in Heidelberg with honors. And I hope to do well today."

"*Mon dieu!*" The general gave a sharp laugh, then sobered abruptly. "I hope you do, Ensign. I hope you do. Your commanding officers should have lined up the men. No doubt they will take care of their duties shortly." He gestured toward the plain. "See those Prussian columns?" Franz nodded. "They will advance against you, and you will exchange fire. Do you know the drill?"

Franz straightened his shoulders. "Yes, sir."

"Very well, then. Just do your duty. Don't try to be a hero."

"No, sir. I mean . . ." Franz broke off helplessly.

The general looked at the men again. "Someone go and get the officers," he bellowed, "and the rest line up. You look like a damned herd of cattle."

They scrambled, found their places, and presented reasonably organized lines.

Luszinsky shook his head and turned back to Franz. "Remember, Ensign," he said in a lower voice, "no heroics. If you desert your place to engage the enemy, you will risk the colors, and with the colors gone, the men will run."

Franz nodded, ashamed that he had thought to use his sword.

A sudden burst of rifle fire made him jump. On the plain below him strange puffs of smoke blossomed. Franz gaped at them. The general cursed in Polish and spurred his horse to gallop back to the general staff. A cavalry officer crossed in front of him at a trot, and he checked momentarily. Franz heard the crack of another rifle shot from the line of trees to his right and turned his head.

A horse screamed, then someone shouted. When Franz swung around again, the general staff was galloping off in all directions. The cavalry officer's horse had unseated its rider. His foot was caught in a stirrup as it dragged him away.

Franz was still staring after him when the middle-aged sergeant shouted, "Hurry up, sir. The skirmishers have started. We'll be moving right away."

Franz ran. He remembered the colors and pulled them from their leather cover, shaking out the blue silk with the emblem of the virgin as he ran, and fixed them to the standard with shaking fingers. Then he took his place in front of the line. The battle had started.

Riflemen, green-coats from both armies, moved across the open ground toward each other, flinging themselves to the ground to fire, then running again. Where they found them, they used shrubs, ditches, stacks of rotting hay, a tumbled down barn for cover.

They were called *Jaeger* because they were recruited from hunters. Their rifles carried farther and were more precise than the muskets issued to the infantry. They had to take out as many of the officers and ensigns as possible before the columns moved. To protect the colors, each ensign had a sergeant assigned to him to step in his place if he fell.

On the Prussian side, a blare of a trumpet was followed by a rattle of drumbeats, faint at first, then louder as the tambours and pipers joined in. The Prussian advance had begun. Salzburg still waited, listening to the cacophony of musical notes and gunfire. Bullets passed over Franz's head and flicked into the grassy ground. Once someone cried out behind him. Franz hoped the command to advance would come soon. He did not relish standing there being shot at.

In the town of Freiberg the church bell struck seven. It seemed earlier. The sun had finally come up but could not pierce the thick cloud cover or the brown haze from campfires. The battlefield was cast in a dismal twilight.

Then a strip of cloud broke apart, and a fierce sulfur-yellow light fell over the land. The advancing Prussian uniforms looked green in this light. They were already much closer than Franz had thought.

"Salzburg will advance!"

The command came from the rear, repeated by subalterns and sergeants through the ranks. Franz straightened his back, held the colors more firmly, and glanced down the line of men beside him. The drum struck up, the fifers fifed, and they began to march.

They moved in tight formation, in lockstep to the rhythm of the drummers and pipers.

Franz kept his eye on the Prussian column General Luszinsky had pointed out. They were headed toward each other and nothing could stop them, not even the enemy fusiliers. When someone was hit, the others stepped over him and closed ranks.

Elsewhere more drum rolls joined in. The regimental flag flapped in the wind, and a great exultation of sound and fury seized Franz. He could feel the same surge of excitement in the men with him. Someone cheered. The drum beat quickened and Franz marched faster. They kept step beside him, behind him. The ground was even and descended toward the enemy. Franz felt the steady boom, boom, da-boom, boom boom, da-boom of the drum in his blood. His heart beat to the rhythm. His eyes were fixed on the enemy line. Was it less than one hundred yards yet? That was when he would order them to start firing.

More bullets whistled past, another man screamed, and someone else cursed loudly. His sergeant shouted, "Close rank," and they moved on without missing a step. Franz stared at the approaching Prussian line. Any moment now. As soon as I can make out the Prussian dogs' faces, he thought, as soon as I see the color of their eyes. He wished he had a musket. They were only fifty yards apart now.

Varel's regiment to their right stopped to release its first volley. Then the Prussians halted. Through the noise, Franz heard their own sergeant's shout, "Halt!"

Franz came to a stop, stepped aside, and called out, "Front rank, kneel!" His voice squawked, but they obeyed anyway. He took a breath. "Aim! And . . . fire!" The crashing sound nearly deafened him, and acrid smoke burned his eyes. "Second rank . . . aim and fire!" Another volley. Before he could call, "Third rank!" a Prussian volley raised a din of screams among his men and shouts from the sergeant to close ranks. Franz closed his mind to everything but the sequence of commands.

He shouted. They knelt, they aimed, they fired. Then they reloaded, and those behind them fired over their heads. Taking turns, they went through the familiar motions in practiced sequence, delivering a barrage of ragged fire. Someone screamed, fell forward, and another man took his place.

Franz squinted through the smoke. Impossible to gauge enemy casualties. The volleys crackled painfully against his eardrums, and the smoke burned his nose and made his eyes water. The Prussians exchanged volley for volley, and he knew the lines were too close to miss each other. On both sides, sergeants shouted again and again to close ranks, and bullets whistled and struck the ground at his feet.

He wondered if he was invulnerable—caught in a dream. He no longer knew where he was, just that he must stand with his colors and shout orders to fire until it was time to advance again.

A mounted officer appeared out of the smoke beside him. "Are you deaf?" he shouted from his height, "Left! Turn left! Now!" and wheeled away. Franz stared after him, bewildered. The order was passed on by others, and the men scrambled up and turned, running at a trot, bayonets pointing forward, and Franz, clutching the colors, finally moved, caught up, still confused and lost.

When the smoke cleared a little, he saw the Prussian cavalry bearing down on them. Someone shouted, "The hussars. Form square! Form square!"

The men struggled to change their lines into a hollow square bristling with bayonets, but it was too late. The enemy was already upon them, wild-eyed horses, huge and powerful, forcing their way into their ranks, hooves flailing, running men down, their riders shouting and slashing down with curved sabers.

Franz found himself surrounded by soldiers using their bayonets to defend the regimental colors. The air was filled with the screams of horses and men.

A Prussian hussar on an enormous black horse forced his way toward them, his eyes on the colors, teeth flashing white under his mustache. His saber slashed and men fell or jumped away, and suddenly there was nothing between Franz and the hussar.

Franz clutched the standard to himself with his left hand and drew his sword. Somehow, he remembered to jump clear to the rider's left and to strike upward. He missed. The hussar swung his horse about and came again. Franz waited, twisting aside again at the last moment. The hussar delivered a glancing cut to Franz's left shoulder, but Franz cut the man's right thigh. The hussar wheeled, and this time he tried to run Franz down. The horse reared above him. One of its flailing hooves caught the side of Franz's head. He felt the colors torn from his hand and began to fall through a red mist. The noise, the stench of blood, the pain reached a crescendo, then died away.

The assassin did not join the battle. As soon as he had hit his mark, he left the woods, abandoning the green coat on the way. A little later, he reported to his commanding officer in his regular uniform.

His superior was watching the progress of the battle through his glass and shook his head. "Salzburg's in retreat. I knew they were hopeless. A ragtag regiment made up of children and old men." He collapsed the glass. "No point in risking more men. We're pulling back. Tell Marshall Stolberg we'll halt at Burkersdorf and then follow us."

The assassin saluted and watched the general ride away. He was not surprised. The old man did not want honors; he wanted to protect his regiment to sell the men's services for the next battle.

He scanned the confused battlefield. The Prussians seemed to be everywhere, and the action had moved westward. It would take only a few minutes to make sure he had not missed, but he might get caught up in the fighting. He decided to postpone it.

When Franz came to, he lay on his back. Heavy gray clouds scudded across the sky. He heard thunder and thought *I must get up and go inside. I must close the shutters because Mama is frightened of thunder and lightning.* But he felt too tired. After a little, the thunder began to sound strange. Something told him that he was not at home, was not lying in the grass of their garden. And this was not thunder. This was artillery fire.

His head hurt, but he turned it and looked. He was alone. Both armies, infantry and cavalry, had disappeared as if swept away by a storm. Instead the muddy field was covered with bodies of men and horses. More men than horses—proof that regiment Salzburg had been defeated by the enemy cuirassiers.

Memory returned slowly. The noise of battle now came from a distance, punctuated by the booming of heavy artillery. Franz heard it through a curtain of pain. There were other sounds nearby: a man wept, another moaned, a third cried for help.

Franz looked back at the gray sky and took stock of himself. He felt blood on his face and seeping down his back. The worst pain was in his head. It throbbed mercilessly. He tried to roll onto his side, felt a violent bout of nausea, and almost passed out. After that, he lay very still and concentrated on the rest of his body. Something was wrong with his left arm. It felt wet, stiff, and numb all the way to his fingers. His legs seemed all right, though. He moved each foot at the ankle, and then bent his knees. His right arm was merely sore, and the palm of his hand felt raw.

That was when he comprehended that he had lost the colors and wept. His failure was monumental. Within minutes of engagement, he had lost that which he should have guarded with his life. He had lost the colors because he had not given the order to turn and form square in time. With the colors lost, the men had run.

Shame overwhelmed him, but it also gave him the strength to sit up. He looked around, fell back twice, but eventually managed to get to his feet. The dizziness caused him to vomit, but he felt a little better for it. The colors were gone, but he found his sword and staggered toward the sounds of battle. When he passed the first body, he saw a dreadful saber wound across the man's face and averted his eyes. The next man was still alive, but in his chest a single wound had opened like a blossom and turned the white cloth of his uniform red. The soldier stared up at Franz with glazed eyes. "*Mutter?*" he whimpered. "*Bist du's, Mutter? Es tut so weh.*"

Franz stammered, "*Gleich*—in a moment. It will be better in a moment."

The man smiled and closed his eyes. Franz looked around for help, but he was the only one standing. When he looked back down, the man was dead. Would his mother be told, or would she wait for months and years for the son who would never come home again? He turned away and stumbled on among the wounded and dying, sometimes stopping to pray with them or give assurances of help that would not come in time.

Along that terrible route, his head cleared a little, and he became aware of the saber cut in his upper left arm. The cut had opened again when he tried to help one of the wounded, and the blood now ran down over his hand, but it seemed to be a mere flesh wound.

Then he saw the drum and the small body curled around it. Afraid, he went closer. One of Carl's hands still clutched the stick; the other was flung out to the side, a child's hand. The boy's head lay a few steps away, his tricorne near it. A frail child's slender neck was no obstacle to a sharp saber swung by a powerful hussar's arm. Carl's eyes were wide open, staring into the distance. There had not been time for the child to cry out for his mother or father.

Franz turned away. The tears of his shame and grief poured again, and his stomach heaved. This time he nearly blacked out when he vomited. He straightened, his face blubbered with tears, mucus, and vomit, and he wiped it with his sleeve. Then he started looking for his regiment.

The battlefield had shifted to the south and west. The infantry now fought for the small hillock someone had called *Trois Croix*. The Prussian and imperial cavalry were engaged near the Spittal Woods.

Sword in hand, Franz started toward *Trois Croix*. Three crosses. Golgotha. He had lost the colors and did not want to live without at least an attempt to redeem himself.

Almost immediately he came across another casualty, a captain. He lay on his back. Franz recognized the light blue and white uniform of the Kurpfalz dragoons and stopped beside him. The wounded man was still alive, his eyes fixed hopefully on Franz.

"Thank God," he said. His voice was fairly strong and sounded desperate. "Can you help me?"

Franz knelt to look for wounds, saw blood stains only on the white trouser leg, and said, "It doesn't look too bad, sir. Just a leg wound. Someone will come soon. I must get back to my unit. I'm with the Salzburg Seventh."

The officer was not much older than Franz. He snapped, "Don't be a fool, Ensign. I'm done for. Shot in the back. Can't move my limbs. Reach into my coat and take out the letter. You're from the Seventh? From Kurpfalz?"

Franz had just realized that this must be the same officer who had been dragged by his horse earlier and was distracted by the fact that the back of the captain's head was a mass of blood and raw flesh. "Surely," he said, "it's just temporary. Perhaps the effect of the blow to the head."

The young officer closed his eyes for a moment. "Don't waste my time. I'm dying. Take the letter. Take it to my father. I'm Christian von Loe. Promise you'll do that?"

Franz put his hand inside the coat and found the letter. It was bloodstained, and the officer's shirt felt soaked with blood. He doubted he would survive this day himself, but there was no point in arguing. "I promise," he said, putting the letter inside his own coat, "but when you find that you've been mistaken, I shall return it to you. God be with you." He gave the officer an encouraging smile and grasped his right hand. It lay cold and unresponsive in his, but the bloodless lips murmured, "Thank you, Ensign. Be careful. Guard the letter with your life."

It was a strange request, but Franz was already up and running toward the action again. Somehow, he found soldiers from his regiment with another unit. They were in disarray, firing listlessly at a company of Prussian infantry without making much headway. Franz picked up an abandoned musket but dropped it again. His left arm was too stiff to load and aim a gun, even if he had bullets, powder, and flint.

A moment later a stray cannon ball tore through the lines, wreaking such bloody havoc that bits of human flesh landed near him. The other company turned and ran, the men from the Seventh joining them. Franz shouted, "Stop, you cowards! Stand and fight!"

Some of the Seventh turned and came back. Others followed. To Franz's amazement, they still obeyed an order. His order!

He waited, sword in his good hand and his bloody left arm hanging by his side. He knew he must be a shocking sight with his blood-covered face and coat. When there were enough men, he raised his sword. "Form line and advance!" They cheered. His sword raised high, he took them up the hill at a run to where a company of Bavarians were in hand-to-hand combat with Prussian dragoons. His men fell upon the dragoons with sword and bayonets to the cheers of the Bavarian soldiers.

It was butchery. The enemy fought for every inch of ground. Franz used his sword viciously, furiously—for the drummer boy Carl and for the young man who would never see his mother again. He shouted his fury and was filled with a strange joy. When a big Prussian sergeant stepped in his way, Franz cut open his belly and was past him before the man doubled over and fell. A Prussian officer was next. Sword against sword.

The other man was an experienced soldier, but Franz parried and slashed, and severed the man's sword hand. The officer, a captain with a small gray mustache and soft blue eyes, could have been Franz's father. He stood, cradling the bleeding stump with his left arm and waited, looking calmly at Franz from his blue eyes. Perhaps he intended to surrender, but Franz had no time to discuss the matter. He ran him through and saw a look of astonishment, almost of outrage at a betrayal, on the dying man's face.

But Franz had to jump aside because a Prussian soldier roared his rage and rammed a bayonet toward his belly. "You bastard!" the man screamed. "You killed him and him without a weapon!" He came at Franz, sobbing and cursing, and Franz half-turned and slashed his throat.

And so he hacked, slashed, and yelled along with his men until the Prussians backed away from this madman to look for easier prey.

Half-dazed with exhaustion and sickened by the bloodshed, Franz finally paused, lowered his sword, and looked around. They had taken *Trois Croix*.

At the moment of his triumph, something took his legs from under him. He fell hard. Before the darkness took him, he knew the battle was over for him.

When the assassin got to his victim, the battle was over. The hillside and plain below lay deserted except for corpses and abandoned gear. Several hundred yards away, some medics bent over the wounded, but the body he wanted was much closer. He found it quickly, made sure the man was dead, then searched him.

Nothing. He straightened with a frown when a voice asked, "A friend of yours, Lieutenant?"

A Catholic priest stood by his side and looked at him curiously.

He nearly jumped but controlled himself with an effort. "Yes, Father. I looked for something to send to his family but found nothing."

"Ah. I saw him talking to another officer earlier. He seemed not too badly wounded so I delayed," said the priest and sighed. "Now it's too late."

The assassin stared at him. "Do you know the man he talked to?"

"No, but he was an Austrian officer. An ensign, I believe. And yes, I think there was a letter. Or some papers at least. The Austrian took them and walked straight back into the fighting. A brave young man. They're all brave young men." The priest bent to mark the cross on the dead man's body.

Mouthing a curse, the assassin left.

# 2

# 1763 Lindau

*A woman is a lonely, solitary creature without a man.*

Thomas Shadwell (1642-92)

Augusta Anna von Langsdorff pulled her woolen shawl more closely around her and reached into the darning basket by her feet for another pair of woolen stockings. Her mother dozed in the large chair next to the kitchen stove, an open Bible on her lap. The cat *Volteur* slept curled up on the pillow behind her mother's head—making a large gray and black fur cap for his mistress. Between them, these two seemed to absorb all of the feeble warmth that came from the small fire on the hearth.

Augusta cast an impatient glance at her mother. It was ridiculous not to have enough wood to warm at least the kitchen properly on New Year's Day. The *Kachelofen* in their parlor, a handsome tiled stove that could be stoked from the kitchen, had been unused all winter. Instead, they huddled here. This past autumn, before the snows came, Augusta had wanted to gather kindling in the woods. She had borrowed their neighbor's tall basket to strap on her back, but when her mother found out, she had forbidden it. The thought that a von Langsdorff would be seen at such menial work, "work that was only done by poor old women and maids", scandalized her.

Poor old women indeed! They were as poor as anyone in Lindau. And when it came to maids, Augusta could have gone into service two years ago when she turned sixteen. She would have been warmer, and certainly better fed.

Augusta pushed the wooden darning egg impatiently into the next stocking, threaded the needle with black wool and started the weaving which would fill the large hole she had worn into the heel. Regardless of how neatly she darned her stockings, they ended up with clumsy welts of wool that rubbed her heels raw. It seemed unfair that she should have been born to a name that obligated its owner to the pretense of nobility without a commensurate income.

Not that there was anything very noble in her background. Her father had been a younger son in a family that had converted early to the Protestant faith. The religious wars of the past century had cost them most of their lands but, being a stubborn breed, they persisted, passing their small holding and title to the oldest son, sending the next to the university to become a clergyman, and any others into the military.

Augusta and her brother loved their father deeply, but Pastor von Langsdorff had been an unworldly man without ambition, too caught up in his studies of religious writings to inspire his congregation with rousing sermons, and too improvident to gain their respect. His charities were indiscriminate and when they exceeded his own purse, he spent freely from the tithes. The church elders demanded his dismissal when they discovered that their money had benefited poor Jews and Catholics. The Langsdorff family left the large parsonage in Heidelberg and moved into this modest house in the Fischergasse in Lindau.

The shock of his unexpected dismissal had been so great that Pastor von Langsdorff suffered a stroke. Not even the beauty of the lake and the gentle climate could heal the wound to his trust in God. He lingered a year as an invalid, then died.

Their house was part of his wife's dowry and survived their father's charitable disposition. There was barely enough money left to send Franz to the university in Heidelberg.

When Pastor von Langsdorff's pension ceased with his death, Augusta had offered to go into service. Her mother would not permit this and sold her jewelry and the family pictures, as well as their father's library and some of the furniture. But those funds eventually also ran out. Franz had left the university to go to war, and now the money he had sent was also mostly gone. Augusta bit her lip. How could their mother have permitted Franz to offer up his life to her foolish pride?

Frau von Langsdorff made a sudden sound very much like her husband's final death rattle, causing the cat to wake and hiss, and Augusta to stick the needle into her finger. Her mother mumbled something, then started snoring gently, her chin resting on the lace fichu at the neck of her black silk gown.

*Volteur* arched his back, cast a baleful look at Augusta, and jumped down, stalking off with his tail twitching. Franz had given him his name; it was French for "Jumper" and sounded like "Voltaire," her brother's favorite author. The cat was forever bounding up to the tops of shelves and wardrobes, whence he would look down at them with a disdainful expression.

"Bother!" muttered Augusta and sucked her bleeding finger. Thick darning needles hurt when rammed into the fleshy part of one's forefinger. She resented her mother for leading this dull, sedentary existence when she was in perfectly good health. Augusta was young and active and did not want to spend her life sitting by the fire, mending stockings. Sunday church service was about the only outing she ever got. If only Papa had not died.

She sighed, gathered up the sock and finished darning it. Then she let the wooden egg slip out and fall to the tiled floor. The crash sounded like a shot, and the egg rolled under the stove. Frau von Langsdorff's head jerked up.

"Wha—someone's at the door. Go to the window and see. Dear me. I hope it's nobody."

She meant nobody of consequence, and Augusta was about to tell her there had been no knock when there really was. She ran to the parlor to peer out through the front window, then went back to report, "It's only Herr Seutter, Mama."

Her mother jumped up. "*Only* Herr Seutter? A man who sits on the city council?" Her hands fluttered helplessly between her dress and her cap as she looked around the kitchen. "How do I look? Oh, dear, I wish there were a fire in the *salon*. What shall we do?" She patted her cap in a distracted manner.

The *salon* was the parlor. Augusta saw no point in giving simple rooms French names. "He'll have to come in here," she said practically. "Maybe he won't stay."

Her mother cast up her eyes. "How rude you are! We have little enough company, and Herr Seutter is an important man. It is kind of him to call on us. We must be pleasant."

The knock came again. Augusta sighed and turned to let their guest in.

"Augusta!" wailed her mother. "Put away that basket of mending. Do you want him to think we live like common people? It's bad enough we don't have a girl to answer the door."

Augusta moved the basket into a corner.

"And take off that apron."

Augusta removed the apron and dropped it into the basket.

Her mother looked at her with a frown. "That dress is getting much too short. I can see your ankles."

It was also getting too tight across the chest, but Augusta only said, "Shorter skirts are quite the style, Mama."

The knocking was repeated.

"Go! Hurry! What are you waiting for? The poor man will think he isn't welcome."

Augusta opened the front door to a snowy street. Jakob Seutter, in a brown, fur-trimmed cloak and cocked hat, stood on the doorstep, looking every inch the substantial burgher. He raised the hat with a flourish. "Good morning, *Fräulein* Augusta," he boomed. "I see you're your usual beauteous self this fine day."

He was a large man. Bourgeois substantiality, no doubt. As if proud of his broad chest, he fancied bright, embroidered vests. Today's was yellow silk sprinkled with blue forget-me-nots. Augusta quickly raised her eyes to his red face. "Good morning, Herr Seutter," she said, suppressing a giggle. "I hope I see you well."

"Very well indeed," he said with satisfaction. "I called to deliver my New Year's wishes to your mother and your pretty self." He made a sweeping gesture, revealing a small boy in the street below him. The child clutched a basket that seemed larger than he. "Come, Hanserl, don't stand there like a dolt. Bring it in, bring it in."

The child was about eight or nine and looked blue with cold. Augusta stepped aside quickly, but Herr Seutter walked in first, cast a glance toward the parlor, saw it dim, empty, and cold, and said, "I thought you and your Mama would be in need of cheering up on New Year's Day."

The boy managed to stagger up the steps. Augusta went to help him, but before she could, his half-frozen fingers slipped, and the basket crashed on the stone floor. The contents clinked in protest, and Herr Seutter was upset. "Careful, Hans. I hope you haven't broken anything." He bent to check the basket while Augusta closed the door on an icy blast of air.

The boy whimpered, "S-sorry, s-sir. I didn't mean to do it. It s-slipped." His teeth chattered as he breathed on his stiff hands.

"I'm sure all is well," Augusta said quickly. "I'm afraid in your great generosity you have overestimated the child's strength, sir. He looks frozen. You must both come into the kitchen and warm yourselves. It's bitterly cold outside."

"Nonsense." Herr Seutter abandoned the basket, took off his hat, and slipped out of his fur-trimmed cloak. "A brisk walk is good for growing boys." He hung his cloak and hat on the hook beside the door and told the child, "Pick up those things and be quick about it, Hanserl. You can take them into the kitchen and then run home. I'm sure Maria has chores for you to do." He brushed his curly brown hair into place, straightened the sleeves of his blue coat, and proceeded toward the kitchen.

Augusta's dislike of their visitor was not improved by this scene, but she followed without comment. Her mother was back in her chair, wearing her false curls under a fresh cap. Her cheeks looked unnaturally rosy, a color—Augusta knew—she had produced by painful pinching.

She greeted Herr Seutter with a gracious smile and extended her hand.

He said, "A very healthful New Year to you, dear lady," and eyed her hand for a moment before shaking it firmly.

Frau von Langsdorff tittered. "Oh, dear. Always so very forceful, my dear sir." She shook a finger at him. "An eligible bachelor like you can benefit from a little advice. You must bow and kiss a lady's hand to gain her heart."

Seutter stole a glance at Augusta, who suppressed a smile and busied herself with unpacking the basket. It contained bottles of wine, a whole ham, a side of bacon, a loaf of bread filled with nuts and corinths, another of fine wheat flour, a quarter of a whole wheel of cheese, a chunk of butter, and a roasted goose. Her mouth watered at such riches.

The boy crept closer to the meager fire and stretched his hands toward the glowing coals.

"Home with you, young rascal." Herr Seutter clapped his hands, and the boy fled, slamming the front door behind him. His master came to help Augusta. "I took the liberty," he said, "of bringing a few things to cheer your Mama and you."

"Oh, you dear man." Frau von Langsdorff tripped over to put her hand on his arm and gave him a melting look. "To know that another heart beats with affection for two poor lonely and helpless females . . . I'm quite overcome by such goodness. Come sit by me, dear sir.

I feel a little faint. Augusta, run and bring in your father's chair from the *salon.*"

Seeing the foods spread out on the kitchen table, Augusta was in a humor to forgive Herr Seutter. She was even more favorably inclined toward him when he followed her out to carry back the heavy oak settle.

"God love you, my dear," he said in the cold parlor, putting his large hand over hers on the back of the chair, "but this will be my duty. I'm not the sort of man who likes to see a tender female put to such heavy work. A young lady deserves a better life than this. A man must strive to make things easy for her."

Augusta snatched back her hand. The chair was certainly not beyond her strength, and she had no wish to discuss her situation with him. Instead she held the door open.

Frau von Langsdorff directed the chair to be placed just opposite herself and close enough that their knees would almost touch. She smiled at their guest. "Perhaps a glass of that lovely wine you have so generously provided? Since it's a holiday and I'm a wee bit faint still? Bring the good glasses, Augusta."

Augusta returned to the parlor and took two wine glasses from the cupboard. They dated back to better times and had not seen the light of day since her brother's last stay.

She thought often of Franz and grieved. They had not had news in months, but her mother thought this was due to the difficulties of getting mail from the theater of war. Perhaps so. Both he and their mother seemed to consider his military service quite safe for officers, and he was an ensign.

She took the glasses to the kitchen, wiped them with a clean cloth, and watched Herr Seutter open the bottle and pour.

"Only two glasses?" he asked. "Will you not join us?"

"I rarely drink wine," Augusta said.

"But, my dear Augusta, you would make me very happy if you joined us in our little celebration. Surely you will not turn down an old friend's request?"

"Go ahead," said her mother impatiently. "It's the New Year after all. Get another glass and pull up that stool."

Frau von Langsdorff had hardly tasted the wine but seemed already in high spirits. Augusta could hear her tinkling laughter all the way to the parlor. She was ashamed of her ill feelings toward Herr Seutter who had, after all, brought them delicacies they had not tasted for many months. And he had also lifted her mother's spirits and caused her to laugh again.

She made an effort to be pleasant. This became easier as she sipped the warming wine and consumed a little ham and cheese with the soft white bread and then nibbled a slice of the very rich almond cake, all helped along with another glass of wine or two.

When Herr Seutter finally recalled other obligations and left—on this occasion bending over Frau von Langsdorff's hand—it seemed quite natural that he should take Augusta into a brief fatherly embrace in the hall.

The basket of food lasted through January, and so did Herr Seutter's visits. Augusta's mother took to baking dainty cakes and tarts and added ribbons and laces to her caps. Herr Seutter was not as welcome to Augusta, but his frequent generous gifts—which included a delivery of firewood—and her mother's pleasure forced her to be civil. Still, she found excuses to leave them alone together as much as possible.

Toward the end of the month, an official-looking letter arrived for Frau von Langsdorff. It bore a military seal. Inside was a brief communication to the effect that Ensign Franz von Langsdorff had been wounded in the battle of Freiberg, October 29, and wished his family informed. It was to be hoped that Ensign von Langsdorff would continue to make good progress and be able to write himself.

"God in Heaven!" cried Frau von Langsdorff, turning pale. "Wounded? How can that be? Franz is an officer. How can he be wounded? Perhaps he was careless, but you would think they would take better care of the young gentlemen."

Augusta would have laughed, had this been a laughing matter. Even if her mother had managed to suppress her maternal feelings with foolish assumptions about military campaigns, she should have tried harder herself to talk Franz out of this desperate undertaking.

Wondering where he was, whether in a hospital or private home, she looked at the letter more closely. She could not make out the name of the town, but when she saw its date, black fear seized her. The letter was more than two months old! What if Franz had died from his wounds and the news had not reached them yet?

She looked at her mother who was wringing her hands helplessly and felt only anger. "Mother, this letter was written two months ago. Why have we heard nothing else? What has happened to Franz?"

Her mother gaped at her. Then her mouth went slack, and she burst into tears. "No!" she wailed, raising her hands toward heaven. "Dear God, don't let me lose my Franzerl! You've taken my husband and left me poor. You cannot take my son, too. He's all that I have left."

"You have me, Mother," Augusta snapped, ignoring this paroxysm of grief. She was casting about for some way to get more information about her brother's fate. In the end nothing occurred to her but to ask Herr Seutter's help.

"Oh, yes," agreed her mother quickly, dabbing at her tears. "Of course. He will know what to do. Run to the dear man and tell him I need his wise counsel."

Herr Seutter's was the finest house in Lindau. His family had made its money in trade and banking, and when their former house had burned in the great fire some thirty years ago, Jakob Seutter's father had called on an Italian architect to rebuild it. The new house was five stories high, and its façade managed to combine princely splendor with bourgeois probity. The yellow plaster walls bore elaborate frescoes, many large windows looked out on the square, and broad, curved steps led to carved double doors that were set between two pairs of slender Corinthian pillars supporting a handsome semi-circular pediment.

Augusta felt intimidated as always, but today she overcame this and ran up the wide stairs to knock loudly on the massive door. It was opened by a middle-aged woman in a black bombazine dress and starched white apron. Short and top-heavy, she was all bosom and arms and large head made larger by her black, frizzed hair and starched cap. She looked sharply at Augusta from black eyes like small elderberries and pursed her lips.

"Yes?"

"Is Herr Seutter at home?"

"Who wants him?"

"I'm Augusta von Langsdorff. Herr Seutter is a friend of my mother's. We need his advice in a family matter."

The elderberry eyes narrowed. "Family matter?"

Augusta blushed. "Please inform your master."

The woman snapped "Wait" and slammed the door in Augusta's face.

Augusta stood and shivered, humiliated by the curious looks from people in the market below. Only tradesmen, servants, and maids were left standing outside.

A moment later the door opened again, and Herr Seutter himself appeared. "Maria, for shame! You should have asked our guest in." Herr Scutter smiled at Augusta, and bowed her in with effusive apologies.

"What a happy surprise," he said warmly and raised her cold hand to his lips—quite as if she had been a lady. "How cold you are!" He warmed her fingers between his hands. "There's a nice fire in the good parlor." He helped her with her cloak and gave it to the woman with the elderberry eyes. "Put this away, Maria, and then run instantly and bring us hot chocolate and a few of your almond cakes." Tucking Augusta's arm under his, he said, "Come, my dear, we'll soon have you warm again."

The "good parlor" in this house was truly a *salon*. It was large and bright, and the *parquet* floor was laid in a French pattern and so highly waxed that Augusta was afraid she would slip and clutched his arm more tightly. White stucco garlands wreathed the ceiling, doorframes, and windows, and the walls were painted a soft blue. On the floor lay a thick carpet, and a settee and dainty chairs stood there, all covered in sky blue velvet. Elsewhere she saw inlaid, bow-fronted chests with marble tops, small gilded tables, and—oh, wonder!—a painted harpsichord.

Her host said, "I've had this room refurnished recently. Do you like it? It was a dark place only suitable for a crusty old man living by himself, but I had a notion to make it more pleasing to female eyes. You will know better than I if it was well done. Pray let me have your advice."

"Oh, it's very beautiful," said Augusta, a little dazed. "Mama would think it quite perfect."

He chuckled. "Ah. But you? What do *you* think?"

"I think it's the loveliest room I've ever seen. And what a very beautiful harpsichord!" She let go of his arm and went closer to admire the Greek maidens with fluttering veils who danced around the outside of the instrument, and the many black and white keys, a whole six octaves of them.

He followed her. "By any chance, do you play, my dear Augusta? I confess it cost me a good bit of money, and I have no use for it myself. I lack the finer skills, you see." He blushed.

She looked at him, wondering why he should have bought the instrument, and saw both pride and shame in his face. How odd, she thought, to have so much and yet feel so inadequate. "Mama plays beautifully," she said, then corrected herself, "I mean, she used to play. We no longer have an instrument."

"Ah! But you? Do you not play a little? Would you? Just any little thing, so I can hear what it sounds like."

Eight octaves! Augusta's fingers itched to try it. "It's been years, and I never was very good."

"Please? As a great favor?"

So she sat down on the bench, and after a moment he sat beside her to watch as her stiff fingers picked out the notes of some songs she remembered: "*Nachtigall, ich hör dich singen*" and "*Ach, Blümlein blau.*" As she used to do years ago for her parents, she sang the ballads softly as she played, and her heart melted at the memory of happier times—until that memory reminded her of Franz, and she dropped her hands in her lap.

She was ashamed to have forgotten so quickly and, rent by a sudden conviction that Franz was dead, she burst into tears.

"God bless me!" cried Herr Seutter, putting his arm around her. "Oh, my dearest girl. Please, tell me how I may serve you, how I may help. Oh, please, do not cry. It breaks my heart to see you so."

Augusta turned to him—somehow she found herself embraced—and sobbed into his blue vest. After a little while, during which he made soothing noises and stroked her back awkwardly, she sat up again and brushed away her tears. "Forgive me, sir," she said, sniffling and embarrassed. "It's only . . . the song brought back happier days . . . and I forgot my reason for coming to you."

"I should not have asked you to play. Pray forgive me, my dear. I would not have caused you pain for anything. Come away from the stupid instrument and tell me what is wrong." He led her to the settee and made her sit beside him, taking both her hands in his. "Now then, what brought you?"

He regarded her with such earnest and kind interest that Augusta felt guilty for having disliked him. "We got this letter, sir," she said, taking it from her pocket and handing it over. "Franz has been wounded. But only see how old this letter is. And there has been nothing else. Not a word." Her fear and grief brought fresh tears to her eyes.

He *tutted* and squeezed her hand. "Please don't cry again, my dear Augusta. I cannot bear it. Let me see what this is all about." He read the letter twice, while she twisted her hands in her lap. Then he nodded. "Well, the post is very unreliable in wartimes. No doubt, your brother has recovered and is back with his regiment. I saw in the *Gazette* just a day ago that there will be a peace finally. It's quite definite. Your brother will be home in no time, you'll see. But meanwhile I shall make inquiries and report back to you and your Mama."

"Do you truly think so? That there will be peace and Franz will be home? Oh, I'm so glad." She smiled at him through her tears. "Thank you for your help. We were so worried, Mama and I." She echoed her mother's words, "We have no one in the whole world except Franz."

He took her hand again. "My dear girl, you wound me. I'm your most devoted servant. Yours and your Mama's. You may call on me for anything. At any time. You made me very happy today by coming here and letting me be of some small service. That you trusted me . . ."

The door opened, and Maria banged into the room, shoving the door closed with her hip while balancing a tray with porcelain cups and dishes and a silver choco-late pot. These she set on a small table, gave her master and Augusta a very sharp look, and left the room, slamming the door behind her.

Augusta flushed and snatched back her hand. "Thank you, sir. I must not trouble you longer. I'm afraid I've made extra work for your housekeeper."

"Nonsense. Maria has worked for my family for thirty years. It's made her a little peevish sometimes, but there's no harm in her." He poured a thick, fragrant liquid into two cups, then looked at her helplessly. Holding up his large hands, he said, "I'm not much good with dainty dishes. Would you mind?"

She liked him for it and took up a cup with its saucer, added sugar from a silver container, and offered it to him with a smile, then took her own.

Now, chocolate was in short supply in the Langsdorff household, and Augusta was very fond of it. This was especially rich and sweet and creamy, though Herr Seutter seemed less interested in the chocolate than in watching her. He smiled, nodded, and plied her with small cakes. Since he took such pleasure in her enjoyment, Augusta warmed to him a little more. Just so her father had urged her to eat when she had been a little girl and they had still been able to afford small delicacies. But she remembered her mother and, replacing her empty cup on the tray, she rose. "The chocolate was delicious, but I mustn't leave Mama waiting. She's terribly worried, and I don't feel right enjoying myself while she's miserable."

He nodded. "Quite right. We must remedy that immediately. Maria!"

Maria reappeared, looking as angry as ever.

"Wrap up some of the chocolate powder for Frau von Langsdorff. No, make up a small basket. Put in fresh cream and sugar and your own receipt so that she may taste it right away. And a few of the little cakes also."

Maria folded her arms. "There's no cream left. I used it all—except for a bit to put in the sauce for your veal tonight."

"What do I need sauce on my veal for? Pack it up, pack it up."

Maria flung out of the room as Augusta protested that there was no need, that she did not want to upset his household, that they could very well make their own chocolate.

He put a hand on her shoulder and smiled down at her very kindly. "Hush, my dear. It gives me great pleasure. I know quite well that you and your Mama are used to better things. Allow me then this small indulgence."

Augusta flushed. She did not mind being poor as much as she hated being made a charity case. Murmuring, "You are too good, sir," she stepped away from him and looked for her cloak.

"I wish you could stay a little," he said. "I want to show you the rest of my house. I would value your advice on how to make it more comfortable. A man is lost without a woman's gentler influence."

She said firmly, "I must go, sir. Thank you for the chocolate."

He went into the hall and returned with her cloak, placing it around her shoulders and then turning her toward him to hook the collar around her neck. She caught her breath at their closeness. When they walked out of the room together, they found Maria waiting with a small basket covered with a pretty cloth.

Augusta ran all the way home.

Her mother flung open the front door while Augusta was still some distance down Fischergasse. "Where have you been so long?" she called. "I'm half distracted."

Augusta hurried inside and handed her mother the basket. "From Herr Seutter," she said, taking off the cloak and hanging it on its hook. "It's to make chocolate for you. He was very particular about that and had his housekeeper add the receipt."

Frau von Langsdorff looked at the basket, clearly torn between pleasure at the gift and worry about Franz. Augusta took pity. "Herr Seutter said he will make enquiries about Franz, but he thinks it's just a matter of lost mails. He says there will be peace and Franz will come home very soon."

"Oh." Frau von Langsdorff's face broke into smiles. "Oh, the dear man! Oh, he must be right. How very kind! How very thoughtful! To take such trouble with a poor widow like myself. It shows great warmth of heart, don't you think?" She lifted the pretty cloth and peeked inside the basket. "Chocolate and cream also. And sugar. And such delicious little cakes. Ah, he knows what a lady misses most when hard times befall her. Come, Augusta, don't dawdle. I cannot wait to taste chocolate again."

Franz forgotten, she bustled into the kitchen and busied herself looking for the small copper pan and a spoon, then sent Augusta into the *salon* for porcelain cups.

When Augusta came back, her mother was stirring the chocolate over the fire and humming to herself.

The rich smell filled the kitchen. "You know, Augusta," she said, "I have been very remiss. Herr Seutter has been everything that is kind and attentive, and I have done nothing in return. It's time we gave a little supper for him. The poor man is quite alone and at the mercy of ordinary servants. I could make a *fricassée de poulet aux champignons*. Or a *terrine*. Or perhaps a *ragoût de veau en paté*. What do you think? I used to make a very nice *ragoût* for your Papa. It was quite his favorite dish. And my pastry was famous among the ladies in Heidelberg. Perhaps we could have some carrots and a chestnut *purée*, too. Nothing too elaborate. Just a small, elegant supper."

Augusta said, "Mama, we don't have the money. And a man as wealthy as Herr Seutter would not expect it."

Her mother trilled the notes of a song. "Silly girl. It won't take much. All men enjoy a little pampering. Why do you think he comes here? He's as lonely as I am." She handed Augusta a cup of chocolate.

Augusta stared at her mother. The thought that a man might court her mother had never crossed her mind. She found she had lost her appetite and set the chocolate aside untasted.

Her mother sat down and sipped. "Delicious! Drink, Augusta. The dear man. How very thoughtful he is!"

"Mama," Augusta said, "you cannot think that he . . . surely you would not want to marry a man like that?"

Her mother gave her a reproachful look. "Who said anything about marriage? And what do you mean by 'a man like that'? He's one of the most important men in this city. And he's a very handsome figure of a man." She smiled and patted her curls. "Come, you must tell me all about his house."

Of course this was about marriage. Augusta looked at her mother, a small woman who had added weight in spite of their restricted diet and whose brown hair already showed some gray, and she marveled. To be sure, Herr Seutter was probably almost the same age, but this florid man with his bright vests was nothing at all like her dear Papa, who had been a slender figure dressed in black, with pale, elegant features and the kind, vague eyes of the scholar. The very idea was abhorrent. She would not allow it. It was a betrayal of their father's memory. How could her mother sell herself to a man like Seutter just because they were poor as church mice and she missed the finer things? Her mother was blinded by wealth and luxuries. By a cup of chocolate!

But as Augusta saw the happy face, the sparkling eyes, the rosy glow in her mother's cheeks and remembered her sprightly manner of talking and humming, her courage failed her. She sighed and described Herr Seutter's *salon*.

# 3

## Mannheim

*Maxima est enim factae injuriae poena fecisse.*
(The heaviest punishment is the fact of having
done an injury)

Seneca, *De Ira*

He dreamed of the lake. Always. Seasons passed in his dreams. The leaden waters of winter, on which the snow fell like down from gray cloud featherbeds, drawing a veil across the alps, gave way to the azure sparkle of spring amid green shores wreathed with flowering apple trees. In midsummer, the lake's warm waters lapped gently against his boat as he floated, bathed by the heat of the sun under a crystalline blue against which gulls soared and swooped like kites borne by the wind. And in autumn the flaming sunsets spilled their glory of molten gold across its surface and made the trees along the shore burst into flame.

The interims between his dreams were filled with images of torment and death. He wanted no part of them and fought the demons that inhabited this bleak and hellish land until he found his way back to the lake.

He learned to explore his dream world to feel it more intensely. He would let his hand fall over the side of the boat to trail through the cooling, caressing waters and imagine touching and being touched by a lover. At other times, he walked along the lake shore, on and on, passing through small familiar towns with smiling people, resting under trees heavy with ripe fruit—cherries melting sweetly on his tongue, apples bursting into tart juice, pears that tasted of honey—and the bees would buzz and sometimes sting, but even their sting was delicious. He would circle the whole lake endlessly, passing under snow-capped mountains, lying in flowering meadows, kissing pretty maidens in their kitchen gardens, and he would end where he had begun, happy for what had been and eager for the next journey.

Once, only once, in his passionate love affair with the lake, he flung himself into its waters, naked like a lover or a newborn, losing himself in its embrace, mastering it, letting himself be absorbed into its dark and mysterious depths, to die in ecstasy.

*Better to die quickly than to live in terror*, says Aesop.

*Dulce et decorum est* etcetera.

*Death pays all debts.*

*Come unto me and I shall refresh thee*, calls the lake . . .

*Earth to earth, ashes to ashes, and water to water.*

*And so ye shall be reborn.*

But it was not to be. The four apocalyptic specters interjected themselves between him and his consummation.

He thought of them as apocalyptic because they were four, differentiated by their colors. Red, black, white, and a pale ivory. In the *Book of Revelations* the four horsemen are sent to end the world. They ride into battle against a sinful mankind. He had once seen a woodcut by Albrecht Dürer, showing the four horsemen as knights or soldiers with raised swords, looking much like the Prussian hussar who had ridden him down and taken his colors. But his own apocalypse walked on foot now, befitting his insignificance.

*War*

*Death*

*Pestilence*

*Famine*

He was not sure who was what in *Revelations*, but he knew that his red apocalypse spoke of War, and the black one of Death. The white apocalypse brought pain, and the pale one came with the white one, so he thought they must be Pestilence and Famine.

The other two came separately.

He hated and feared all of them, for they warred with his desire to be reborn. They tormented his body and rent his soul. They kept him from fleeing to his lake with its refreshing waters and its island paradise.

However much he resisted, they were slowly winning the battle, for his escapes became shorter and his suffering greater, longer, and more intense.

In time he was to learn that his *chimerae* were mere flesh-and-blood men, but that did not change his fear and anger. The white figure was a military doctor in Austrian uniform with a stained white apron tied around his middle. He worked on the legs, inflicting such exquisite agony that Franz would scream like one of the damned in hell. Sometimes his screaming would produce the nurse Famine with a meager draft of laudanum, the nepenthe of forgetfulness that brought a brief sojourn back to his lake.

The red *chimera* was another military man, in red coat and breeches. His visits were rare in the beginning, and Franz did not know if it was always the same officer. He had a notion that this man had been asking questions that Franz could not or would not answer. At least once those questions concerned Mama and Augusta. He remembered trying to answer but his tongue had refused to obey.

Not that he felt like talking to any of them. The most irritating visitor was the clergyman assigned to him. In his sober black robe and with his harsh voice reminding him to put his trust in God who was the resurrection, he seemed Death personified. Franz knew the way to resurrection and hoped for more laudanum, enough laudanum so that he could cross over and lose himself forever in the lake.

It was not to be.

They had brought him here to this hospital. Drifting in and out of his dream state, he remembered little of the journey except discomfort. He had lain on a stretcher in a covered wagon with other wounded men.

Then he was in this room, and here he suffered more pain, worse than the first, but there was also more laudanum, and he returned to the lake.

The pain did not leave him, but it abated in time. And when it did, there was no more laudanum. The cup the nurse offered to his lips now contained broth, and later soup with bits of meat. At first he refused the food, knowing that it sustained existence, and existence was too painful to contemplate.

Another doctor came and asked questions. Franz answered with grunts. Like all doctors, the man volunteered little himself. One day, Franz strained very hard to speak and managed, "W-wh-hat?"

The doctor gave him a sharp glance over his spectacles and said, "What is the outlook, do you mean?"

Franz had meant to ask, "What is wrong with me?" but this would do. He nodded.

"Well, the field surgeons did the best they could."

They always say that when the news is bad, Franz thought.

"They should have taken your leg off. But as they didn't, I could see that yours was the sort of case we might learn from." The doctor preened a little. "There was an article—published by a Frenchman—his name's Desault, if you've a mind to know—that proposes to deal with necrosis by cutting the rotting flesh away. It seemed the opportune moment to test the theory. Mind you, it was touch and go. I cannot count the bits of bone and metal I had to remove first, and it's a miracle you didn't die from gangrene fever after all. Nasty stuff, gangrene. Your flesh turns black and stinks to high heaven. Well, I kept cutting and cutting, and here you still are."

"M-m . . . m-m?" Franz wondered why his tongue would not cooperate.

"I mean, the leg's still there. Both of them. Though the right knee may be a bit of a problem. Won't be able to bend it or put much weight on it. I'm afraid crutches will be in order. The other one's well enough. Scarred, of course. You're a lucky fellow."

"L-ll . . . l-l . . . l-la?"

"What's wrong with your tongue?" The doctor bent over him and pulled down Franz's jaw, peered inside his mouth and then felt around it with his fingers, pulling his tongue up and down and sideways.

Franz gagged. The doctor's fingers had a disgusting smell and taste of tobacco and other unspeakable things.

The doctor removed his hand and straightened. "Say something!"

"N-na-no!" croaked Franz and glared.

One day, Franz stole a glimpse at his legs while the doctor and nurse were cleaning and re-bandaging them. It was a very brief glimpse, for the pain was, as usual, excruciating. But the sight of his wounds was so unnerving that for a long time afterward he refused to look at them. The flesh was a violent red or purple, puffed up so much in places that the middle of his leg no longer looked like a limb but like something rotten and slimy unearthed from a grave. On the right leg, trickles of blood and pus pulsated from the doctor's incisions like burning lava from small volcanoes. The smell of corruption reached his nose, and he closed his eyes, gagging on his vomit.

The sharp-nosed servant with the odd yellow eyes closed the double doors of the library behind the visitor. The visitor advanced nervously, bowed, and sat down on the other side of the wide, ornately carved desk. "Is it true?" he asked.

His host poured cognac into two glasses and pushed one toward him. "Really, Paul," he said. "You have less self-control than a female. Pull yourself together. It appears there *was* a letter, but it has been five months. We would have heard if it had been delivered."

The other man emptied the glass and set it down with a shaking hand. "Your informant was certain that such a letter was written, but we don't know what happened to it? How can you be so calm? As long as it exists, our lives aren't worth a copper *pfennig.* And surely we have to abandon our plan."

"What plan? There never was a plan."

The visitor raised his glass, saw it was empty and set it back down. "You said a hunt was quite as useful as a battle for fatal accidents. I thought—"

"What?" His host's face had purpled. He rose from his chair. "I never said anything of the sort. Beware of that careless tongue of yours. That sort of thing will get you into trouble."

His guest blustered, "I would never mention the matter outside this room. You mistake me. I am completely devoted to the cause."

The other man glared. "Understand this: there is no cause! There never was a cause, just idle talk of foolish men in their cups."

The visitor looked astonished. He rose slowly. "Well, if that's the way it is . . . and if you are certain all is safe . . ." He saw the other man's face. His voice trailed off, and he turned to go.

After several weeks of fever and pain, Franz became aware that his right leg was no longer straight but made an awkward curve near the place where his knee had been. But both his legs continued to heal—at least the wounds did. The shattered knee cap and the badly aligned bones would never get better. Yet the doctor thought his treatment entirely successful and told Franz that he was writing an article of his own, based on the case. He had saved the limb after it had been nearly destroyed by an exploding canister filled with rusted nails and assorted bits of metal, and the patient had not died from the experiment.

Franz did not thank him for his effort.

By then, he knew that he was in Mannheim, the residential capital of His Serene Highness, Karl Theodor, Margrave of Bergen op Zoom, Duke and Count Palatine of Pfalz-Sulzbach, Duke and Count Palatine of Pfalz-Neuburg, and Elector of the Holy Roman Empire.

The fact that Franz did not speak bothered the doctor enough to bring in his colleagues again. They stood over him, tormenting him for days by poking around in his mouth, squeezing his neck, and assigning him all sorts of speech exercises. In the end, the verdict was that the blow to his head must have deranged something in his brain. One of the learned men seemed to think that his intelligence had been destroyed, or at least severely damaged, and that he was an imbecile who should be given a pension. This, Franz knew not to be true, though he made no effort to disabuse him.

He reached his twenty-first birthday a cripple who could no longer speak normally.

His wounds did not affect his ability to write, and one of his military visitors, the same one who had brought him his decoration and a letter of congratulation signed by General Luszinky himself, suggested that Franz should write to his family. This, Franz declined by shaking his head. Lieutenant Killian offered to write for him, and again Franz shook his head.

But his mother and sister heard of his fate anyway. Letters arrived, which Lieutenant Killian gave to Franz. Franz opened and read these when he was alone and immediately tore them into little pieces. He did this not because they made him angry—they were quite loving epistles, especially his sister's—but because they shamed him. He was not the Franz they remembered, believed in, and expected to return to them. He was an altogether different man, one he did not yet know completely but whom he already despised.

His odd behavior lent credence to the opinion of the physician who had thought him an imbecile. Franz glowered at everyone, miserable in the knowledge that an imbecile was at least blessed with ignorance about his condition. He was haunted, sometimes to the point of madness, by what he had become.

He was haunted more by what he had done.

Another parson sat beside him one afternoon, a thin black figure haloed by the golden light of the afternoon sun in the window, and said, "I am told that your father was also a servant of the Lord. You must find great comfort in that."

Franz turned away his head. After a moment, the parson sighed, patted his arm, and left.

They had raised his rank to second lieutenant—a small and meaningless gesture, since he was unfit for duty. In that at least, Franz found comfort.

Some aspects of his condition gradually improved, while others deteriorated. The pain lessened, and he got stronger until he could sit up, and look out of the window at the slowly greening trees. He sat for hours doing that. Lieutenant Killian brought him books. When Franz refused them, he offered to read to him. Franz refused that also, and Killian sighed and decided to pen a short letter to Franz's mother.

He asked, "Shall I tell them that you feel better?"

Franz looked back at the trees and nodded.

"Shall I say that you miss them and hope to see them soon?"

Franz did not answer that.

Killian said, "I think I shall. They will expect it, you know. You don't want to hurt them, do you?"

Franz shook his head.

"Good. I shall say that you are thinking of them fondly and counting the days."

One day Franz sorted through his possessions in a small trunk. Somehow, these had been dispatched after him, or with him—he could not be certain because he had had no desire to look at them before. There was not much. His uniform—the one he had not worn into battle, a small case containing his razor, comb, soap, and scissors, his decoration, the papers certifying his new rank, a few letters from his mother or Augusta that had escaped his destruction, and one letter that did not belong to him. This letter was fairly thick and stained with a brownish spot on one corner. Franz turned it in his hands and was mystified. It was addressed to someone called Friedrich von Loe, but there was neither a city nor a street. Surely whoever had packed his things had made a mistake. Eventually he put the letter with the others and relocked the trunk.

To Franz's irritation, the kind Lieutenant Killian came regularly and wrote what he thought a loving son should tell his family, and when he was done, he would read the letter to Franz and look at him with pity and friendship, thinking, no doubt:

*There but for God's Grace, go I!*

If Franz had ever had divine grace, he had certainly lost it. As his physical health improved, he was forced to confront who he was, and what his father, a saintly and gentle man, would think of him now. His self-disgust caused him to lash out with angry snarls at anyone who came near him at such times. Not even Lieutenant Killian was spared.

Then, one day Franz remembered the wounded captain. The next day, he asked Lieutenant Killian if he knew a Captain von Loe.

Killian, not used to being spoken to by Franz, was immediately eager to be of use. No, he did not know the name. Could he write it? Franz did. Had von Loe been at Freiberg? Franz nodded.

"W-w-ounded. N-not s-s-sure if a-a-. . ." Franz choked.

"You want me to find out if he survived?"

Franz nodded.

Killian left happily. He had finally established communication with his difficult patient. He asked everyone among the military staff in Mannheim and then mailed letters to Vienna and Munich. The answers were disappointing. Captain von Loe had indeed died at Freiberg.

Franz was saddened by it. The young captain's voice been strong and his request fervent. His death left him with a letter to deliver. "H-his f-father? wh-where?" he asked Killian.

But this time Killian's search brought forth no answer. No one by the name was known in or near Mannheim. Franz pondered this for a few days and eventually decided that he must be mistaken about von Loe's home. He had been dazed and sick from the blow to his head. It was a wonder he remembered anything at all. In any case, it would have to wait until he was well.

His first struggle to stand—an effort that brought back an almost forgotten physical agony—also opened a mental wound. He had to come to grips with his deformity, the misshapen and awkwardly bent leg that could not be hidden in stockings and tight knee breeches. He was a freak in a world that valued physical beauty.

Though he was still doing his best to avoid communication with the living, he could not escape the dead so easily. They came to him at night and haunted his dreams of childhood. His father would look with his blue eyes at the boy Franz, who had drummed too hard and too long on his little drum, and say gravely, "Careful, son, or you may lose your head." And little Franz, in his Christmas Day finery, would answer, "I'm not afraid, Papa," and drum some more. Papa would shake his head and keep shaking it until it flew away, a white-haired cannonball, and Franz would stumble around, searching among the bodies of the dead for his father's head. When he finally found it, his father's head perched on the body of the Prussian captain, who attacked him with a bloody sword. He would wake up screaming and lie, drenched in sweat, wondering if he would have killed his father or if his father would have slain him.

Not all the dreams were the same, of course. Sometimes his father wore a hussar's uniform and rode a big black horse, and Franz would raise his bare hands and cry, "Don't kill me! It's me, Franzerl." And sometimes, most dreadful of all, he fought and killed Prussian soldiers who changed into Carl, the drummer boy, before he could stop himself. Then, when he went to kneel beside the boy's severed head to ask his forgiveness, he saw that he was looking down at his own face.

*Speculum Hominis.*

The city of Mannheim was laid out in a neat grid within the heavy fortifications that guarded the confluence of the Rhein and Main rivers. The palace of the Electors of Kurpfalz dominated the city as the cultural hub of the principality and strove mightily to equal Versailles.

This night, in a steady, drizzling rain, carriages and sedan chairs waited outside the *Hoftheater* adjoining the palace. They carried away those who had attended the latest production of *Olimpie*, M. Voltaire's tragedy, written specifically for Their Most Serene Highnesses, Karl Theodor and Elisabeth Augusta.

It was close to midnight. One man, in a dark cloak and gold-trimmed cocked hat, emerged from a side door of the *Hoftheater* and hurried past a waiting carriage when its door opened and a familiar voice summoned, "*Herein!*"

The man inside was a power at court, and the pedestrian was the assassin.

The great man clearly did not relish the meeting. He looked as if he had bitten into a lemon and wished to get this over with as quickly as possible.

"You botched it," he informed the assassin coldly as soon as he had climbed in and closed the door. "The letter exists."

"That cannot be, my lord. I made certain. Captain—"

"No names or titles!" snapped the other.

"Your pardon, sir. I'm a good shot, and I made sure afterward. He was dead. I searched him. Then I searched his quarters. There was nothing."

"He was able to pass it to another before he died."

The assassin drew in his breath sharply. He had thought himself safe. Months had passed without news. He had assumed that the unknown Austrian officer had been killed and the letter destroyed on the battlefield. "I don't understand. How can this be?"

"Because of your slovenly work. And don't doubt for a moment that your life is lost if you cannot correct the mistake."

The assassin did not doubt it and found that his knees were shaking. He said fervently, "You may count on me, sir. It's a matter of pride and honor. I did not miss last time, and I shall not miss this time. And this time, I shall make sure I get the letter."

The great man snorted. "Oh, no. This time there will be nothing to trace this back to us. We know who has the letter, no thanks to you. By a stroke of luck, he talked to one of the officers in the hospital. The patient wanted to know what had happened to a wounded man who had given him a letter for his father. The officer asked around and, by another lucky chance, I overheard him." He paused to let his heavy sarcasm register. "Fortunately, the man has no idea what he carries. You will get the letter, and this time without using violence and without making him suspicious. But under no circumstances will you approach him here in Mannheim."

"N-not approach him?"

"He will be leaving shortly. His name is Franz von Langsdorff. He will travel by post to Lindau Tuesday next. You will follow or join him and get the letter in such a way that he doesn't realize its importance."

The assassin bit his lip. How much good luck did they hope for? "What if he delivers the letter before he leaves Mannheim?"

"He won't. No one by that name lives here."

Apparently luck was still with them, but the assassin did not trust it for a minute. "Might he not throw it away then? Or open it to get more information?"

The great man stamped his foot. "Curse you for an incompetent knave! You will make sure he doesn't or suffer the consequences. Don't contact me until you have it." He did not trouble with farewell courtesies as he opened the door.

The assassin meekly descended into the rainy night and watched the coach drive away.

It was a difficult assignment. A shot from a distance was simpler and safer, but his livelihood depended on the people he served and he was obliged to play it their way. They had given him a second chance when he had no right to expect one.

# 4

# The Journey Home

*"Do you think," said Martin, "that sparrow-hawks have always eaten the pigeons they came across?"*

*"Yes, of course," said Candide.*

*"Well," said Martin, "if sparrow-hawks have always possessed the same character, why should you expect men to change theirs?"*

Voltaire, *Candide*

Regardless of how much he wished to delay facing his family, Franz had to leave the hospital in Mannheim. By April, he had protracted his departure past all tolerance. He was the last of the wounded officers from the recent war, and the doctors had declared him fit and washed their hand of him. So he shaved off his mustache and put on his old uniform again, dressing with some difficulty because his breeches would not buckle around the deformed right knee and his boot pinched the barely healed leg.

With the uniform and boots gone, the trunk was nearly empty. He decided to abandon it in favor of a light satchel for a clean shirt, shaving kit, letters, and decoration. The undeliverable letter from the dead captain he tossed away at first. But after a moment, he picked it up again and shoved it into his right boot where the leather bit into his crippled leg. Then he took up his crutches, flung the satchel over his shoulder, and made his slow way to the post station inn *Der Goldene Pflug* where he paid for his coach fare to Stuttgart.

He hated the pitying looks and questions from the passengers and reacted by glowering and ignoring their questions and offers of help. After a while, they left him alone.

The coach traveled south along the Neckar River, through Heidelberg and Heilbronn. Whenever they approached a station, the *postilion* blew his horn, and people came to welcome passengers and mail. In Heidelberg, the old capital of the Kurpfalz, the blackened ruins of the castle loomed large above the city where Franz had spent carefree student years. The castle had been sacked and burned by the French in another war, but the swaggering university students he saw from the coach window were innocent of ugly thoughts of battles and casualties.

In Stuttgart, capital of the dukes of Württemberg, Franz had to spend the night before buying a seat in another coach to Ulm.

A cold rain was falling when he climbed out of the coach in Ulm. The posting inn, called *Goldener Adler*, stood in the shadow of the looming cathedral. Three beggars huddled against the inn's wall, stretching their hats and hands toward the travelers who hurried past them through the rain.

"Help a fellow wounded veteran, sir!" begged a young man who had lost an eye and wore a patch over it.

"I've got a starving wife and four kids, sir. Have mercy on them," pleaded the gray-whiskered man who missed a leg.

The third man, pale and red-haired, wore an arm in a sling and was racked by a hollow cough. He said nothing, just held out his hand.

They wore the tatters of their uniforms, an Austrian jacket here, the breeches and gaiters of another regiment there, a vest and bandolier over a torn shirt on the third man. None inspired trust, and the other travelers had ignored them.

Franz, who had been the last out of the coach, stopped, felt in his pocket for money, and gave each some silver he could ill spare. Their misery was worse than his.

They saluted and thanked him fervently.

Inside the inn, he was shown to a seat near the window. As he waited for his meal, he could see the three wretches huddling together in the rain. They were looking enviously his way. A maid brought him a plate with a slice of roast beef and two potato dumplings swimming in gravy. The food looked and smelled delicious, but he had lost his appetite.

After a few listless bites, he got back on his crutches and hobbled outside. The three beggars watched him coming. Perhaps they thought he wanted his money back.

"W-will you j-join me for a m-meal?" he asked, speaking carefully.

They gaped at him, then looked at each other.

"You're asking us to eat with you, sir? In there?" the youngest finally asked.

Franz nodded.

The old soldier with the gray whiskers eyed Franz slyly. "We can't afford the prices."

"M-m-y g-guests." Franz said. "I-it's c-cold and w-w . . . ." He gestured at the rain.

They looked at each other, grinned, and accepted.

The inn's staff was not happy to see three wet and filthy beggars occupying their premises, but since Franz paid, they served them hot food and beer.

Franz watched as the soldiers ate. He felt a little better.

"You just getting back from the war, too, sir?" The whiskered man's name was Hannes Moser. Franz nodded, and Moser guessed, "Freiberg, was it?—where you got wounded, sir?" Franz nodded again. Moser shook his head. "Them Prussians are devils. At least you still got two legs."

Franz said nothing.

The man with the cough was Willi Reiss. He was shoveling in the food and asked with a full mouth, "Where's home then, sir?"

"L-lindau."

Willi choked on another spasm of coughing, washed it down with a draft of beer. "A far way."

The one-eyed youngster grinned and raised his own beer, "Here's to you, sir! May you get home safe."

Franz did not particularly want beer, but it was churlish not to respond and he filled his own mug from the pitcher and drank, then proposed another toast to happier times for them.

They took turns talking about their battles and wounds and where they had served, consuming a large amount of beer toasting fallen friends and famous generals. Franz was thankful that this conversation asked little of him except an occasional nod or grunt and a raised glass. And ordering fresh pitchers of beer. They were talkative enough. He learned that they, too, were on their way home but without money for lodging or post coaches. They would have to spend the night outside in the rain and were reluctant to leave.

Finally Franz was nearly asleep and went to talk to the innkeeper about sharing his room for the night. The innkeeper didn't like the idea but agreed when Franz offered to pay double if he would provide three pallets and blankets on the floor of his room.

This act eased Franz's guilt a little more. He fell into bed in his breeches and boots and slept deeply and without his usual nightmares.

He woke at dawn, heavy-headed, and scratching. The innkeeper deserved a lecture for overcharging him because of vermin-ridden companions when the inn's beds were infested with bedbugs or fleas, or both. Then he became aware of the silence in the room. In the gray light filtering through the closed shutters, he saw that the pallets were empty. He was alone.

Franz sat up and felt for his money purse under the pillow. It was gone. Then he groped for his crutches. He had left them leaning against the side of his bed. No crutches. He got off the bed and hopped to the window to throw back the shutters. Daylight from an overcast sky filled the room. His guests were gone, and so were his cloak and hat from the back of the chair. His leather satchel lay near the door, limp and empty. The old single crutch that had belonged to Moser stood in a corner. Apparently, Moser had traded it for Franz's new ones.

Cursing himself for a fool, Franz checked the room thoroughly. The only things they had left were the clothes he wore and the empty satchel.

The thieving bastards! The ungrateful dogs! So that was what came of charitable gestures. They had taken what he had offered them out of pity and a feeling of brotherhood, and they had made off with his clothes and property.

Now how was he to pay his bill and theirs? Franz had visions of being arrested and thrown into the local prison, to linger there the rest of his life. He could not ask his mother and sister to help him. No, that would be too much. The thought of suicide, carefully kept at bay these many months, surfaced again. A day ago, he had had little enough to live for. Now he had nothing. Nothing but trouble!

But common sense returned. Awkward on one crutch, Franz made his way downstairs, showed the empty satchel, and demanded that the gendarmes be called. Because he was excited, it took him a while to make himself understood. The innkeeper looked at the satchel and the old crutch and shook his head.

"I warned ye," he growled. "But ye young officers are all alike. Ye think nobody but a soldier matters in this world. Now see what ye've come to. And ye a wounded man, too. They'll be long gone by now."

The assassin received Moser's report and the papers taken from Franz with disbelief.

"What d'you mean, that's all there was, you oaf?" he shouted. "The letter I want isn't here. Who in damnation had the gall to keep it? Was it you? Are you holding out for more silver? Curse you for a god-damned thieving swine!" In a fury, he drew his sword and put the point to Moser's throat.

In the end, he had to accept that they had either overlooked the letter in the dark, or that the lieutenant no longer had it. He thought over his options, decided to bribe a maid at the *Goldene Adler* to search the room and, if the letter did not turn up, to go back to Mannheim to make a thorough search of the hospital. He wished he had done the job himself, killing the man and searching the body, but he had been forbidden to use violence.

Foolishness, but best not to inform the great man of another failure. Next time he would do things his own way.

Despite the innkeeper's gruff manner, Franz thought he detected signs of kindness. He offered, "I-if y-you'll allow m-me, I sh-shall pay f-f-- you when I r-reach - h-home. M-my f-family l-lives in L-lindau." He made a gesture of writing.

The innkeeper raised his brows. "Lindau, did ye say?" He pointed to Franz's uniform. Ye're from Kurpfalz, ain't ye?"

"Y-yes, b-b—." Franz took a breath and started again. "I w-was a s-stu - ah -- u-univ-vers--ty - ah - H-hei—d-d--b-b--." The last came out as a mere garbled breath.

The innkeeper sighed. "Never mind." He went to get paper, quill, and inkhorn. "Just sign yer name and write down who ye are and where ye live on the bottom of the bill."

Franz did so eagerly. The bill was large, but the man had been kind and was taking a risk.

"How're ye going to get home?" the innkeeper asked.

Franz looked down at his crippled legs. At least the three villains had left him his boots, no doubt because they did not fit them. "W-walk."

The innkeeper shook his head and left. Franz started toward the door. He needed his second crutch because he could not put weight on his right leg at all and his left leg was still too weak to bear his weight and push him forward.

"Wait, sir." A maid ran after him, a bowl of milk and a chunk of white bread in her hands. "Ye'll need yer breakfast, sir," she said, her eyes filled with pity.

Franz hated the pity but thanked her for her kindness, and sat down on one of the benches to eat. At this hour, the inn's main room was still empty of guests, and he was in no one's way. He finished the milk and bread quickly. He had hardly eaten the night before but hurried more out of shame than hunger. When he was done, he staggered up to return the bowl to the kitchen. Those dependent on charity, learn to be humble before their benefactors. The thought reminded him unpleasantly of the sycophancy of the three soldiers the night before.

The maid was kind, though. She saw him coming and rushed to take the bowl, waving away his stuttered thanks. "A safe journey, sir," she said with a smile, just as if he had been an ordinary customer and not a begging, penniless cripple.

And then more kindness.

The innkeeper returned. "There's a wine wagon outside," he said. "The carter's going south as far as Kempten. He says ye can ride with him if ye like."

Tears came to Franz's eyes. He could not speak, but he shook the innkeeper's hand, then hobbled outside, the innkeeper holding the door for him, to meet a graybeard in rough woolen clothes and knitted stockings, master of a team of sturdy draft horses and a wagon loaded with wine barrels.

Franz got up on the seat with the help of the graybeard and the innkeeper and started on the next leg of his homeward journey.

The graybeard's name was Anton. He was taciturn, and Franz was grateful for this and sat for the long day, sunk into misery. He no longer feared that he would die somewhere in a ditch, but the homecoming now loomed even more hatefully in his imagination. They would see a hopeless cripple who brought them debts instead of his lieutenant's pay. Perhaps this was his punishment—and given his offense, it was mild indeed—so he bore up under it.

The advantage of traveling with a carter who carried wine to customers at various inns on his route was that he was invited to share his meals and found a dry bed in the straw of the inn's stable in Kempten. His companion broke his silence only once, to ask about Franz's regiment, where he got wounded, and where he was bound to. The fact that Franz had trouble speaking put an end to other conversation.

In Kempten, Anton found Franz another form of transport in a farmer's cart. This carried him only a few miles westward, but it brought him the gift of bread and a hunk of cheese. He set out on foot after that. It was a dry, warm spring day, and he moved by leaning on his crutch and swinging his left foot forward. He thought he was becoming handier with the single crutch until he had to rely on it for any distance. The pain the crutch caused to his underarm and shoulder within the first mile was so great that he had to rest frequently. Dying in a ditch seemed once again a possibility, even a release.

But there were kind people everywhere, and someone else found him, took him a little ways, and passed him on to another person. In this manner, he finally reached the lake at sundown.

He was riding backward on the servant's seat of a
fast carriage and only realized where he was when the
road made a bend, and the trees parted.

And there, under a blue and rosy sky, lay the Bodensee. The English and French tourists called it Lake
Constance after the town Konstanz at its western end.
To the Romans it had been *lacus brigantium* after their
city *Brigantium,* now Bregenz. The lake was old and
had seen much of life and death, of war and peace.

As if in welcome, the westering sun turned its surface to molten gold. Small, white-sailed fishing boats
were headed home. Here and there along the shore,
cheerful towns with onion domes and quaint, steeply-
pointed tile roofs lay like jewels in a necklace of green
and flowering trees.

Franz saw his lake through a haze of tears and felt
such a dizzying surge of love, of passionate devotion to
the lake, that he had to clutch the seat or he would have
tumbled off.

# 5

# The Homecoming

*Deformed persons tend to avenge themselves on nature*
Francis Bacon, *Exempla*

Frau von Langsdorff suffered from the warm spring wind that people called *Föhn*. She spent a great deal of time moaning and resting in her bedroom at the back of the house.

Unimpressed by her mother's suffering, Augusta took advantage of the good weather to clean the front windows downstairs. Frau von Langsdorff did not permit her to do such a thing in full view of neighbors and passersby, but the windows were grimy and, to Augusta's mind, this was much more embarrassing than being seen washing them. She put on an apron, tied a scarf around her hair, and carried a bucket of water and some old dish clouts outside, then got the short ladder from the shed in the back garden and went to work.

The day was blue and pretty, with puffy clouds sailing along, and Augusta did not mind the wind. It helped dry the windows more quickly. She made good progress and thought that she would be done well before the church bells struck eight and her mother emerged from her room to nibble something for her supper. They always ate late because "only servants and laborers" had their evening meal before the sun set.

The sun was setting, and she had reached the last window when her neighbor put her head out to call, "Gusterl, look who's coming. That's Franz, isn't it? Oh, the poor boy!"

Augusta swung around, upsetting the water bucket and causing the ladder to wobble. Halfway down Fischergasse, a soldier in a blue and white uniform pushed himself forward awkwardly on a crutch. When he saw her, he stopped. For a moment it almost looked as if he meant to turn and stumble away.

Augusta slid down the ladder, picked up her skirts, and ran. "Franz," she shouted, her voice as joyous as a lark's, "Oh, Franz!" When she reached him, she threw her arms around his neck, half laughing and half crying. "O, Franz, my dear, it's you, it's finally you. I've been watching for so long but you never came."

He did not hug her back and said nothing, and after a moment she let him go to look at him. His crippled leg shocked her. He was also unshaven, thin, and very pale, but there was something worse in his face, in the blue eyes that would not meet hers, in the tight clamping of his lips. It frightened her.

"You look tired," she said in a falsely cheerful voice, more to convince herself that was all it was. "Come, lean on me. Mama will be beside herself with happiness."

He still said nothing and glowered at the neighbors who came from their houses, smiling and curious. They greeted him, asked how he was, patted his shoulders, gave him joy. Many young men had left for the war and not returned.

Franz neither smiled nor spoke. He nodded, shook his head, gestured that he was exhausted, in pain, eager to get home. And so they let him go.

Augusta closed the door of their house, and they were alone. "Welcome home, dearest Franz," she said in the dim hallway. "Oh, how I've prayed to see you here again. How I've promised God anything if He would only return you to us. Why did you stay away so long?"

He said nothing.

She brushed away the tears and hid her anxiety in reproof. "Why didn't you write? There's nothing wrong with your right arm or hand, is there?" She touched the hand and searched his face anxiously.

He croaked, "I-I c-could n-not."

Her happiness to have him back overcame everything else. "Never mind. You're here now. No need to stammer apologies. Mama and I will soon get you well again. You're so thin. Are you really in great pain?"

He was in pain but shook his head and looked down. "I-I'm s-s-sorry b-but I s-seem t-to have l-lost m-my s-speech."

She hugged him. "I know. It's all a little too much. You've been hurt and heaven knows how many horrors you've seen. Come into the kitchen and sit down. I'll put on some soup and then get Mama. She has one of her headaches."

He shook his head but followed her to the kitchen where she made him sit in their mother's high-backed settle and then stirred the coals on the hearth. She put the spider over the fire with a pot of potato-and-carrot soup. *Volteur* jumped down from the top of the cupboard and came to inspect Franz. Franz leaned down to stroke the cat, and Augusta was filled with a dizzying happiness as she gathered earthenware bowls and set out a loaf of bread, butter, and cheese. All would finally be well.

"There. We still have some of the cake Herr Seutter brought, but I think I'd better get Mama first." She took a few steps toward the door, then turned. "Oh, Franz, I have so much to tell you. I've missed you so."

The cat jumped on her brother's lap and settled down, purring loudly. "W-wait, Aug-gusta," he said, making an effort to speak slowly. "Y-you d-don't unders-s-tand." He gestured to his mouth. "Th-this isn't g-g-going aw-way, I'm af-fraid. I-I'm a usel-less c-cripple and a f-freak." He raised his hands from the cat's back and covered his face. A hoarse sob racked him, and he doubled over. *Volteur* hissed and jumped from his lap a moment before Augusta flung her arms about her brother.

"Oh, Franz, don't. It will be all right. We'll make it all right. You'll see. You just need a little time to rest and get your strength back. You're home now. Mama and I will look after you."

"Augusta?"

Their mother's voice came from the hallway. An expression of fear passed over her brother's pale face. He pushed her away.

"Where are you, girl? People are looking this way. I can see them from the window. Has something happened?" Frau von Langsdorff reached the door of the kitchen and gasped.

Augusta stood up with a vague notion of shielding her brother. But of course that was impossible. Frau von Langsdorff shrieked.

"Franz? Is that Franz? Let me see him. Let me see my son, my beloved child, my life!"

She rushed forward, pushing Augusta aside, and flung herself on Franz.

The scene which followed was certainly affecting to their mother, but Franz looked positively terrified. When the torrent of endearments, questions, protestations, hugs, kisses, wails, and laughter began to abate, Augusta interrupted, "Mama, you must give Franz time. He's very tired, and hungry, too, I shouldn't wonder. And stop pulling him about so. You're hurting his leg."

Frau von Langsdorff desisted long enough to say, "His leg? Oh, dear. Yes. Why didn't you tell us you were coming home? There's nothing in the house.

Augusta, run over to Herr Scutter and tell him the good news and beg a few things from his kitchen."

"Mama, we have taken enough from Herr Scutter. We have soup, and I'll slice some fresh bread. We have butter and cheese. And cake for dessert. It will do for now. As soon as Franz is resting, I'll go to the market and buy a chicken for a real feast tomorrow. And you can bake one of your raisin cakes Franz is so fond of." She busied herself, stoking the fire again and stirring the soup. A savory smell filled the kitchen, and hope filled Augusta's heart.

Her mother bridled. "What a cold girl you are to offer such a poor sort of welcome to your brother. And Herr Scutter will be hurt if he's not told right away and made part of our family celebration. Have you forgotten how much he has done to find your brother and get us news of him?"

Augusta said nothing and went into the pantry for the cake. She could hear a one-sided conversation in the kitchen. Their mother chattered on about Herr Scutter, his kindness, his wealth, his standing in the city. In between, she asked if Franz was in pain, how he got hurt, how long he could stay before returning to his military duties, and if the ladies in Sachsen wore their hair powdered. Since she did not leave Franz time to answer, she remained blissfully unaware of his stutter. Augusta returned to the kitchen to serve bowls of soup and to slice some bread and cheese. The bread she buttered generously, and she added a mug of beer for Franz. She and her mother drank water.

Franz fell to hungrily. Frau von Langsdorff finally paused her chattering, but she swallowed her soup quickly. Franz could not be expected to tell his story until he had eaten, and he was taking his time. She finally got impatient and said, "Well, since you refuse to go tell Herr Seutter, Augusta, I suppose I must do it. I'll just change my cap, and we'll be back in a trice. Be sure to have some wine ready. Herr Seutter will wish to meet your brother." And she flounced out of the kitchen.

Franz glowered. "Wh-who is H-Herr S-S--?"

"Seutter," his sister helped out. "He's the man Mama has set her cap for." She giggled.

Franz dropped his knife. "Wh-wha--t?"

"I know it sounds ridiculous, but really they are nearly of an age, and he's very well-to-do and has been extremely attentive. Mama is delighted with the attention. And it would be an answer to our prayers."

He frowned at her. "Wh-why?"

"Well, he's rich. And he's quite nice really, even if he's nothing like Papa. He's not an educated man, you know, but one who had a rich father and is a good businessman himself. He's been very kind to us."

Her brother stared at that. "How, k-kind?"

Augusta felt a little uncomfortable. How could she explain his gifts? Or her visits to the Seutter house to play the harpsichord and, lately, to teach its owner to pick out a few simple tunes. His pleasure and gratitude for this small service knew no bounds. He always treated her to cakes and chocolate and also pressed other gifts on her—a pair of embroidered gloves, a silk scarf

with exquisite lace trim, a ring set with pearls and dia-
monds. She had refused the ring and passed the gloves
and scarves on to her mother—who received them without surprise and considerable satisfaction. Augusta had
begun to covet such things and could easily convince
herself that he almost stood in place of her father. Still,
his relationship to her mother remained unsettled.

"Oh," she said lightly, busying herself with the dishes, "he sends Mama a few delicacies now and then and
offers his advice on matters. He helped us find out
where you were when we were frantic for news of you."

The last was inspired and effectively stopped Franz's
disapproval of the relationship. When Frau von
Langsdorff returned with a beaming Seutter, the meeting between the two men was fairly polite.

On the part of Seutter, it was much more than that.
He made a great effort to be pleasant to Franz, expressing his joy at meeting him and having him back with his
family. As Augusta's mother bustled about, fussing over
her son, slicing cake and pouring wine, Augusta managed to whisper to their guest that her brother found it
difficult to talk. Seutter took the hint and carried on a
conversation that let Franz answer with nods or mono-
syllables. Still, Augusta heaved a sigh of relief when he
took his leave.

She returned to the kitchen to find that her mother
had discovered Franz's speech defect.

"Dear God," she greeted her daughter, "isn't it
enough that those monsters crippled him? Did they
have to take away his speech? What will he do now?
What can he do? He cannot be a soldier, and certainly

not a preacher. Why, he cannot even be a teacher or a lawyer. Oh, this is misfortune indeed! What will people say? What will they think when they hear him?"

Franz sat frozen, his face very pale, his eyes like blue quartz.

"Mama," Augusta pleaded, "please stop it. Franz has been wounded but he'll get better. It will take a little time, but he will be well again."

"N-no!" Franz levered himself out of the settle and onto his crutch. He snarled, "I-I'm a c-c-cripple *and* a-an i-imb-becile. G-get used t-t-to it, M-mama." Pushing Augusta roughly out of his way, he hobbled out of the kitchen.

The best inn in the free city of Lindau was called *Zur Sonne.* The assassin took a room, giving his name as Georg Koehl from Salzburg. He stayed several days, pretending to enjoy his visit so much that he kept delaying his departure. The innkeeper was delighted. Not only was this guest paying for the best room, but he took all his meals there and ordered a bottle of the best wine with his dinner. Moreover, he frequently invited guests to a beer or *schnapps* in the evening.

Herr Koehl did enjoy his visit, though he never lost sight of his objective. He learned all he could about Lieutenant von Langsdorff, and this familiarity bred contempt. The man was not only a pitiful cripple with a badly deformed leg, but he stuttered so badly that people avoided talking to him. Furthermore, he seemed slightly mad or so melancholy that he might easily do away with himself and thus relieve the assassin of the chore.

Still, there was the letter, and Koehl took pains to observe the cripple's family and their position in the city.

Position, as he knew only too well, was everything. A man in good position might dare anything and get away with it. A poor man, on the other hand, were he ever so obedient and hard-working, would be consigned to an ignoble hanging without much more than a shake of the head.

The cripple and his family were poor. The assassin had not been so different, but he had taken risky steps to rise in the world. Now he must move carefully or lose what he had gained. He decided to make use again of one of the men who had bungled the theft in Ulm. This time, however, he would pick the youngest because he could be molded to his purpose.

After his mother's outburst, Franz kept to his room and refused to speak to anyone but his sister. His hair was dirty and hung to his shoulders. He let his beard grow and rarely changed his linen. Frau von Langsdorff complained bitterly, first to Augusta, then to Herr Seutter, and after a month had passed, even to her neighbors. By then she had decided her son's "illness" did not reflect on her after all; rather it bestowed on her a mantle of martyrdom. She made the most of it, even to the point of exaggerating his condition so that, instead of being thought an imbecile, Franz was now believed to be mad. The day Franz found out, he kicked the cat and pushed his sister out of his way so roughly that she wore a bruise on her arm for a week.

His mother did not hear her son's nighttime terrors. She slept with wax plugs in her ears, claiming that the ringing of nearby church bells kept her awake all night. But Augusta did hear and on his first night home came rushing to his room to see what was wrong. He explained that a nightmare had woken him—he did not describe it, though the torn bodies, rearing horses, and flashing swords remained as vivid as they had been when he slept—and thus reassured, she had left. But the nightmares returned, and finally he locked his door against her pity.

Whenever he encountered his mother's or sister's concern, he responded with snarls, sometimes roaring at them to leave him alone. Once he raised his fist to his mother and frightened her into fearing for her life. After that she left him to Augusta's care and fled whenever she saw him coming. Augusta did not fear her brother, but she worried that he might do himself some mischief and watched him closely.

Twice, after dark, she followed him out of the house to the lake shore. But he only stood, staring out across the dark waters, and eventually turned away to hobble home.

Strangely enough, Herr Seutter was not taken in by Frau von Langsdorff's description of her son's madness.

One day, when a mild, warm summer had settled over the lake and the island of Lindau, Augusta came out of the house into the garden to hang some laundry on the clothesline that stretched between the pear tree and the corner of the house. Franz sat reading on the bench under the old tree. When Augusta put down the basket of wet laundry, he looked up. She gave him a smile, then bent and stretched to hang sheets and petticoats, shifts and shirts, stockings and breeches up to dry in the warm summer air. She liked their clean smell and the way they fluttered in the breeze. When the basket was empty and she picked it up, she saw her brother staring at her with a curious expression.

"What is it?" she asked, but before he could answer, the back door opened and Herr Seutter joined them.

"Ah, so here you are," he called out. "What a pretty day to be outside. I trust you feel much stronger these days, young man?" He made a little bow to Augusta, then sat down beside Franz.

Franz gave his sister a furious look and reached for his crutches—he had two again—to make his escape, but Herr Seutter put a hand on his arm. "A moment, if you please," he said, becoming serious. "I came to see you, Franz. I hope you'll think of me as a friend and I trust that someday soon you may think even better of me." He blushed a little and glanced quickly at Augusta, who waited, surprised and curious. "But we won't talk of that yet. I've been coming here from time to time this summer, very pleased to visit and to see you mending day by day. It occurred to me once or twice that time must hang heavy on your hands. Your Mama—mind you, I think her a most estimable lady—is not perhaps always the best companion for a young gentleman like yourself." He cleared his throat and gave a nervous little laugh. "In short, I thought you might like an excuse to get away for a bit every day. Am I right?"

Augusta forgot the rest of the laundry which had yet to be scrubbed, rinsed, and wrung out. She had fretted over her brother's refusal to leave the house and go among people. Though she knew he was not insane, she was afraid his odd behavior was due to some inner despair that was getting worse rather than better.

There was, for example, the matter of the missing money. Franz received a small amount each quarter for his military service. He turned this over to his mother after he arrived, and they used it to buy food. It would be almost another month before more would arrive, and Augusta had hoarded the few *talers* carefully in an empty stoneware pot that normally held pickles. Several days ago she had gone to get some market money and found the pot empty. She thought Franz had taken the money, or their mother, but she could hardly remonstrate with either. Franz was entitled to it, and Frau von Langsdorff would merely fall into another bout of self-commiseration and blame Franz for their poverty. So she kept the matter to herself and used some of the money she had put aside for a new shift.

Now she saw her brother's anger flare up that Herr Seutter should intrude into his private life and take it upon himself to guess what his thoughts were. She was afraid that he would lash out, perhaps even strike their guest. His fits of anger were unpredictable.

But he did not strike their visitor. He growled, "M-my m-mother s-says I'm m-mad." Then, with a bitter laugh, he taunted, "G-go on! R-run or I m-may k-kill you."

Herr Seutter did not run. He chuckled as if Franz had made a joke. "I know, I know. She's a dear lady but sometimes she says some very silly things. I daresay your Papa used to have his hands full with her."

This comment clearly startled Franz. He shot Augusta a look of astonishment. She said quickly, "It's true. Papa spent most of his day locked into his study, and Mama would tiptoe past his door with a finger to her lips, telling us not to disturb him at his work." She smiled at the memory.

"Ha, ha, ha," laughed Herr Seutter, "I thought so. A most charming lady, of course, but a man needs some time to himself. So I've been thinking. You see, my dear Franz, I know a lawyer who needs a bright young assistant. It's only a matter of writing letters and taking notes about his cases. And perhaps some reading-up in his law books. Someone who knows a little Latin. We don't seem to have many educated young men in Lindau these days, and so right away I thought of you. What do you think? Doesn't it sound like a capital idea?"

Augusta clasped her hands and held her breath. Oh, if only Franz would say yes. It would answer all of her prayers. Franz would have respectable employment and begin to take an interest in the world again. It would give him back his confidence, and, oh, how badly they needed the extra income!

Her brother stared at Herr Seutter. "Y-you c-cannot be s-serious," he sputtered. "Wh-what m-makes y-you th-think anyone w-would want t-t . . . s-someone like m-me?"

Herr Seutter raised a brow. "You mean your leg? Or because you speak a little more slowly than other people? What can that signify in a lawyer's chambers? No, no, what's needed there is a learned head and a good hand."

Franz looked away. "N-no. You d-don't unders-s-stand. P-people s-say I'm m-mad. N-now go away!"

Herr Seutter looked at Augusta. His face was stern when he got up. "Your sister needs you," he said to Franz. "Look at her. She's a beautiful young woman and should be thinking of dances and pretty gowns. Instead she's working in rags like the poorest maid."

Augusta shrank into herself. Her old summer dress was much too tight and too short, but it had seemed good enough for laundry day. She had left off the kerchief of bleached cotton that she normally tucked into its bodice because it was hot and kept coming undone as she worked. Franz looked at her and flushed crimson, and she felt the color of shame hot on her own face. She snatched up the empty basket.

Herr Seutter turned back to Franz. "If you won't face people for your own sake, do it for her," he said quite angrily.

Augusta fled into the house. To her dismay, he followed and caught up with her in the hallway, catching her by an elbow. "Forgive me, child," he said. "I wouldn't have hurt you for the world, but I had to shame your brother into action. He wasn't getting any better."

She stood, her head bowed, and knew he was right. He had spoken out of kindness. Overcome with gratitude and trust, she laid her head against his embroidered vest and wept.

He hesitated, then held her lightly. "Ssh! Don't cry," he murmured. "I know it's been very hard for you, but it will all come right. I promise I'll see to it that you'll be happy again."

It was very comforting to be held. She let herself go for a few moments, then realized that his hands on her back were trembling, and that his breathing was becoming heavy, and pulled away. "Thank you, sir," she whispered. "Thank you for all you have done for us. You're as kind as only a father could be."

He left quickly then and without bidding farewell to her mother.

Augusta went back out into the garden where Franz still sat, his book closed beside him. He glowered at her.

"Oh, Franz," she said, brushing away tears, "don't be angry at him. It was kindly meant and it would make us all happy."

He exploded. "H-how d-dare he! S-such a man—a mere s-s-stranger—m-meddling in affairs th-that are n-none of his bu-business."

"He's not a stranger. He's courting Mama."

"I f-forbid it. P-papa w-was a gentleman and s-scholar, a m-man of taste and learning. He's n-nothing but a t-tradesman." He reached for his crutches.

His stutter had improved with his temper, a hopeful sign. Augusta smiled through her tears. "Oh, come, Franz. He's on the city council and has been very kind."

But Franz did not return the smile. Taking up his crutches, he stood and said coldly, "You l-look like a t-trollop—showing off your b-breasts and l-legs to a man."

"Franz!" Her hands went to her bodice.

"I've s-seen less b-bare flesh on whores."

"I have no other clothes. Only my good gown for church. This is for work around the house. And I cover it with Mama's old shawl when I go to the market."

"*K-kruzif-fix! Zum Teufel!*"

The blasphemous cursing shocked Augusta. Franz had never cursed before.

"I'll m-make Mama b-buy you s-some c-c-clothes," he sputtered and started for the house.

Augusta thought of the empty pickle jar. "No, Franz," she cried. "You mustn't do that. We don't have the money. I can fix this dress so it won't offend you. I'll add a hem and make a new bodice from an old dress of Mama's." She looked down at herself. "I must have grown. And I'm getting fat."

He turned to look back at her with blazing eyes. "Dear G-god! Wh-what has this f-family c-come to?" he muttered.

Augusta glared back. She was both ashamed and angry at Franz. She knew that she was little more than a scullery maid, someone who did all the rough work because they could not afford help. Perhaps that was what made him think she was a loose woman.

He said roughly, "You m-must know how you l-look to s-strangers. You shouldn't have l-let S-seutter see you like this."

"He thinks of me as a child. A daughter. He comes here for Mama's sake only."

Franz snorted.

Augusta remembered the embrace in the hallway and how Herr Seutter's hands had trembled on her back. Suddenly there was a small doubt in her mind about Herr Seutter's intentions and a very large one about the future.

But her unhappiness was short-lived. The next morning, Franz appeared in the kitchen freshly shaved and with his hair tied neatly in back, wearing a clean shirt, and his old blue coat and buff breeches. His mother gaped at him. He looked grim but nodded to her, then told them haltingly that he was going to see Herr Seutter about the job and left.


Not far from the city wall's westernmost corner stood a solid tower topped by five pointed turrets. The turrets were covered with colored tiles and the walls with ivy. This cheerful building was the Thieves' Tower, the local dungeon.

The assassin had selected this place for the meeting because it amused him to meet a thief there.

Max had miraculously regained sight in his left eye since Ulm. With his blond curls and without the eye patch, wearing leather knee breeches and a neat green jacket instead of a soldier's rags, he looked like a harmless country lad. The man who called himself Koehl knew better than most that Max was gallows' bait.

He did not bother with a greeting. "Well? Did you get it?"

Max Bauer grinned and shook his golden locks. "Your honor's in a hurry? What's it worth to speed up the enterprise?"

Koehl scowled. He held a fist under Max's nose. "Dog! Remember what you are and what I know about you." He pointed upward. "They call this the Thieves' Tower. I hear they have plenty of leg irons."

Max Bauer paled a little. "You've no cause to make threats, your honor," he said, sounding aggrieved. "I been doin' as you told me. I had bad luck, that's all. I watched the place every day, but they didn't all leave till Sunday. For church, I figured. I went in then, thinkin' to search the house from top to bottom."

Koehl frowned. "Get on with it. What happened?"

"T'was easy. They don't lock their doors. Nothin' worth stealing there. Proper poor, even if they make out like they're gentry. I went in the backdoor, bold as brass, and searched the parlor, hall, and kitchen." Max fingered the coins in his pocket. "Then, just as I was startin' on the bedchambers, I see the cripple coming home early. I had to scamper to get away."

"Damnation!" Koehl kicked a small rock into a patch of weeds.

Max Bauer regained some of his *sangfroid*. "I'll go back tomorrow, your honor. It'll be a pleasure." He chuckled. "I got my eye on the girl. Her ma keeps her close and works her like a slave, but she's ripe for the pluckin', if you get my drift."

Koehl slapped him. "*Lumpenhund!* I'm not paying you to fornicate. I want the letter." He stalked off muttering to himself.

# 6

# Nepomuk Stiebel

*I defy the wisest man in the world to turn a truly
good action into ridicule.*
Henry Fielding, *Joseph Andrews*

ranz found Herr Seutter in his office—a room
that had nothing in common with the late Pastor
von Langsdorff's book-filled retreat.   Seutter's
workplace contained little more than a large table,
shelves with ledgers, and a tall desk at which a clerk
stood, making entries in another ledger.

Seutter received Franz warmly.   "Now here's a day
to celebrate.   I'm happy to see you up and about, Franz,
and doing me the honor of a visit.   Come and have a
seat."   He moved an oaken settle beside his desk.
"How's the leg this morning?"

"F-fine."   Franz looked at the clerk—a pimply-faced
young man who stared back at him—and thought that

his right leg was still too weak for him to work on his feet all day long. His courage faltered. He bit his lip. "You s-said yes-s-sterday th-that you kn-know s-someone wh-who n-needs h-h-elp."

Seutter clapped his hands. "I do! Indeed, I do. However, allow me to introduce Kaspar Geiss, my clerk. Kaspar, meet my friend, Lieutenant von Langsdorff."

Kaspar Geiss, perhaps impressed by the military rank, bowed. Franz nodded back and felt a little better.

Seutter said, "It's very good of you to offer your help. You would do my friend a great favor, a very great favor."

Franz blushed a little, aware that he was the one who needed the favor. "I h-hope so, b-but it m-may not s-serve." Catching the clerk's eyes on him, Franz flushed again.

"Pah." Seutter rose. "It will serve capitally. Most capitally. Shall we go right away? Do you feel up to it?"

Franz nodded. "You're v-very g-good," he murmured. The clerk now stared at Franz's crippled leg as Franz took up his crutches and hobbled awkwardly to the door.

This was going to be hard, and not just because he was a cripple.

Privy Councilor and attorney Nepomuk Stiebel had his chambers in another. patrician house at the opposite end of the market. A finely lettered brass plate announced, "*Doctor Juris Nepomucus Stibelius, Advocatus Ordinarius*," and in smaller letters in German, "offers his services in all legal matters."

Doktor Stiebel turned out to be elderly and of such short stature that Franz at first took him for a dwarf, a very odd-looking dwarf performing in some Italian pantomime. He perched on an enormous carved chair behind an enormous carved table. An old-fashioned full wig shed powder over the shoulders of his brown velvet coat like snow dusting barren winter fields. On his nose rested thick spectacles, and his hand held a very long quill. Beside his desk, a small, brown bird chirped in a gilded cage.

The little lawyer peered at them over his glasses and became animated. Hopping down from his chair, he cried—in a voice that was surprisingly strong and clear for such a small person, "Seutter, you old devil. What have you done now? Don't tell me. Dipped into clients' funds? Robbed a poor widow of her mite? Or murdered an inconvenient blackmailer?" He cackled and came to shake Seutter's hand.

Standing, he had gained some stature but he was still short in spite of a pair of very high-heeled shoes with large gilt buckles. Franz wondered if the velvet suit, time-yellowed lace jabot and rich lace cuffs, silk stockings, and shoes had once belonged to a long deceased courtier.

Seutter, who had received the aspersions on his probity with rumbling laughter, introduced Franz.

Stiebel made Franz an elegant bow. "A great pleasure, young man," he said. "My friend here has spoken so highly of your talents that I fear my needs are well beneath your abilities, but he seems to think that you would not be completely averse to them at the present time?"

Franz muttered an affirmative.

Stiebel's narrow face stretched into a smile and his eyes twinkled over the spectacles. "'*O diem laetum*,' as Pliny said. You make my day joyous. Pray be seated, gentlemen."

The interview was strange in that Stiebel both asked and answered his own questions, leaving Franz no more to do than to nod or shake his head. Seutter listened with a smile, or made noises of approval and comments like, "There! Didn't I tell you so?" "I knew it would serve perfectly," and "What happiness!"

So Franz became a lawyer's clerk.

Max Bauer made his second attempt on the Langsdorff house toward noon. He had been watching since dawn and had almost decided to try a daring night-time entry while the family was asleep when he saw the cripple hobbling away and shortly afterward his mother setting off with a basket over her arm. That left the girl, and the smoke from the chimney told him that she must be cooking. He knew well enough that the kitchen was in the back of the house while the stairs to the bedrooms were in the front.

He walked boldly up to the front door and knocked very softly. After a short wait, he tried the handle and slipped in. The hall was dim, but he could hear the clatter of pots from the kitchen. He sniffed the air.

Cabbage and onions. It smelled good and he was hungry. His employer had not paid him because Max had not produced the letter.

He listened, heard only the normal kitchen noises, and tiptoed to the stairs. His foot hovered over the lowest step when the girl came out of the kitchen, saw him, and froze.

For a moment, they stood staring at each other—perhaps equally frightened. Max pictured himself with a noose around his neck, and she was a mere girl and must be terrified to find a strange man in her house when she was alone. It was a wonder she had not started screaming yet. Max recovered and put his foot back on the tiled floor.

"Beggin' your pardon, miss," he said in his humblest voice and in a wheedling tone. "I knocked and was sure I heard you call out to come in. I hope I didn't give you a fright."

"You did," snapped Augusta. "And I did not hear you knock. What do you want?"

Max bowed his head and twisted his hands. "Just a piece of bread, miss. I'm that hungry. I'd be glad to work for it."

He peered cautiously at her and saw that she was undecided. Good. The noose could be avoided once again. "For the sake of our Lord," he pleaded, then shuffled back a step or two. "Beggin' your pardon. I can see it's not a good time. I'll try elsewhere." He bobbed his head and reached for the door handle.

"Wait," she said. "When did you eat last?"

"Yesterday, miss. Or maybe the day before. I can't hardly recall. I don't like to ask for food but I haven't had work since the war."

This was inspired, for she came closer and took his arm. "Oh, you're one of the poor soldiers. Perhaps you've been wounded like my poor brother?"

When he saw her face close up and filled with pity for him, he was almost too overcome to speak. She was as beautiful as an angel, an innocent angel, and he was ashamed of what he had thought to do with her not so long ago. "Yes, miss," he lied humbly. "Took a bullet in my leg. 'T wasn't nothin', but I fell and must've been kicked by a horse. Now my head gets dizzy with the pain sometimes."

"Oh. I'm sorry for you. I know it's hard for a man to come back from the war and have no work and feel the constant pain. Well, come into the kitchen. The soup's not ready, but I have bread and butter, and some sausages. We won't need them all for our dinner. I can cut up a bit of bacon instead." She drew him after her into the well-lit kitchen and made him sit at the table. Here they looked at each other properly. Max saw a young woman, or rather a girl just at the point of turning into a young woman, with a dainty figure in a faded dress and large white kitchen apron. Shining brown hair was pinned under a white ruffled cap, but a few curls escaped and trembled against the rosy cheeks. Amazingly—to Max, who thought brown-haired girls had brown eyes—her eyes were a clear, deep blue. And now she smiled at him with those pretty lips and white teeth, and Max fell in love.

Franz's life fell into a routine that would have given him pleasure if he had not still woken up on a strangled scream most nights. The days at least took on some semblance of normalcy, though that was not the word to use for Doctor Stiebel.

Nepomuk Stiebel had never been married. He slept above his chambers and kept no servants. His only companion was the small goldfinch who lived in the gilded cage which its master carried daily from bed-chamber to work chamber and back again.

In time, Franz became aware of other eccentricities. At first glance, the legal chambers had seemed ordinary enough: six large rooms that occupied the lower floor of the house and were arranged on either side of a hallway that contained only the pale stone floor, dark oak wain-scoting, dark oak staircase to the upper floors, and a dark oak bench where callers awaited their turn. The room to the right of the front door was Stiebel's office. The other two on that side communicated with it and each other and contained bookcases filled with leather-bound legal tomes. To the left of the entrance was a meeting room with a large oak table and six plain side chairs presided over by a carved settle with grotesques snarling from its back and arm rests. Its dark green vel-vet upholstery bore traces of the same white powder as Stiebel's velvet coat. The rest of the downstairs was taken up by a legal documents room and a storage room.

It was the latter that contained an odd assortment of objects that seemed to have no purpose there. A dusty glass case held a dead snake, a moth-eaten owl looked down from its wooden perch, a gilded harp leaned against one wall and a violin against the other, a series of stands held wigs of every description and color, a clothes' form was dressed in an old-fashioned white silk court suit, the skirt of its coat and waistcoat heavily embroidered and trimmed with tarnished silver. The walls were covered with pictures, some of them oil portraits of frowning old men, darkened with age, and others prints of famous places. The rest of the collection, if that was what it was, resided in a number of carved trunks and two large wardrobes.

Franz had little time to inspect the hidden treasures. He was put to work in the first of the two book rooms, at a chair and table under the window. Here he resided for the next months under the benevolent but strict eye of councilor Stiebel.

He arrived punctually at seven every morning to receive his instructions for the day. At eight, the waiter from the *Goldene Löwe* across the square arrived with a pot of steaming coffee, two cups and plates, hot rolls fresh from the bakery, and butter. Stiebel produced a jar of jam made from plums or strawberries, and they would share a pleasant breakfast discussing politics or the state of the postal system. Legal business was taboo during meals, and Stiebel did most of the discussing.

When the church bells rang the noon hour, the waiter returned to clear away the breakfast dishes and set out the midday meal. This was always specific to the day of the week and never changed, except for the preparation and seasonal adjustment of vegetables. Mondays was beef, Tuesdays chicken, Wednesdays sausages, Thursdays veal, Fridays fish or *Käs' Spätzle* (Stiebel was Catholic), and Saturday pork. Franz used to wonder what his employer did about meals on Sundays, but he was grateful that he did not have to eat at home. It saved money, and he avoided his mother's chatter.

Matters did improve dramatically at home. The day Franz returned from his first day's work, his mother not only did not run away but rushed to greet him.

"My dear boy," she cried, "how proud I am! My son a secretary to the best advocate in our city! His confidential secretary! Oh, it's a most respectable and promising career for a clever young man." She embraced Franz, who bore it in guarded silence and looked to Augusta for an explanation of this change of heart. Augusta raised an eyebrow and made a face, but her eyes danced. It reminded him of when they were children and shared a secret. Franz felt almost light-hearted.

When his mother released him, she said triumphantly, "And Herr Seutter made it all possible. He is the dearest of men to be so devoted to me." She cast up her eyes and pressed her hands to her bosom. "Oh, it fills my mother's heart to overflowing to know that I have helped my son rise above his terrible affliction!"

Frau von Langsdorff wasted no time in informing all her neighbors of her hand in the miraculous cure of her son's madness.

Meanwhile Franz was not only fed well at Stiebel's, but he received a generous salary that was increased when he had learned enough to require little instruction. Most of this money Franz turned over to his mother, except for a little pocket money and something extra for Augusta.

Frau von Langsdorff purchased fabrics and paid a seamstress to make dresses for herself and her daughter. Soon, there was also a very young maid, a farmer's daughter who wanted to learn housekeeping in a city household.

The fact that he made all this possible went a long way toward allaying the seething anger that had plagued Franz's conscious hours.

He worked contentedly six days a week, often until late into the night because Stiebel seemed loath to part with him in the evenings. It did not matter. Franz had found some peace at last, a modicum of it at home, and a great deal more in chambers. There, he really did begin to heal. His right leg improved enough that he learned to do without the crutches and used a cane instead. His speech was less slurred also.

But the dreams still haunted his nights, and one or two incidents signaled that he had not left the horror behind.

The worst of these happened soon after he had started work, on a warm summer afternoon. Franz was bent over a legal tome, following the strangely-shaped gothic font of the text with a finger so he would not misread any letters. He jotted down his translation as he read. Near him lay a Latin-German dictionary, though he rarely consulted it. His Latin was very good, thanks to his father's teaching and the university. Only certain medieval corruptions stopped him.

This work required his utmost concentration as well as a knowledge of legal matters, and so he did not notice that the light outside had changed. He looked up only when a particularly violent gust seized the half-opened window, slammed it inward, and lifted loose papers from his desk, scattering them over the floor.

The sky was an angry charcoal gray. A chestnut tree near his window tossed its branches in the wind, and the first thick drops hit the window pane when Franz forced it closed and pushed the latch in place. A summer thunderstorm. It was nearly dark in the room. He bent to gather up the sheets of paper, pale rectangles against the darkness of the flooring, when a flash of blinding bluish light filled the room as suddenly as if some curtain between time and eternity had been rent. The darkness that followed was denser and more suffocating than he could have imagined, and then the world cracked apart with a noise as of a hundred cannons exploding beside him, above him, all around him.

In an instant he was back on the hillside near Freiberg. All around him men were stabbing, bleeding, dying. Cannons belched smoke and hurled death. Giant hussars appeared, sabers flashing, and braying black horses reared above.

He threw himself down and screamed again and again, long past the final roll of thunder. Then the nightmare of severed heads and hands, of the sight, feel, and smell of blood returned, and he retched and sobbed until the next clap of thunder made him scream again.

He felt the hands first, tugging, shaking. Then he heard a voice. Words filtered through the shell he built around himself with his screams until it cracked and sense leaked through.

"Franz! Franz!"

As the fragments of the shell broke away on all sides, he wondered who Franz was. And then, having found him, he wondered who was calling.

*Judgment Call?*

He opened his eyes to face an angry God at the very moment when the blue light flashed again and blinded him, just before the divine wrath crashed down, crushing and obliterating him. He sobbed and curled up with a whimper.

But still the voice called and still the hands tugged. He reached out, clutched a hand, and cried, "Stop! Stop! There's too much death. Too much blood!"

The thundering barrage came again, and in the end, he just held on and wept.

When the thunder finally died away and lightning merely flickered across the murky darkness, Franz came to himself and knew where he was and who held him.

Stiebel said, "My poor boy. Are you hurt? Did you fall or did the lightning strike you?"

Thunder and lightning were common occurrences in the summer months over the lake. As a child, Franz had watched the jagged fire in the night sky dancing across the water and had found it beautiful. But such sounds and sights, even the slightly sulfurous smell in the air, were now too close to the sights, sounds, and smells of the battlefield where the heavy artillery plowed bloody furrows through the lines of soldiers.

He sat up. His body was bathed in sweat; he was shaking and deeply ashamed. Stiebel still knelt beside him, looking worried. "N-no," Franz said. "I'm unh-hurt. I b-beg your p-pardon, s-sir. It w-w-was exc-ceedingl-ly s-s-stupid!"

"Not at all. Are you sure you're quite all right?"

How to explain such terror? Only small children were frightened of thunderstorms, and even they did not make such scenes. He wanted to crawl away and hide in his room at home again, but Stiebel had been kind to him and he owed him an explanation.

"I-it was th-the n-noise. S-so s-sudden and l-loud. L-like the c-cannon f-fire," he said.

Stiebel was silent for a moment. Then he said, "Ah, yes. I see. Does this happen often? I mean, do loud noises frighten you?"

"N-no!" But that wasn't entirely true. He had ducked one day when a carter had snapped his whip with a sound like a gun shot outside his window. His heart had raced for minutes after that. And there had been other noises. His sister dropping a kettle in the kitchen had started him shaking, and he had spilled the beer from his glass. A child screaming after a fall had made him see the headless body of the drummer boy Karl again. The memory had been so vivid that Franz had burst into tears and hurried away.

He said more honestly, "S-sometimes. You s-see, what h-happened is always w-with m-me. I h-have n-nightmares."

"Hmm," said Stiebel, getting up and extending a hand to him. "That must be very unpleasant. Have you told anyone about it? Consulted a doctor perhaps?"

Franz stood and wiped his face and neck with a handkerchief. The old fear of being thought mad was back. He looked at Stiebel, who merely looked serious but might well be thinking of dismissing him. The thought horrified Franz. He had come to like, no, love his work here. Yes, he had even come to be fond of his employer. "I-I'm n-not m-mad," he said, pleading for belief. "I'm n-not. D-don't s-send me aw-way! I p-promise n-no one w-will know."

Stiebel's eyes widened with shock. "Send you away? Don't be absurd! How would I get along without you? No, no, there's no fear of that. But what can we do? It grieves me to see you like this."

Franz felt like weeping with relief. "Th-thank you," he mumbled, turning away.

Outside the rain had slowed. Single drops still landed on the window and made their way downward. The world looked brighter but fractured into kaleidoscopic patches of color.

Stiebel put a hand on Franz's arm. "Come join me in a small glass of cognac. I feel the need for it."

They sat in the meeting room and talked like friends—or perhaps like uncle and nephew—sipping fine French brandy from small glasses. The spirits spread a comfortable warmth through Franz's belly and loosened his tongue enough to talk about that day at Freiberg.

"S-so, you s-see," he said, staring into his glass and thinking about it with revulsion, "I k-killed so m-many men, h-helpless m-men. And I m-made a terrible m-mistake when I d-didn't give the order to f-form s-square and the hussars rode us d-down. It was m-my fault C-carl died, m-my fault that all of them died. All b-but the one that gave me the l-letter, but I failed him, t-too."

"Well, now," said Stiebel, "your not giving the right order does not seem so terrible to me. They sent an untrained youngster into his first battle. And what were you to do but kill or be killed? You were wounded yourself. Most likely you were half out of your mind. What did they expect? What's this about a letter?"

"A captain—I d-didn't think he w-was s-so badly hurt but he d-died—g-gave me a l-letter to his father. Only I f-forg-got all about it t-till I was ready t-to come home. And then there was n-no one by that n-name in M-mannheim. All that w-weighs on m-my c-conscience."

Stiebel said practically, "Then you must bring the letter tomorrow and together we'll discover how to deliver it."

"You're very k-kind, sir. I should not b-burden you with my t-troubles."

"I take it as a compliment."

# 7

# Max

*Calms appear when storms are past,*
*Love will have his hour at last:*
*Nature is my kindly care;*
*Mars destroys, and I repair.*
*Take me, take me while you may;*
*Venus comes not every day.*

John Dryden, *The Secular Masque*

Augusta was greatly relieved when Franz took the position in lawyer Stiebel's chambers and liked his work. She was even more relieved when his employment and his absence from home ended her mother's wailing fits, and peace as well as some prosperity returned to the family.

But at the same time, her life became emptier that ever. Franz was gone. Her mother spent her time with neighbors or in planning little treats for Herr Seutter or in adorning her person with new caps, curls, and crinolines. Running the household fell to Augusta's duties, but the little maid Elsbeth did most of the housework, and time hung heavy on her hands. She had never had friends in Lindau and had long since lost interest in such ladylike interests as romances, embroidery, or painting in water colors. These days, her only amusements were the lessons on the pianoforte at Herr Seutter's house, and these were more of a burden than the daily housework she no longer did.

For all that Herr Seutter treated her like a dainty figurine made from fine china, she felt awkward around him and embarrassed by the obligations they all owed him. This embarrassment increased with the many small gifts he bestowed upon her—the silk ribbons, lambskin gloves, a set of finely wrought silver buttons like so many tiny roses, scent bottles filled with French perfume, sets of gilt-edged stationery, lace pocket handkerchiefs, and a small china shepherdess that had reminded him of her. The most unnerving gift had been a laced kerchief to be worn around her neck and tucked into her bodice. Herr Seutter had presented her with it shortly after Franz had questioned her modesty on that hot day in the garden.

When Max Bauer walked into her life, it changed. He reminded her of the real world, of how lucky they were and how frivolous she had become. Fate was more cruel to some soldiers than to others. Franz had an education, a family to come home to, and friends who found work for him. Max had none of these.

She fed him some bread and sausages and a small pot of beer, and he blessed her. Then he blessed himself for having had such good luck that day. All this for a simple meal!

When he told her a little about himself, tears had come to her eyes. She could see he was a simple young man, but strong and well-made. With his blond curls and clear blue eyes he made her think of the image of the archangel Michael on the window of the Catholic church. Max had no wings, being quite earthly in most respects, but he had the same shy smile.

She told him about Franz to give him courage and hope and to show him that she understood. He was unconvinced.

"Your brother, Miss, was an officer. There's a world of difference between officers and corporals."

"Not so much, Max. We're all God's creatures and feel the same pain and fear."

He bristled at that. "I wasn't afraid. It's not the war I blame, nor even the Prussians. From what I could see, they're the same poor devils as us. It's what ordinary folk think of common soldiers comin' back. To them I'm nothin' but a beggar and a thief. They think I'll steal their chickens and rape their daughters."

Augusta blushed hotly at this, and Max apologized, turning beet red himself. Augusta said, "Not all people are so mean. I trusted you right away."

Max looked at her and then down at his clenched hands. "You're an angel, Miss," he said, his voice choking a little. "Yes, you're as beautiful and good as an angel. But you shouldn't have. There aren't many angels about, and God help me, most men are devils."

Augusta blushed again but, thinking of the archangel on the church window, she managed a little laugh. She had received very few compliments in her young life. "I don't believe it," she said. "It's strange you should mention angels when you look uncommonly like the archangel Michael yourself."

He stared at her, bereft of words for a moment, then burst into speech. "God love you, Miss. Me? I'm more like one of the devils." He jumped up, looking quite fierce suddenly as he towered over her. "Don't you go invitin' in men like me, bringin' them into your kitchen and showin' them your kindness, Miss. And you all alone and as pretty as a flower. It would tempt a saint. It's more than a weak and foolish man can bear." He turned and stormed out of the kitchen. A moment later, the front door slammed.

Augusta sat stunned. What had come over him? Then she got up and went upstairs to peer into the small mirror in her room. Apart from being rather pink, her face looked unremarkable. Then she remembered her brother's anger at her revealing dress and looked down at herself. Was it her body that tempted and infuriated men? This young man, Max, had not been her brother, and yet he had been angry.

She wasted a few more moments considering what brought men and women together, got properly hot and ashamed, and returned to the kitchen to clean up and look after the soup.

The next day, Max returned and knocked at the back door. Frau von Langsdorff and Augusta were in the kitchen with the little maid who was being instructed in darning socks.

Max came in, bowed to Frau von Langsdorff, and said he wished to thank them for their charity and to offer his help with any chores they might have.

He looked neater than the day before and seemed to have washed and combed his curls. Frau von Langsdorff eyed him appreciatively and said, "Hmm. You look strong and healthy. Augusta, what can he do?"

Augusta was embarrassed. "There's no need to do any work, Max," she said. "It was only a bit of bread and a glass of beer."

Her mother frowned at her. "Nonsense. It's quite proper that he should offer to repay us by his labors. Do not deprive him of the opportunity. We must be charitable to the less fortunate."

Max nodded, looking from mother to daughter. "Thank you, Ma'am. I'm very strong, Miss. I can carry wood. Or split it. Or patch the roof. Or move furniture. I can mend stairs or fences. Or maybe clean out your stoves. Please let me do somethin'."

"Well," Augusta murmured, "I suppose the windows upstairs are very dirty. Elsbeth is afraid to stand on a tall ladder."

Max looked eager and asked where he could find a ladder and a pail of water. Augusta gave him some clean rags and a pail and told him to fill it at the well in the garden. "The ladder's behind the shed," she said. "But be careful."

Max gave her a heart-melting smile. "I will, Miss. I won't break anythin'. I'll make your windows so clean it'll be like lookin' through air. You won't even know they're there."

Frau von Langsdorff smiled benevolently. "Be sure to put a little vinegar in the water, and clean each window before the sun gets to it or it will streak." She caught herself and added quickly, "Of course, I have never washed windows myself, but that's what my maids have always said."

Augusta gave her a look and fetched the vinegar.


Max Bauer had to report another failure to his employer, but after weighing the pros and cons of the situation, he decided that the protector of thieves had smiled on him again.

Compared to having tumbled head over heels into love with Augusta—he murmured her name to himself over and over again—facing the unpleasant Koehl was nothing. Max would have slain dragons for Augusta.

It turned out that no courage was required. They met again at the wall. Max was early, impatient to lay out his plan. It was sunset, and the ivy on the sun-warmed wall stirred in the warm breeze. Max leaned against it, watching birds wheeling in a faintly lilac sky. A beautiful day.

"From the smirk on your face, you've finally met with success," said the unpleasant voice, startling Max from romantic dreams.

"Almost, your honor," Max said. "Wait till you hear."

"Almost? What do you mean? Do you have it or don't you?"

"Nay," protested Max, "it's a risky business, breakin' into houses in the daytime." He gestured up at the thieves' tower. "It's my neck, as you said yourself, your honor. But you're so cursed pressin' that I made the attempt. Well, I was caught."

"What?"

"The girl—her name's Augusta—caught me starting up the stairs. Bad luck, except I turned it to my advantage. I told her I was hungry and lookin' for work. She has a soft heart, that one. She fed me, and I'm to come back tomorrow to clean the windows." Max grinned. "Upstairs. Where the cripple's room is."

Koehl stared at him, then allowed his lip to twitch. "Got to give it to you. You're not without a certain native wit. And I suppose the silly female fell for your blond curls and fawning manner. All right. You've got a bit more time, but do not disappoint me."

From the very beginning, Max impressed Augusta with his willingness to work and work hard. No, more than that. He put his hand to many things he had not been told to do. Soon, the pear tree in the garden had its dead branches trimmed off and a neat stack of firewood resided next to the shed. He kept the small vegetable patch and the single rose bush watered and pulled the weeds. One day, he appeared carrying a load of roof slates in a leather sling and set about repairing the roof.

This gave Augusta a fright, for the roof was very steep, and she trembled lest he should slip and fall and break his neck—a very handsome neck, as she had observed.

The Langsdorff property had been long neglected by the two women. They had not had the funds to make repairs even when they realized they were needed, and mostly they did not. Franz had neither the time nor the interest for such things these days and left the management of the household to the women.

But Max saw and knew what had to be done, and he set about it. He showed up at sunrise, accepted a breakfast of milk, bread, and cheese in the kitchen, and then went to work. He did the work cheerfully and without making great demands on their funds.

Frau von Langsdorff abused his good nature shamefully, sending him on errands to hat makers, seamstresses, shoemakers, haberdashers, drapers and mercers, and even had him follow her about town to carry her parcels. Augusta begged her mother not to do this, but to no avail.

"What?" asked her mother. "Am I not entitled to a little help? I see no reason why we shouldn't keep a footman. After all, your brother's a gentleman. And Max is very accommodating—besides being quite handsome."

Augusta agreed that Max was handsome; but for all that she liked Max herself, she did not approve of the way her mother became increasingly attached to him.

Their little maid Elsbeth, who was all of fifteen years old, also fell into a fervent infatuation with Max, following him about and gazing at him with trembling lips.

Only the relationship between Max and Franz, the master of the house, seemed somewhat strained. Franz largely ignored the new servant except for an occasional nod. Augusta ascribed this to Franz's preoccupation with his new profession. But Max's behavior defied explanation. He made determined efforts to stay out of her brother's way, and she had caught an expression of fear and loathing on his face when he looked at Franz.

"Max," she asked one morning after Franz had brushed past Max on his way out of the house and Max had shrunk against the wall as if he wanted it to swallow him, "are you afraid of my brother? Has he said or done anything to upset you?"

Max flushed. "No, miss. Not at all. He's always a very polite young gentleman."

"But I think you're not comfortable when you're around him," Augusta insisted.

Max studied the plate of bread and cheese she set before him. "Beggin' your pardon, miss," he finally said, looking up at her shyly, "it's just that I'm reminded of the difference. Between him and me, I mean. Our station in life. Someone like me could never measure up to someone like him. Or you."

Augusta read a fervor in his eyes that made her face grow warm. "Oh, Max," she exclaimed, "you mustn't feel that way. We're ordinary people with little wealth and no position in the world. And besides our Papa raised us to know that respect is due to all those who are kind and good. And you are one of the kindest men I know." She blushed and saw that he blushed also.

He snatched her hand and kissed it. "Bless you, miss, for the angel you are," he said and turned to his breakfast. When she left the kitchen, she heard him mutter, "Lord help us, I'm not good enough for her."

This exchange preoccupied Augusta for days afterward, and she became shy around Max, who seemed equally tongue-tied around her.

But then the pears ripened on the old tree, and Augusta got the small ladder and climbed up to gather an apron full of the luscious, honey-scented fruit. She was just reaching for another, leaning far out to grasp a sunwarmed, smooth, and gently rounded pear in her hand, when she heard Max call out, "Careful, miss! Let me—," and slipped.

Max caught her before she took a painful tumble. For a moment, they were both startled and out of breath—he holding her hard against him, one arm around her waist, the other on her hips—she clutching his neck—their faces only inches apart.

Augusta looked from his eyes to his lips. A strange desire to kiss them seized her, and she raised her lips to his.

"That was well done!" boomed a familiar voice.

Augusta pushed away from Max who set her down quickly. Like guilty children, they jumped apart and turned toward Herr Seutter, who stood beaming in the doorway.

"Well done, young man," he said again to Max as he came toward them, and to Augusta, "My dear girl, you made my poor old heart stop when you came tumbling out of that tree. You look quite flushed still. Come, let us sit on this bench until we catch our breaths again."

Augusta allowed herself to be led away and sat, with Herr Seutter's arm supporting her back and her hand in his large, warm one, while he admonished her to take greater care of herself. She felt unaccountably emotional. His kindness brought tears to her eyes, and her hand trembled in his. These days her heart behaved like a team of run-away horses.

Max picked up the pears she had dropped, inspected them for bruises, and then climbed the ladder to gather more. He left a generous pile under the tree and walked away without a glance or word, hanging his head.

She felt she had somehow wronged him and drew away a little from Herr Seutter's comfortable embrace. "I'm sorry," she murmured, "but you startled me."

"Forgive me, my dearest girl. I wouldn't for all the world have seen you injured on account of me." There was a brief silence, then he asked, "Augusta, who is that fellow? What is he doing here?"

She gave a little laugh. "Oh, Max? He's one of the poor soldiers back from the war without a home or work. He's been truly wonderful. He works for so little pay and is grateful for every crumb. You have no idea how many things he has fixed and how devoted he is to

Mama." She was babbling and wished Herr Seutter away so that she could go to her room and calm the strange fluttering in her breast.

"You don't say." Herr Seutter looked concerned. "He's not a local, I think. You know you must be careful these days about the people you ask into your house and family. There are many desperate men about."

She protested, "Not Max. He's the soul of gentleness."

"Is he now? Well, perhaps I'll ask a few questions to make sure."

Augusta was appalled. "Oh, no. You mustn't. It could cause trouble for him and . . . it would shame me."

Herr Seutter gave her a long, searching look. "Indeed?"

"Dear Herr Seutter," she begged, "you must trust me in this matter. Please."

He sighed and patted her hand lightly. "We're old friends, Augusta," he said. "Might you not call me by my Christian name?"

She looked at him blankly. "Your Christian name? But I don't know it."

He smiled and said, "Jakob."

"Jakob. If you wish it, but it seems improper."

"Never improper among friends. And that reminds me. I came to beg another lesson on the pianoforte. It's been a long time since the last one."

It had been weeks, but Augusta had been busy setting their new servants to work and had forgotten all about the lessons. Indeed, she wished he would not ask for them now.  But gratitude for past kindness made her apologize and promise to come the very next day.

# 8

# Mesmer

*We may lay it down as a Maxim, that when a Nation*
*abounds in Physicians it grows thin of People.*

Joseph Addison, *Spectator*, 1711

When Franz took up the study of law under
Stiebel's guidance, his days became even
longer, but he found moments of pure happiness again. Most of these concerned his legal work,
but when Stiebel responded with genuine interest to the
mysterious letter, Franz felt a great affection for his employer.

"People do change their names and titles with inde-
cent frequency these days," Stiebel said, turning the en-
velope this way and that. His nose quivered with
curiosity. "Perhaps we should open it?"

"Oh, n-no!" Franz was shocked. "S-surely n-not, sir. Not s-such a letter between s-son and father. N-not his f-final words."

Stiebel rubbed his nose. "Hmm, yes, I see your point. It could be a little indelicate. I tell you what: Mannheim is the seat of the elector now, but it used to be in Heidelberg. Chances are this family has followed the court to Mannheim. I still have friends in Heidelberg who may find the von Loe name in old records. Allow me to write to them."

"Oh, th-that would serve very well. Th-thank you. W-will you be s-so good as to t-take charge of the letter? I'm n-notoriously careless, and our house is f-full of new s-servants who s-seem to t-take a great interest in my p-papers."

Stiebel chuckled and locked the troublesome letter up in his strongbox.

With this off his mind, Franz began to look at his future more hopefully, but the dreams still haunted him every night, and his guilt weighed on him every day.

He also feared thunderstorms. He could not control the attacks of panic, no matter how hard he tried. Eventually he learned to cover up his defect. At the first sound of thunder, he would go off by himself so that he could cower in a corner, shaking in abject terror until the storm passed. But often sudden loud noises caught him unawares and his reaction made people stare. Rumors of his madness resurfaced.

One morning that summer, when the chestnut trees had scattered their red and white blossoms on the cobbles outside, and the farmers were making hay in the fields, cutting the tall grass, raking it into rows and turning it to dry in the hot sun, Stiebel greeted Franz with great excitement.

"We're going to see a famous doctor," he announced. "I've ordered a post chaise. It's a fine day for a trip." He rubbed his hands in glee and cackled at Franz's astonishment. "We'll close chambers. Breakfast's waiting and the chaise will be here any moment."

Stiebel never did anything without careful forethought and hated upsetting his domestic and professional routine. Franz stammered, "Wh-what d-doctor?"

"Mesmer himself!" Stiebel cried in a tone of triumph. When the name did not produce much reaction, he added, "Only the most brilliant man in the world. And what do you suppose? He's your fellow countryman. Born and raised in Iznang on the lake, son of the forester to the Bishop of Konstanz. Studied philosophy at the University of Dillingen, theology at Ingolstadt, took his doctorate in medicine in Vienna, and is not thirty yet. He's the great man in Vienna, known for remarkable cures—but it's all good science as he will tell you himself." Stiebel slapped his head and raised a cloud of powder. "What am I doing? We're wasting time. Come." He took Franz's arm and drew him into the dining room, where the usual breakfast waited, evidently ordered an hour before its customary time. "Eat, while I tell you."

Franz obeyed, listening with astonishment and a good deal of emotion. Stiebel had taken Franz's cure for his personal task and made inquiries. When he heard that Mesmer had returned for a brief visit to his parents, he had right away ordered the post chaise to take them to Iznang.

Franz did not believe in a cure, but he had not the heart to talk Stiebel out of his plans. The chaise arrived, a cheerful yellow two-wheeled vehicle with a postilion perched in back and the driver astride one of the horses. The black top was folded down.

They traveled under a cloudless sky. The lake glistened to their left, the sweet smell of hay was in the air, and the steeples or onion domes of churches, the half-timbered houses, the vine-clad castles rose before them, passed, and rapidly disappeared behind as if by magic.

Franz looked at Stiebel beside him, a friendly gnome from some ancient fairy tale, as he chattered about animal magnetism, healing hands, and the miraculous cures this strange doctor had performed in Vienna. Stiebel's finery heightened the other-worldly effect. He had tied on the gold-trimmed hat with the gray ostrich feather, but the breeze blew small clouds of powder from his periwig. His buckled shoes swung with the swaying chaise, and his white-gloved hands gesticulated like a pair of fluttering doves.

To Franz, Stiebel was a greater miracle than anything Mesmer could perform. Why does he take such care of me, he wondered. How have I deserved so much love from this man who is neither my father nor my brother—I who am the least worthy of men? What can he possibly hope to gain by taking such trouble with someone like me?

But this love was not given with an ulterior motive, and Franz felt humbled in its presence. The eccentric Stiebel became very dear to him.

The idea of revealing his scars, his weakness, his repulsive deformity to yet another doctor—to be prodded at, frowned over, and made a fool of—sickened him. But he would allow it to happen. It would be hellish, but he could do no less in the face of such love.

They stopped for a meal in Konstanz. Roasted meats, fricassees, and fine wines appeared and disappeared, but Franz hardly knew what he ate.

Their arrival in Iznang caused a small sensation. People gaped at the chaise and horses, at the postilion who jumped down and held the door for his passengers, at the strangers who had come to see the local genius.

Mesmer was young, not yet thirty, dapper and elegant, of middling height, clean-shaven, and energetic. His blue velvet suit was of the most recent cut, and the lace of his jabot and wristbands was very white and very rich. His brocade vest bore silver embroideries. But when Franz raised his eyes from the clothes and past the man's incipient double chin, he met a sharp and penetrating glance from the brown eyes.

Mesmer was clearly not impressed by their appearance, but perhaps he welcomed a scientific challenge. Franz let Stiebel do the talking and bore the doctor's frequent scrutiny with some resentment. When Stiebel mentioned the nightmares, Mesmer's interest peaked.

"Such dreams are often symptoms of a more deeply seated illness," he said in a more animated voice. "I suspect this is the case here. You may have heard of the remarkable work of Father Gassner?"

Stiebel clapped his hands. "Yes, of course. The famous exorcist. Do you then think that the illness is in the soul?"

The discussion was taking an unpleasantly religious direction. Even his love for the kind Stiebel would not make Franz submit to an exorcism. Mesmer, as he knew from Stiebel's account, was a Catholic and had studied theology with the Jesuits before taking up medicine. He said sharply, "I'm n-not p-possessed!"

Mesmer laughed heartily. "Of course you're not. Father Gassner's work resembles in some ways my own treatments, but he puts quite another interpretation on his healings. No, indeed, science does not deal in evil spirits; rather, it searches for the physical causes of disease."

That sounded better, and Franz subsided with a nod.

"Because you dream," Mesmer continued, "you have particular insights into the nature of your illness. It will be a simple matter to heal the wounds of the mind—or soul, if you permit the word—once we heal those of the body."

"B-but my wounds have h-healed."

"Some patients carry the invisible marks of their wounds with them for years after they are seemingly healed."

That sounded reasonable to Franz. Indeed, now that he thought about it, both the nightmares and his reactions to thunder were related to what had happened during the battle. But this did not explain his speech defect.

Mesmer questioned him about the injuries he had received, had him roll his knee breeches up and his stockings down, and felt the scar tissue on both legs. Franz cringed, but he submitted for Stiebel's sake.

Mesmer said, "The wound to your leg is responsible not only for the poorly aligned bones, tendons, muscles, but also for a blockage of veins and fibers that run through the body, carrying the fluids of life. Having become blocked, they are creating imbalances elsewhere. It will be necessary to promote a freer flow. You are educated men and aware of the influence of the planets on the tides?"

Franz nodded.

"It is my theory, based on work by the English scientist Isaac Newton, the Viennese astronomer Father Maximilian Hell, and others, that the human life force can be influenced from outside the body much as the tides are by the moon. I call this connection between the fluids coursing through our bodies and the forces of nature 'animal magnetism.' The word *animal* is to be taken as a descriptive term and refers to *anima*, the soul or spirit of life."

Franz was confused and glanced at Stiebel who smiled back, nodding approval. Stiebel asked, "Then you can help my young friend, Doctor?"

"A proper treatment would take many months, and I shall have to return to Vienna in another day."

Stiebel said quickly, "But could you please make a start?"

Mesmer agreed. He moved his chair so that he faced Franz and their knees touched. Placing his hands lightly over Franz's wound while his eyes—light brown eyes with golden flecks in the irises—looked deeply into Franz's, he said, "Close your eyes. You must feel completely at ease to allow the magnetic force to have an effect."

Franz closed his eyes. He felt Mesmer gently stroking his knee. The experience was oddly pleasant. His touch was gentle and moved from his knees along his thighs and hips to his torso, and thence to his face and head and back again as if tracing the secret channels of his blood. Warmth flowed from Mesmer's touch, a warmth which gradually relaxed his tensed muscles until he was seized by a great lassitude and drowsiness.

Right away, the dream returned, the headless bodies, the bloody swords, the Prussian officer. He screamed and awoke.

A smiling Mesmer sat across from him. "Good. How do you feel?"

Had he screamed or merely dreamed the scream? It must have been in the dream, he decided. He wondered how he could have dozed off. Stiebel and Mesmer were looking at him expectantly. "I feel fine," he said, putting aside the weight of guilt in his mind and consulting his body instead. "I was . . . dreaming of the battle again. How did you . . .?" He stopped. He had not stumbled once over the words. His stutter was gone. He asked, "Am I c-cured?" and felt foolish and disappointed that he was not.

"Not quite," said Mesmer, getting up and putting his chair away. "But it looks promising." He took a small black object from a leather box on a table. "Here, take this magnet. It may do some good. When you have leisure, relax and move it back and forth over your knees and then up and down your body as I just did. You will not fall into a trance and relive the occasion of your injuries again, but it may move some of the blocked fluids. Be sure to write to let me know if you improve. That is all I can do for now. We must hope."

Franz parted from Mesmer in a daze. He saw Stiebel hanging back to exchange some words with the famous doctor and pass a well-filled purse into his hand, but the little lawyer climbed into the chaise without comment.

"Herr Koehl," the innkeeper called out, "you have a visitor. I put him in the *Stüble.*"

The assassin was puzzled; he expected no one. If Max had the gall to call on him here, he would tear him limb from limb. But the *Stüble,* while not exactly a private room reserved for a person of importance, was not the sort of place Max would have been invited to. Frowning, he opened the door to the small room with its red-checked tablecloths and leaded windows and saw a stranger waiting at a table.

The man was no longer young but favored the bright clothes worn by students who wished to impress young women. His knee breeches were yellow, his jacket sky blue, and his vest mustard-colored. He wore a powdered wig in the latest style—with two horizontal curls over each ear and the rest caught in a black silk bag in back . A cocked hat lay on the table next to a bottle and a glass of red wine.

"You wished to speak to me?" the assassin asked coldly.

The dandy raised his glass and drank, insolently letting his eyes scan the assassin's figure. He had green eyes under carroty brows. Smirking unpleasantly, he set down the glass and gestured to a chair. "Right. Have a seat, sir. We're private here, so there's no need to look so glum."

The assassin made no move. "Who are you?"

Another smirk and a wink. "No names. Let's just say both of us work for the same master. A great man in Mannheim."

Suppressing his rage at the familiarity, the assassin went to sit down. Close up, the stranger inspired even less confidence. The thin face, sharp nose, and narrow eyes reminded him of a fox. Given the man's speech and appearance, he put him down for a valet with ambitions. His resentment increased.

The foxy man took a letter from his jacket and handed it over, watching him expectantly. The letter had neither superscription nor seal. Putting it in his pocket, the assassin rose. "Thanks."

The foxy fellow grabbed his sleeve. "Not so fast, my friend. Read it."

The assassin flushed with anger. "I'm not your friend. Take your hands off my arm or you'll be sorry."

The stranger pursed his lips, but he removed his hand. "As I'm to report what you say and do, I think you should be more polite."

The assassin glared, but he took out the letter again, broke it open, and read.

It was short and unsigned: "Return immediately with the man who brings you this."

Fury resurged. He knew the handwriting and expected a tongue-lashing. It was galling to be treated like a hired man. He was of good birth, at least as far as people knew. As always, resentment for his parents rose like bitter bile. His mother had been a fool who had allowed his father to renege on his promise to legitimize their relationship. When the old man had died, there had been nothing but a commission for his son. He had lived by his wits and by making himself useful to men in power. A glance at the messenger told him that the repulsive creature guessed his circumstances.

"The post leaves in an hour. I've paid our fares."

The assassin scowled. "I've employed a man on behalf of your master and must speak to him before I leave."

The foxy fellow cocked his head. "You'd best hurry then."

Muttering curses, the assassin returned to his room to throw his belongings into a *portemanteau*, then paid his bill and left his bag to be picked up later. He glared at the innkeeper who stifled his questions and regrets, and walked quickly to the Fischergasse.

Turning over his situation in his mind, he felt the insult to be almost unbearable. He had obeyed his employer's instructions even though he was in danger as long as the cripple lived. It was time he looked out for his own skin before he lost his life.

He found Max on top of a long ladder, whistling merrily as he polished the windows of the modest house. After catching Max's eye by bumping into the ladder, the assassin strolled to the end of the street where he stopped to stare into a silversmith's shop window.

Max joined him with a cheerful, "Hey ho!"

This irritated the assassin further. "Mind your manners, dolt." He lowered his voice. "The plan has changed. I have to leave. The cripple has to go." He saw Max's face fall and reached into his pocket. "Here. Fifty *taler* on account to take care of him. You'll get another hundred when it's done." It was an empty promise, because he would be long gone by then, and there was no Georg Koehl.

Max took the money and looked at it. "Take care of him?" he asked dully. "What d'you mean?"

"Don't be a dunce. Kill him."

"No!" Max pushed the silver coins at him. "I may be a thief, but I'll not murder a man."

"Not so loud. You've been a soldier and killed plenty of men."

Max drew himself up. "It's not the same. They don't hang you for that. They give you medals."

"I have no time to argue the point. Use your head. Neither of us wants a hue and cry. A quick bash with a cudgel and throw the body in the lake. It'll be taken for an accident or a suicide."

Max backed away, shaking his head. "I can't."

"Hell and damnation! If you don't do it, I'll lay charges against you for attempted robbery, and Moser will testify to your past activities. They'll hang you for certain then."

Max turned pale. "You devil. I hope you get your just rewards," he muttered, but he shoved the silver in his pocket.

The assassin smiled thinly. "I take it we're no longer friends. Never mind. If you do as I say, you'll be safe and richer by a hundred and fifty pieces of silver. A young man can make a start at a new life with that. He can even take a wife. In fact, I may add another fifty as a wedding present for a job well done." Seeing Max's face turn red, he barked a laugh and walked away.

Stiebel was quiet on the homeward journey, but he looked happy. Supper was a brief affair of bread, cheese, and cold roast chicken. Stiebel ate, sipped his wine, and smiled at Franz.

Franz was afraid to speak in case his stutter should worsen again. He did not want to disappoint Stiebel. Mostly, however, his heart was too full of gratitude.

When the sun set behind them, its golden light turned the finials on church steeples into flames and drew sparks of fire from the surface of the lake. The rhythm of the hoof beats mingled with the sound of the turning wheels, and the outrider caught the measure and began to sing. Stiebel joined the symphony with a gentle snore. Gradually, the sinking sun's fiery energy burned itself out, and a soft, lilac-colored haze fell over the land. The outrider's song died away, and by the time they approached Lindau the lights of the city blinked like stars against the dusky mirror of the lake.

It was fully dark when they stopped at Stiebel's house. Stiebel wanted the chaise to drop Franz off first, but Franz refused. His mother and Augusta would besiege him with questions, and his heart was too full. He parted from Stiebel with an awkward embrace and muttered thanks and walked away as quickly as he could.

The streets were empty. People were at their dinners or in the inns for a glass of beer or wine with their friends. There was hardly any moon, but Franz wanted to see the lake at night and listen to its waters lapping at the shore and think of Stiebel's kindness. At the Brettermarkt, he turned into an alley that led toward the water.

Almost the only sounds were his steps—irregularly spaced: one heavy step, followed by the sharp click of his cane striking the cobbles, and then the light shuffle of his right foot, followed quickly again by the firm step.

Not even the great Mesmer could fix a cripple's limp.

He looked ahead for a glimpse of the water and thought about Mesmer and the magnet in his pocket, and about Stiebel and all the gold he had had to pay Mesmer, and about his affection for the little man when he noticed that another sound had joined the rhythm of his steps—a quick, soft, regular footfall. A man's. Close.

He swung around awkwardly, but the fellow was already upon him, a dark figure muffled in something, a hat pulled low over his face. It was too dark to see much, but Franz knew a raised cudgel even in a dark alley.

With his crippled leg he could not move quickly, but he had his cane and brought it up like a sword to deflect the man's blow and then to lash across his attacker's face viciously. The cane broke, but the villain cursed with the pain. Lights came on in the nearest house, and Franz shouted for help. With another curse, the villain struck once more.

This time, Franz was not so lucky. The cudgel caught the side of his head and sent him reeling into the house wall. He lost consciousness.

When he came to, he was lying on the ground, and a woman was shaking his arm.

"Get yourself home, swill pot!" she snapped. "Shame on you! Disturbing the sleep of honest, hardworking folk with your drunken brawls. Get on with you, I say, or I'll call the guard."

Franz somehow got to his feet. His mouth was full of blood, his jaw felt broken, and his head hurt dreadfully. He made no attempt to explain to the angry female. His speech would simply prove to her that he was drunk.

He found the pieces of his cane by the lamplight from the woman's doorway. She slammed the door a moment later, and he stood swaying in the darkness, spitting out blood.

# 9

# The Proposal

*O Love, what monstrous tricks dost thou play with thy*
*votaries of both sexes! How dost thou deceive them,*
*and make them deceive themselves! Their follies are*
*thy delight!*

Henry Fielding, *Joseph Andrews*

As it turned out, Augusta did not keep her appointment with Herr Scutter. When her brother staggered into the house, white and bloody, and collapsed on the tiled floor—where he vomited and passed out—the Langsdorff household was thrown into turmoil. Augusta sent Elsbeth for the doctor and applied cold compresses to her brother's head while her mother wailed and tried to join him in a fainting fit.

The doctor arrived quickly, and Franz came round, muttering unintelligibly something about robbers. Augusta and the doctor supported him up the stairs and into his bed. Her mother sobbed downstairs and called for Elsbeth, who hovered pale-faced on the stairs.

When the doctor finished examining Franz, he shook his head. "Attacked on the street? What is this town coming to when a man is no longer safe on his way home at a decent hour? And a cripple at that."

Franz turned his head away. Augusta's anxiety made her voice sharp. "My brother will not thank you for calling him a cripple."

The doctor raised his brows. "I daresay," he remarked coldly. "Well, bed rest for two days. Nothing stronger than some veal broth if he'll take it. Call me if he should fall to raving. That will be two *taler*, if you please."

The comment about raving frightened Augusta into meekly fetching the gold and seeing him out without further argument.

That night she sat beside her brother's bed as he slept fitfully, twitching and moaning now and then. He did not show any signs of delirium, but every sound he made sent Augusta into a panic. When he finally woke, it was daylight. He mumbled about an aching head and wanted to know what time it was.

Relieved, Augusta said, "Gone past eight. You're to stay still and have nothing but broth for a day or so."

"Past eight?" he cried, sitting up. Clutching his head, he grimaced and swallowed. "Why the devil didn't you wake me? Oh, God, it hurts!" he muttered.

"But I should be at work. What will Herr Stiebel think?"

Augusta was not sure what to make of his condition but did not want him to risk getting up. "Max can take a message," she offered.

Franz sank back into his pillow and closed his eyes. "Very well."

"Franz?"

"What?"

"Your stutter's gone."

His eyes opened. "N-no! It can't be. How–?"

"Don't think about it. Just speak. Did Dr. Mesmer cure it?"

He frowned. "I don't know. Perhaps. B-but it may c-come back."

"Never mind. Rest now. I'll send Max to Dr. Stiebel."

But when Augusta got downstairs, Max had not arrived yet, and she sent Elsbeth with the message. Then she made breakfast for her mother, her ailing brother, Max, Elsbeth, and herself. She never found time to eat because she had to urge some white bread soaked in warm milk and sweetened with honey on her brother, in hopes that it would serve as well as veal broth. Franz was irritable and uncooperative. He also refused to talk. She was still in the midst of begging him to eat a little more, when her mother came in to fuss over her son.

Augusta went back to the kitchen to make a list for the day's marketing. She had no peace for the rest of the morning. Franz slept or dozed, but her mother came to argue about the marketing and to complain that Max had promised to fetch her new hoop petticoat.

Where was Max? It was not like him not to show up. Augusta, her head full of the attack on her brother, began to fear for Max. She was up to her elbows in soapy water, washing the breakfast dishes while reasoning with her mother, when a pounding on the door sent her rushing to open it. Two uniformed gendarmes stood on the steps.

The older touched his cocked hat. "Sergeant Steiner, miss. And Corporal Radl." The Corporal stood at attention. "We got a report of a gentleman of this household having been attacked last night, miss," the sergeant rasped. "Can you confirm the matter?"

"Yes," said Augusta, wiping her hands on her apron. "My brother was indeed cruelly beaten on his way home."

"Ah," said the sergeant. "Von Langsdorff's the name? It's the right place then. We must have a word with the gentleman, miss."

"He did not see who it was," she said. "And he's resting."

"If you don't mind, miss," insisted the sergeant. "It's a matter of the law."

With a sigh, Augusta took them to her brother's room and left them with a warning not to tire him.

They did not stay long, but by then their mother was in another tizzy about the absence of Max and the marketing that had to be done. Augusta had hardly seen her off with Elsbeth, when there was another knock at the door.

Augusta had never met her brother's employer. Franz had said that Doctor Stiebel was shy around women. Now she saw a very small, odd-looking person, who peered up at her over his spectacles and made her an elaborate courtly bow. When he straightened, his wig was askew. His brown jacket was buttoned crookedly, and one of his white silk stockings sagged around his ankle.

"Oh," he said nervously, "I do beg your pardon. I know it's quite outrageous. But the occasion . . . you will forgive this intrusion? . . . I have been distracted with worry. And at such a moment, too. I mean when all seemed so hopeful. Mesmer, you know. Oh, forgive me, my dear. You must be Augusta. I'm Stiebel."

Augusta suppressed a smile. "Yes, of course, *Herr Doktor.* Pray come in. I'm very glad to meet you, sir. Franz speaks of you often." She remembered his description of the lawyer's eccentricities and added too quickly, "With the greatest respect and affection, of course." And blushed.

Fortunately the small gaffe passed by the little man who looked around distractedly and asked, "How is Franz? It's not too serious, I hope. Though I was told a blow to the head . . . still, he's young . . . but then the brain is such a delicate matter . . . especially in his case. I took the liberty to notify the authorities. Oh, dear." He looked at Augusta beseechingly.

"Yes, two gendarmes were just here. Franz did not see the men who attacked him. He's feeling better but keeping to his bed on doctor's orders. He was so determined to go to work this morning that I had to restrain him." She wondered if she should tell him that the stutter was nearly gone. But perhaps Franz was right, and it was only a temporary improvement. So she said, "I am anxious to know what you think of his condition, sir. He will be glad to see you. Pray come upstairs."

Stiebel hurried after her and into Franz's bedroom, crying, "My poor fellow!" and peering anxiously at Franz with his bandaged head, "How are you feeling? The doctor has seen you. What was the verdict?" He scurried around the bed and hopped into the armchair beside it.

Franz smiled. "You're very good to come, sir. Nothing's broken—except my thick head a little bit. I'm to rest just today and shall be as good as new tomorrow. I shall work very fast to catch up on Steinhilber vs. Wagner."

"Bless my soul, never mind that." Stiebel smiled, patted his hand, and laid it back on the cover. "Don't, for heaven's sake, trouble yourself with that, my dear boy. Allow your charming sister and your mama to pamper you a little longer. I've a free day today and shall take the case in hand. *Pars sanitatis velle sanari*, as you know. You must wish to get well first." He paused to nod. "Your charming sister tells me that you did not see the villains. Tell me, do you think this attack had something to do with the letter?"

Augusta asked, "What letter?"

Franz glanced at her. "Oh, it's nothing. I promised to deliver a letter but could not find anyone by that n-name. Doctor Stiebel offered to make enquiries for me." He turned back to Stiebel. "It's just a letter from a s-son to his father, sir. And besides, no one knows about it. I think last night must have been a footpad in hopes of my purse."

Stiebel chewed his lip. "Strange. I asked because someone broke into my chambers while we were in Iznang. It's never happened before, and I cannot account for it."

Franz looked astonished. "Broke in? Was the letter taken, then?"

"No, no. The strongbox was attempted, though. They searched my desk and yours. Nothing was taken, I think, and they were careful not to disturb things." He sighed. "Except my little bird. The scoundrels let him out and he's gone. I'm sure, by now the neighbor's cat got it. It had a very complacent look about its whiskers this morning."

"Oh, I what a pity," Augusta said quickly. "But do leave the window open. Perhaps it just wanted a taste of freedom and will return. And now, will you take a glass of wine, sir?"

But Stiebel was in a hurry to get back, either to work on his papers, or to look for the lost bird. At the front door, she asked, "Don't you find Franz's speech much improved?"

"Do I? Oh, indeed, I do!" The little lawyer brightened. "It was the great Mesmer, you know. I cannot tell you how happy I am my little scheme worked so well."

"If it is so, dear sir, we're most deeply indebted to you."

"Not at all. Not at all," Stiebel cried and dashed down the steps to escape so much gratitude.

Augusta had to deal with still another visitor. This time, she opened the door to Herr Seutter and remembered the lesson on the pianoforte. She burst into apologies, mentioning Franz's injuries and his having been attacked the night before.

He listened with great concern. "Do not, my dear girl, fuss yourself about the lesson," he said, taking her hand and leading her into the parlor. "It don't signify. How is Franz? Are you all alone?" He looked around the room and frowned. "Your Mama is with the patient?"

"No, Mama's gone out. Oh, dear. The bells are striking twelve. I must see to his broth. I wish Mama were back." Augusta brushed a distracted hand over her curls. "The doctor said he must have broth, but I haven't had time or veal bones . . ."

"Ssh! We'll send your servant to my house. There must be some broth to be had there."

"Oh, you're very kind, but Elsbeth has gone with Mama."

"What of that hulking big fellow I saw the other day?"

"Max didn't come today." She went to the window to look out. "I can't imagine what happened to him. He's never late." Her voice trembled.

Herr Seutter joined her. "Augusta," he said firmly, "you must calm yourself. Allow me to take some of these cares from your shoulders." Saying this, he laid his warm hands on her shoulders, and Augusta choked back a giggle. "What's the matter? Why are you laughing? I came to talk to you about something, but maybe this isn't a good time."

She apologized, feeling vaguely resentful at the way life seemed to derail all her efforts to keep control. Only Max had been there to help, and now he, too, was gone. She sat on the settee and twisted her hands in her lap, fighting tears and wishing Herr Seutter gone.

But he came to sit beside her and took her hands. "Augusta, forgive me for speaking to you now when you are troubled, but my poor heart cannot bear to see you so distracted. You know that I've been alone since my dear Susanna died and took our boy with her. It's been hard, living alone in that big empty house of mine. Seeing you and your dear Mama struggling since your Papa passed away has made me realize that I'm not the only one. It pained me to see two gentle ladies in such straits. And it's made me think that all this can be put behind us in a moment. I made up my mind a long time ago and have been patient, counting the months until your next birthday before speaking to your Mama, but I cannot wait any longer. I'm afraid if I don't speak now, I may lose my happiness forever."

She looked at him, surprised, blinking away her tears. Why did he need her approval? Pressing his hand, she said with a smile, "But why should you wait for my birthday? I assure you, I have no objections whatsoever. And as for Mama, why, I think she'll be excessively happy."

His face glowed. "Oh, my dearest girl!" he cried and pulled her into an embrace so fervent that it imprinted every button of his waistcoat on her bosom. "My very dearest girl. You make me the happiest man alive. And the luckiest. My dearest life! Oh, my joy! I'm blessed beyond anything."

Augusta had begun to struggle against the painful clasp, when the parlor door opened and her mother and Elsbeth came in. They stopped. Her mother gasped and then shrieked.

Herr Seutter released Augusta and jumped to his feet. "My dear lady," he cried.

"Villain," screeched Augusta's mother, pointing a shaking finger at him. "Viper! Oh, that I had to live for this day! I feel faint." She swayed on her feet.

Elsbeth stood, struck speechless and paralytic, her mouth open at the drama that unfolded before her eager eyes. Herr Seutter rushed to support her mistress. When Augusta's mother saw that she was about to find herself in his arms, she uttered another shriek. "Don't touch me, you monster!" she cried and tottered to a chair where she collapsed. From the stairs came the thumps and curses of Franz coming down, and Augusta realized the magnitude of her mistake.

Herr Seutter had been proposing to *her*.

In spite of her shock and confusion, she managed to get up and say quite firmly, "Mama, there has been a misunderstanding."

Her mother blinked, then searched her bodice for a lace handkerchief. "What misunderstanding, you unnatural girl?" she quavered. "Your perfidy was clear as day."

"Yes, what misunderstanding?" demanded Franz from the doorway, barelegged in his nightshirt and with his head bandaged. He was pale and supported himself against the doorframe as he looked around the room. "Your servant, Seutter," he said to the visitor. "Mama's screams brought me down. What happened?"

Herr Seutter was red with embarrassment. "I took the liberty to make my intentions known—" he began.

Augusta interrupted, "Herr Seutter asked me if Mama would welcome his suit. When I told him, she would, he was overjoyed and embraced me. That's all that happened."

A startled silence fell.

Her ears burning, Augusta turned to her mother who gaped at her over her lace handkerchief. "Mama, you have shamed me and our kind friend. And Franz should be in bed. I think it will be best if we leave you to make your apologies to Herr Seutter." She started for the door.

"Not so fast, Augusta," growled Franz.

Dear God, she thought, don't let him suddenly take an interest in us now. Not when he wasn't here for all those months and years when we needed him.

Franz did not move aside.

Augusta's despairing eyes fell on Elsbeth, who seemed fascinated by Franz in his nightshirt. "Please, Franz," she pleaded. "You're not dressed. Let me help you upstairs."

Behind her, Herr Seutter cleared his throat. "I beg your pardon, Franz. This is my fault and my mistake.

I'm sorry for it and I also beg your pardon, madam. I should've spoken to both of you first. You see . . ."

The disastrous truth would come out after all. Augusta clapped her hands over her ears and closed her eyes. What would her mother do to her for having stolen Herr Seutter's affection? Mama had never loved, or even liked her. How much would she hate her now? She felt her brother's hand move her aside and opened her eyes.

He went to stand beside his mother, his hand on her shoulder. Frau von Langsdorff wept in earnest now and clutched her son's hand. "Go on," Franz said in a dangerous voice.

Herr Seutter looked terrified. He raised, then lowered his arms helplessly. Augusta's heart went out to him. "I," he started, blushing with embarrassment, "I was speaking to Augusta. I mean, it was Augusta's hand in marriage I was asking for. Only—" he faltered and gave Augusta a despairing look that twisted her heart.

"You did what?" Franz cried. "You had the gall to come here and pay court to a mere child? You dared to seduce my sister? An innocent girl who's barely past childhood? You, a man old enough to be my father and hers? My skin crawls at it. Oh, yes, I see what you were up to. With me at war, you saw her unprotected and used false charity to gain the confidence of two naive women. You toyed with their affections so you could lay your dirty hands on an innocent child. What will you say to the good burghers of this city when these charges are brought against you?"

Augusta rushed to her brother and, ignoring his injury, shook him hard. "No, Franz! No!"

He thrust her aside. "Leave the room, Augusta! We will speak later."

Augusta felt sick, She wished her brother's stutter had prevented his speech. Turning toward Herr Seutter, she saw how pale he was and made half a move to go to him, but he held up his hand and she dared not defy her family. Tears of pity spilled over as her silence shamed her.

They looked at each other for a long moment, then he bowed his head, and walked out. Nobody spoke until they heard the sound of the front door closing.

Franz bent over his mother. "That damned villain! I'm sorry, Mama. It's better to know a man's true character, even when such revelations are painful."

Frau von Langsdorff dabbed at her eyes. "You shouldn't have left us alone, Franz," she whimpered. "It was too much for me. I couldn't be expected to cope. Without a decent income, too. I was busy making ends meet and pinching pennies. How could I see your sister's deceitful ways in going to his house all the time. She said it was to teach him the pianoforte. Hah!"

Augusta dashed away her tears with clenched fists. "Shame on you, Mama, for saying such filthy things. And you, Franz, you had no right to hurt a kind man who has treated all of us—yes, you, too—with nothing but generous friendship. He has never taken liberties with me. And I only showed him how to play his pianoforte. That was all. He's the soul of kindness and courtesy. If you want to know the truth, if I hadn't

thought he was courting Mama, I would've been deeply
honored by his proposal." She burst into fresh tears.

Franz glared. "Are you mad? Why, the very
thought of this . . . this common old man . . . touching
you—it should disgust you."

Augusta gasped. She had never been so angry with
her family in her life. Wishing they were strangers, she
ran from the room.

Max spent the night in the Catholic church. He prayed
and wept and cursed Koehl. At sunrise, the priest
found him stretched out on the cold stone floor, sobbing softly. He asked, "Are you troubled, my son?"

Max had not heard him approach on soft-soled
shoes and jumped up to flee.

The priest, an old man in a black cassock, blocked
his way. "This is the house of God," he said soothingly.
"You're quite safe here. It is a sanctuary even for those
who have committed a crime."

Max backed away. "How did you—?" He broke off
and took a deep breath. Then he wiped away the tears
and saw that his hand was bloody.

"If you'll come into the sacristy, I'll wash off the
blood and apply some ointment to your wound."

"It's nothing. A fight. That's all it was. I've got to
go, Father. Thanks." Max tried to slip past him.

The priest looked more sharply into his face and put
a hand on his arm. "Don't go, my son. If you need to
unburden your soul," he gestured toward the confes-
sional, "I have time to listen."

Max shuddered convulsively. "No. Not now. Another time."

The priest sighed and released him.

Max ran from the church. At the fountain outside, he washed his face and drank thirstily. He caught a glimpse of himself in the water. His left eye was swollen shut above the raw cut across his cheekbone. He looked bad enough to frighten children. The sun was up and people would soon be on their way to work. He had to find out what he had done.

He walked quickly to Fischergasse, but stopped to peer around the corner at the house. It looked as always in the morning sun. Then the door opened, and Elsbeth came out. She walked off toward the market. It all seemed quite normal. Perhaps the news had not reached them yet.

But then he saw the two gendarmes coming down the street. At the von Langsdorff house, they stopped and knocked.

Max's stomach heaved, and he fled. He had killed a man. He had murdered his angel's brother. He should sooner have taken his own life than bring her grief. Wandering about blindly, he muttered to himself. People got out of his way, and a man cursed when he stumbled over his dog. Go ahead, he thought, call the gendarmes. Have me arrested. This time I'll hang, and it serves me right.

At some point—he was not sure when—he stood in the market near a flower stand. An old woman sat among the pails of phlox, dahlias, zinnias, and every other kind of flower in every shade of the rainbow. He was lost in the multitude of hues and shapes and scents. Augusta loved flowers. His hand felt for the silver in his pocket, the Judas silver he had earned for killing her brother. Nausea rose again, and he turned away.

"Here," urged the old woman, holding out a bunch of asters and daisies. "Been in a fight? Give flowers to her, and she'll give you plenty of lovin' instead of what you deserve." She cackled.

Sick, Max cursed her and turned away.

That's when he saw them. In front of the vegetable stands. Augusta's mother in a sprigged gown and lacy white cap under a straw hat. And Elsbeth in her apron and with the market basket over an arm. Shopping!

It couldn't have been news of murder that the guards had brought.

An enormous weight lifted, and he laughed out loud and skipped a little. The flower woman grumbled sourly, "Drunken fool!"

But Max was puzzled. He knew his cudgel had made contact with the lieutenant's head before the door of the house opened and he had to take to his heels. Even if he hadn't killed him, he was still in plenty of trouble. What if her brother had recognized him? What if the guards had been there because Langsdorff wanted to lay charges against Max? Were they already searching for him? He touched the cut on his cheek. The lieutenant had been too handy with his stick.

He had botched the job, been sick before the attack, had vomited afterward, and still got queasy thinking about it. He wasn't a killer, he was a thief. That probably accounted for it. His heart hadn't been in it. That and the woman coming out of her house. But his employer's threat still hung over him. That devil would make sure that Max would hang—one way or the other.

In spite of the danger, he went back to the house and arrived to see the lawyer Stiebel leaving. He wondered if the queer little man knew that someone had searched his place. Probably not. His back door had been easy—he hadn't needed to force the lock. Too bad the strongbox hadn't yielded as well. He could have used the gold, and if the letter was there, it would have got his employer off his back. Maybe he could try again, with better tools. He was a better thief than a killer.

Then Seutter arrived. Max caught a glimpse of Augusta when she let him in. Max didn't like Seutter. He had a nasty suspicious way of looking at Max. And that day when he'd caught Augusta falling out of the pear tree, Seutter had looked fighting mad. She would have kissed him, if the old bastard hadn't walked in on them.

The memory of that missed kiss was sweet enough to make Max risk his life. He went to the house through the back alley and the garden, slipping into the kitchen just as the front door closed behind Seutter.

# 10

# Travel Plans

*Innocence never finds as much protection as guilt.*
François, Duc de la Rochefoucauld

The incident with Seutter upset Franz's recuperation. He realized how very ill he felt when Augusta left the parlor in tears. His mother had collapsed into hysterical weeping, and Elsbeth still stared at his bare legs. His headache had reached a blinding ferocity, his stomach heaved, and he reached for the chair back to support himself in a sudden fit of dizziness. Heaven forbid he should faint. His misery made him even angrier.

"Don't you have things to do in the kitchen?" he snarled at Elsbeth through clenched teeth.

The girl squeaked, "Yessir. Sorry, Master," and disappeared with the full market basket.

He turned to his mother. "Come, Mama," he said as firmly as he could manage. "No harm was done, thanks to your timely arrival. If you will see to the household affairs, I'll return to my bed."

She burst into angry speech. "How can you say 'no harm was done'? What of my feelings? What of the gossip? I shall not be able to hold up my head before my friends. The scandal will spread all over town. I'm ruined. No harm indeed! You are very unfeeling, Franz."

He closed his eyes and clutched his throbbing head. "Hush. Nobody will know. Seutter will hardly spread the tale." Then he remembered Elsbeth and knew he would have to have a word with her.

"That's not the point at all," his mother cried shrilly. "What of my broken engagement?"

He lowered his hand and looked at her. "What broken engagement? Are you telling me that Seutter has proposed to you and you accepted?"

His mother looked away and dabbed at her eyes. "We had an understanding," she said with a sniffle.

"Surely," Franz said severely, "that was quite improper. I knew nothing of it. Why didn't you speak to me?"

She began to cry again. "You are so hard. What has made you so hard? Don't you know my heart is broken? Why do you torment me?"

It dawned on Franz that the "understanding" had been one-sided. And she had probably informed her friends of her expectations. He sighed again. "We'll discuss it later. Perhaps you should also lie down for a little. Elsbeth can bring some chocolate to your room. You may feel more yourself by evening."

To his relief, his mother nodded. "I do feel very weak. Your arm, if you please. And tell Elsbeth to bring some of those almond cakes with the chocolate."

He saw his mother to her bedroom. On the way back, he passed Augusta's closed door and thought he heard weeping. He regretted that he had been so harsh with her and knocked softly. "Augusta?"

There was no answer, but the weeping stopped. When he tried the door, he found it locked. This angered him again, and he turned away. Remembering Elsbeth's fascination with his bare legs, he put his banyan on over his shirt before staggering downstairs again to deliver his mother's instructions.

The girl was talking to someone, so he called to her from the hall.

She put her head out of the kitchen door. "Yessir?" Franz noticed the broad-shouldered figure of Max disappearing through the backdoor.

"I see Max finally showed up," he said sourly. "About time, with the house in such a turmoil." Though it was probably too late, he added, "Elsbeth, you are to speak to no one about what happened just now in the parlor. Do you understand?"

Elsbeth flushed and nodded.

"Your mistress is resting. Take up some hot chocolate and almond cakes. Then see if you can fix a plain meal. Anything will do."

She looked doubtful. "There's some soup left, Master. And I can cook potatoes and a bit of bacon."

Franz suppressed a wave of nausea. "Anything. Perhaps Miss Augusta will be down later." Feeling dizzy again, he turned and climbed back up to his room, where he fell into bed and closed his eyes with a moan.

The assassin returned to Mannheim in the company of the vulpine messenger. He felt like a prisoner being taken to face his judge. The nasty creature maintained a stubborn silence about his fate, but he smiled a good deal.

*Schadenfreude!*

In a mood of mingled fury and fear, he was delivered to a large private house near the palace. The fox led him to a paneled and gilded library filled with paintings, globes, and comfortable chairs.

The "great man" surprised him with a courteous, "I hope I see you well, my friend," and dismissed the fox, saying, "*Entre nous: le petit reynard est trés utile, mais je ne l'aime pas.*"

Offered a comfortable chair and a glass of burgundy, the assassin—who positively hated the little fox—permitted himself a cautious smile. "A strange creature," he murmured and raised his glass to study its ruby lights before tasting. The wine was superb, and that was as strange as the friendly reception. Was this the condemned man's last drink? He did not think so. "Frankly, I wondered how much he knows of our business."

"Almost nothing, and he's devoted to my family and would never speak against me or mine. His usefulness lies in the fact that he pays close attention to all I do business with."

"I see." He felt a fresh twinge of unease.

The great man eyed him over his glass. His voice purred as he said, "Reynard will report to me later." His white, plump hand with the heavy gold ring twirled the stem, and the candles drew ruby sparks from the wine.

As red as blood, the assassin thought, and the old anger returned. "If it concerns me, I'll warrant I can do that better, sir."

"Mmm. Perhaps, perhaps not. But I have more important matters to discuss." He set down his glass and leaned forward. "I take it that you still do not have the letter?"

The assassin burst out angrily, "There is no letter! If there ever was one, it's long gone."

The great man raised a hand. "Pray, do not excite yourself. I'm inclined to agree. Will you take part in the hunting this fall?"

The assassin contained his surprise and relief at the change of subject. "I have no plans but am at your service as always, sir," he said cautiously.

His host refilled their glasses. "There will be another official hunt this year. In Schwetzingen." He made a face. "I get no pleasure from the killing of trapped animals, but you rather like that sort of thing. You know Schwetzingen, of course."

He was beginning to get nervous again. "Certainly."

"I doubt His Highness will stage the hunt far from the comforts of the summer palace. You'll get an invitation."

He guessed wildly at what was coming. The thought struck him with horror.

With a faintly sardonic smile, the great man said, "You look stunned. Surely such an entertainment is the very thing for a man of your parts."

The assassin's hand trembled, and a small amount of wine splattered on his frilled shirt cuff. This, too, looked like blood. "I . . . I . . . you cannot have considered, sir. It would be much too public!" He heard the panic in his voice.

The bushy brows rose, and the smile was gone. "I beg your pardon?"

He sweated and put the glass on the table, clenching his hands together. "Please consider, sir, the crowd of spectators."

"You surprise me. As a soldier you should know that life is not without a few risks." The great man laughed. "I dare say it will be much like Freiberg. Guns fire, blood flows, and when it's all done, there is a winner."

He knew there would be a great difference. During a royal hunt, those with guns are few, and they are watched by many. Every man with a rifle had several guests and servants beside him.

The great man emptied his glass. "The plans aren't final. My true purpose for calling you back was to assure myself of your continued loyalty. Her Highness needs all the friends she can find." He turned cold eyes on the assassin. "You have mismanaged this other business badly, and I had to make sure. You do understand that matters have gone too far for you to withdraw now?"

The assassin cast a frantic glance around the room. He was trapped. What a fool he had been to think he was master of his fate while serving this man's political ambitions. He was being used just as he had used Max. Gulping down the rest of his wine, he said angrily, "You do me an injustice, sir. I proved my loyalty at Freiberg."

"Let us not speak of that matter. It was poorly done and dangerous. And you have been paid generously with your current appointment. If you prove more reliable in the future, you may do even better."

The assassin bowed, deciding against another warning about the dangers of killing a ruling monarch in front of his assembled court. Time would show him a way to extricate himself and emerge victorious. Already his mind turned over possibilities. The reward would be enormous, unimaginable.

The other man became all complacency. "I recently received the privilege of suggesting appointments. Quite often, a title and an appropriate estate accompany such appointments."

That was more like it. Title and estate would certainly take care of what fate and his parents had denied him. The assassin bowed again. "My felicitations, sir. You will have, as always, my utmost loyalty and support."

The great man refilled their glasses. "Let us drink to success."

He raised his glass. "To the glory of *Kurpfalz!*"

Franz slept the rest of the day, waking only to find darkness outside his window and silence in the house. He got up to use the chamber pot and drink some water from the pitcher in his room and went back to sleep. The next time he woke, the sun was up and his head felt much better.

The house was quiet. He got up, splashed some water on his face, combed his hair as best he could around the bandage and tied his queue in back with a black silk ribbon. Then he dressed and opened the door to listen. He heard Elsbeth clattering pots around in the kitchen, but otherwise there was no noise. His mother must still be asleep, and perhaps Augusta also.

He felt a little cowardly, because he was going to turn his back on the troubles of his family and go directly to work. Sharing a house with three emotional females was hard on a man. Young Elsbeth was all prying eyes and ears and seemed to follow him about, and while he should be used to his mother's silliness and hysterics, she still managed to upset him. He found it difficult to show her the respect due a mother. And now even Augusta's behavior had become quite shocking. She had been such a quiet, sensible girl. What could have possessed her to pay visits to a man like Seutter? And without so much as a maid to lend some respectability? Was she so blinded by wealth that she did not care, that she did not mind Seutter's age and appearance and—worse—his lack of culture?

He tiptoed downstairs and slipped outside, closing the front door softly behind him.

He found Stiebel with the servant from the inn who had just served him his breakfast. Not having expected Franz, the little lawyer insisted on first ordering another breakfast. Then he looked Franz over carefully and asked, "Are you quite sure you are well enough? You still look very pale. Come, take a seat." He pushed his cup toward Franz. "Have some of my coffee. I'm sure it will set you up in an instant."

Coffee was a luxury the Langsdorffs had never succumbed to. Feeling the need for clear thinking, Franz accepted gratefully and asked if he might have Dr. Stiebel's advice in a family matter.

Stiebel's face grew grave. "My good friend Seutter came to see me yesterday. He was in a very distraught state. If it's about that, then I think we should wait until after breakfast."

"The man's a scoundrel!"

Stiebel said nothing.

"Augusta is not yet seventeen. A child! And he, a man old enough to have fathered both of us, played with her affections and tempted her with his wealth. He may well have ruined her. I say he's a scoundrel."

Stiebel sighed. "You forget that I've met your sister. She is not a child. She is a young woman. A very charming young woman. Why should not a man fall in love with her? Is love reserved only for the young? *Amor idem omnibus*, says Virgil."

Franz floundered. He thought of the scene in the garden when Augusta had shocked him by displaying a good deal of bosom. Seutter had seen her nakedness also. No doubt the damage had been done that day. It was disgusting but true that even a man Seutter's age might lust after her. "Perhaps," he said, "Augusta has been too careless in her dress, but I'm convinced it was done quite innocently. In fact, I had to have a word with her about it. I'm afraid my mother has not paid sufficient attention while I was away."

Stiebel looked grave again. "Poor girl. What must she have thought? I trust you have made amends?"

"Amends? She knows how improper their behavior was. To sit alone with a man, allowing him to hold her hand—and God knows what else—is surely the height of brazenness."

They were interrupted by the inn's servant bringing Franz's breakfast. Franz had lost his appetite and seethed with impotent anger.

"Eat," said Stiebel, turning his attention to his own meal.

Franz knew better than to interrupt breakfast. He made an attempt to eat and found that he was hungry after yesterday's abstinence. They ate silently, Franz turning over in his head the arguments he meant to bring in the Seutter affair. He had just about arranged them cogently when Stiebel removed his napkin, dabbed his mouth and fingers, and leaned back in his chair to regard Franz.

Franz hurried to swallow his last bite. "Sir?"

"This attack on your poor head—it hasn't by chance addled your good sense?"

Franz flushed. "Not at all, sir," he said stiffly. "In fact it seems to have taken away the stutter. I feel quite well and am ready to go to work."

"As to the stutter, yes, it seems to be gone. An excellent thing, though perhaps it may rather be ascribed to Doctor Mesmer's treatment. But that is not what I meant. You have confirmed what my friend Seutter told me, and it seems to me that you owe your sister and him apologies."

"Apologies?" Franz was shocked. Stiebel's manner reminded him of certain occasions when his father had looked and spoken to him in just such a way. But he had been a boy then, and he was a man now, and the head of his family. "I have certain responsibilities, sir," he pointed out. "You cannot know what that feels like. You have no family."

Stiebel was silent. Then he said bleakly, "You're right. I beg your pardon." He rose. "Let's go to work then."

Franz jumped up and limped after him. "No, I beg *your* pardon, sir. I don't know what came over me. Perhaps I'm not quite myself yet. I would not for the world have offended you."

Stiebel stopped. "Well, my boy," he said, "perhaps I shouldn't have spoken as I did. Only, being a lonely man, I have long since formed a habit of imagining myself in the shoes of others. In a manner, I try to live their lives for a little while, to see the world through their eyes, to feel their pain and joy, to understand why they act the way they do. It is quite an extraordinary exercise and has occasionally been useful to me in my profession. As you show an interest in the practice of law, you might try it."

"I shall try, sir."

"Well, there's no more to be said, then." Stiebel turned and disappeared into his office.

Franz stood for a moment, trying to grasp that Stiebel, who only two days ago had been the kindest and most affectionate friend he had ever had, was angry with him when he should have understood. Then he took his wounded self to his own desk.

The morning passed slowly. Franz tried to work but his mind was not on it. He felt the pain of Stiebel's re-proof acutely and blamed his family for it. If they had not created the scene the day before, Stiebel would not have taken against him. And Seutter, no doubt, had represented the situation in a light favorable to himself while blackening Franz's character.

The lying villain!

Around noon the post came. Since all of it was usu-ally for Stiebel, Franz paid no attention. Perhaps a new case or two would be added to his chores. He did not care.

Suddenly the door of his room flew open, and Stiebel shot in, periwig and coat skirts flying. He waved a letter in his hand. "We have it!" he cried and hopped on a stool next to Franz's desk. "We know who he is! Wait until you hear."

Franz blinked. "What?"

"Von Loe, silly boy. Von Loe! How could you for-get? The man your letter is addressed to."

"Oh," said Franz. "Yes."

"Listen to this: 'My dear Nepo,'—he's always called me that, ever since we were boys together at the university—'my dear Nepo, I am happy to be able to clear up this mystery for your young friend. It is indeed a fascinating tale. Your von Loe is none other than Baron Friedrich von Winkelhausen. He is chamberlain to His Most Gracious Highness, the Prince Elector of the Palatinate. Born into the von Loe family of Heidelberg, he still bears that name, along with his new titles. When the court moved from Heidelberg to Mannheim, this branch of the von Loe family moved also.'" Stiebel lowered the letter. "You see? It's just as I guessed. And he's a great man." He glanced at the letter again. "Well, there's more here but mostly about himself. Now, what will you do?"

"Do?" Franz did not know what to think. The dying captain had been the son of a senior court official. "I suppose," he said reluctantly, "I shall have to go to Mannheim to deliver the letter."

Stiebel nodded eagerly. "Of course, you must. It might pertain to a matter of the highest political importance. In fact, it's most probable that it does. I cannot like what has been happening. Thieves robbed you in Ulm. Someone broke into my chambers. And then someone tried to kill you." He shook his head. "That attack makes me afraid for you."

The way the muffled robber had swung his club could have cost him his life if he had not parried with his cane, but Stiebel's suspicions were outlandish. "Surely he just wanted to steal my money," Franz said.

"I don't know. You did say this dying captain seemed desperate. And he told you to be careful. Would he have done that if it was just an ordinary letter?"

"I was going back to the fighting. I'm sure he wanted the letter to reach his father. That's quite natural. Perhaps it contains his will. Perhaps he had a wife and children."

"His will. Yes. Possibly." Stiebel pursed his lips. "It must be very easy to murder a man during a battle," he mused.

Franz laughed a little. "Oh, being in the legal profession, you make too much of it." But as he spoke, a memory nagged. When the captain had galloped toward the generals, there had been the sound of a shot, and Franz recalled turning his head toward the woods behind him. Then the rider had fallen and been dragged away by the horse. Why had he turned his head? No shots should have come from their own troops at that time. Another thought crossed his mind. If someone had fired, he could have aimed at one of the generals and hit von Loe by accident. And yes, the captain had said he had been shot in the back—surely an impossibility if it had been enemy fire. But he must be imagining things.

His face had given away his uneasiness, because Stiebel said, "We will go to Mannheim together. I don't like the idea of you taking that letter by yourself. And we will be quick about it. I shall hire a chaise for the morning. Meanwhile, keep the matter to yourself.

We shall be back within the week. Until then I trust your mother can manage without you."

# 11

# The Betrothal

*As the ancients agree, brother Toby, said my father,
that there are two different and distinct kinds of love,
according to the different parts which are affected by it—
the Brain or the Liver—I think when a man is in love, it
behoves him a little to consider which of the two he is
fallen into.*

Laurence Sterne, Tristram Shandy

Unlike her brother, Augusta did not sleep. Neither did she eat. Elsbeth knocked on her door later that terrible evening, calling out, "Miss? I brought your supper. Miss? Shall I set it on the floor?"

In a thick voice, Augusta answered, "Take it away. I don't want it."

The girl was persistent. "Are you sick, Miss? Shall I go for the doctor?"

Augusta dabbed at her eyes. "No. It's just a migraine. Please go away." It was not a migraine, but her head felt stuffy enough after hours of weeping.

Elsbeth left then, reluctantly, no doubt; the girl took the greatest interest in her employers' private lives. If the scene in the parlor had not been so truly awful, Augusta might have smiled at Elsbeth's fascination with Franz's bare legs, but now this interest in Franz seemed prurient. Franz had complained that Elsbeth searched his room in his absence, disturbing his papers, and snooping through his clothing. Such suspicions had never been on Augusta's mind until her mother and Franz accused her of carrying on a "secret" relationship with Jakob Seutter. Now she felt wretched and unclean.

The memory of the shock and pain on his kind face tore at her. What must he think of all of them? She had lied to avoid a scene, but he must have seen it as a cruel rejection. He must have thought she felt such revulsion for him that she could not admit he had offered her marriage. Her shame for the lie and her pity for him occupied most of her thoughts.

Later she also thought of what her life would be like in the future, now that she had lost the affection of both mother and brother and had no one who cared about her. That was when she wept for herself. She had never been so alone.

After this long afternoon and night of weeping and wringing of hands, she made a decision that had the strange effect of drying her tears and stiffening her resolution.

Since they had all offended Herr Seutter so cruelly, she would go to him. She would make her own apologies and to try to explain away her mother and brother's ill manners.

As for herself, she would have to make the best of her life in this house. Her mother would be very angry for a long time and would find ways to humiliate her daily. But surely in time she would relent. Franz must be made to understand. She needed his support if she was to continue her life with them.

And so Augusta dipped a towel into her basin of cold water and applied it to her swollen eyes. This took patient reapplication and frequent checks in the mirror, but when the sun came up, she thought her appearance was passable. Putting on her second best dress, she tied an apron around her and ventured down into the kitchen.

Elsbeth was chatting with Max—who had a black eye and a plaster on his cheek. When he saw Augusta, he shot up from the chair.

"Miss," he said, looking anxious, "are you feeling better? I was that worried when Elsbeth told me you were sickly."

Augusta was touched. "It was just a migraine," she lied again with a glance at the round-eyed Elsbeth. "What happened to you, Max? Your face? It looks terrible. And I missed you yesterday."

He blushed. "Thank you, miss, for caring. I don't deserve your kindness." He hung his head. "There was a bit of a fight, miss. Night before last. I had too much beer. The gendarmes ran us in. I do beg your pardon, miss."

He looked so crestfallen that she only said, "You shouldn't fight, but I'm glad to see you." She urged him to continue his breakfast, then asked Elsbeth, "Is my brother awake?"

"Master's been up and gone this hour, Miss. Slipped out the door, quiet-like. When I went to look, there he was, walking away to his work as usual."

Augusta frowned. "Oh, dear. He wasn't well yet." She smiled at Max. "We seem to be a sickly household of late."

Max cleared his throat. "I was that sorry to hear about your brother, miss. I wish I'd been there. I would've shown that villain a few things. Did he get a look at him?"

Augusta poured herself some milk and cut a slice of bread. "Thank you, Max. No, I'm afraid he didn't see the man's face." A thought came to her. "Perhaps I'd better look in on him at Dr. Stiebel's to see how he fares." Her real errand might escape her mother's notice that way.

Max pursued the story. "Elsbeth says the gendarmes have come. Did they catch the black-hearted swine?"

"No. It was dark. My brother cried out and woke up a woman who frightened the villains away. She was quite unkind to Franz, but perhaps she saved his life."

Max departed on one of his self-imposed chores outside, and Elsbeth washed the dishes while Augusta ate her breakfast. She had no appetite but was afraid to embark on this errand light-headed from hunger.

Her mother had not yet emerged from her chamber when she left the house, a dark shawl draped around her shoulders and her small straw hat tied on over her cap.

When Maria saw who stood outside the heavy door of the Seutter house, her face became pinched with anger. "You!" she said, her voice low but sharp. "Haven't you done enough? Go away and don't come back." She tried to close the door, but Augusta took a desperate step forward and pushed. An unseemly struggle ensued that brought tears of shame and frustration to Augusta's eyes. "How dare you?" she said. "You're a servant. How dare you refuse to admit your master's friends?"

"You're no friend, you hussy!" spat Maria, shoving.

But the door was open far enough, and Augusta's skirts were not very full. She slipped through the opening and stood in the entrance hall.

"Get out!" shouted Maria, infuriated by the invasion.

"No," cried Augusta, chin high and eyes flashing.

The shouting brought Herr Seutter from his office. He looked tired and was in waistcoat and shirt sleeves. His hand still held a quill.

"Augusta," he said, shocked. Then he took in the confrontation between the two women. "Maria, please make some chocolate and bring it to the parlor."

Maria folded her arms across her starched breast. "I will not. She's trouble, and I will not have you insulted by people spreading vile gossip. You know very well that she shouldn't be here. You should never have let her into this house. She may be young, but she's a slut for all that."

Augusta gasped. Herr Seutter turned first red and then pale. "Maria, pack your things and leave. You have no place in my house. The rest of your wages will be sent to you."

Maria's mouth opened, but no sound came from it.

"Oh, please," Augusta said, horrified, "please, sir, don't be rash on my account. Maria was quite right. I should not have come. I only came for a last time to ask your forgiveness."

He seemed at a loss what to do or say. Shaking his head, he made a helpless gesture with his hands. Then he turned and held the parlor door open for her.

Augusta walked in, pulling her shawl a little closer. This was going to be very hard, but it must be done. Perhaps it would be mercifully quick. She turned to face him, and saw that he still stood by the door as if afraid of her. Then he closed it, his head bowed.

She clenched her hands until the nails bit into her flesh and said quickly before she lost courage, "I'm very sorry for the lie I told. It's true I was confused at first. But when I told my brother that you had come to court Mama, I knew it wasn't true. It was cowardly of me. I came to say how honored I was by your offer. How very deeply I feel your goodness and regard." Oh, dear, tears were filling her eyes again. She blinked, and went on, "My brother and my mother spoke without thinking or knowledge. I would give anything to make those things unsaid." She stopped because her voice was breaking.

He remained near the door but raised his head to look at her. "It's very kind, Miss Augusta, but you really shouldn't have come here," he said. "They were quite right to be angry, and now they'll be angrier still.

It doesn't matter about me. I'll go on as I have been." He looked around the room sadly. "My money makes sure of that. But you must guard your reputation. In so far as I've been the cause of any damage to you, you or your brother need only mention what will satisfy and I shall make amends. And now perhaps . . ." His voice, which had been quite firm and even cold, stopped abruptly and he held the door open for her.

The moment he had started to speak, calling her Miss Augusta, she felt completely bereft and could not stop her tears. What was she to do? Her family did not want her. Where was she to go? The tall figure of Jakob Seutter swam before her watery eyes, and her knees felt weak. She knew she must leave and was ashamed of her weakness, but he stood at the door and besides she did not think she could walk that far. She tottered to the settee. In a moment she would be stronger, she thought, and blinked her eyes furiously.

"Please don't cry." He sounded desperate. "You know I cannot bear to see you unhappy. Tell me what I must do. I'm only a simple man, but I would gladly give my life and all I own to make you happy."

Augusta sniffled, her heart too full to be rational. "Then marry me," she said and gasped at the audacity.

He said nothing, but she saw through her tears how shocked he was. She wiped her eyes and swallowed. "Yesterday you came to propose marriage. If you're still of the same mind, I accept. Only let it be soon. Let it be now. I don't want to go home. I never want to go home again," she wailed, covering her face, hoping for she knew not what and afraid that she had made things much worse.

He closed the door and came to sit beside her. "Augusta," he said gently, "I cannot. Not without your family's approval. You're not of age, you see. In any case, I had meant to wait at least until your seventeenth birthday, but I was afraid I might lose you, that you might fall in love with someone else."

She dropped her hands and looked at him. "I would never do that," she cried. "But Mama and Franz may lock me up, and then I cannot come to see you ever again."

His face softened. "Oh, my dear, you don't need me. Be patient. Surely it won't be as bad as that at home. I'm sorry that you should have this trouble on my account, but you're very young, and your whole life is ahead of you. There will be someone else, someone your mother and brother will approve of, someone you can love."

She looked down at her hands and bit her lip so she would not cry again. Love? She thought of all the nights she had lain in her narrow bed, looking through the window to the night sky above the steep roofs of the houses, and dreamed of love. Dreaming dreams of dashing cavaliers to carry her away with them, and more recently and guiltily of Max's arms around her and his lips on hers. It now seemed childish and unreal. Jakob was real. Jakob. She tasted the name silently on her tongue. His warm hands had held hers the way a nest held a tiny bird. He had wrapped her cloak around her and held her against him like a mother would a child.

That was what love was: gentleness and protection. That was what she wanted.

She raised her head to entreat him again, but he got up and went to the window, his back to her.

"Oh," she said, her heart breaking. "I see. You've changed your mind. And why should you not? I'm being foolish. We have all been making demands on you, and now Franz has insulted you so grievously. I . . . shouldn't have come." She got up to escape from this shameful scene.

"No, wait." He caught up with her, catching her shoulders and turning her to face him, then dropped his hands and stepped back. "Augusta," he said, looking anxious, "never think that I shall forget you. And never forget that you need only call on me, whatever the case may be. As long as I live, I'm yours to command in everything."

She stamped her foot, angry and frustrated. "Then why don't you prove it?"

"Prove it?"

"Hold me, Jakob. I need to feel your strength because I've been cast adrift and will surely perish if you don't save me."

He put his arms around her then and held her, fiercely, muttering endearments and upsetting her starched cap when he stroked her head. She felt his buttons pressing into her chest, and his warm hands on her back, and felt safe.

It was some time later that they wondered what had happened to Maria and the chocolate, but they decided it was more important to hold hands and talk about the future. Neither knew how a reconciliation with Augusta's family might be achieved, but Jakob accepted that Augusta had made her choice for better or worse.

And later again, Jakob took her through the house, proudly and nervously in case she should not like it. He told her in every room that she might make any changes she wished, and she said that all was quite perfect as it was.

They came to the kitchen last and interrupted an intense exchange between the servants. Shocked silence fell. Maria sat at the big table with the cook and several housemaids, her eyes red from weeping. Young Hans was in the scullery, polishing his master's boots while listening to his elders. All of them stared at the intrusion of their master and his loose woman.

Jakob smiled at them all. "I'm glad to find you here. It's to be a big secret yet, but you may wish us happy, though how I could be any happier I don't know." He chuckled and took Augusta's hand to kiss it. "Here's Augusta, er, Miss von Langsdorff. She's just agreed to be my wife, bless her. This house will be full of joy again after all these years. I know you will serve her as devotedly as you've served me and my dear Susanna."

They gaped, then muttered congratulations. Maria's voice was flat as she spoke the obligatory well-wishes and welcome to Augusta. Augusta thanked them all, and in Maria's case she added the hope that the housekeeper would help her learn the ways of a large household. Maria curtsied, casting an uncertain glance at her master, who nodded with a benevolent smile. In his joy, he had evidently forgotten that he had dismissed her.

Augusta went home happy, warm in her new security, touching from time to time the ring inside her bodice. Jakob had given it to her as the symbol of their betrothal, but they had agreed to keep it to themselves until he could make peace with her family. She wore it under her clothes on a fine silk ribbon Jakob had fastened around her neck and then he had kissed her tenderly on the lips. Augusta reveled in her new status, in the fact that she belonged to Jakob now, that she was loved.

And what of Franz and Mama? They would have to accept what they could not change, for if they did not, she would go to her betrothed without their consent. And if they locked her up, Jakob would come and get her. She laughed a little at the thought of him climbing a long ladder to her window and felt at peace.

Elsbeth had told Max with considerable relish that Miss Augusta had been caught snuggling with Herr Seutter, and that her mistress had shrieked and fallen into fainting fits, and that Master Franz had come in his night shirt, his poor legs all bare, to vent his fury on Herr Seutter. "What d'you think?" she had asked, goggle-eyed with excitement. "It'll be a duel fer sure, right? And poor Master Franz a cripple, what with that leg of his. What if they bring 'im home dead?"

Max's opinion of Franz in a duel was somewhat better than Elsbeth's, but he cared more about his angel

Augusta. How dare that rich bastard lay his filthy hands on her? There was no way an innocent like her would invite such behavior. Max had a good mind to show that dirty dog a thing or two. In that, he was of one mind with her brother. The young were meant for the young. His angel needed his protection.

According to Elsbeth, both mother and brother had turned against Augusta, who had run to her room, "crying her eyes out." After expressing his outrage that they should reject their own flesh and blood, it struck Max that Augusta's misery might well push her into his own eager arms.

Thus, he felt a proprietary love when he finally laid eyes on her. He could tell she had not slept. Her beautiful blue eyes were dull, she had dark rings under them, and her eyelids were red and puffy from weeping. And yet in her misery, his angel had pity for his black eye and cut cheek and forgave him for the drunken brawl he offered as an explanation. He decided to press his luck by buying her that bouquet of flowers in the market.

When he returned with an enormous armful of zinnias—after long deliberation, he had decided the mix of strong red and orange, pink and purple, white and yellow was certain to cheer up even a dying man—he found Master Franz had come home in the middle of the day and was closeted with his mother in the parlor.

Elsbeth, the source of this news, was confounded by the flowers. "Mary and Joseph! What's this? Did the mistress send you for them?"

"No. I got them for Miss Augusta. To cheer her." He handed them over. "Here, put them in some water, will you?"

Elsbeth's eyes flashed. She dumped the flowers on the table. "Do it yourself. And just for that I won't tell you why the young master's home."

"Well, here," said Max, plucking a few flowers from the bunch and handing them to her, "the white ones were meant for you cause you're as sweet as . . . sugar."

She blushed and pressed her nose into the blooms. "Aw, the things you say."

Max found a large earthenware pitcher, filled it with water from a bucket and shoved Augusta's zinnias into it. "So what's this about the master?"

Elsbeth hugged her flowers. "Only that he's going away. Early in the morning. To Mannheim, with that lawyer he works for."

Max froze. "What?"

Elsbeth made eyes at him. "You really like me, Max? You're not just saying that?"

Max frowned. "I like you. Go on."

"I like you, too, but you like Miss Augusta better." She pouted.

Max, intent on information, seized Elsbeth around the waist and laid a wet and crushing kiss on her lips. "There! That's how much I like you." When he released her, she was breathless and rosy-cheeked. Max considered that such sacrifices were a small price to pay. In fact, Elsbeth might well turn out a windfall for an enterprising lad embarked on a difficult quest. He smiled at her.

She smiled back. "Would you walk to church with me next Sunday?"

"Don't push me, girl," Max growled. "I don't hold with church and such. Get on with your story."

She was disappointed, but he got his report. "I was listening at the door, thinking it was more talk about Miss Augusta and her beau, but it wasn't. He said how he had to go right away, and not to go talking about it."

"Why not?"

"It's a secret. And you should've heard the mistress. She wanted to go with him. She said it was just the thing to take Miss Augusta away right now. But he wouldn't have none of it. Got real fierce with her, he did."

Elsbeth was clearly fascinated with the dynamics of the von Langsdorffs' family relations, but Max was not interested. "So what? A man's got to be firm with womenfolk."

Elsbeth gave him a soulful look. "I like a man to be masterful. Anyway, the mistress said it would be on his head if his sister ends up a spinster or worse. And then she was sniffling 'cause he had no pity on her, what with the evil things her friends was saying. And how she was mortificated. How her consternation couldn't take no more. How could she lay eyes on the faithless man after what he done to her? She meant Herr Seutter, I think."

Max nodded impatiently. "Never mind the old biddy. Why's he goin' to Mannheim? Did he say?"

"He's takin' a letter. He did say he was comin' right back. But there's the post for sendin' letters."

Max stared at her. He suddenly saw a way out of his predicament. If he let his employer know about the impending arrival of Franz with the elusive letter, he was rid of all his problems and might earn himself some good will besides. But he must be quick about it.

Augusta slipped into the house silently to avoid her mother, but the moment she closed the front door behind her, she heard the voices in the parlor. It was midday, and Franz and her mother were arguing behind the closed parlor door.

She thought her mother had discovered her absence and sent for her brother. For a moment she was afraid, but then she remembered Jakob and straightened her shoulders. Heart beating and hand touching the ring inside her bodice, she opened the parlor door and walked in.

They looked up from their heated exchange. Her mother instantly glared, but Franz merely said, "Ah, there you are, Augusta. Good. I shall need clean shirts and stockings for my trip. Will you see to it? Mama is upset."

She gaped at him. "Where are you going?"

"Doctor Stiebel and I will take coach for Mannheim tomorrow. I shall be gone five or six days at the most. Four shirts, my good ones. And brush and press my uniform. Elsbeth cannot be trusted."

The old Augusta would have asked many questions, but she was now a grown woman with a life of her own and was willing to let her family go about their business without confiding in her. She nodded and left the room.

Let him go on his trips. It would mean one less person to berate her. She could manage to avoid her mother as much as possible in the few weeks until her birthday, and Jakob had promised that he would have their banns called the Sunday after.

She went upstairs and changed into a house dress and kitchen apron. Then she collected the uniform from Franz's wardrobe and counted out his shirts, cravats, and stockings. There were enough clean ones, except for one pair of stockings, and these Elsbeth could wash and hang out to dry. The uniform, shirts and cravats she took down to the kitchen.

It was empty, but on the table stood a pitcher with an enormous bunch of colorful zinnias. Zinnias flowered in village gardens and were not at all her mother's sort of flower. She wondered where they had come from. She moved them to the sideboard and put the iron on its stand into the hot coals. Then she stirred up a small bowl of potato starch for the shirts and cravats. The uniform had been cleaned and mended after Franz's return and only needed brushing and smoothing out.

Surely Franz was not returning to military duty. What could he and Stiebel want in Mannheim? But this was no longer her business. She was betrothed. And come to think of it, once she was Frau Seutter, she would no longer have to clean and press, though she would be happy enough to do so for her husband. She smiled to herself. How good it would be to have him always near her.

She was almost done—a clean uniform and four starched shirts lay neatly folded on a chair while she pressed the cravats on the kitchen table—when Max walked in. The autumn sun slanted through the kitchen window and made a halo of his blond curls: the archangel Michael come to earth.

He stopped and looked at her with a smile that was almost tender. His teeth were very white and his eyes crinkled at the corners. Even with the bruised eye, he was beautiful. "Are you ready for your food, Max?" she asked a little breathlessly. "I'm almost done here."

"Did you like the flowers?"

"The zinnias? They're beautiful. Such colors. Where did they come from?"

"The market. I knew you'd like the colors."

Augusta blushed. "You bought them? Oh, Max, there was no need."

"Every need, miss. I couldn't help seein' you were cast down."

Augusta did not know where to look. "It was very kind, but you really mustn't do such things."

"It gives me pleasure," said Max and sat down across from her to watch her work. He made her so nervous that she hurried, creasing the last cravat.

"It gives me more pleasure to look on you," he said softly. "A man would be the luckiest man alive to come home to such a wife."

Shocked, she looked at Max just as a cloud passed over the sun and extinguished his halo. The black eye

looked sinister and his smile predatory. She was suddenly afraid and wished for Jakob. Taking her hand
from the iron, she touched the ring inside her bodice
and saw that his eyes followed it. She shivered with a
mixture of fear and pleasure, and then felt foolish. He
was only Max, even if he looked at her in a way that was
. . . not really predatory perhaps, but intent. She
thought of their embrace under the pear tree and grew
warm.

When she snatched the hot iron from the cravat, it
had burned the corner.

Turning away, she quickly put the iron back on its
stand and folded the cravat with unsteady fingers.

"Could I ask a big favor, miss?"

"A favor?" She gathered Franz's clothes, holding
them protectively against herself, ready to escape upstairs.

"A letter, miss. To my old auntie. I've never been
to school, and I'd be so very grateful if you could write
it for me."

Ah, so that was why he had bought the flowers. She
said warmly, "But of course, Max. Let me put away
these things, and I'll be back with paper and ink, and
you can tell me what to write."

Poor Max, she thought, not to be able to read or
write! Perhaps, now that they had Elsbeth and him to
do the menial work, she might try to teach him.

When she returned with sheets of her own letter
paper, her ink well, and a quill, Max looked so humbly
grateful that her heart melted. "Now," she said, smiling
and settling herself to her task, "what shall it be?"

"Beggin' your pardon, but I hardly know how to put the matter," Max said, looking ashamed. I don't have the gift of words. Auntie Rosa's sent word that she's been in such pain, she's hardly been able to walk even with a crutch, miss. I got her some medicine from the apothecary on the market. He said it was the best thing in the world for the rheumatics, and to put it in some hot wine and take it every night. I'll put the medicine on the post coach tonight, but she won't know it's waitin' for her when it gets there. A letter would tell her. If you please, could you just say it's waitin' and greetings from her loving nephew Max?"

"Oh, Max, that was very thoughtful of you," said Augusta warmly. "I hope your auntie will be much better for your kindness. Suppose I write, 'Dear Auntie Rosa. Knowing of your poor health, I have found you a medicine that is said to be excellent for rheumatic pain. You are to take it every night mixed in some hot wine. I am sending it by post, and it will be waiting for you at the post station. Hoping to see you well very soon, I am your loving nephew etc.' Will that serve?"

"You have the gift of words, miss. No need to mention the wine or the rheumatics. The apothecary put it on the medicine and auntie can read pretty well. Maybe if you'd just write, 'What you want is on its way. I done my best. Now it's up to you, dear auntie. You'll be rid of the crutches and sticks and pratin' lawyers, too. Haha.' The 'haha' tells her I'm making a joke. She's forever blamin' her rheumatics on her landlord and wants to take him to court." He chuckled.

Augusta did not think this an improvement on her own version, but Max's aunt would recognize her nephew's manner of speaking. She carefully copied down his words, only correcting his grammar a little. "There." She held up the letter. "Shall I write at the bottom that it was written by me as dictated by you?"

Max grinned. "Yes, miss. Write 'This was written for me in Lindau by an angel called Miss Augusta von Langsdorff.'"

Augusta wrote all but the angel part, then dusted the ink with sand. "Now, how shall I direct it?" she asked, folding the sheet.

"Direct it?"

"Yes. Your aunt's name and where she lives."

Max slapped his forehead. "I'm a fool. I left her letter in my room. But never fear, Miss. I can copy that well enough. I'll do it myself." He stretched out his hand. "Thank you from the bottom of my heart, miss, and my auntie thanks you, too. She'll be ever so glad to get this."

# 12

# Gods and Kings

*Order is Heaven's first law, and this confest,*
*Some are, and must be, greater than the rest.*

Alexander Pope, *Epistle 4*

The assassin read Max's clever letter and cursed. "What god-damned nonsense is this? 'What you want is on its way. I done my best. Now it's up to you, dear auntie. You'll be rid of the crutches and sticks and pratin' lawyers, too. Haha.' The bastard calls me auntie? He must've been drunk."

But on second thought, Max could not read or write, and it said very clearly that the letter had been written by the cripple's sister. He studied it again, and finally light began to dawn. "What you want is on its way." That must be the letter. But wait. "I done my best" and "now it's up to you" surely means he didn't get the letter and wants me to do it." He frowned. Not good! "Crutches" and "lawyer" refer to the cripple and

Stiebel. Max must mean that they are on their way with the letter. Yes, that must be it.

He decided to show this to his employer. At the very least, it would prove that he had left someone behind to carry out instructions.

The great man was in a pleasant mood. He listened to the assassin's story, read Max's letter with interest, and said, "This man has more brains in his little finger than you have in that big head of yours. And the man can't even read and write."

The assassin started to protest.

"Shut up! This will be handled by my good Reynard. You can leave."

Stiebel and Franz journeyed to Mannheim in a hired chaise with four post horses, stopping only to change horses and postilions and staying a mere two nights in inns.

Stiebel was distracted and spent most of the jolting, swaying journey clinging to the leather loops beside the windows and peering impatiently through the dirty glass. Once a delay caused by an overturned lumber wagon caused him to wonder aloud if he should have brought his pistols.

"Are you worried about highwaymen, sir?" asked Franz. "Surely there's nothing to be afraid of. Besides, I have my sword." He had purchased it for the journey and was inordinately proud of it.

"Hmmph," said Stiebel and shifted to the other side of the coach to get a peek at the road ahead.

To distract him, Franz raised the subject of his sister and Seutter again. "I have decided to let the matter slide," he informed Stiebel, feeling quite magnanimous. "Nothing good can come of making it public."

The ploy succeeded. Stiebel turned a shocked face to him. "Surely that never crossed your mind?"

Franz flushed. "It did at first. I was very angry. But Mama will see to it that Augusta behaves in the future."

Stiebel grunted and fell into another lengthy abstraction. The roads improved, and the coach rolled more smoothly and steadily. He finally dozed off until the next post station.

They reached Mannheim late on the third day. Their inn was on the Paradeplatz. Stiebel had sent ahead to arrange for rooms. Franz climbed out first, stiff after sitting for so long. He was helping Stiebel down when a short dapper man in black appeared at their side, bowing over his folded hands.

He had sharp, pale features and wore the small powdered wig lately fashionable among young dandies. Bidding them welcome, he said, "The name's Reinhard. At your service, gentlemen." Then he waved over two liveried servants who seized their baggage and carried it in while Stiebel paid off the coachman and tipped the postilion.

The inn resembled a large private house with its comfortable furnishings and handsome paintings on the walls. As usual, Stiebel's liberality made Franz uncomfortable because he did not know how to repay it.

They signed the guestbook, then followed the servants upstairs. Reinhard skipped ahead, chattering about the fine fall weather and his hopes that their stay would be comfortable. Stiebel climbed slowly, grasping the polished banister and pausing from time to time to catch his breath.

When they reached their rooms—very handsome adjoining ones with fine beds and more pictures—Franz said, "You must rest, sir. This journey has tired you out. They can bring us dinner here."

"Of course," cried the dapper Reinhard. "Allow me to make the arrangements. I'm sure we can please the gentlemen with the finest dishes the kitchen can provide."

"No, thank you, Reinhard," said Stiebel. "Later perhaps. We have an errand first. Would you happen to know where we might find Baron von Winkelhausen at this hour? He's chamberlain to the Kurfürst, I believe."

One of the footmen said, "He'll have an apartment in the palace then."

"Thank you. Very convenient." Stiebel pressed some coins into the footmen's hands and turned to Reinhard to reward him also.

Reinhard accepted the silver piece with a bow, then eyed their clothes. "If you'll allow me, gentlemen, you'll need your court suits for a visit to the palace. And your honor," he said to Stiebel, "may wish to replace the *peruke.* I know a very good man who can bring a selection immediately."

"What's wrong with my wig?" demanded Stiebel, patting it. "It was made by the French king's own *perruquier.*"

Reinhard looked at it. "Was it indeed, sir? Which king was that?"

Stiebel snapped, "Louis XIV, of course. The sun king. It's exactly like his. And what is it to you anyway?"

Reinhard immediately clasped his hands and bowed. "Your pardon, your honor. Nothing at all, I assure you. Several of the elderly gentlemen still wear the full wig. It does lend an air of dignity. Pray accept my humble apologies."

Stiebel grunted and looked around for his *portemanteau*. "You can press the clothes in that for tomorrow," he said. "Today we must go as we are."

Franz decided the dapper man had a point. Under the fur-trimmed traveling cloak, Stiebel's brown velvet suit looked dirty and rumpled. "Perhaps," he suggested, "a good brushing for now?"

"Nothing simpler," cried Reinhard and dashed off.

Stiebel shook his head. "That footman knows nothing about hair, but he's very accommodating. You'd better change into your uniform. Here,"— he delved into an inner pocket of his cloak—"take the letter. The sooner that's delivered, the better. I confess, I'll be very glad to be rid of it."

Franz took the letter and his own *portemanteau* into the next room. Pouring water from a very handsome pitcher into a very handsome bowl, he washed his hands and face, then combed his hair over his healing scalp wound, and retied the black ribbon of his queue. He changed his shirt and put on his uniform and boots.

When he was dressed, he took up the letter. It was badly creased from the time it had spent in his boot. With a sigh, he put it in the pocket of his coat and returned to Stiebel.

The dapper Reinhard was back, vigorously flicking a brush as Stiebel turned. The sprucing up was deft and expert. Reinhard's fingers flew from straightening the collar band and ruffling the lace jabot to tucking-up stockings and dusting buckled shoes. He adjusted the wide cuffs and pulled down the skirts of the coat, unbuttoning and re-buttoning to achieve a perfect fit. When he was done, he stepped back to study the effect. "Much better, your honor."

It *was* much better, and Franz let the clever fellow give his uniform the same attention. Another silver piece passed hands, Reinhard bowed, and they set out for the palace.

Franz had seen little of the city beyond his hospital room and the road to the post station. Now he looked with wonder at the wide paved streets and modern buildings. Mannheim was nothing like Lindau or other cities with their narrow, winding medieval streets. The avenue they were on ran straight as an arrow from the Paradeplatz to the palace gates. All was order and clarity in Mannheim, and at its center was the enormous palace. He remarked on this to Stiebel.

The old man grumbled, "All the princes have a mind to be sun kings. This looks a good deal like Versailles."

"But where does the money come from? The Kurpfalz is a very small country compared to France. How do they do it?"

Stiebel snorted. "Taxes and debts, I think."

The palace gates stood wide. Coaches and pedestrians passed in and out between uniformed guards standing at attention. Stiebel headed for the central building.

Franz gaped. Surely Versailles could not be larger. East and west wings embraced an enormous *cour d'honneur* and extended on either side as far as his eye could see. It was dusk, but lights glimmered everywhere, from lanterns on carriages, walls, and doorways, and behind hundreds of large windows. There must be thousands of candles. A fine church stood at one corner, to show that an enlightened ruler could also be a good Christian. It was an impressive and intimidating display of power and faith, and yet, with its lights and pale colors, it was beautiful and welcoming.

"What are all these people doing here at this hour?" Franz asked.

"Some festivity, no doubt."

The liveried footman at the door looked down his nose. "Baron von Winkelhausen no longer resides here."

Franz caught sight of the hall, three stories high and entirely of white marble. Oversized marble statues of the elector Karl Theodor and his wife Elisabeth Augusta stood in marble niches, and the shining marble floor was like a sheet of shimmering ice. A massive double staircase, its marble banisters adorned with gilded lanterns and marble *putti* at play, led up to some heavenly realm. Franz's dazzled eyes took in an enormous ceiling fresco of richly dressed men and women mingling with ancient gods and goddesses. It looked as if the palace roof opened directly onto paradise or Mount Olympus—he knew not which.

He returned to earth reluctantly. Stiebel was speaking in French to a gentleman in a suit of rich dark blue silk with gold lacing.

Franz's French was not altogether fluent, but he understood the gentleman to say that Baron von Winkelhausen had retired to his country house in Schwetzingen. He added, "His health has been indifferent since he lost his only son last year. May I be of some assistance? My name is Moritz."

Stiebel bowed. "Nepomuk Stiebel, privy councilor from Lindau. And this is my friend, Franz von Langsdorff. He served with the baron's son at Freiberg."

"Did he indeed? An honor, Lieutenant." Herr Moritz looked at Franz with interest, taking in his crippled leg and the cane. "If you will both come with me, we shall enquire about the baron's condition. You arrived for a special court concert. Young Mozart is to perform. Everybody is here tonight."

They climbed the stairs, slowly, to accommodate Franz's limp and Stiebel's age. Franz's eyes were drawn again to that magnificent ceiling. He was ascending into a realm where humans conversed with gods, perhaps toward an apotheosis. Filled with exhilaration and awe, he wondered if that forbidding-looking gentleman on the next landing was about to pass along some portentous message or warning.

The marble staircase did not lead to paradise or Olympus but to more splendor. They turned down a wide corridor and then passed through a series of beautiful rooms lit by enormous chandeliers and gilded sconces. They walked on glossy parquet floors inlaid with arabesques and across deep carpets adorned with flower garlands. The flower garlands also festooned the walls in gilded stucco, and more gold sparkled from the frames of large oil paintings and the ormolu detailing on furniture. Large mirrors reflected lights of crystal chandeliers, and enormous tapestries depicted tales about the gods.

Franz gazed and gazed, trailing heedlessly behind Stiebel and Moritz. Violins and flutes accompanied their progress, weaving melodies so light and gay that even a cripple might wish to dance. He was floating on an invisible cloud toward some grand destiny.

When a pair of wide doors of gilded ebony opened onto a large gathering of men and women, he was disappointed that they were mere mortals. To be sure, they wore gowns and suits in such colors of rainbows that they took his breath away, and he realized that these were the gods and goddesses of this world, amusing themselves in their Elysian fields.

The women in their low-cut dresses wore flowers and pearls in their powdered hair and at their breasts. Augusta could have made four fine gowns out of their enormous skirts, and they showed far more of their bodies than Augusta did the day he had told her she looked like a whore.

These elegant creatures, these goddesses, sat or stood, moving their fans languidly to the sound of the violin, tapping dainty feet in beribboned shoes to the rhythm of the clavichord, and Franz was besotted by their beauty.

The center of this magnificence was the elector. Karl Theodor sat in a large gilded chair and looked still quite handsome, while his wife, the Electress Elisabeth Augusta, was a matronly figure beside him.

Zeus, the all powerful, and Ceres, the bountiful, Franz thought.

But then his eyes moved on to a beautiful little girl who sat on the elector's other side, a little princess, twelve at most, but already a *grande dame* in miniature. Half child, half woman, her perfection seemed unearthly.

But all eyes were on another child, on a little boy, who played the harpsichord like a master. He was so small that someone had placed several hefty tomes on his bench so he could reach the keys. His tiny hands flew back and forth like playful birds, and sometimes he laughed out loud with delight.

When the piece was finished there was great applause, and an older man with a violin stepped forward to announce that "Wolferl" would now play one of his own compositions. The violins and flutes were silent, and the boy played—so happily and cleverly from memory, that Franz smiled with everyone else.

That, too, was a wondrous thing, for he thought he had forgotten how to smile. Enchanted, his eyes moved back and forth between the talented boy and the young princess.

Perhaps she felt his gaze, because she turned her head and looked at him. Her eyes were cornflower blue and wide with curiosity as they swept over him— and then she smiled.

Such a smile!

Franz put his hand over his heart and bowed.

At that moment the music stopped. Applause. Movement, and chatter, and she turned away.

Stiebel nudged Franz. "Wake up! Herr von Moritz wishes to introduce us to the baron's doctor."

Franz bowed to this Doctor Mai, and then to a Colonel von Rodenstein, a Count Schönborn, and another colonel, whose name escaped him. A small group of men, some in court dress, others in uniform, gathered around them.

"The lieutenant served at Freiberg," Moritz explained. "He carries a message from poor Captain von Loe to his father. Lieutenant, this is Doctor Mai, who can speak to the baron's condition."

The doctor wore a fine dark blue velvet suit and a very elegant lace cravat. He looked sharply at Franz. "I think I must advise against a visit," he said. "The baron is in poor health and should not be upset."

Franz's hatred for doctors flared up. He said stiffly, "Thank you, Doctor, but under the circumstances, I think we must go to see for ourselves."

Doctor Mai's face reddened. "Surely you are not so heartless as to trouble a sick man, especially with such a message?"

Stiebel intervened. "We will certainly wait until tomorrow. Perhaps then we may catch the gentleman on one of his better days."

Rodenstein, tall and somewhat corpulent and with the broad ribbon and diamond-studded order of the White Eagle of Poland on his heavily laced uniform coat, addressed Franz, gesturing at his leg. "*He* was injured during the recent campaign?"

"Yes, sir. At Freiberg."

"We lost many fine young men there besides von Loe. Why has *he* come to see Loe's father?"

To be addressed in the third person like those of lower rank was disconcerting, though common enough. Franz said, "I'm the bearer of his son's letter, sir."

"In that case, *he* can surely leave it with someone."

"By your leave, sir, I think I must attempt to deliver it. It . . . it's a matter of honor. I've given my sacred word as a soldier and a gentleman."

Colonel Rodenstein frowned and turned away. The others were silent.

Stiebel touched Franz's arm. "Come, we have troubled these gentlemen enough."

On the way back, Stiebel was preoccupied with his own thoughts, and Franz thought of the little princess in her magnificent palace, and the enormous distance that separated crippled lieutenants from goddesses and men of privilege.

Later, during dinner, he asked, "Who was that small boy playing the clavichord?"

Stiebel looked surprised. "God love us, where was your mind? All the talk was about the *Wunderkind*. His name's Wolfgang Mozart. He's seven and travels with his father and older sister from court to court, giving performances. They've come here from Vienna where he played for Empress Maria Theresa. I'm told the empress took him on her lap. She's a very motherly lady—quite unlike this princess, I think."

Franz thought of the little princess with the cornflower eyes. "Surely she is much too young to be motherly?"

Stiebel laughed. "Too young? Elizabeth Augusta's nearly forty. And probably barren. She finally had one pregnancy last year, but the little prince died the next day. A hard birth, they say, and no chance of another. So there's no hope of an heir."

"But whose children were those?"

"They belong to Elizabeth Augusta's sister, the Countess Palatine of Pfalz-Zweibrücken. Another dynastic house of the Wittelsbach family. The Count Palatine Michael is Karl Theodor's heir, by the way. Gossip has it that the Countess Palatine had an affair with an actor, got pregnant, and was banished by her husband. She's said to be in a convent. Elisabeth Augusta is raising her daughters."

Repelled by these details, Franz grumbled, "I don't see where the marital troubles of the sovereigns are any of our concern."

Stiebel pushed away his empty plate. "You're quite wrong about that. There's a good deal of ill will between Karl Theodor and his wife, as well as heirs waiting to succeed him. It makes for a delicate political atmosphere."

Franz digested this. "But why this talk about lovers?"

Stiebel raised his brows. "I've noticed before how very prudish you are, Franz. Colonel Rodenstein has been warming Elizabeth Augusta's bed for a decade. Did you notice the Polish Eagle? She bestowed the decoration on him. He's her Master of Ceremony. Elisabeth Augusta favors military men."

"If it is indeed true that these women have taken lovers, why don't their husbands divorce them?"

"The Count Palatine is protecting his children, and Karl Theodor is Catholic and  . . . well, they are cousins, but hers is the direct line. Her grandfather made certain she would rule by making the marriage a condition for Karl Theodor's succession. Karl Theodor consoles himself with actresses."

Franz did not want to think about royal affairs, not merely because he disapproved on moral grounds, but because he thought his little princess—innocence personified— would sooner or later be exposed to such a life.

That night he did not have one of his usual nightmares. He dreamed instead of the gods and goddesses in green forests. Nymphs and satyrs danced to the flute of the goat god Pan, and he himself chased after a half-dressed nymph who cast teasing glances back at him and beckoned with a dainty fan. His crippled leg dragged, he stumbled, nearly lost her, but persisted with superhuman effort and finally caught her. They fell laughing into soft green moss, and he bent to kiss her. A moment later, she slipped away, her cornflower blue eyes full of mocking laughter.


The great man was at his desk, and a smirking Fox lounged against one of the book cases.

"Ah, there you are," said the great man coldly.

The assassin suppressed his irritation. "Could we speak in private, sir?"

"*Reynard* is a man of many special skills. He has done us a great service today." The great man held up a very dirty and creased letter. "One that you have signally failed at."

Anger curled like a lit fuse in his belly. So the odious creature had managed to steal the cursed letter. He glared at the fox. "What special skills?"

"I used to be a pickpocket." The fox wiggled his fingers and grinned.

The assassin turned back to the great man. "I'm the one who warned you of their coming."

"But it was *Reynard* who got the letter. And let me point out that it was your carelessness that caused the trouble in the first place." He held up the letter again. "Take a look."

"He stole the wrong letter?" the assassin asked hopefully.

"Oh, it's the right letter. See the blood stain? But take another look at the seal."

"They haven't opened it!"

"Precisely. Too honorable for their own good." The great man broke the seal and unfolded the two sheets of paper. He read, pursing his lips.

The assassin watched impatiently. The letter had already caused him enormous trouble. He was not sure if he wanted the contents to be harmless. Yet, if the dying captain had been in possession of certain details, then he might have told the cripple something of the affair, perhaps even mentioning names. Especially his own.

The great man looked up. "Not so very dangerous after all," he said, then held the letter into the flame of his candle. It caught fire and flashed up, illuminating for a moment the faces of the three men, their expressions distorted into ugly masks.

The Fox detached himself from the book case. "So I wasted my time, did I?"

"Not at all, my good *Reynard*. You did well." The great man opened a desk drawer and took out a fat purse. "You may go to bed now."

The Fox snatched the purse and bowed. "A thousand *remerciements*, your honor." He smirked and left the room on silent feet accompanied by a soft clinking of coin.

The assassin bit his lip. "What was in the letter, sir?"

"Nothing of importance. You may forget about it."

So he was not to be trusted. "Well, I suppose that finishes our business then," he said resentfully.

"Not quite. You've left me in a difficult position," said the other, studying his fingernails. "When that young man and his legal friend discover the loss of the letter, they will get suspicious. They will almost certainly try to make contact with the old man, and he will smell a rat. He is our greatest enemy." He shook his head and glared at him. "I wish I had never taken you into our confidence. If this has further repercussion, I shall hold you responsible. And I do not forget those who have injured me."

The assassin was speechless, but it did not matter. The great man waved him away with a peremptory, "That's all. Good Night!"

# 13

# Highway Robbery and other Crimes

*Murder most foul, as in the best it is,*
*But this most foul, strange, and unnatural.*
William Shakespeare, *Hamlet*

The day before Franz's departure for Mannheim, Augusta's mother, angry with both of her children, withdrew to her room and emerged only when she wished trays of delicacies brought to her. Augusta was relieved.

She was also relieved that Franz seemed to have forgotten about the scene in the parlor. She went about her household chores, buoyed by a quiet happiness. Soon, very soon she need never again fear her mother's ill temper or her brother's censure.

Franz left at dawn in a carriage hired by Doktor Stiebel. His mother did not see him off, but Augusta got up to fix his breakfast. He ate it absent-mindedly and in a great hurry. When he pushed his empty plate away for Augusta to remove, he looked at her as if he had only just remembered her existence and said, "I'll only be gone for a few days. I trust you and Mama will manage for that long, and that you will consult Mama before you go out."

Consult her mother? He clearly did not know that she had taken care of this household for many months now, and that Mama rarely emerged from her bed-chamber until midmorning. But she bit her lip and only said, "We shall manage."

This was clearly not enough. His frown deepened. "You are not to have any contact with that man, do you hear?"

Her anger flared, but nothing was to be gained by another violent argument. Franz would be gone in a little while. She turned away and went into the scullery with the dirty dishes. "I hope you have a safe journey," she called back to him. "Pray give my regards to the good *Doktor.*"

"Augusta!" He sounded impatient. "Come back here a moment. I want to make certain that you under-stand—" he broke off because—blessedly—the sound of a carriage stopping outside sent him to the front door instead.

Augusta waited as long as she dared, then emerged to wave goodbye from the door. But Franz had his back to her and was supervising the loading of his *portemanteau*, and only Doctor Stiebel raised his cocked hat and smiled. Franz climbed inside and slammed the door without another glance.

Augusta dropped her hand and looked after them as they disappeared down Fischergasse. Her brother had not even raised his hand to wave farewell. She mattered less to him than Elsbeth—except in so far as she was an embarrassment to his pride. With a sigh, she went inside and closed the door.

Elsbeth appeared soon after, having been woken by the sound of the carriage, and soon Max also arrived. The three of them set about the daily chores.

When Augusta's mother came downstairs much later, she was dressed for going into town. Augusta wished her a good morning. Her mother pursed her lips and did not respond. Her face was set in a tragic expression as she sipped her morning coffee interspersing every sip with deep sighs. Augusta made no attempt to carry on a conversation. She felt that in this instance she had been—and still was—the victim. Between sighs, Frau von Langsdorff made a good meal of her coffee and several slices of yeast bread spread liberally with butter and peach jam, then left on her errand.

Augusta, having nothing else to do, went out into the garden with one of the books that had belonged to her father. She had chosen it because she felt a need to be close to her father in her loneliness.

The day was warm, but autumn had already brought chill nights, and she had to brush yellow leaves off the bench before sitting down. She found that that the book contained poetry by Angelus Silesius. Opening it in the middle, she read:

> *Jesu, du mächtiger Liebesgott,*
> *Nah' dich zu mir,*

I. J. Parker

*Denn ich verschmachte fast bis in Tod*
*Für Liebesgier;*
*Ergreif' die Waffen und in Eil'*
*Durchstich mein Herz mit deinem Pfeil,*
*Verwunde mich!*

She was profoundly astonished that a Christian poet should address Christ as the god of love, speak of languishing in desire, beg to be overcome, to be wounded, to be pierced by His arrow. Just thinking about it made her feel warm.

Was loving God like loving a man? If so, she did not love God as Silesius had. She was not even sure that she loved Jakob with such fervor. Confused, she looked up into the pear tree where the blue of the sky mingled with the gold and green of the leaves and searched her heart for such passion.

"There you are, Miss."

She started, shutting the book quickly. Max was striding down the garden walk. With the sun on his curls, he resembled the archangel again, an archangel who carried a nosegay of red roses and smiled in that way which always made her heart beat faster.

"What is it, Max?" she asked in an unsteady voice, clutching Silesius to herself.

He extended the roses. "For you, Miss."

"More flowers? Why?" she cried, uncomfortable with such attentions because she was not sure that she did not want them, and that wanting them was surely wrong.

"For helping me with the letter . . . and because it pleased me." He gave her a melting glance.

She put her nose into the roses so she would not have to look at him. The petals were cool as silk against her lips, as deep a red as blood, and their scent was sweeter than any she could remember. "Thank you, Max," she murmured, "but you mustn't bring me flowers. Did you put the letter in the mail?"

"Yes, Miss. Auntie'll have it before the sun sets. Isn't it a grand thing how fast the post is these days?"

"It is indeed, Max." She did not know how to end this conversation but knew she must.

"Augusta! Where are you?"

For once, her mother's call was welcome. "I must go," she murmured and, holding Max's roses and the Silesius pressed to her breast where Jakob's ring also rested, she dashed into the house.

Her mother was in the parlor, taking off a fetching new bonnet. On the settee lay a number of parcels. She looked excited and happy. Apparently she had soothed her wounded feelings by spending money on herself.

Augusta meant to avoid irritating her again at all costs and said, ""Yes, Mama," as humbly as she could manage.

"What have you there? Roses? Very pretty. Wasted under the circumstances, but it shows the right spirit." She came and took the bouquet from Augusta and smelled it. "And a book? Such an old one. Is it a romance?"

"No, Mama. It is one of Papa's. I was reading it when you called."

"Oh." She tossed the book on a chair. "Sit down. I've come to a decision."

This did not sound like her mother and made Augusta uneasy, but she sat down and waited.

"I've taken two seats on tomorrow's coach," announced her mother triumphantly. "We are going to Mannheim!"

"What?"

Her mother twirled around the room with a happy laugh. "We are going, my girl. You and I. Why should Franz have all the fun? I'm quite angry with him for being so selfish. In fact, I was unable to sleep and felt very ill this morning, but the fresh air did me good. I was in the middle of trying on some bonnets at Madame Annette's . . ." She interrupted herself to peer into the mirror between the windows. "What do you think? Isn't it most charming? The violet ribbons match my eyes. Anyway, I was trying on bonnets when I had my idea. Why can't we follow Franz by post coach? He'll be glad to see us, and even if he's put out, it will be too late by then." She turned around, smiling broadly at Augusta. "Now what do you say?"

Augusta had listened in horror. "You can't, Mama," she said. "Think of what it will cost. And what will we do when we get there? I'm sure a city like Mannheim will be much more expensive than Lindau. You know we must manage our money, especially now that we have to pay wages."

"Tralala!" sang her mother, picking up a heavy purse from among her purchases and shaking it so that Augusta could hear the clinking of coins. "We have plenty of money. One hundred *gulden.*"

"One hu . . . how did you get that?"

"Look around you, girl. I'm a property owner. I borrowed the gold on the house. Quite easy."

"Oh, Mama! What will Franz say? Oh, you shouldn't have done that."

"And why not? The house is mine. I can do with it as I wish. I cannot imagine why I didn't think of it before."

"But Mama, how will we pay back the money?"

"Don't be silly. We won't have to."

Augusta tried again. "Mama, it is a loan. You have to pay back the money. With interest. How will you do that?"

Her mother laughed. "Foolish girl. Once we get to Mannheim, we'll find you a rich husband. Someone of good birth and with a position at court. Someone who will help Franz with his career and see to it that I'm taken care of."

Augusta was aghast. "What makes you think some stranger in Mannheim will want to marry me?"

Her mother cocked her head and eyed her speculatively. "You're not bad looking, you know," she said, astonishing Augusta who had never heard her mother say anything of the sort and thought herself plain. "With the right clothes and hair style you'll look charming. Franz must seek *entrée* among the best people at court and introduce you to his friends. Nothing could be simpler." She laughed and raised the fat purse again, shaking the gold inside. "We'll order new gowns to be made in the latest fashion and have our hair done once we get to Mannheim. Now go and pack your best dress and enough shifts and stockings for a week. You can wear your second best in the coach."

It was mad. And awkward. And somewhat laughable. Here she was, secretly betrothed to Jakob, a man as wealthy as even her mother could wish, but she would be snatched away from him and paraded in Mannheim as if she were a heifer at a cattle market because her mother was piqued that Jakob had preferred her daughter.

Of course, she had no choice but to make this foolish trip. If she refused, her mother would go by herself, and Augusta was afraid of what would happen then.

She would have to let Jakob know of her mother's plan, but there was little chance of slipping away while Mama was organizing her madcap journey. In her room Augusta sat down and wrote to him, her first love letter. It did not read like any love letter she had ever read in books, and after rereading the matter-of-fact statements about her imminent departure (she did not mention her mother's intentions of finding her a husband), she added, "I shall miss being near you, dear Jakob, but surely it won't be long until I may see you again." It was true, even if it lacked the warmth of desire expressed by Angelus Silesius. She sealed the missive and, still feeling it inadequate, she kissed it, though Jakob would not know that she had done so. Then she put it in the pocket of her apron and went in search of Elsbeth.

But Elsbeth was busy with her mother. They were sorting through her mother's wardrobe and gathering a large pile of skirts, shifts, caps, and kerchiefs that Frau von Langsdorff wanted mended, taken in, washed, pressed, or otherwise improved before their departure.

Elsbeth was not a safe messenger in any case. The girl could not keep her mouth shut. Augusta looked for Max instead and found him stacking firewood behind the shed.

"Max," she said, blushing a little, "would you take this note to Herr Seutter for me? Be sure to give it into his own hand. It seems we are to go on a journey tomorrow and neither Mama nor I have time to see him before we leave."

Max took the letter, but he looked angry. Perhaps he did not like being sent about like her errand boy. "I'm sorry, Max," she said. "I wouldn't ask this favor if I had another way to send the message."

"You should not go running off to Mannheim like that," Max said. "It's not safe for two females to travel on their own. It's especially not safe when one is taking quite a lot of money."

So her mother had already shared the news with her servants. What else had she shared? That she planned to find a husband for her daughter? Augusta said, "We won't be gone long, and my brother is in Mannheim. But I thank you for your concern. We shall be careful."

The assassin had made up his mind to murder the old man only because he had no choice. What happened at Freiberg had been easy and safe, but this was different. He nearly panicked several times and was in a state of nerves all the way to Schwetzingen, his hands so wet with perspiration that he could hardly hold the reins.

Thank God, horses were sure-footed creatures in the dark, or he might have taken an awkward tumble. His mind was not on the road but on what he was about to do.

He was very comfortable with a gun, a marksman of distinction, but a gun would not serve this time. This must look like a natural death. He was neither a burglar, nor could he claim any experience with the *garrote*, but that was what he carried in his pocket. He thought to string the body up by a noose afterward, somewhere near a toppled chair to make it look as though the old man had hanged himself out of grief over the loss of his only son.

But strangling a man required getting close enough to the victim to lay hands on him. What if he did not cooperate and raised an outcry? And even if he was quiet, what of having to hold him as he choked to death? He felt nausea rising from his stomach and swallowed down bile.

He pictured the bulging eyes, a mouth wide open in a silent scream, a swollen tongue pushing out like some slimy creature. He imagined the choking, rasping sound coming from a collapsed windpipe, the smell of sour old age, the weak struggle faltering, and the worn-out body sagging in his arms. To come so close to the moment of death should never have been part of his service to the great man's cause.

And there was the danger. He might be caught. Even if he was not caught, he might not be able to do it. But he hardly dared to think what another failure would mean. The old one knew far too much to be allowed to live.

The manor lay quiet in the moonlight. Not even a dog barked.

Trembling a little with nerves, he left his horse out of sight from the road and walked cautiously toward the main house. All was silent and peaceful. He had prepared an explanation, should he be stopped, but no one stopped him. The baron shared the house with an elderly couple, who occupied the top floor, while he had his rooms downstairs. Old people sleep soundly, he thought, trying to give himself courage.

The baron's rooms were in the back. He walked around the building into the small, formal garden and was momentarily unnerved by the black shapes of trimmed bushes, standing there like so many strategically placed sentries. He stopped to calm his breathing. Somewhere water trickled—a fountain. The gravel crunched softly under his soles, and he moved off the path and onto the dirt of a bed of late roses that shone ghostly white in the moonlight. The scent of roses was in the air, and somewhere an owl hooted.

The rooms on the lower floor opened by glass doors onto the terrace. He tried the doors one by one. Somewhat to his surprise, the door to the old man's room was unlatched. Very careless, thought the assassin and was suddenly filled with confidence.

He eased open one wing. It squeaked a little, and he stopped to put his ear to the opening: nothing but a soft snoring sound. The old were deaf, but what if there was a servant sleeping nearby? His information about the inhabitants of the house might be faulty. He bit his lip and slowly opened the door a little more until it was stopped by heavy velvet draperies. A thin line of light showed between them. Pushing the curtain aside, he slipped into the room. The draft caused a candle to flicker beside the curtained bed, but the sleeper still snored.

No sign of a servant, and the door to the adjoining room was closed.

Inside the bed curtains, he could make out the form of the sleeper. A book he had been reading when he fell asleep lay open on the turkey carpet next to a pair of slippers. A chamber pot peeked out from under the bed. On the small table beside the candle stood a brown medicine bottle and an empty glass with a spoon in it. A sleeping potion, the assassin hoped.

He crept up to the bed and peered at his victim. The old man slept on his back, his mouth slack under the white mustache, a trail of saliva trickling on the pillow.

Disgusting. The old had no business clinging to their miserable lives. The assassin felt for the *garrote* in his pocket when he saw the large bolster beside the sleeper. Perhaps it had propped up the old man's back earlier while he was reading.

Holding his breath, he reached across, his eyes on the sleeping man's face. The snoring sound changed, became more guttural, then stopped. The assassin snatched the bolster, pushed it down over his victim's head, and pressed.

A hoarse cry, followed by a mewling sound, came from under the pillow, then the old man's sticklike arms came up to push and tear at the pillow and flail about. His legs pulled up and kicked at the cover. His body arched.

Damn! The old bastard was stronger than he had expected and making more noise than was desirable. Climbing onto the bed, the assassin straddled the heaving, twisting body and forced his weight down hard on the bolster. The arms flailed more violently and one caught the glass. It fell with a clatter of the spoon but did not break. Nearly frantic now, the assassin lay down bodily on top of the old man to stop his thrashing. He pinned down the old man's legs with his, caught the flailing arm, and held the bolster in place with his weight, pressing his face down on it.

As he lay thus, feeling the convulsions of the other body beneath his, he thought that this murder was astonishingly similar to rape. The struggle against his body felt just like having an unwilling woman under him, an exciting experience he had savored several times in his life. He felt himself grow hard. At first this reaction shocked him and he tried to control it, but the urge was too powerful and the stimulus too insistent. He came just as all movement ceased under him.

He staggered off the corpse and out of the room, hardly aware of what he was doing. Not until he was well clear of the estate, galloping back to Mannheim as fast as he could make his horse go, did he regain some mental equilibrium.

He had ridden like this on moonlit nights after spending a night with a woman. Not all those times had involved rapes, of course, but several of the women had been married, and the excitement of secrecy and danger had been similar. And so was the feeling of physical well-being, of satisfaction, of pleasure consumed. In fact, murder had been more exhilarating, had brought such a rush of energy and such an orgasm that it exceeded all sexual encounters in his life.


Max was angry. How dare the old biddy pack up his angel and depart for Mannheim to find her a husband. Someone should keep an eye on silly females. And she had that great bag of money with her. A very tempting bag of money. He had been tempted himself.

His first instinct was to follow them, but he could not go to Mannheim. Koehl was there and had paid him to kill his angel's brother.

That did not mean that he intended to deliver her letter. After having seen the ladies and their bags and trunks safely stowed in the post coach, he returned to the house. In the empty kitchen, he took the letter from his pocket and kissed it. He thought he still detected a trace of her scent, though he had slept with it under his cheek all night. He wanted to keep it, knew it was much safer not to, but in the end he tucked it back in his pocket.

Then he went out to dig over the vegetable garden. Elsbeth was there, bent over to pour some milk into a bowl for the cat. The wind lifted her skirts and petticoat, revealing sturdy legs and thighs. The white wool stockings stopped above the knee. Max eyed the firm rosy flesh appreciatively. Perhaps waiting for their employers' return would not be without its compensations.

Of course, Frau von Langsdorff was incapable of keeping her plans and her ample purse to herself on the journey. Augusta tried warning glances, squeezing her mother's arm, and even interrupting her chatter. Nothing stopped her. Two female passengers— an old lady traveling with her companion—became her confidantes. The other passenger, a clergyman in black, glanced her way disapprovingly from his corner, then turned his back on them and opened his Bible.

Other travelers came and went. Augusta examined them all anxiously for signs of moral turpitude, but none showed particular interest in them or their money. She began to relax a little and even took some consolation from the fact that her mother's excitement saved her from silent ill temper or renewed accusations.

They reached Ulm without mishap but had to spend the night because there was no connecting coach to Mannheim until the next morning. Frau von Langsdorff had not counted on this and complained bitterly about the inconveniences of the postal system.

Yet she ate well and slept like the dead, while Augusta, who had pushed a chair under the door handle, barely closed an eye.

The night passed without interruptions, as did the next day and night. The company in the coach on the final leg of the journey looked harmless enough: a well dressed young woman with two small girls and the disapproving parson who had spent the previous days' journeys reading his Bible. There were also two young men, apprentices by their looks, who rode outside, but they only went as far as the next town.

Her mother instantly struck up a conversation with the parson, greeting him like an old friend. He listened to her reminiscences about being a minister's wife and her dear husband's sterling qualities and saintly character but said little himself. Eventually, she gave up and drew the young woman into a conversation. Augusta looked out of the window at the passing scenery, and having been deprived of sleep, dozed off. She woke to the same chatter, except that her mother was once again embarked on her plans for Augusta's marriage. The parson had returned to his Bible study.

Augusta sat, listening to her mother's hopes for her brilliant future. Mama's reasoning was beginning to make perfect sense: by taking this sudden trip, she had left behind unpleasant gossip about her own failed aspirations and would spend an enjoyable time shopping for clothes and attending parties, which would take her mind off the Seutter scandal. Even better: Mama would rid herself of a troublesome daughter and do so in a way that would benefit herself.

There was something almost endearing in her mother's optimistic pursuit of self-gratification. Since she had fallen into this happy mood, she had treated Augusta with surprising mildness. Perhaps Augusta had not been forgiven completely, but there definitely was a truce.

Disaster struck after they entered the Black Forest. The coach slowed because of the mountainous terrain and the winding roadway. There was much cursing and snapping of the whip from the driver, and once or twice the postilion got down to push when the road went uphill, or to hold back the horses on a steep downward course. Inside the coach all was peaceful. Augusta's mother had finally run out of steam and dozed off. The young mother had made her little girls comfortable and was reading a fairy tale to them as they rocked and swayed through the forest. The tale of two children lost in the woods and a witch with a gingerbread house seemed appropriate, and Augusta smiled, remembering her father reading the same tale to her when she was small.

As the coach swung around a sharp bend, the parson rose to lower the window and lean out with his upper body. Perhaps, thought Augusta, the swaying of the vehicle was making him sick. One of the little girls had complained of nausea earlier.

Then she hard shouts, and next there came a gunshot, and the coach shuddered to a halt. The young mother dropped her book and cried out. Augusta reached to lower her own window and look out, but the parson pulled his head back inside and said quite sharply to her, "Sit still and nothing will happen to you."

"There was a shot," objected Augusta. "We should try to do something." She did not know what, but sitting still in utter ignorance seemed worse than knowing what was happening outside.

Her mother, sleep-dazed, sat up and looked around wildly. "A shot? What? Where?"

The young woman was quiet now, but she had turned very white and drawn her children close to her. The girls began to cry.

The parson drew a pistol from his pocket. This he pointed first at the young mother and her girls, causing them to cry out, and then at Augusta who was getting up. "Sit down and hand it over," he snapped.

"What's happening?" asked Frau von Langsdorff, trying to see out of the window and pushing the pistol-holding hand out of her way.

The parson pointed the gun at her face. "Shut up, you infernal old baggage. Give me your money. Yes, the money you've been bragging about. And your rings and chains and other jewelry. You, too." He gestured with the gun at Augusta and the young mother. "Hurry up, or someone dies on the count of five."

They stared at him, paralyzed with fear.

"One!" He held out his free hand.

Augusta slipped a small ring from her finger and put it in his hand, then looked at her mother, whose purse was attached to her petticoat and hidden under voluminous skirts.

"Two!"

The young woman added several rings and a brooch. Augusta's mother pushed another ring and a few gold and silver pieces at him. He dropped them in his large pocket.

"Three!"

"That's all, you villain," Augusta's mother cried, outraged that he still pointed the gun at her face. "Go away and may God have mercy on your soul for you'll be hanged for this."

The robber struck her viciously across the face with the pistol and said, "Four!" She shrieked and covered her face.

Augusta, in a panic, cried "Mama, please," and then dug around under her mother's voluminous skirts. She found the purse, untied it with shaking fingers, and pulled it out.

"Five!"

The robber snatched it from her hand, then opened the door and jumped down. Another man brought up a horse, and he climbed into the saddle.

With the robber gone, Augusta tried to stench her mother's blood by pressing her handkerchief against her face. Outside, more shots were fired, and the coach jerked forward.


Max was frustrated. The foolish maid thought a few turns under the featherbed constituted a proposal. No, he told her, he liked her well enough, but he could not marry her.

This brought an angry storm of tears and reminders that she was now used goods and no man would have her for wife. Besides, she might turn up with child, and what then?

Max made the mistake of pointing out that it takes two to make a child and that she had practically pulled him into her bed. Now, Elsbeth threatened to tell all to her mistress, and Max realized that he would be dismissed unless he married the girl. He protested his devotion and hoped for a reprieve.

His relationship with Elsbeth took on a depressingly domestic tone. She clearly thought herself his wife already, cooking and serving his meals while regaling him with plans for their future. They would go back to her father's farm and settle into the attic there, helping with the dairy herd and starting a market garden behind the stables. In time, and with a legacy from her parents, they would have enough for another small homestead or a house in the village where they would raise their children. She could take in sewing and he could find work managing the local lord's fields and woods.

Max had Elsbeth's measure: she would not let go of him if he remained. He frequently kissed Augusta's letter and thought with longing of her. Then, one day, he had an idea.

# 14

# Small, Helpless Creatures

*Plots, true or false, are necessary things,*
*To raise up commonwealths, and ruin kings.*

John Dryden, *Absalom and Achitophel*

The morning after their arrival, Franz found Doktor Stiebel dressed and standing at the open window, looking down on the Paradeplatz.

"There you finally are," he said. "It's already past eight of the clock."

"Good morning. I'm sorry, sir. I'm afraid I overslept. And you? Did you have a good rest?" He saw that his friend looked less tired, if not in a very happy mood.

Stiebel made an impatient gesture. "Adequate. We should be on our way. I ordered breakfast."

A pot of coffee and a basket of fresh breads, assorted jams, pale slices of ham, boiled eggs, and butter waited on a table. Franz was hungry and said, "I cannot think that we should call on the baron before ten or eleven, sir. After all, the old gentleman is said to be in ill health. Won't you join me?"

Stiebel grunted, but he sat down with Franz and poured himself coffee. "I have this feeling all is not well—that we will be too late," he said after drinking half a cup.

"Impossible." Franz patted his pocket where the letter still rustled. "We shall be rid of the task today. Even if the Baron isn't in his right mind, we'll leave the letter with him. My duty will have been done, and we can go home." And none too soon, he thought, for Stiebel's lack of interest in such delicious food troubled him.

Stiebel nibbled abstractedly on a piece of bread roll with a little butter and jam, while Franz consumed several fresh rolls with butter, ham, and honey, interspersing them with a couple of soft-boiled eggs. When he looked up from his empty plate, he saw Stiebel smiling at him.

"What's the matter, sir?"

"You did not cry out last night." Stiebel said. "It gives me great pleasure to see you so very nearly well again. I confess that you've become dear to me, my boy."

Franz felt his eyes moisten. "Please promise me that you shall not make yourself ill on my account. I have come to curse this infernal letter."

"Not at all. Not at all," murmured Stiebel and looked away, embarrassed.

They left soon after in a hired carriage, both made silent by their emotion. The drive was comfortable in dry fall weather and on a remarkably smooth road, but gray clouds began to gather ahead. They arrived in the small town of Schwetzingen before the rain, got directions to the Baron's house, and pulled up before its door just as the church clock struck ten.

The villa was new, like several others that had sprung up around Schwetzingen and near the palace. It was a charming two-storied building in pale stone with blue shutters at its large windows. In front was a wrought iron gate and a graveled drive, and in the back rose the trees of a garden. The house looked deserted, except for some odd-looking chickens and a neat two-wheeled vehicle with two horses tied up outside. Franz looked about him curiously. The chickens were fancy birds, some speckled, other pure white or glossy black. Perhaps the absence of servants was accounted for by the Baron's poor health.

He climbed down and helped Stiebel, who eyed the waiting carriage with a frown. "I wonder who's here. You have the letter?"

"Yes, sir. Be calm, I beg you. We're almost done."

Franz pulled the clapper of a copper bell beside the double doors. When that brought no response, he repeated his summons more impatiently. The clangor should have woken the dead.

Stiebel said tersely, "Someone's here. Try the door."

Franz did and found it unlocked. They stepped into an empty hall with a black-and-white-tiled marble floor. A life-sized painting of a bewigged gentleman in red velvet looked back at them from the opposite wall. Somewhere people were talking. A female voice sounded agitated.

"Hallo!" Franz called out. "Is anyone here?"

A door beside the bewigged gentleman opened, and a youngish man with round brown eyes and a small powdered wig looked out. When he recognized them, he frowned. "Not you again! Go away!"

He was the physician they had met the night before. Astonished, Franz said, "I beg your pardon, Doktor Mai, but you may recall that I bring news of Baron von Winkelhausen's son."

Doctor Mai stepped fully into the hall, closing the door behind him. Today he was soberly dressed in a black suit over a burgundy brocade vest and eyed them coldly. "You have wasted your time. His son is dead, and now so is he."

Franz gaped. "The baron is dead?"

Stiebel stepped forward and bowed. "I collect we have the honor of speaking with Baron Winkelhausen's physician?"

"You do."

The door behind him opened again, and an elderly woman in a gray dress and white apron and cap joined him. Her eyes were red-rimmed from weeping.

"Frau Schaller, there is no need," the doctor said impatiently. "I'll handle this. Go back and have a brandy to calm your nerves."

"Thank you, Doctor, but I'm all right. He would have wanted me to take care of things."

Doktor Mai gave in with ill grace and turned back to Stiebel and Franz. "I was sent for about an hour ago. This is Frau Schaller, the baron's housekeeper. She found him this morning, dead in his bed. So you see you have come too late."

Stiebel said heavily, "Too late!" and then, "Was the death natural?"

The doctor looked shocked. "Certainly. The baron was elderly and had been in poor health for some months. He simply died in his sleep. A merciful way to go." He turned to the housekeeper, who was weeping softly into a handkerchief, and put his hand on her shoulder. "Isn't that so, Frau Schaller?"

She mumbled, "*I* didn't expect it, sir. He was just as usual last night. Ate a good supper. Veal with mushrooms. It was his favorite." She broke into sobs again.

The doctor patted her back. "Now, now, my dear, you must be strong." Glancing at Franz and Stiebel, he said, "She's served him all her life. Even if not unexpected, this is a great blow for her."

Stiebel looked as if he wished to argue the point, but Franz apologized for their untimely visit and expressed his condolences to Frau Schaller. They left quickly.

Stiebel climbed into the carriage with a set face. When Franz joined him, Stiebel told the coachman, "Back to Mannheim and be quick!"

"Why the hurry?" asked Franz, still a little dazed by the news of the baron's death.

"Let me see the letter."

Franz dug it out of his pocket. "I suppose we might as well throw it away." Stiebel snatched it out of his hand. "Just as I thought," he said grimly.

Franz saw with surprise that the paper looked somehow different—cleaner and newer than it should. "What . . . ? How did that get into my pocket?" He searched his pocket again.

Stiebel unfolded two pages and held them up for Franz to see. They were blank. "We've been duped," he said. "If I'm not mistaken, that very accommodating little villain at the inn picked your pocket last night and substituted this."

"Impossible. I would have noticed. Besides, why would one of the inn's people steal a letter?"

"I'm beginning to doubt he works for the inn. And it was no ordinary letter you've been carrying. People have been trying to get it for months now." He turned to check the road behind.

"Well, whatever secret it contained, it no longer matters. Both the letter and the man it was intended for are gone. Please do not get agitated. It's not good for you."

Stiebel snapped, "Are you dense? We were expected and met in Mannheim, and the baron died a few hours later before we could see him."

Franz saw that Stiebel's hands were clenched and shaking. He was suddenly afraid and made an effort to reassure Stiebel. "In that case, whoever wanted the letter has it. I'm sorry I failed Captain von Loe, but he should have warned me." Actually the dying man had stressed the letter's importance. "I almost wish we had opened it," Franz added.

Stiebel said nothing but he looked quite miserable.

"It's over, sir. Let's leave this place behind and go home." Franz thought wistfully of the little princess, and that delightful world of gods and men he had so briefly strayed into.

"I'm afraid," Stiebel said heavily, "that our visit was responsible for the baron's death."

"Oh, come," protested Franz, "you heard the doctor. It was a natural death. It was expected."

"His housekeeper was surprised." Stiebel fidgeted. "I don't know, Franz. I don't know what we're dealing with here, but judging from what has happened, this is no ordinary matter and, given the baron's position at court, men of power are involved. We're already too deeply involved for our own good. Whoever is behind this may suspect that the dying captain told you something of this matter."

Franz felt a slow horror creep up his spine. This time, *he* turned to check if they were being followed. "He didn't tell me anything. I swear it," he said weakly.

"I know, my boy, I know." Stiebel patted Franz's knee. "Franz, I have a confession to make. I'm ashamed to tell you that I did open the letter. I beg your pardon for doing so, but my lawyer's mind would not let me deal with the case without having all the evidence. After my office was searched and you were attacked, I was afraid for your life."

Franz gaped. "But it was still sealed."

"In my profession one learns all sorts of useful tricks. A hot knife blade inserted behind the seal allows it to be lifted without breaking it."

"You know what was in the letter?"

Stiebel nodded.

"Well, what did it say?" Franz did not know whether to be angry or glad.

"I didn't understand all of it. The young man was careful to use some sort of code, pseudonyms instead of names. Apparently he and his father were in the habit of referring to acquaintances in that manner. It may be possible to ascertain who some of them are, if we can gain knowledge of the court and the various players in this conspiracy.

"Conspiracy?"

"I think the captain warned his father that someone close to the Kurfürst was a danger to the monarch. As I told you, Karl Theodor's wife is by birth the direct heir. Her grandfather, the previous elector, wished to see a male on the throne and arranged the marriage. It is by all accounts unhappy. Add to this that Karl Theodor has enemies because he supports the Catholic cause and opposes powerful factions of libertarians and masons, and I worry about an assassination. Whoever is involved in this is playing a very dangerous game."

"All that was in the captain's letter?" Franz asked dubiously.

"Oh, no. The letter seemed just what you would expect: a son's affectionate recounting of his experiences in that frustrating war and assurances that he was well and expected to be safe during the upcoming battle. He was *aide de camp* to Fieldmarshal Prince Stolberg , a position that apparently involves only the carrying of messages from Stolberg to commanding officers during a battle."

Franz nodded. "Yes. That's what he was doing when he was shot. It was just as the action started." The memory of that gray, chilly morning returned to him with shocking clarity. As yet innocent of the bloody deeds he would witness and commit, he had watched the general staff discussing the enemy's position. There had been those white puffs of smoke in the valley below as the first Prussian skirmishers fired, and then Captain von Loe had galloped across his field of vision and been struck by a bullet. In the back. Franz swallowed and said, "Oh!" He remembered that he had turned his head at the sound of that shot because it had come from the woods behind him. Horrified, he said, "He was shot by someone on our side. I didn't realize it then, but that's what happened."

"Yes. He was murdered because he knew something."

"Dear God! Did he know his danger?"

"I doubt it. Perhaps he didn't even realize it after he was wounded. The letter didn't tell of any fears for himself. But he mentions an overheard conversation in camp one evening when he took a note from Prince Stolberg to Count von Meyern. That was where he suddenly referred to people by names taken from the Ancients. He spoke of Spartacus and Cato, and Minos and Ptolemy, and several others I do not now recall."

"But how are we to know who they are? Both father and son are dead."

"We know a few things about the political situation here, and those names are very much in the style used by certain prohibited groups to hide their identities. Some of these groups are opposed to rulers and support the overthrow of governments."

"You mean like the Illuminati? They are masons, I think."

Stiebel nodded. "Yes, perhaps. I happen to know some very powerful and respectable men who are associated with the masons, but there are splinter groups that are quite fanatical, and Karl Theodor is known to hate freemasonry for its attacks on what they call the 'despotism of princes'."

"So you think someone is planning to assassinate Karl Theodor?"

"Whatever is going on, it's serious enough for someone to kill von Loe and attack you because they fear that the dying son passed on some dangerous knowledge."

"Oh, God," said Franz, "and I have drawn you into this! You must go back to Lindau immediately. You must be seen to have nothing more to do with me. Dear heaven, I hope it's not too late."

This amused Stiebel because he chuckled. "Of course it's too late. But it's certainly not your doing. I pushed myself into this affair. No, don't concern yourself about me. I've had a very satisfactory life. You're the one who is still on its threshold."

"That's a ridiculous way of looking at it," snapped Franz, then recalled himself. "Sorry, sir, but you must

know I couldn't bear to lose you over something that I
have done . . . or lose you at all."

Stiebel reached for a large handkerchief and blew
his nose. "Thank you, Franz," he said a little unsteadily. "That means a great deal to a lonely old man."

An embarrassed silence fell. They had reached the
outskirts of Mannheim when Stiebel said with a sigh, "I
think we have no choice but to find out what is going on
and who is behind it. It is our duty as human beings.
Besides, neither of us will be safe unless we stop these
blackguards."

"The danger will surely be greater if we stay and ask
questions."

"Oh, certainly. But we will be on our guard, and I
confess it has put me on my mettle." Stiebel chuckled.
"You know, it makes me feel quite young again and
ready to risk everything. Surely you would not deprive
an old man of his second childhood?"

Franz laughed. "You're being very foolish, you
know," he said affectionately, but the truth was that he,
too, hoped for an adventure.

"Very well then." Stiebel rubbed his hands. "Here's
what we'll do."


Murdering the old man had changed the assassin. It
had been that enormous sense of power at the moment
of his sexual release. Nothing like it had happened
when he had shot the old man's son on the Freiberg
battlefield. At best, he had been satisfied with his

marksmanship in hitting a moving target at precisely the correct moment.

Now he felt his fortunes were finally changing and he need never put himself at the command of the great man again or take risks for rewards that were both slow in coming and uncertain. As a gentleman by birth and education, he resented too bitterly the reprimands and threats, and the odious comparisons with that pick-pocket Reinhard.

Besides, a certain person had spoken to him lately with a warmth that promised more. Women were easily captivated by his good looks and manner. Should he succeed in that direction, then the tables would be turned, and he would be the one to give the orders.

Meanwhile, there were still the cripple and his companion, and much depended on what they would do next, but he was perfectly capable of dealing with any threat from that direction. He felt lucky.

The assassin did not bother to report to the great man. Feeling vindicated as a man of action and ability, he took care of personal business.

On his way to the palace that evening, he checked on the visitors from Lindau and learned that they had returned from Schwetzingen, paid their bill, and ordered a post chaise to take them home. Excellent news. He had harbored a niggling worry that the crippled lieutenant knew more than was good for him. Their rapid departure proved otherwise. He decided to forget about them.

That night he spent most pleasantly at court, so well received by his lady that he engaged her in outrageous flirtation. Convinced of his own invincibility, he murmured his devotion to the woman who might hold his future in her soft white hands.

She took it amazingly well; so well in fact that it confirmed him in his decision to break with his unsavory past and devote himself entirely to his official duties. They offered a far more secure future than the dangerous schemes of the great man. Who knew, he might even some day step into the great man's shoes.

Stiebel paid their bill in Mannheim and ordered a post chaise, telling the inn's clerk they were returning home. Then he asked what had happened to the very accommodating man who had welcomed them on their arrival.

The clerk was dumfounded. "I assumed the fellow was the gentleman's servant, sir. I hope nothing untoward happened? The world's full of trickery these days."

Stiebel agreed.

As soon as they left the city behind, Stiebel told the coachman they had changed their minds and wanted to go to Schwetzingen.

While the coachman enjoyed the food and beer at the Schwetzingen inn, Franz and Stiebel returned to the baron's house, passing through streets that seemed filled with music and song. A female voice warbled some operatic aria in one house while sounds of flutes and oboes came from another.

"What is happening here?" Franz asked in wonder, his eyes on an upper story window where a young man was playing the violin to a flower box crammed with scarlet geraniums.

Stiebel looked up. "Yes, charming," he muttered. "It must be the court's arrival. None of our business, I'm afraid."

By the time they reached the baron's house, the gayety of the town was forgotten and thoughts of death and danger were with them again.

"We'll be too late to get a look at the poor dead gentleman," said Stiebel, "but that was always unlikely. I have hopes of talking to that housekeeper, though."

The chickens were gone, the front door stood open, and the house already had an empty, dead feeling. The housekeeper and her husband were sitting hand in hand on the oak bench in the hall. They looked as if their world had crumbled around them and there was little point in doing anything about it. When they saw Stiebel and Franz, the husband got to his feet with the slowness of painful joints. Franz wondered again why the baron had not provided himself with sturdier servants.

"Yes?" the old man asked. "How may we be of service?"

His wife got up more quickly and came to peer at them in the dimness of the hall. "It's the gentlemen from this morning, Walter," she said. "The ones that came about the young master."

Stiebel nodded to her and extended his hand to her husband. "Please forgive the intrusion. I'm very sorry to trouble you again in your grief, but we have traveled a long way, my young friend and I. We came to speak to your master about his son's death, and we couldn't leave without talking to you. I expect you both knew young Captain Christian von Loe?"

She said, "Of course we did, and a better boy there never was. It was like the world had come to an end when we got the news. The master was like a madman at first. He paid off all his servants, sold his horses and carriages, and came here to be alone with just the two of us." She paused and put a hand to her mouth. "Mary, Mother of God! What's to become of us now?"

Franz said quickly, "I'm afraid I didn't know his son, but I can tell you that he died bravely in the service of his country and with his father's name on his lips."

She pulled herself together. "God bless you, sir. It's sad that the master could not hear you say that, but God's will be done." She glanced at Franz's crippled leg. "War's a terrible thing." Her husband nodded and murmured something unintelligible.

After a brief, mournful silence, Stiebel said, "We're both troubled by the baron's sudden death, especially when you hadn't expected it."

She sighed. "He was as hale and hearty yesterday as any day before. We thought he was getting over his boy's death. His Grace wanted him to come back to court. I blame myself." She cast a glance at the bowed figure of her husband and began to weep again.

He patted her shoulder awkwardly and found speech. "The master walked in the garden every day and fed his chickens. He loved them. Very fancy chickens, they are. What will be done with them now?"

"I'm sure provisions have been made for you and the house and its contents," Stiebel said.

"It's that nephew will get everything," he muttered. "The master never did like him. He's a cruel and tight-fisted man who's already come to put a price on every-thing while the master was still alive. We'll be turned out, and the chickens will go into the pot."

"Never mind that now, Walter," his wife said. "We should ask the gentlemen in. They've come a long way to pay their respects. The master would've wanted it."

Franz and Stiebel found themselves seated in a pret-ty salon where Frau Schaller served them coffee and small cakes from delicate painted porcelain.

"He loved these cups and plates," she said. "They're from the Frankenthal manufacture. His Grace and my master started the factory to give people work and bring some money to the country."

Stiebel raised his cup to the light. "They're as fine as the Sèvres ware I saw in Paris. I thought it was a se-cret process."

"They have the way of it in Meissen, your honor. His Grace brought back the receipt from there."

Franz, impatient with chatter about cups, asked, "Was there no illness to account for your master's death? We were told that the loss of his son had affect-ed his mind and body and he'd become too ill to work."

She gave a snort and said darkly, "There are those that tell lies because it suits them. It's true he wasn't in his right mind at first, and it's also true that grief made him harsh with people. But he was as bright a man as ever. It's because they turned against him that he wanted to leave and be in peace."

"You must have been a blessing to him in his loneliness," said Stiebel soothingly. "Did visitors come to trouble him often?"

"No," she said, shaking her head emphatically. "Nobody's been here for months except the nephew and the doctor. Yesterday was like any other day. He walked a bit, fed his birds, worked on his accounts and gave me some money for shopping, had his rest, and then he spent the afternoon in his library, sorting through old papers. He was writing a history about his work under Prince Karl Theodor. I called him to dinner at seven. A roast of veal with mushrooms, roasted potatoes, and a salad. He ate well. He always did like my cooking." Her eyes welled over again, and she brushed the tears away with her sleeve. "He went to bed at nine with a book. I made sure he had his sleeping draft, and then Walter locked up, and we went to bed."

"Was there anything out of place in his room when you found him?" Franz asked.

She shook her head. "He'd dropped his book, but he often did that. And the candle had burned out." She thought a moment. "There was this large cushion he had in his bed to prop himself up with. It was a bit wet. I wondered if he'd spilled some of his draft on it when he knocked the glass over."

"He knocked his glass over?"

She nodded. "Walter thinks it must've been when he took his last breath. It proper bruised his poor wrist. He must've fought against death."

"Yes," said Stiebel heavily. "Yes, I think that very likely. Could a draft from the door have blown over the glass."

Walter spoke up. "There's heavy curtains across the doors, keeping out the night air. And the doors were closed."

"Were they locked?" Franz asked quickly. "Someone could have come in during the night."

Walter glared. "Not on your life. I lock all the doors every night."

His wife said, "You do, Walter, but sometimes the master opens his door again. He likes to hear the fountain. He says it helps him sleep."

A silence fell. Then Stiebel asked gently, "Was the door unlocked this morning?"

She nodded unhappily.

"He wasn't murdered." Walter sounded belligerent. "And we'll thank you not to spread such lies. We both saw him, and so did the doctor. There wasn't a mark on him other than that little bruise."

Stiebel said quickly, "You misunderstood. We didn't mean to imply a crime took place, but rather that there might have been an accident. Perhaps he got up and fell but managed to get back into bed before he died. Or he had a fright and his heart failed."

They looked confused. Clearly the death was a mystery to them, but neither wanted to be thought careless. They preferred the doctor's diagnosis. Franz and

Stiebel bade them goodbye and expressed the hope that the heir would have the humanity to look after them and the fancy chickens.

"It's silly, but I grieve for those chickens," said Stiebel outside. "They remind me of my little bird. We pay too little mind to small, helpless creatures and their feelings. It's a cruel world for the old and the weak."

Franz shuddered and turned to look back at the house, but the *allée* of linden trees was empty, and only a finch trilled briefly in the branches above, then flew away. "Surely that was murder," he said.

"Oh, I think so. That wet bolster. So easy to suffocate an old man who's taken a sleeping draught. He had no idea he was in danger, or he wouldn't have been satisfied with just two old servants in the house. Or left his door open. You, know, in a way, this death was quite similar to his son's. That, too, offered a perfect opportunity for his killer to commit a murder without raising suspicion. The villain seized his chance and struck. And now he has escaped the law again. He's a very dangerous man. I'm afraid that it was our coming here that caused the baron's death."

Franz said, "It's horrible that human beings can bungle along with the best of intentions and yet cost some hapless fellow creature his life."

"Indeed. But ours are not the hands that commit the deeds."

Franz said glumly, "Is this the purpose for which God spared me at Freiberg? It weighs heavily on my soul that I killed men there, and here I am, adding to my heavy sins unknowingly. Even your little bird's demise was my doing."

Stiebel stopped. "We're in enough trouble, Franz, without you beating your breast and crying *mea culpa*. No, we must see this through and leave the verdict of our actions to a greater judge."

Franz hung his head. "What can we do?"

"As the elector and his court are to come here, I have a mind to stay. We shall dismiss the coach and take a room. *Iacta est alea!*"

# 15

# The Earthly Paradise

*It is a great pity but 'tis certain from every day's observation of man, that he may be set on fire like a candle, at either end provided there is a sufficient wick standing out.*

Laurence Sterne, *Tristram Shandy*

The die was indeed cast; there would be no going back.

Their driver was agreeable to the change in plans because he had another party for the journey to Heidelberg. Stiebel paid, tipping him generously, and told Franz, "It couldn't be better. Since he continues on to Heidelberg, no one in Mannheim will know that we have broken our journey here."

Luck was still with them when they got the last room at the inn. The court's imminent arrival in Schwetzingen brought its usual influx of hangers-on and *demimondaines* who were in hopes of making their fortunes. The Elector Palatine was thought to be more approachable here than at Mannheim.

As for the *demimondaines,* Franz ran afoul of one almost instantly on his way upstairs. When she swept down, he, supported on his cane, could not avoid the collision quickly enough. He staggered back, tried to catch her fall, and both went tumbling down the stairs. Somehow, he found himself on his back on the inn's floor, grasping a soft and scented figure firmly to his chest.

It had fortunately not been a hard fall, and she was a charming burden as they lay there, he looking up at her and she down at him. Both liked what they saw and smiled, and neither was in a great hurry to get up.

The inn's servants pulled them apart and put her back on her feet. Franz, propped on his elbows, looked up at a dainty creature in a gown of green-sprigged muslin trimmed with black velvet ribbons, her small head of dusky curls topped by a lacy cap, her black eyes sparkling, her red lips moist. An enchanting beauty patch was placed cunningly on one white breast just above the tightly laced bodice. She giggled, then saw his cane and the crippled leg and gasped instead. "O, *mon Dieu! Le pauvre gentilhomme! Je vous demande mille pardons!*"

Franz struggled to his feet, flushing a deep crimson with mortification. The beauty meets the beast, he thought. "*Pas de tout, Mademoiselle,*" he said with a bow, worried about his limited French.

It was almost worse when she shifted to German, heavily accented German, though from her lips the words fell with a particularly musical sound. "Eet vas my mistake, *Monsieur.* Are you pained badly?"

"Not at all." His crippled knee hurt furiously, but he was not about to admit to it. Instead, he became miserably lost in admiration of this altogether bewitching creature. Stiebel finally took his arm and pulled him away. Climbing the stairs feeling her eyes on his back was sheer agony. Nothing could hide his deformed leg, and the pain in his knee was so agonizing that perspiration ran down his back and he bit his lip bloody to keep moving.

"That was one of the actresses," remarked Stiebel when they gained their room.

It was of an adequate size, but they would have to share the bed, and their bags took up much of the remaining floor space between the bed, a large wardrobe, and a small desk. Still, above the desk was a window which looked out over the town's market and, being open, it let in the sounds of music and song.

"How do you know she's an actress?" asked Franz, taken aback. "She was very well dressed. I took her to be the daughter of some visiting French gentleman."

Stiebel's eyes twinkled. "Trust me, she's an actress. The inn's full of players. Princes like theater, and there are always players about the court. The females make good money if they're young and pretty—or talented. Yours was clearly young and pretty." He paused. "Dear me. It was unkind of me to assume that she's not talented."

Franz was oddly disappointed. This enchantress, hardly older than Augusta, was an actress? Franz knew that such women were thought to be only a small step above ordinary prostitutes. The students in Heidelberg had frequently bragged about their affairs with them. "I'm a great fool," he said sadly. "I thought she liked me. Proper women have no time for a penniless cripple."

Stiebel smiled. "Franz, you cannot have looked in the mirror lately. You have just such a face as girls swoon over and a nice manly shape to your body. And never underestimate the power of a uniform. That small defect with your leg makes you more interesting rather than less. A hero who has been wounded in battle arouses the tenderest feelings in a woman's breast."

Franz said bitterly, "You're quite wrong, and besides I'm done with all of that." He thought it nothing but the most barefaced flattery from his friend but, like all flattery, it worked in insidious ways; he wondered what an affair with the little actress would be like and felt quite warm at the thought.

Stiebel watched his face and cocked an amused eyebrow. "I confess I hadn't thought of it, but since you seem to have settled for the life of a monk all too unwillingly, I think you must reassure yourself at your earliest convenience. Abstinence can lead to madness, you know. So let us rest a little and then descend to the public rooms to take our supper with the other guests. I hope to learn some things while you're about the business of making eyes at the little lady."

When the assassin finally called on the great man, he found him at breakfast in an elegantly appointed dining room with pearl gray paneling and Dutch still-lifes of dead fowl among fruit on the walls.

"Where the devil have *you* been?" the great one snapped.

"I beg your pardon?" the assassin said, raising his brows.

The other's scowl faded, and his tone became slightly warmer. "Oh, what does it matter? Sit down, sit down." He waved to a chair and called a servant. "Another cup and more coffee."

He sat. "Thank you. No coffee. I'm in a hurry."

"In a hurry?" The great man's cup stopped halfway to his mouth. "What's the matter with you? I expected you sooner."

The assassin studied his fingernails. "I've been rather busy with my own affairs."

The great one set his cup back down. "Why this double talk? I take it you heard of the baron's death?"

He said nothing and smiled.

Turning rather pale, the great man said, "You don't mean . . . what did you do?" . . . you surely didn't think I'd send you to—" He broke off, his eyes startled.

Just what had the pompous bastard expected him to do? The assassin controlled his temper. "Sir, I may do a friend a favor, but I shall not be *sent* to do his bidding like a common lackey."

The great man's jaw sagged. "Dear gods," he muttered. "You must be mad."

The servant came in with fresh coffee, and nobody spoke. The assassin drew out his pocket watch and clicked it open. He waited until the servant had left the room, then said, "You worry too much. An old, sick man died, that's all. As I said, I have no time for coffee. The court is to go to Schwetzingen. There will be an Italian opera and perhaps also Voltaire's new play." He tucked his watch into its pocket and rose. "I shall be busy for the coming months."

The other man still looked sick. "Yes. The last occasion for the year—except for the hunt."

"Hunts no longer interest me," the assassin said grandly. With a very small bow, he departed—happy in the knowledge that he had left the great man looking very worried.

When Stiebel and Franz entered the public room that evening, they found all the tables occupied. At one end of the room was a large and cheerfully noisy party of young people who—a waiter informed them—were musicians and players with the court theater. Franz found his French charmer among them, and gaped, struck by the easy manner of such men and women. They laughed and talked with the familiarity of old friends or siblings.

She was one of five females and six or seven males gathered around two tables that had been pushed together. To Franz, she was the youngest and most beautiful of the women, though all were quite handsome in looks and fashionable clothing.

He was still staring when she saw him. Her dark eyes widened, and she sent a devastating smile and a wave of her small hand his way. As a gentleman cannot ignore a lady's welcome, Franz said to Stiebel, "Surely we should at least introduce ourselves."

Stiebel smiled. "But, of course."

They went across, bowed, and Franz kissed the pretty actress's hand.

"*Mon chèr ami blessé!*" she cried, dimpling. "All dis time I 'ave been 'oping to see you again. *Le voilà,*" she said, turning to the others at the table, "Dis is de 'andsome 'ero I talk you about."

They all smiled, the men rising and making their bows. One of the women joked about the wounded hero having wounded Desirée's heart, and Franz blushed. Introductions followed, invitations to join them were given. Franz hesitated in spite of a fervent wish to sit beside the delectable Desirée—never was woman more aptly named! Before he could speak, Stiebel accepted for both. Room was made, food and wine appeared in abundance, and Franz thought he would never spend a more pleasant evening than this. It brought back memories of happier days with fellow students in Heidelberg. But this was immeasurably improved by the presence of an adoring woman.

Because she was something of a distraction, he missed a good deal of the general conversation, but when the talk turned to the Elector's imminent arrival—Franz was dimly aware that Stiebel had raised the subject but he had been looking too deeply into pansy-brown eyes to follow the exchange—someone praised the gardens of the summer palace, which were said to outshine even those of Versailles.

"Oh, you 'ave not seen?" asked Desirée, opening her pansy eyes in surprise. "You must. Eet is *très charmante*. We walk dere many days."

Greatly daring, Franz said, "I would enjoy it above anything with such a guide as you, *Mademoiselle*."

She giggled and slapped his arm. "I vill not deny you, *mon brave*."

And so Franz climbed the stairs to their room that evening happy in the prospect of taking *Mademoiselle* Desirée to the palace gardens very soon.

"A useful evening," said Stiebel as they undressed for bed. His eyes twinkled. "I trust your own investigations also bore fruit?"

Franz blushed. He had quite forgotten about the baron's murder. "Did you really learn anything useful from them?" he asked.

The little lawyer draped his fusty brown velvet coat lovingly over the back of a chair and chuckled. "Indeed, yes. Never underestimate your actor for knowing all the intimate details of the lives of the great. They tell me that His Highness is bedding another member of their troupe, a dancer by the name of Françoise. Actresses hope to catch a great man's eye so they can retire from the boards. And a handsome young actor may do equally well with a great lady."

"But surely their reputations will be lost," Franz protested, thinking of his Desirée. "It sounds both mercenary and immoral. Not much better than—" He broke off.

Stiebel removed his large wig and placed it over a wig stand he carried in his trunk. Franz saw that his own hair, cut very short, was white and so pitifully thin that his pink scalp showed through. It struck him suddenly that his beloved friend was quite as old as the murdered baron and might not live long.

Stiebel, unaware, said, "No, not much. Though to be truly successful at that sort of seduction takes a good deal of beauty and talent. I had the pleasure of meeting the French king's *maîtresse* once. She's the Marquise de Pompadour now, an extraordinary woman with great style, charm, and intelligence, in addition to being an enchanting beauty. All the foreign ambassadors pay her every attention because she has the king's ear. Here, both the Elector and his wife have their favorites. He's on familiar terms with dancers, while his lady prefers military gentlemen."

Franz said, "I cannot hope to compete with such information, sir. We only talked of the local sights. I'm to be shown the gardens the day after tomorrow." Then had the grace to blush and added, "Perhaps I should not have accepted?"

But Stiebel's eyes twinkled. "Go on, my boy, enjoy yourself. Why not look in on a rehearsal tomorrow? Keep your eyes and ears open for more gossip from the actors. I shall manage quite well on my own."

Franz hardly laid eyes on Stiebel the next day. They breakfasted together, then parted to meet again over dinner, but Franz was too full of the delights of the

opera rehearsal, the beauty of the music, and the inde-
scribable charm and talent of *Mademoiselle* Desirée,
who had a small but impressive dancing and singing
part between acts. Stiebel listened, but he seemed distracted or bored with Franz's enthusiastic descriptions,
and Franz eventually fell silent.

The following day, the actors made up a party for
the palace gardens. Besides Franz and Desirée, there
were two young men and two of the younger women.

Desirée wore a black and white striped silk gown,
tightly laced and long-waisted, with a froth of lace barely
covering her breasts above the bodice and a larger froth
peeking out under the full, rather short, skirt. Below
the skirt, Franz spied dainty white-stockinged ankles
and red high-heeled slippers. A lace cap with red ribbons perched on her dark curls. He looked at her, lost
in admiration, and then blushed for having stared.

Later he recalled little of the conversation among the
three couples and retained only the vaguest memory of
laughter and a sense of his own great happiness that
these friendly young people accepted him into their
midst with such camaraderie. They teased each other
freely, and after a while they also teased Franz and
Desirée with gentle hints of romance.

Desirée had taken Franz's arm right away and sent
many melting glances up at him. He still could not
quite believe that any woman would take an interest in
him, even if Stiebel had pointed out that his crippled leg
might have that effect on a soft female heart. She was
such a pretty creature, one who could have had any
man she wished, and yet she seemed to want him.

Though there was an autumn chill in the air, he felt warm all over and, willy-nilly, he fell half in love.

It did not help that the princely garden was another Eden, fraught with a million seductions of the senses. The scents of ripe oranges and lemons hung about the *orangerie*; intricate patterns of flowers, colored sand, and clipped box accompanied neat paths; fountains rose into the limpid blue sky with the shimmer of molten silver and fell into marble basins with the liquid music of a multitude of glass harps. It was a place made for strolling arm in arm down broad *allées* of clipped trees and for playing innocent games of hide and seek in dense *bosquets* so green and secretive that a man might snatch a kiss without blame. Marble temples beckoned—belvederes to see all the beauties of this world spread out below and make a young man feel godlike and randy and his nymph breathless with desire.

The temple of the god Apollo was such a place. Its gilded cupola and white columns crowned a small hill. Inside a slender, white marble youth stood under a golden sun, holding a lyre.

"The German princes all think they are sun kings," said one of the actors with a laugh. He said it in French, but then added in German, "Apollo, god of the sun and of poetry. What a pity, he's left-handed." He laughed again.

And so he was, and the others mocked the sculptor's mistake, but Desirée squeezed Franz's arm and whispered, "'E is beautiful. 'E looks like you. Come, we go up."

Franz blushed a little—the god was quite naked—but he let her pull him away from the company and into a dim grotto underneath. It was dark and cool there, with the smell of earth and mold of a grave. Desirée shivered and clung to Franz. He held her close. Through a narrow, winding tunnel they climbed upward—slowly, very slowly, because the darkness and the contact of their warm, young bodies hampered their progress to the light. But eventually they reached the top, and Franz blushed again when Desirée directed his eyes to the god, whose nakedness was all too close now, and whose left-handedness reminded him of his own imperfection.

They stood together and looked down upon the Elector's gardens and across the lush greenery into the adjoining hunting preserve. All the beauties of this world seemed spread out before them.

Franz was thoroughly seduced by all this earthly beauty and fell into sin more readily than Eve.

They descended into the grotto again, where they kissed passionately and hungrily, letting their hands explore each other's bodies. Once out of the damp darkness, they found a hidden place in some thick shrubbery, and there in the smooth grass, Desirée lay down with Franz.

He was taking and giving pleasure—oh, Desirée, my desired one!—far from the Elector's palace and its playing fountains and white marble gods, when a cool voice drawled, "Well, well, what have we here? A satyr at play with his nymph?"

Franz froze. Shame and fury fought with a wish to hide Desirée's face and bare breasts.

The intruder continued, "What very white buttocks you have, my goatish fellow. And whose charming thighs are wrapped around you so passionately?— What? It's not our Desirée, by God?"

Desirée muttered a French expletive and pushed Franz away. He was still trying to extricate himself, when he felt a stinging pain across his buttocks.

"Up, cripple!" snapped the voice.

Franz snatched down the girl's skirts and pulled up his breeches with his other hand as he stumbled to his feet and turned. He was livid.

The man, a gentleman by his fine clothes, had a sword in his hand and a look of cold hatred on his handsome face. Apparently he had used the flat side of the blade to strike Franz—an odious offense.

"You, sir, are a scoundrel," snarled Franz, aware that he only had his cane and was standing above the little actress in her disordered clothes while still holding up his breeches with one hand. He made a ridiculous figure, something from an Italian farce. In fact, the whole incident seemed theatrical, almost staged. His voice unsteady with the shock of the insult, he said, "I demand satisfaction. Be so good as to appoint a time and place."

The other man laughed. "Why as to that, my awkward swain, dueling is against the law hereabouts. But then I daresay your rustic amusements are proof of your ignorance of civilized manners."

Franz took a step forward and struck the stranger across the face with such force that the man staggered back. An ugly outline of Franz's fingers spread across his cheek. With a curse, he raised his sword.

"*Non!*" screeched Desirée, jumping up from the mossy ground in a flurry of black-striped silk, white petticoats, and pink breasts. She flung herself down on her knees before the stranger, and wailed, "*Je vous en prie, mon chéri! Pas de scandale!*" Pressing her breasts against his thigh, she seized his hand and kissed it. "*Pour le Bon Dieu, mon amour.*"

He snatched away his hand and slapped her face so hard that she collapsed with a cry and lay there, her shoulders shaking with sobs.

Franz snatched up his cane and raised it.

The other man curled his lip. "As you may have gathered by now, I'm the injured party in this case. It is for me to ask for satisfaction."

Franz understood finally and was ashamed. He had allowed himself to be seduced by Desirée without taking thought to her character or her connections. Perhaps these two were even man and wife. He let his arm sink helplessly.

The other man turned to Desirée and pulled her upright by her hair. "I'm afraid God has small regard for loose women," he said coldly. "You're a harlot. As for any past between us, I had no idea you offered your quim so readily and with so little discernment to every country booby." Reaching down, he squeezed one of the girl's breasts viciously and said, "I know you like it rough, my dear, but this is ridiculous." She gasped and cried out. "Very well," he said, releasing her. "I'll let him live this time. But you will come to me tonight. I have a sudden taste for country manners." Turning on his heel, he left.

Franz quickly rebuttoned his breeches and tucked in his shirt. The insult of being struck like this had been gross, but this man had had a relationship with the willing nymph. They were lovers rather than married, but that still meant he had been justifiably angry. The charming Desirée was a faithless slut. But as he watched her covering herself and weeping softly, his disgust faded.

"He hurt you."

"Do not concern yourself, *chéri*," she said sadly, finding one of her shoes and putting it back on.

"Who is he? What is he to you?"

"Eet is my business. I must obey 'im." She gave Franz a pleading look. "Do not make ze trouble, *mon ami. Il est très dangereux.* 'E vill 'urt me and 'e vill keel you."

Franz did not think the man dangerous. What mattered at the moment was what lay between the girl and himself. Desirée had given herself to him freely and generously—if not perhaps virtuously. She had suffered pain for it and would suffer more. Franz touched her face gently. "My dear Desirée," he said, tipping up her chin and kissing the moist lips, the wet cheeks, the brimming pansy eyes. "Do not go back to him. Promise me. I cannot bear to have you hurt again. Nothing is worth that. I'll take care of you. I'll find a way." He faltered.

He could not seriously consider marrying a French actress who evidently fell from one man's bed into another's without much thought.

She kissed him back and laughed a little. "You're very sweet. But *non*, eet is over, *mon brave*. Eet vas only *un plaisir— une galanterie d'un après-midi.*" She gave him a little push, whirled, and was gone.

Very well. But what would Stiebel say? No, he could not possibly tell his kind friend and mentor what had happened.

He thought of finding this man, of challenging him and, being a fair swordsman, perhaps killing him. Better for Desirée to be free of such a villain. Satisfied of having somehow soothed his injured honor along with his debt to Desirée, Franz started back to the inn.

Stiebel was writing a letter. He looked up at Franz and chuckled. "The young lady returned in some disorder a few minutes ago," he said. "And here you are, looking not much better. I see grass stains on the knees of your breeches. What have you been up to?"

Franz flushed, brushed at his knees, and tucked in an errant shirt tail. "Nothing much, sir," he lied.

Stiebel pursed his lips. "If your amorous pursuits were as successful as I think, I trust you were prepared for them?"

"Prepared?" Prepared for what? For being attacked in *flagrante delicto* by the lady's lover?

"With a French letter, Franz. Armor for the encounter. These women often harbor the pox."

"Oh." Yes, he should have known better. He shook his head. He had bigger problems to deal with.

"Well, we must hope for the best. I should have reminded you."

Stiebel's familiarity with gallantry was not as shocking to Franz as his own naiveté. He had actually thought himself in love with a wanton. But even as he thought this, he felt pity for women who must lead such lives. Whatever Desirée might be to other men, she had made no demands on him but had treated him with kindness, nay, perhaps even a little fondness. What had happened was not her fault.

# 16

## The Good Daughter

*Is it not better to be freed from cares and agues, from*
*love and melancholy, and the other hot and cold fits of*
*life, than like a galled traveler, who comes weary to his*
*inn, to be bound to begin his journey afresh?*

Laurence Sterne, *Tristram Shandy*

Frau von Langsdorff moaned and wept during the rest of their journey to Mannheim. Every jolt of the carriage produced a cry of pain. After they got some water, Augusta placed cold compresses on her mother's swollen, bloody face. At first she worried that the nose and cheek bone might be broken, but as the hours passed, the compresses reduced the swelling, and her mother managed to breathe through her nose again. At last, she fell into a restless sleep.

The stage coach stopped at Heidelberg and reported the attack to the local gendarmes. They stared at Augusta's mother, nodded wisely, and took down descriptions of jewelry and monetary losses. Augusta was not sure how much gold had been in her mother's purse, and her mother was in no condition to talk.

"A lot, was it?" said the officer with a shrug. "That's a pity. They'll be long gone and the goods with them. The Parson—that's what they call him, though he's nothing but a thieving clerk—mostly works between Ulm and München. Strange, he should've come so far north this time."

Not strange at all, thought Augusta. Her mother had told one and all that she carried a small fortune in gold.

They approached Mannheim after dark.

"Will your brother meet you?" asked the young woman with a glance at the softly moaning Frau von Langsdorff.

"He doesn't know we're coming." Augusta peered out of the window at the lights ahead, then lifted the hem of her skirt to unpick a seam. She removed two gold pieces she had sewn up there while still at home and tucked them in her bodice. She had intended to buy a present for Jakob with them. Now the amount was pitifully small for their needs.

"Oh, how clever of you!" cried the young woman. "But surely that's not enough for two females alone in a strange city?"

"No." Augusta saw that they were pulling into an inn yard. "But it may pay for a room where my mother can rest while I make inquiries."

"Surely she cannot stay by herself. She should have a doctor. And you cannot walk about alone at night."

Augusta, suppressing her rising panic, snapped, "We will have to manage."

The young woman was offended. When the coach stopped, she cried, "There's my husband, God be praised. What a dreadful journey!"

She gathered her things and was the first to step down. A very tall, pleasant looking man greeted her with a fervent hug and a peck on the cheek, listened to her excited tale, then lifted down his daughters. They went off together.

Augusta thought with longing of Jakob. He seemed so far away that it was almost as if she had lost him. She shook her mother's arm. "Mama, we're here. We're in Mannheim."

It took the help of the coachman to remove a limp and moaning Frau von Langsdorff from the coach. As soon as her feet touched the ground, she collapsed in a heap in the dirt of the inn yard.

Augusta nearly wept with frustration, but the young woman's husband came back. "Allow me," he said, scooped her quivering and sobbing mother into his arms, carried her into the inn, and set her down in the first chair he found. Augusta followed, and someone brought their bags.

The inn was modest but clean. The innkeeper assumed that they were guests. Augusta's funds would barely pay for food and accommodations as well as a doctor. Still, if she could find Franz quickly, they might manage. She asked for a room, then turned to thank the young husband.

"No trouble at all," he said, looking at her anxiously. "I'll carry her up, if I may. It's a very great shame that she was hurt, though I suppose we must be grateful that no worse happened."

She nodded.

He glanced back at the door where his wife and the two little girls hovered, looking impatient.

She took his meaning and said, "There was some shooting but I think they fired into the air. They just wanted the gold."

The room being ready, he took up his moaning burden again and climbed the stairs as if she weighed nothing.

A kind man.

Augusta settled her mother in bed and sent for a doctor. He, a young man, rather finely dressed for some social appointment, arrived, looked the patient over quickly, and pronounced her to have suffered only minor bruising and a loose tooth. He left a bottle of laudanum to help her sleep and departed with one of the gold pieces.

Augusta waited only until her mother was asleep, then threw her hooded cloak about her and set out to find Franz. Downstairs, the innkeeper waylaid her. He had heard of the robbery and wanted to be paid in advance. Augusta, her heart beating with panic, put on a haughty mien, pressed the other gold piece in his hand,

and told him that her brother, Lieutenant von Langsdorff, would take care of any future bills.

To her relief, the posting inn was in a central part of the city, and the streets were wide and well lit. She asked one of the grooms about the best inns and set out at a fast pace, praying that her mother would not have some dreadful setback, that no one would mistake her for a woman of the streets, and that she would find Franz as soon as possible. It had been the most dreadful day of her life, and she dared not even consider what the loss of the money would mean to all of them in the future.

Her brother and Doktor Stiebel had in fact stayed at the second inn where she asked, but, alas, they had departed only that afternoon.

For a moment, the blow staggered Augusta and she reached for support. The inn's servant scanned her waist and asked if the younger gentleman was her sweetheart.

"My brother," she said, taking his interest for kindness and pouring out her tale. "We've come to join him, Mama and I, only we were robbed on the journey. Mama was hurt. And now I don't know what to do." Tears stung her eyes. She blinked and gulped some cold air to subdue her nausea. "What are we to do?"

The servant's eyes widened. "What? You were on that post from Ulm? Everybody's talking about it. Here, if you give me half an hour, I'll be free. I'll buy you a hot meal and some wine to hear the story." He leaned closer to push back her hood and whistled. "It's my lucky day. You're a beauty, sweetheart," he said with a leer.

Augusta backed away, pulling up the hood again. "I can't stay. I must get back to Mama."

She ran all the way back. Oh, Jakob! That silent cry for help reminded her that she still had one item of value, his ring. It rested between her breasts, tied to a thin cotton string so as not to arouse her mother's curiosity. For that reason and because the highwayman had wanted her mother's purse, it had escaped him. She could not give it up, but knowing that she must, she started crying in earnest.

Her mother was snoring soundly when she slipped back into their room. The candle had almost burned down, but Augusta found another in the drawer of the small table and lit it. Then she took a sheet of writing paper from her case and her quill and small bottle of ink. She had meant to write to Jakob about Mannheim and her new clothes, but now she had to beg for his help instead.

"Dearest Jakob," she wrote. "I hope you will find it in your heart to forgive me for troubling you so greatly again. Max will have brought you my note by now. Believe me, I did Mama's bidding against my better sense. She—may God forgive me, but she is a very foolish woman—not only borrowed a very large sum of money but talked about it on the coach so that somewhere in the mountains between Ulm and Mannheim one of the passengers drew a pistol and robbed us. Mama at first refused to give up her gold and was badly beaten for it."

She paused to check on her mother, whose breathing sounded stertorous, but it turned out to be nothing. Then she finished her letter, naming the inn where they were staying and telling Jakob that Franz and Stiebel had left Mannheim and were on their way home, leaving them in dire straits.

"It is with the greatest sorrow, my dear Jakob," she told him, "that I shall have to pawn your ring in the morning in order to post this letter and buy a little food for us. I pray you will forgive me for doing so and for making such demands on you again. I promise that I shall try to make it up to you by being your most faithful and loving wife.

Yours forever, Augusta."

She folded and sealed the letter, addressed it to Jakob Seutter in Lindau, then blew out the candle, slipped out of her dress, and crawled under the covers beside her mother.

Desirée's lover stopped short of killing her but only just. Desirée lay curled around her pain and sobbed. She had been a fool, and it was just that he should be furiously angry at her. She tried to convince herself that such violence showed how much he cared for her. He had been careful not to bruise her face. Other parts of her body could be hidden by clothing, and she would still be beautiful to her audience. She loved the stage, was besotted by the applause, and would do anything to keep working.

Even this.

His house was empty; he had brought no servants, and so her cries went unheard. He had spent nearly the whole night alternately beating her and then raping her like an animal. In the end she had stopped resisting and let him do whatever he wanted.

After the first bout of punishment and sex, he had made her crawl to him on her knees to beg his forgiveness.

After the last, he left her in the half darkness of closed curtains, lying tangled in the blood-stained bedding. The room smelled of blood and sex, and she thought she would never be clean. Or able to walk.

The door opened. "Well?" he asked. "Not up and around yet?"

Terrified, she moaned, hoping he would leave her alone.

He came to the bed and shook her. "The man you were with, where does he stay?"

She saw the expression on his face and cringed. "At the inn," she said and felt ashamed.

Poor boy! Poor, gentle boy.

He was satisfied. "Very well. Take your time, but make sure you're gone by nightfall. You can burn the sheets. When you get back to the others, say that you're ill. A female complaint." He laughed. "That should buy you some time. If you behave yourself in the future, I'll see about getting you a good part in the next play."

She said nothing.

"And be sure to air out the room before you leave," he said on his way out. "It stinks."

Augusta woke when her mother shook her shoulder. "How can you lie there, fast asleep, when I'm at death's door?" she demanded.

Daylight came from the window. Augusta peered at her mother blearily. To be sure, she looked a fright. Some of the swelling had subsided but one eye was still swollen shut and her upper lip was split, giving her a lopsided leer. The bruising, from her temple to her jaw on one side, had darkened. "I'm sorry, Mama," she said, sitting up. Her throat felt strangely tight. "Are you in much pain?"

"Don't be stupid. I'm in agony. And I cannot see. I'm going blind." Her mother whimpered. "Where's Franz? Go fetch him. I don't want to die without seeing my son."

Augusta felt the good side of her mother's face and found it cool to the touch. "You're not dying. And your sight will come back when the swelling goes down." She got up and washed her face in the frigid water from the ewer, then dipped the cloth into the water and placed it on her mother's face.

"How can you be so cold?" her mother muttered. "You have no feeling at all."

Augusta shivered as she slipped on her dress and found her stockings and shoes. She hardened her heart. "I'm sorry, Mama, but there's more bad news. Franz has left and is on his way home. As we have no money, the innkeeper is likely to throw us out in the street."

This made her mother sit up in bed, dropping the wet cloth. "They've left? How do you know?"

"I found out last night. They left before we got here." She stepped into her shoes and put on her cloak.

"Where are you going? You cannot leave me here."

Augusta sighed and held up the letter. "I have written for help to Jakob Seutter."

Her mother gasped. "I forbid you to write to that man, do you hear! Isn't it bad enough that you've given away all of our gold? What we could have done with that! Oh, why did I have to be punished with such an unnatural child?"

This was too much.

"How dare you, Mama, when you were the one who borrowed it and then told all and sundry in the coach how much money you had with you? You were begging to be robbed."

Her mother turned alarmingly red and raised a fist. "It was you," she screeched, "you who gave that monster our gold! Or have you forgotten that?"

"He would have killed us all if I had not. How can you have a moment's doubt of that after what he did to your face?"

"Oh, I'm ruined. I'm dying and will be thrown into the gutter like a beggar." With a moan, her mother sank back into the cushions and began to cry.

Augusta left, slamming the door behind her.

The innkeeper had been keeping watch for her. "Found your brother yet, Miss?"

Heart beating, Augusta said, "I'm on my way now. Pray send some warm milk and white bread up to our room." Then she swept past him and out into the street.

She had noticed a pawnbroker's sign the night before. In broad daylight, the city had lost its fearful aspect, and she walked quickly. The shop was open for business. An elderly man inside looked her over carefully. When she untied the string and pulled Jakob's ring from her bodice, he stretched out a gnarled hand for it. Taking a deep breath, she handed it over.

He peered at it closely, then reached for a pair of small scales. "It's nicely wrought," he said. "A fine ring, but I can only value its weight in gold. Are you selling or borrowing?"

"B-borrowing," she stammered.

He gave her a sharp glance over his spectacles. "Five *taler* is all I can advance. If you'll sell it, I'll go as high as ten."

Five *taler* were a pitiful amount. However quickly Jakob would come to her—and she had no doubt that he would—they could not subsist on so little. Tears rose to her eyes. She bit her lip and nodded. "Very well."

He counted out the ten pieces of silver, then, seeing her looking at the ring with tears in her eyes, took some pity. "I'll hold it for you for a week."

She gave her name, thanked him, and went back to post her letter, paying extra for the express service. Then she returned to her mother.

Jakob Seutter bore the separation from Augusta poorly. The happiness he had found so unexpectedly—and that he felt unworthy of—once snatched away, left him as bereft as if an arm had been torn off his body. It was an added burden that his friend Stiebel, who might have kept him informed about his dearest girl, had left for Mannheim. Only his fear of causing Augusta more misery kept him away from the house in Fischergasse. But he walked the streets and the market daily, hoping to catch a glimpse of her from a distance.

One day, in the course of some unrelated business dealings, he heard that Frau von Langsdorff had mortgaged her house to the tune of 100 *gulden,* a stunningly large sum. It suggested some catastrophe to him, and he sought out the lawyer who had secured the loan and asked some questions. Because Seutter was a banker and known to buy secured debts, the man rubbed his hands and informed him that the lady had borrowed the money in order to marry off her daughter advantageously.

"It's a very safe loan and soundly secured," he said eagerly. "In my opinion, she isn't likely to pay it off. A less businesslike creature cannot be imagined. There's a good bit of money to be made out of the property."

Seutter hid his dismay. "Are there prospects for the daughter?"

The man laughed. "They went off to Mannheim where the young woman's brother is expected to find her a man of rank and wealth. The mother is—shall we say— overly sanguine? Are you interested?"

Seutter bought the paper. It cost him an additional fifty gulden, but he was in no mood to bargain.

From the lawyer he went to Fischergasse, where he found Max and the young maid at their ease in the good parlor. They were dining on roast beef from the family's best dishes and drinking beer from wine glasses. When they saw him, they jumped to their feet and looked guilty.

"When did your mistress and Miss Augusta leave?" he asked, looking pointedly at the table. The answer shocked him more. Augusta had left without a message to him. He eyed the two servants suspiciously.

"Does your mistress know how you two live here?" he asked Elsbeth.

She turned a fiery red and twisted her apron in her hands.

"Do your parents know that you're staying alone with him?"

She raised her chin. "We're betrothed."

Max shot her a glance. "Now, Elsbeth! You shouldn't say such things. Nothing's settled. You're too young."

Elsbeth looked hurt. "You promised. You said soon, Max."

Jakob thought of Augusta who was also very young. The fear that he had no right to her returned painfully. But the servants' morals were none of his business. He looked sharply at Max. "Did Miss Augusta leave a message for me?"

Max mimed sudden recollection. "Oh, sir, now that you mention it . . . it clear went out of my mind . . .

there was a note." He boxed his head. "Now what did I do with it? I meant to give it to your boy. Did I? The mistress was not to know about it, so maybe I didn't right away." He looked distracted, then ran his hands through all his pockets and came up with Augusta's crumpled letter.

Jakob took it, glowered at Max, and went home to read his dear girl's letter in private.

It confirmed what he had been told and made him miserable. If Augusta's mother planned to introduce his dear girl to high society, who was he to stand in her way? Why should she not see the world she belonged in? Why should she not meet handsome young men and attend dances and entertainments in pretty gowns?

He sat up most of the night, holding her letter and grieving for his love. A thousand times he decided to give up his claim on her.

But the next morning changed all that. As he was taking a listless breakfast at the Post, he heard of the robbery of a post coach near Mannheim. The tale was garbled, but the times fit and the victims were said to be gentlewomen traveling with a great deal of gold on their persons. Lurid descriptions of what the villains had done to them turned his stomach and sent him into frenzied preparation to hire a private coach and six.

He was just throwing a few clothes, money, and letters of credit into a satchel when Max showed up. He looked shamefaced and asked for work because he could not remain in Fischergasse.

"You saw how it is, sir. Elsbeth's set her cap for me. It isn't right. She's too young, and I have no mind for a family, not when I can't give 'em a roof over their heads. But she won't listen."

Scutter thought him a scoundrel, but he needed an able-bodied servant on the road, and Max was available. So he packed a loaded pistol in his satchel, and told Max he could ride beside the coachman.

Augusta tended to her mother silently for another day and night, refusing to engage in more verbal battles or to defend herself against the accusations. She was not feeling well herself. As her throat became too sore to speak much and her head hurt and she was generally too listless, it was not much of sacrifice. When her mother slept or kept an offended silence, she rested, her thoughts with Jakob.

But the next morning, she could not bear the close room any longer. She went outside for a breath of fresh air. Her mother had improved sufficiently to eat and drink with a good appetite and had taken to issuing new orders. Augusta was to search out the high-ranking persons whom Franz had met on his stay here—especially the baron whose letter he had delivered—and ask for their assistance. Augusta said nothing. She had no appetite herself and felt feverish.

As she stood outside in the sun, the innkeeper approached her again. "I know where you may find your brother, Miss," he said.

She stared at him. "How do you know?"

"A postilion's just come back from a run to Heidelberg. I happened to mention the plight you and your mother were in after the robbery of your stage. He's the very one took your brother and an older gentleman day before yesterday? You just missed them."

Disappointed, she nodded. "I know."

"Seems they decided to spend a few days looking at the summer palace in Schwetzingen."

Hardly daring to hope, Augusta asked, "How far is Schwetzingen?"

"Nine miles on a good road. Your brother could be back here by tonight if you were to send a note by the post. He's staying at the inn in Schwetzingen. Or if you like, you can go yourself. That coach there is just leaving, and there's a seat left outside."

Augusta hesitated only a moment. It was mad, but she could not bear the thought of spending another day with her mother. She gave him most of her remaining money and said, "Please tell my mother I shall be back with Franz before night falls. The money is for her food and someone to look after her." Then she ran for the coach and climbed on.

Two hours later, stiff, chilled to the bone, and blown about by the wind, she climbed down in Schwetzingen. She had never traveled outside on a stagecoach. Not only was it bitterly cold, but she was jolted and bounced about mercilessly. She had eaten nothing that morning and very little the day before, but the swaying of the vehicle had made her ill. The headache was back, pounding furiously behind her eyes.

The posting inn was large. Feeling ill and light-headed, she stumbled through its door. A pair of young men were leaning against the banister of the stairs, engaged in a boisterous conversation. They stared when they saw her. She brushed back her disheveled hair. Their bold looks made her blush, but she asked if they knew a Lieutenant von Langsdorff. To her dismay, her throat hurt worse, and she could barely speak.

They looked at each other, and the taller one laughed. "Poor Desirée," he said. "She'll have to share her Apollo."

The other one grinned and bowed to Augusta. "Why, yes, my dear. We met the lieutenant, and a very pleasant young man he is. May I know who's asking for him?"

"I'm his sister Augusta."

"His sister?" He exchanged another glance with his friend. "Well, then, Miss— or is it Mistress?"

Augusta did not like their familiarity. "Miss von Langsdorff. Where may I find my brother?"

"He's gone out. Afraid he didn't tell us where. Could we offer our services? You look proper chilled, Augusta. Perhaps a glass of mulled wine?"

Relief that Franz was still here mixed with disappointment. She did not feel at all well. Her knees began to tremble, and she sat down quickly on the stairs, murmuring, "Oh."

They sat down beside her and were solicitous, holding her hands, peering into her face, and distressing her more, but she did not have the strength to get up again.

"What's going on here?"

The voice was educated and commanding. Augusta looked up hopefully. A well-dressed gentleman looked down at them. "Why aren't you at rehearsals? We have a play to put on, remember?"

The two young men shot up and bowed. The stranger was older than they but quite handsome and clearly someone with authority. Augusta pulled her wits together and stood up also.

The taller of the young men explained. "Just offering assistance to a young lady who's been taken ill. The sister of Lieutenant von Langsdorff. She's just arrived on the stagecoach."

The gray eyes of the officer measured her. "Oh, I see. Well, you're excused then. But hurry up and get to the theater. I'll see to the young lady." He made Augusta a bow. "Allow me. My name is Karl von Eberau, major in the Kurfürst's army and director of the court theater. I'm sorry if the young scallywags have frightened you. They're harmless enough, but actors behave more freely than gentlemen, I'm afraid. Now, how may I be of assistance?"

Gratefully, Augusta poured out the story of their misfortunes and her urgent quest for her brother.

"Why, I believe I know the young man. Does he walk with a cane? And is he traveling with a very short older gentleman?"

"Yes, indeed. The older gentleman is Doktor Stiebel, a lawyer and Franz's friend and employer. They came to Mannheim to deliver a letter. I thought they had completed their errand and left again, but then the innkeeper in Mannheim told me they stopped here."

"And so they did. For some sightseeing, I believe, and perhaps to attend a performance or two. The court is shortly to arrive here and there will be all sorts of shows and musical and theatrical entertainments. I hope you and your Mama will be able to attend. The young Mozart from Salzburg is to perform again on the pianoforte and violin. He's only seven and on a tour of all the major courts in Europe. Have you heard of him?"

Augusta shook her head. "I'm sure it will be quite magnificent, sir, but at the moment my brother is rather urgently needed."

"Forgive me. Of course. If you will wait just a moment, I shall make inquiries."

She waited, leaning against the wall and feeling fainter by the minute. Ravishing smells came from some of the dishes servants carried past her to the dining rooms. Outside the church clock struck one.

Herr von Eberau returned quickly. "Good news," he cried cheerfully. "I believe I know where they are, and my chaise is just outside. Come."

He took her arm as they went to a neat little vehicle with a pair of fine horses. Helping her in, he said with a smile, "What very good luck that I happened to meet you this morning."

With a sigh, Augusta sank back into the soft leather seat and closed her eyes.

# 17

# A Question of Honor

*Honor's a fine imaginary notion,*
*That draws in raw and inexperienced men*
*To real mischiefs, while they hunt a shadow.*

Joseph Addison, *Cato* II,iv)

Franz was too ashamed to mention the encounter in the palace garden to Stiebel. As he hoped, his friend thought his reticence was due to embarrassment about his sexual naiveté and changed the subject after the merest questioning look.

"Well then, what about that chatty group of actors you were with? Have you learned anything?" he asked.

Franz hung his head. "I'm afraid not, sir. The talk was of entertainments and how many great people would be in attendance on this last of the annual visits of the court. There will be musical performances, ballets, plays, and even a staged hunt."

Stiebel sat up. "A staged hunt? Barbarous affair. They drive the poor creatures into an enclosure where they'll be massacred. But that's neither here nor there. Will the Kurfürst attend?"

"I suppose so, since he ordered it." Franz was a little surprised that this negligible bit of news should be significant.

Stiebel raised his brows. "Surely it's obvious. If there's a plot against the prince, he is in imminent danger. Remember that our assassin specializes in such scenarios."

"Oh." Franz, his head full of his own problems, had some trouble thinking about Karl Theodor's. "I suppose we must warn him."

Stiebel got up to pace. "Indeed, though he's not easy to approach. I wish we knew who is involved and what they want precisely." He stopped and frowned at Franz. "You'll have to be very careful from now on. People are arriving every hour. The man may already be here. If he sees you . . . "

Franz thought he was quite likely to die in the duel anyway. He used to be good with a sword before Freiberg, but his crippled leg put an end to that. And pistols? The chances were only slightly better, for he was a terrible shot. He supposed that Desirée's protector would have the choice of weapon. Strange that he should have wished for death so frequently in the past year, only to fear it now when it was thrust upon him.

Stiebel's voice droned on while Franz wondered if he should have insisted on satisfaction. The insult to his honor had been serious. What if the man talked, boasted about what he had done?

"Franz?"

Franz blinked. "I'm sorry. I was distracted."

"Really, Franz, I wish you'd get your mind off that little actress and pay attention. I was speaking of men who might expect preferment from Elisabeth Augusta if she were to take her husband's place. Truth to tell, I confess to a strong contempt for those who hope to advance in the world by seducing or allowing themselves to be seduced by women of power. It is said that Catherine of Russia made herself empress by having her husband, the czar, cast into a dungeon. Now she changes lovers with the rapidity that men change horses."

"These men you suspect are lovers of Elizabeth Augusta?"

Stiebel said testily, "Pay attention. Colonel Rodenstein has served the Kurfürstin in war and peace for well on fifteen years now. There's an ugly rumor that the prince who died may have been Rodenstein's son. You do recall meeting the colonel?"

Franz nodded. The heavy pompous man with the large order of the Polish Eagle pinned to his broad chest. "What about Dr. Mai?"

Stiebel pursed his lips. "I don't know. As her private and confidential physician he is well placed, and he was physician to the baron. The sleeping draft may have contained a poison. But surely he was not at Freiberg. There may be other men who hope to be Rodenstein's successors, military men. She's said to prefer them. Why do you look so horrified? Affairs are common among the great. You recall Elizabeth Augusta's sister, the one who married the Count Palatine Michael and carried on an open and torrid affair with a Mannheim actor last year? You must accustom yourself to the idea, Franz. Not everyone lives up to your sainted Papa's ideals."

No, not even his only son, thought Franz bitterly. Oh, how very far had he strayed from the teachings of his youth. And now he had not only failed Stiebel but got himself into a situation he did not know how to handle. He felt sick.

"Come, don't look so miserable, my dear boy," said Stiebel, clearly sorry for his sharpness. "Go change your linen, and we'll see what we can learn during supper."

But Franz could not face another evening with the actors—who would by now have learned of the events in the garden—and begged off. He wanted to think through his options while Stiebel was busy elsewhere.

She was charming, the little sister. Quite young still—he judged her to be seventeen or eighteen at the most—and wholly trusting.

He glanced at her sideways as he guided the horses toward his house. Her eyes were closed, and she looked innocent, a sleeping angel. What would it be like to make love to an angel?

Lust stirred and reminded him of Desirée, the latest of the long string of dancers, actresses, and chambermaids he had bedded. There was a tiresome sameness to such affairs, though last night had made for some sport, as the inventive French Count de Sade had promised.

There was no time to make a plan regarding the young Augusta. He had simply taken advantage of a chance to avenge himself on the man who had dared steal his woman.

But abducting young gentlewomen was even more severely frowned on than dueling. Elizabeth Augusta would not countenance such a thing. He tried to think of a way to have the little virgin and get away with it but failed.

When they stopped at his house, she awoke. "Are we here?"

It struck him that she looked feverish and seemed to find speaking painful. "Yes. Allow me to take you inside. There's a comfortable room where you can wait while I get your brother."

She let him help her down and lead her into the house. He took her to a settee in the small salon. It was a dim room. The shutters were closed and there was no fire. She sat down quietly, shivering a little.

"Forgive me," he said, "but this is a summer residence, and I arrived only yesterday. The servants are in Mannheim. I wish I could offer you some refreshments."

"It doesn't matter," she said and pulled her cloak around her more closely. "You are most kind."

He stood for a moment. Ah, it would be so easy. All he had to do was to push her back, fling her skirts over her head, and get between her thighs. There would be nothing she could do. The idea of rape brought back a memory. It stirred his lust so powerfully that he left the room before it was too late.

He went upstairs to his bedroom and opened the door. Good, Desirée was still here. And she had cleaned up like an obedient little slut.

She jumped up from a chair and stared at him, pale and terrified. "*Pardon, monsieur,* I go now."

"*Non, ma petite,*" he said. "You will stay a while longer."

The brown eyes filled with tears. "I am not well. *Je vous pris!* Tomorrow per'aps."

He laughed. "Don't worry. I haven't come to bed you. I need you to play chambermaid to a young lady. You will make her comfortable. She's a little feverish."

Desirée's eyes narrowed. "You want me to go like zis?" she asked, pointing to her blue silk dress.

"Go find an apron and cap. There must be something left behind by the servants." He raised a monitory finger. "Remember, my girl, if you behave yourself, I'll reward you. But if you mention our dealings to anyone—least of all to the girl below stairs—you'll regret it."

She nodded, and he saw with satisfaction that the look of hopelessness had returned.

The angel was nodding off again on the settee and jerked upright when he closed the door of the salon behind him.

"My brother?" she asked anxiously.

The rosy color brought on by the fever suited her well, he thought. He shook his head. "I regret that the young man has escaped us again. You look a little feverish. Are you feeling quite well?"

"I . . . I shall be all right as soon as I find Franz." She made an attempt to stand but swayed on her feet.

He came to steady her. "You must rest here. I found one of my maids. Tell her what you need, and she'll procure it. Meanwhile, I shall go hunt down the elusive Franz."

She gave a little sigh and sank down again. "Thank you. You're very kind. It's too much trouble, but I do feel a little dizzy."

He stood for a moment, looking down at shiny brown curls, charmingly tangled about the graceful curve of neck and shoulder, and imagined what lay beneath the plain woolen cloak. "Would you like a little water? Or wine?"

"No, thank you. Nothing."

She had deep blue eyes ringed with soft lashes. Small beads of perspiration shimmered on her upper lip. The situation was delicious. Should he help her off with that heavy cloak and those dusty shoes? Make her stretch out on the settee? What a very fine neck she had! How he longed to kiss that small ear and then slowly uncover the hidden charms. He felt the stirring of lust again and controlled himself with an effort. With a bow, he took his leave, repeating his promise to leave no stone unturned in his quest for Franz—which was no more than the truth after all.


With the gentle snores of Stiebel in his ears and the warmth of his body close by, Franz lay stiffly, staring into the darkness. All his blackest thoughts returned, angry demons with outstretched claws and open mouths that denounced him for murder, cowardice, disloyalty, lust, and weakness.

He had failed at everything he had ever attempted. He had failed his father by not following in that good man's footsteps, failed as a soldier by leading his regiment to destruction, failed to be a support to his family, failed to be a friend to Stiebel, failed to protect poor Desirée, and now he was about to fail himself, for he was afraid to face a duel.

The question of whose honor had been injured most was murky at best. True, striking Franz in such an indelicate manner and at such a moment could not be allowed to pass. But there was the matter of Franz's flagrant act of copulating with the other man's woman. Perhaps the matter could have been settled at that point with an explanation (on Franz's part) and an apology (on the other's), but Franz had then slapped the man.

By morning, Franz had decided that he must confront Desirée's lover as soon as possible. Then perhaps they could discuss the situation while they were both calmer. Feeling his ears burn at the lie, Franz told Stiebel at breakfast that he thought he would pursue their inquiries on his own that day.

Stiebel sighed. "Very well. I have a mind to visit the summer palace today and make the acquaintance of someone close to Karl Theodor. We need to get an audience with the prince. But I can manage by myself."

Franz had no intention of joining the actors, who would be engaged with rehearsals until the afternoon, or of meeting Desirée. Instead he took his sword and walked to the nearest woods.

In a clearing covered with a layer of multicolored leaves like a fine Turkey carpet, he reviewed the moves of swordplay.

He had not drawn his sword since Freiberg and swallowed down the bile rising at those memories. He had killed many men with his sword then and now proposed to kill again or be killed.

He managed the salute creditably, but that was the first and last of the approved moves his crippled body could assume. His right knee would not bend and, as he was right-handed, that was the knee employed in lunge, attack, parry, counter parry, *demivolte, coupe,* and *reposte.* It was a crucial joint, and no manner of agility of wrist or strategy of mind made up for it.

But he forced himself, taking fall after fall, until his knee burned like fire, until he lay groaning on the ground and knew that even an untrained swordsman would skewer him within seconds. Bathed in sweat, he eventually gave up all pretense.

He was a cripple. He could no more use a sword than the left-handed Apollo could play his lyre.

Stiebel—who loved all the weak things in this world and grieved for the baron's chickens and the loss of his little bird—had adopted him because he, too, was one of the weak in need of care.

In a contest between the weak and the strong, the weak must lose.

Franz gathered himself up from the gaily colored leaves—how beautiful nature was in death—picked up his useless sword, and limped home.

Desirée's lover was waiting outside the inn.

Franz stopped, leaning heavily on his cane. They measured each other. The other man noted the sword and, smiling coldly, drawled, "A word, if you please, Lieutenant Langsdorff."

Franz took a breath. "You have the advantage, sir, but I'm very glad to meet you," he said. "Having thought the matter over, I find that I also behaved badly. Under the circumstances, I'm willing to overlook the incident and apologize for my part in it. I assure you I had no idea the young woman was your . . . friend or I wouldn't have . . ." His voice trailed off when he saw the sneer on the other man's face.

Desirée's lover took a visiting card from his coat pocket and handed it over. "What, are you a coward besides being a scoundrel?" he asked.

Franz stood up a little straighter. "You mistake, sir." He glanced at the card. "I'm perfectly willing to meet you, Major, but my injury"—he gestured at his leg—"makes swordplay awkward."

The other man raised a brow. "You should have thought of that before you insulted me."

Franz flushed. "As you wish it, sir, swords it shall be."

"No. I'll not be blamed for killing a cripple. We'll use pistols. But no seconds. As I told you, duels are forbidden. Keep the matter to yourself."

"Of course. But I'm afraid I did not bring pistols and am a stranger here."

"I'll bring a set of dueling pistols. You may inspect them. Shall we say midnight tonight? At twelve paces? There is to be a moon tonight." He curled his lip. "And what more suitable place than at the feet of Apollo—where you committed the offense."

Franz bit his lip and bowed.



Desirée could not understand what her tormentor had seen in this girl. She was plain, without a bit of paint to her face, or powder on her hair, and her clothes—*mon Dieu!*—such a fusty gray cloak and such worn black shoes. She must be very poor.

And she had fallen asleep.

"*Mademoiselle?*" Desirée asked, bending over the strange guest.

The girl opened her eyes, looked at her blearily, and struggled upright. "I'm sorry," she said hoarsely. "I'm not feeling well. My brother, is he here yet?"

Desirée put out her hand to touch the girl's forehead, then snatched it back. "*Mademoiselle, vous êtes malade.* Is fever!"

"Some water, if you have it, please," murmured the sick girl. "It's very hot in this room." She frowned at the empty fireplace, then struggled with her cloak. She managed to take it off, revealing a dark blue dress with a bit of lace at the high neck and sleeves. The lace was good, and Desirée, who had a shrewd eye for such things, revised her estimate of the girl. She was of good birth but little fortune, perhaps a schoolmaster's daughter. She felt a twinge of pity for her, both because she was sick and because she was in the Major's clutches.

"I go fetch water," she said, making a little curtsey, and tripped from the room.

Stiebel was frustrated and uneasy about the lack of progress. While all sorts of possibilities had occurred to him, he had no proof that they were, in fact, related to any adulterous behavior of the Kurfürstin or her spouse. The actors talked freely and with some pride of such liaisons, citing case after case of actors, actresses, or dancers becoming official lovers of kings and princes and being given noble titles and large properties. But it seemed to Stiebel that Karl Theodor, and anyone who supported him, had more reason to have his wife murdered than him.

The very air of Schwetzingen seemed filled with the electricity of imminent catastrophe. He feared that Franz was as helpless as a newborn babe in the face of such danger. By involving him in the investigation, he had hoped to give Franz the self-confidence that was so sadly lacking after his experiences in the late war, but instead he had made things worse. He had pushed the boy into the arms of a French vixen and caused no telling how much additional damage. Something had happened during the rendezvous, and Stiebel thought that Franz having caught the pox was the least of his worries.

It was time to make an end of this mad excursion and take the boy home. Stiebel decided to take his surmises and suspicions to the Kurfürst himself, and thus rid himself of his responsibilities. He dressed with some care. The brown coat and breeches were brushed and assorted spots removed, and the old periwig was freshly powdered by the local barber, who also shaved him. And thus he presented himself at the summer palace and requested an audience.

He was told to join a number of other gentlemen and a few ladies, all of whom waited patiently in the anteroom. He sat on a fine but uncomfortable chair, his feet not quite reaching the floor, and watched as soberly dressed officials passed back and forth through the fine doors to His Highness's rooms. At no time were any of those waiting called to the double doors.

After an hour, Stiebel slid down from his chair and went to speak to a haughty individual with a beak of a nose. "Have you passed my request to His Highness?" he asked.

The man looked down his nose at him. "What request?"

Stiebel raised himself on the balls of his feet. "As I told you quite a long time ago, I am Nepomuk Stiebel, attorney at law from Lindau, and I have urgent information of the greatest importance to His Highness. How long will it be before I may speak to him?"

"His Highness is very busy with affairs of state, sir. Besides, he rarely sees anyone without a proper introduction. You will have to wait."

Stiebel went back and sat down again. He felt very tired, but he was determined. And patient. The sun reached its zenith, and many of the others left, discour-

aged or in search of their midday meal. Stiebel sat on.
A lackey replaced the man with the beak, so that he,
too, could refresh himself.

It was not until nearly two o'clock that Stiebel saw a
familiar face. It belonged to the same accommodating
gentleman who had taken him to the music room in the
Mannheim palace. Moritz, that was his name. Stiebel
hopped down again and went to meet him with a smile.

"My dear Dr. Stiebel," Freiherr von Moritz said,
shaking his hand warmly. "I had no idea that you were
still in our country, let alone here in Schwetzingen."

Stiebel sighed. "I have been waiting to see the
Kurfürst since early this morning. Not so very long as
such things go, but I'm an old man, and I confess I'm
no longer up to the challenges of court attendance. I
was about to declare myself defeated." It was true. He
felt positively lightheaded with exhaustion.

"Well, I'm afraid I cannot be much help. His
Highness worked all morning and has now gone to rest
a little before this evening's entertainments. But perhaps you will do me the honor of taking a glass of wine
with me and telling me what brings you here?"

Stiebel accepted. They repaired to a small room on
the ground floor, furnished as a gentleman's study with
bookcases and a writing table. Here Herr von Moritz
produced a bottle and two glasses from behind some
books and poured. The port did much to give Stiebel
back some of his spirit and determination. He decided
that he must trust this man. Moritz had no ties to Elisabeth Augusta and was all old-fashioned courtesy and
kindness.

"You'll be aware," Stiebel began, "that Baron von Winkelhausen died before my young friend could deliver the son's letter?"

Moritz nodded. "Yes. I was sorry to hear of the death. He had served His Highness with great loyalty. But you seem to attach some significance to the event?"

"The timing, rather. We arrived the very morning after. That in itself might have been a tragic coincidence if not for the fact that the letter had been stolen and a substitution made. Naturally, this raised our suspicions, especially since both my young friend and I had been attacked and robbed before. Franz is a very honorable soul and had not opened the original letter, but I, being in the legal profession, suspected from the start that this was no ordinary communication. When Franz was nearly killed by a footpad in Lindau and my house was searched, I was afraid that the letter was putting his life in danger. In short, I decided to read it."

Moritz's brows shot up. "Did you indeed? And?"

Stiebel shifted uncomfortably and took another sip of port. "I'm rather ashamed of going behind my young friend's back and breaking a confidence, but you see, there was a reason for us to rush to Mannheim. The son was warning his father about a dastardly plot against His Highness."

"What? What sort of plot? Who is involved?"

"I wish I knew. Alas, the letter was not at all clear. Captain von Loe used a sort of code, perhaps because he thought his mail might be opened." Stiebel had the grace to blush. "Whatever he suspected, he did not expect to be murdered for it."

"I thought he died in battle."

"No. My young friend saw him get shot. It happened very early, before the troops engaged. He thought the bullet came from our side."

Herr von Moritz's face closed. "Forgive me, but this is an extraordinary tale—if it is true."

Stiebel felt this comment like a stab to his heart. He gasped a little, then slid from his chair. "I'm afraid you take me for a senile fool, sir—or worse. It will be best if I give up my endeavors on behalf of your master—who is not in any case my sovereign but merely a fellow human being—and concentrate on protecting my young friend instead. I bid you farewell." He made a slight bow.

Moritz rose. "Wait. I'm sorry if I have offended you, but you, being a lawyer, must surely see that I cannot take this tale to His Highness without proof."

"Perhaps not, sir. We're dealing with a very clever murderer. But I have discharged my moral obligation and leave the warning in your hands." And with that he turned to go.

"Sir," pleaded Moritz. "Can you not tell me anything else? Anything at all?"

Stiebel paused. "Who among Her Highness's particular attendants served at Freiberg?"

Stiebel saw thoughts chasing each other on Moritz's expressive face. "I'm not sure. I think perhaps Eberau did. He's the theater director and reports to her. But he served directly under General von Meyern, and Meyern withdrew before the battle was over. It caused considerable comment later. I shall enquire about others."

Stiebel nodded. "Thank you for the port, sir. I wish you well."

Franz went upstairs. After sending for paper and ink, he sat at the small table by the open window and wrote his will to the accompaniment of the violins and flutes of musicians.

It was customary to settle one's affairs before a duel, though he had little enough to bestow. His simple will left his meager possessions and whatever was still due of his pension to his mother. He enclosed the will in a letter to Stiebel in which he explained the circumstances of the duel and that he did not expect to live. He begged Stiebel's pardon, asked him to serve as his executor, and then poured out his heart in gratitude for Stiebel's friendship and in grief that he had proved a disappointment. He wept a little, moved equally by his wasted life and the melting melodies produced by a particularly fine violinist, then added as an afterthought a request to assure his sister Augusta of his brotherly love and his hope that she would be guided by wiser heads than his. These two documents he sealed and left in his *portemanteau.*

A separate note to Stiebel explained that something had happened and he would be late returning. He left the note on the table. It was the truth, after all—though he did not think he would be back.

Franz dared not stay in case Stiebel returned, but he changed into a clean shirt and combed and retied his hair. Then he put on his sword and his cocked hat and left the inn. The sun had set, and he was uncomfortably aware of a gnawing hunger. How persistently the human body clung to life!

He spent the next hours in the Catholic Church of St. Pankratius, not in worship but in idle speculation about a faith that filled its churches with an abundance of art and beauty, ornamentation, and color until they resembled the palaces of princes. Where was the soul in all of this celebration of the abundance of life? For that matter, how was he to leave all he held dear about his life—his home, the lake, Stiebel, music, and the love of women—when all about him touched on the senses? The paintings and statues of Christ and all the saints showed him human beings filled with an excess of life and emotion. The very angels had been transformed into cupids, fat laughing babes with wings, and the mother of Christ was a voluptuous figure in shimmering blue silk.

He heard the clock strike the hours and half hours, saw men and women enter, kneel, and pray, and then leave again, watched the light fade and the windows turn dark. A priest came to light candles on the main altar and in the altar niches on either side. He passed Franz with a nod and a smile. What did he know of agony?

Eventually Franz could not bear it any longer and left to wander about the dark town. Long as the wait was, it was also all too short. The clock struck eleven, the streets grew empty and quiet, and Franz turned his steps toward the summer palace.

# 18

# The Duel

*It is easier to be wise for others than for oneself.*

La Rochefoucauld, *Maxim* 132

Stiebel's bitter disappointment translated into activity. He would find Franz and arrange for their
passage home on the next coach.

As he passed the theater, the sounds of music and
song from within reminded him of the actors. Thinking
that perhaps Franz had followed his *inamorata* here, he
went in. An Italian opera was being rehearsed. The
stage set suggested ancient Rome, and the soldiers wore
short tunics, dainty gilded boots, and ostrich feathers on
their helmets.

Stiebel took little interest in the performance, but he
saw one of the young actors from the inn and approached him.

It appeared that the opera was *Sofonisba*, the tragic tale of the Numidian queen captured by the Romans, and, no, neither the director nor Franz was here. The director had stopped by earlier but left again. The actor thought that Franz might be with the charming Desirée who had not shown up for rehearsals, and then he suddenly recalled that a young woman had arrived by coach, claiming to be the lieutenant's sister.

"Young Augusta here? In Schwetzingen?" Stiebel was thunderstruck. What could have happened at home? "When did you see her, and where is she now?"

"It was just striking one o'clock, sir. She must've got off the coach and walked into the inn. As to where she may be, I don't know. Herr von Eberau arrived just then and sent us off to rehearsal."

Stiebel stared at him. "Dear God in heaven, I hope it doesn't mean what I think it means," he muttered.

On the stage, Sofonisba drank her cup of poison and collapsed. The orchestra struck up heavy, tragic chords, and the curtain came down.

Stiebel ran nearly all the way to the inn. There he gasped out questions about Augusta but was told that nobody knew anything about her. There might have been a young woman on the coach but she had not asked for lodging.

Filled with anxiety, Stiebel asked where Eberau stayed in Schwetzingen.

The distance seemed farther than Stiebel had thought. He had to rest frequently and developed a painful stitch in his side. The house, when he finally reached it, was shuttered, and there was no answer to his pounding on the door. Stiebel sank down on the steps. He felt ill and confused.

After a short rest, he started back, his feet leaden and his breathing so painful that he almost despaired of reaching the inn.

When Eberau returned to his house, he had hit on the method of having the girl with none being the wiser.

Desirée, looking tempting in her little apron and cap, met him at the door. She reported that his guest was very ill and resting in one of the bedrooms upstairs.

"Excellent, *ma petite*," he said with a smile and tweaked Desirée's cheek.

She narrowed her eyes. "*Elle est très malade, M'sieur.*"

"Not too ill for a little sport, I trust," Eberau said lightly. "Don't worry, my dear. Your time will come again." He climbed the stairs briskly.

"*M'sieur,*" cried the little actress, "*je vous en prie. Ze* fever! She must see ze doctor."

Von Eberau paused to look down at her. "Nonsense. She's young and healthy. Clean in body and mind. And that's more than I can say for you." He drew a stoppered brown bottle from his coat pocket. "*Voilà.* I bought some medicine. I have a soft heart for innocence. Tincture of poppies will soothe her pains." He laughed and continued upstairs.

The girl lay in the bedroom next to his own. He tiptoed to the bed, a narrow one with curtains à la Polonaise but adequate for what he had in mind. She was asleep, deeply flushed, and breathing raggedly. For a moment, he faltered, but he saw that Desirée had helped her undress. She wore only a thin shift. The heat of the fever had caused her to push away the covers. One charming leg lay bared to the middle of her thigh, and her breasts swelled deliciously under the thin lawn of the shift.

He went to lock the door and undressed down to his shirt. Taking the brown bottle, he poured some of the liquid into a wine glass. Then he sat down beside her on the bed, and looked at her. He was very tempted to touch her—here and there—lightly so as not to wake her. But safer not. Putting his hand on her shoulder, he shook her gently. "Wake up, my dear. Here's some medicine to make you feel better."

Her eyes opened, and she stared up at him. "Mmm . . . who are you?" she muttered, her voice thick.

"I'm your doctor," he lied, smiling at his jest. "I'm here to ease your suffering and make a new woman out of you. Here, just take a sip of this medicine. I promise you'll be better in a moment."

She frowned and looked about. "Where's Mama? I don't feel well. Please call Mama."

"In a moment. Now come, drink this." He put his arm under her shoulders and lifted her, holding the glass to her lips. She drank a little, than pushed the glass away. "Mama?" she called, her voice louder and filled with panic.

"Ssh!" he said. "People will hear. Come, just another sip."

"No." She tried to push him away.

Impatiently, he grasped her firmly and forced the rim of the glass between her lips. She gasped for breath and swallowed the rest of the laudanum. "There," he said, releasing her, "isn't that better? Now let me make you comfortable." He set the empty glass aside and reached down for the hem of her shift. Raising her again to a sitting position, he pulled it up over her head.

She gave a soft cry and struggled against him, but he gloried in feeling her hot, naked body in his arms. Flinging the shift aside, he caught both of her wrists behind her and lifted her so she straddled his lap. Fully aroused by now, he bent to kiss her breasts— such charming breasts—when she suddenly vomited all over him.

With a curse, he flung her aside and jumped up. A large, sticky, and malodorous stain dripped down his shirt.

"*Diable!*" he muttered through clenched teeth. His lust evaporated. He glowered at her. "I'll be back to teach you better manners, my girl. And when I do, you won't get a soothing draft of laudanum to save you from what I have in mind." She cowered away from him, her eyes wide and glazed.

He stripped off his stained shirt, dropping it on the floor, then scooped up his other clothes and left, locking the door behind him and taking the key.

Desirée hovered in the dark hallway, staring at his nakedness.

"What do *you* want?" he snapped. "Find me a clean shirt."

At that moment, the sound of knocking came from the front door. He took a step toward Desirée and clamped his hand over her mouth. "Not a sound," he hissed.

Stiebel returned to the inn and climbed the stairs, gasping for breath, hoping against all hope to find Franz in.

He was not, and Stiebel read the note on the table with a gnawing fear. Why had he not been more careful of his charge? Franz was very young and no match for a murderer.

He recalled the strange mood Franz had been in the night before—not at all excitement or male pride, but rather as if he had a very guilty conscience. Stiebel decided to search Franz's possessions. The sword was gone, and on top of Franz's clothes in his *portemanteau* lay a fat letter addressed to him.

Stiebel tore this open, saw the will, and read Franz's apology with horror. He glanced out of the window. The sun had set. Was it already too late?

He put the letter in his coat and started down the stairs. Halfway down, he suddenly felt faint. He swayed as the banister started to float up. Then the steps beneath his feet dropped away.

He came to in his bed. It was dark outside. By the light of his candle he saw an old man sitting beside his bed. He was a fusty-looking individual and wore an old-fashioned periwig like his own. Stiebel wondered idly if that scoundrel in Mannheim had been right and it was time to get a new wig made.

The man nodded and smiled. He had crooked yellow teeth. "Ah, we're awake," he said in an oily voice. "Good. Drink this." He held a cup to Stiebel's lips, and Stiebel drank. It tasted bitter, and he made a face. "And how do we feel?" asked the man solicitously.

Stiebel glared. "*My* shoulder hurts and so does *my* head. I've no idea about your condition, sir—or who you are. What is that vile draft you just gave me?"

"Ha, ha, ha. I see we're quite ourselves again." Such good humor grated. "I'm Thomas Winter, apothecary, at your service, sir. The innkeeper called me when you fell down the stairs. Nothing's broken, though there will be some nasty bruises on your legs. And I expect you wrenched your shoulder a little when you tumbled. The medicine is to make you sleep."

Memory returned, and Stiebel started up. "Hell and Death!"

Thomas Winter pushed him back. "Oh, no, we mustn't. Rest is indicated. We'll feel sleepy in a moment. We must lie still and doze a little."

"No . . . you don't understand . . . Franz . . . the young man with me. I must stop him . . ." But it was no good. His head and limbs felt very heavy and after a brief struggle, he gave up.


On his way to meet his death, Franz found life and sound and beauty again. The windows of the summer palace blazed, carriages awaited their owners, and sounds of music came from the theater. Franz wondered if the little princess was inside. He grieved for her, a child still but on the threshold of womanhood. What lay ahead for her? An arranged marriage to a princeling who had no interest in her except as a vehicle for mandatory procreation while he found his pleasure in the arms of women like Desirée. All of them would be cheated of love.

Love? No, better not to think of Love. It was a cheat.

When he entered the garden, he saw that the glazed doors of the summer palace stood open and paused. Inside, crystal chandeliers blazed with many candles above a gaily dressed crowd. Not far from him, a man bent his head to the woman beside him and whispered something. The woman laughed with a peculiar and melodious sound, not unlike that made by the plashing fountains and purling violins. Just so his ears had been seduced when he had walked here with Desirée. It now seemed to him that the woman's laughter was false, as insubstantial as a bubble floating in the fountain, a practiced delusion and an invitation to the male.

The game of love.

And yet, and yet . . . oh, to be thus seduced again, to fall into the arms of Venus and become godlike again!

The distant clock struck the half hour. He had a mere half hour of life left. Turning his back on the glittering palace, he passed silently through the dark garden, passed silently the small hedge-enclosures where lovers moaned softly in each others' arms as they approached consummation—*the little death* some poet had called it.

Leaving behind the straight open paths and *allées* of clipped trees and hedges, he lost himself in the darkness of winding trails. The gardens were still under construction, and parts resembled primeval forest. They would be laid out in the English style, the actors had told him, a new Arcadia where the lords and ladies of this country could play at the pastoral life of ancient shepherds and shepherdesses—or satyrs and nymphs.

His eyes searched for the snowy marble temple of Apollo where he and Desirée had found their own Elysium, but the trees were too dense. At night the area looked different, and the moon was little help. It merely elongated the shadows and turned trees and shrubs into black shapes, much like *Scherenschnitte*, those delicate scissor cuts of images from black paper. Only here the background was not white, but rather a slightly paler darkness studded by stars.

He blundered about, increasingly tense, for the clock must strike soon, and he was afraid to be thought a coward. It mattered that he do this final thing right— not because he wanted to kill the man who had put him in this position—he would delope rather than take another life—but because he must prove to himself that he was a man.

And because he owed a death to those he had killed at Freiberg.

By the time the tower clock of St. Pankratius struck midnight with twelve slow, somber peals, he was bent on death with a single-minded frenzy. When he finally burst from a stand of trees, and saw the Apollo temple just ahead, he laughed out loud with relief. He had come to his belvedere, to the white marble monument on a hill. It shone brighter than the moon. Only a few paces to its left was the green dell where he had made love to Desirée and where he would end his life.

Franz thought he saw the major in the temple above and started forward just as someone called his name.

He started to turn but felt a sharp blow to his upper back and heard the sound of a shot. He stumbled and fell. He lay looking up into the shimmering sky where stars danced measured minuets along the milky way . . . to the music of a laughing boy who was playing a pianoforte . . . for him and the little princess.

# 19

# Of Dark Deeds and Darker Desires

*Get place and wealth, if possible with grace;*
*If not, by any means get wealth and place.*

Alexander Pope *Epistles of Horace*

For so well-laid a plan, it should not have gone wrong. He had arrived well ahead of the appointed hour and had hidden his rifle on a high shelf in the grotto underneath the Apollo temple. From the temple itself, he had a perfect overview of the green dell. There was an adequate moon and the distance was slight.

Afterward he mingled with the guests at the palace, chatting about the opera they were rehearsing and about the precocious child from Salzburg who was to give another performance tonight.

Near midnight, he slipped away as if for a breath of fresh air. In the grotto, he retrieved his rifle and primed the gun, then he climbed up to the temple and waited. A green youngster like Langsdorff would be early, he thought, smiling. Early for a duel that would not happen because duels were risky affairs, even for a marksman like himself. Honor was a vastly overrated commodity.

When he heard the church clock strike midnight, he became uneasy. What if the coward had backed out? He waited a little longer and was just getting to his feet to leave when he saw the cripple coming from the wrong direction.

It did not matter. The bullet would be fatal either way. He raised his rifle and sighted. Yes. His finger was tightening on the trigger when he heard shouts and then saw two people running toward Langsdorff.

His heart missed a beat. Now what? What was he to do now? In a moment, it would be too late.

The sound of the shot deafened him before he realized he had fired. His mind went blank, but the instinct for self-preservation took over. He dove down into the grotto, shoved the rifle into its hiding place, and ran.


Franz felt the pain on his head first. He muttered a protest and opened his eyes to a fierce, blinding light. Even behind his closed lids, the harsh brightness burned like the sun.

Phoebus Apollo, the sun god. Or his father's God? Dante had been deemed worthy to look into that blinding light.

Something pressed against the pain in his head, and he flinched away. "I'm s-sorry," he muttered. "I'm s-sorry. I t-tried, but I wasn't g-good enough. B-brave enough. S-s-stupid." The stutter was back—another flaw in his fatally flawed being.

"Yes," replied a voice, sounding angry. "You were very foolish, my boy. Hold that lantern still so I can see. There's a good deal of blood."

The painful pressure returned, bringing back the memory of a narrow alley and of an angry woman shaking him. He peered cautiously through his lashes. The light was still too bright, but he could make out shapes.

"Hold still, for heaven's sake," snapped the voice, familiar now.

Fingers probed, and Stiebel's face was bent over him. It was lit up strangely from one side and seemed to float in the darkness. What was Stiebel doing here? He muttered, "What?"

"It's just a cut," said Stiebel. "I thought you'd been shot. You must have hit your head on a stone."

Another voice said, "He was luckier than poor Brandt. The bullet got him in the eye. He's dead."

"Oh, the pity of it! Poor man. He saved the boy's life."

Franz returned to the world.

Shading his eyes against the light, he struggled upright. Stiebel, kneeling beside him, dropped a bloody handkerchief. "Lie still," he snapped. "I'd just got the better of it."

Franz felt warm blood trickling down his face and dug out his own handkerchief. "W-what happened? S-someone shot at me?" Holding the cloth to his aching head, he looked around. Night. In the park. A stranger held the lantern that had blinded him, and a little way off lay a body. A servant in livery. In the distance, the park was coming alive with shouts and torches.

Stiebel asked, "Did you see him? Was it Eberau?"

Franz made a face. "No. I was late and hurrying to meet him when it happened."

"Hah!" said Stiebel grimly. "The coward was making sure of you. You'd be dead, if the brave Brandt hadn't pushed you down."

"But I told you. I was late. We were to meet in the dell below the Apollo temple. Eberau was bringing pistols. He would not have fired at an unarmed man."

Stiebel rose with a grunt. "Franz, I'm much too tired to argue with you. And here comes a whole crowd of people. I'm afraid it will be a long night. You'd best get up and prepare to tell your story."


Eberau slipped into the festival hall from the *orangerie*. The Mozarts were giving their performance. The court, in full attendance on their Highnesses, stood in two large groups, gathered around the Kurfürst at one end of the room, and his wife at the other. The little Mozart boy was playing a pianoforte whose keys had been hidden by a piece of velvet. His father and older sister accompanied him on their violins. When the musical piece ended, applause broke out.

Eberau used the moment to move through the crowd toward Elizabeth Augusta. Young Mozart hopped down from his stool and made his bow. He wore a fine little velvet suit with gold lacing and a small

powdered wig—exactly like a miniature courtier, except
that he jumped and clapped his hands in childish glee
and then scampered across the shimmering parquet
floor to climb on the lap of the Kurfürstin and throw his
arms around her neck.

*Lèse-majesté!*

The guests gasped, and Her Highness's somewhat
protuberant eyes bulged alarmingly. Mozart senior
started after his son, but Eberau was quicker. He slid to
a halt before Elizabeth Augusta and snatched the boy
from her lap. With a chuckle, he told the child, "My
boy, your eye for beauty is even better than your ear for
music. You dared what the rest of us only dream of."
Abandoning the prodigy to his father, he turned to his
sovereign and looked deeply into her startled eyes.
Placing a hand over his heart, he said fervently, "Oh,
that I had been that child, *Madame.*"

Elizabeth Augusta fluttered her fan. "He is a terrible
liar, Karl. I'm an old woman and well past such foolishness."

"Never!" Eberau sank on one knee and kissed her
hand. "You wound me, my goddess. I would die for
you. Nay, I would die happily to hear one kind word."

To his delight, she did not take her hand away. Her
smile was warm, but her teeth were bad. Eberau quickly lowered his eyes to the white bosom, most of which
rested invitingly before his eyes and swelled with every
breath. Tight lacing and low-cut dresses did wonders
for the full breasts of older women, he thought, and was
half tempted to lean forward and kiss them, when Her

I. J. Parker

Highness finally bethought herself and detached her hand. "Not here," she said softly.

Eberau thought he had not heard correctly. Flushing with pleasure, he murmured, "I shall become a hermit then," and rose with a long, warm look into her pale eyes. As he moved aside, his eyes met those of the lady's husband across the room. The Kurfürst glowered. Was the old goat jealous? Surely not. His ill temper was more likely directed at Elizabeth Augusta. Everyone knew there was no love lost between the two. Eberau placed his hand over his heart again and bowed toward His Highness. He planned to console the lonely lady.

At that moment, there was a disturbance. A servant entered and walked quickly to Baron von Moritz, who sat near Karl Theodor. He whispered to him, and Moritz turned to Karl Theodor, who started up, crying, "Shot? What does he mean: the fellow was shot?"

The room fell quiet. Eberau stepped behind Elizabeth Augusta's chair and watched, his heart pounding. The Kurfürst looked agitated, and questions buzzed among the guests like a swarm of angry bees. A lackey closed all the doors to the garden.

Elizabeth Augusta turned and pulled his sleeve. "What happened, Karl? Who was shot?"

"I don't know, *Madame*. Allow me to find out for you."

As he crossed the room, he heard the name Brandt and wondered who the devil Brandt was, and what had happened. There would be an investigation, and he would be kept in the palace all night.

He looked back at Elizabeth Augusta and saw her watching him. She smiled and nodded. The prize was his, but he must first play his cards well. Once he was in her bed, all would be accomplished.

Franz and Stiebel, both a little unsteady on their feet, walked to the palace and told their story to the local gendarmes and the Kurfürst's officials. Stiebel said he had attempted to prevent a duel and had followed Franz with the unfortunate Brandt, who knew the park better than he did. Franz admitted that he was to meet Freiherr von Eberau at midnight in an affair of honor.

They were told to wait.

Sometime later, Eberau was brought in to confront Franz. The major denied having made the assignation. This astonished Franz, who pressed him about the duel. Eberau admitted to having exchanged words with him the day before when he found him engaged in copulation with one of the actresses in broad daylight and in the palace garden.

"Instead of showing shame, he had the stomach to challenge me," he told his listeners. Hostile faces turned to Franz, who could not deny it and flushed guiltily.

"And did I not," continued Eberau, waving a finger at him, "inform you at the time that dueling is against the law here?"

"Yes, but—"

"Then clearly your tale must be a lie." Eberau turned to the officials. "I reprimanded him and the girl because the players are in my charge and it is my duty to watch over them. Her Highness is very strict about their morals. In any case, a man of my rank does not engage in duels over a French strumpet."

The officials nodded, and Eberau departed. Franz looked for help to Stiebel, but his friend merely compressed his lips and shook his head.

In the end, they let Franz and Stiebel go because a search of the park and gardens had turned up nothing, and Franz had no weapon. It was decided that the shot had come from the adjoining game preserve, where a thief or poacher had been careless, and thus Brandt's death was likely an unfortunate accident.

It was getting light when they left the palace: a gray and chilly day with clouds scudding overhead and an icy wind blowing. Franz saw that Stiebel looked exhausted. He was deathly pale, and his lips had a bluish tinge. Feeling guilty, Franz refrained from further protests and was silent on the way back. They were near the inn, when Stiebel suddenly stopped.

"Franz," he said, gasping a little, "I forgot. Augusta's lost."

"Augusta?" Franz stared at him.

"The dear girl followed us." Stiebel grasped Franz's arm for support. "She was on the coach from Mannheim." He took a few steadying breaths. "Yesterday. You must hurry and find her." He swayed a little and gasped again.

Clearly the events of the night had been too much for Stiebel. Franz said, "I'm sure you're mistaken, sir. Augusta would never travel so far alone. Come, lean on me; you need to rest. We shall order some hot food brought to our room."

Stiebel clutched his arm more desperately and stared around. The dark clouds scudded across the sky, and a gust of wind caught his hat. Franz caught it and returned it. Stiebel muttered, "I don't feel well. That apothecary and his sleeping potion. Find Eberau. Quick."

Franz feared that Stiebel's mind had become deranged. "Come, sir. You must rest."

Stiebel gave him a sorrowful look and fainted.

Colonel von Rodenstein received the summons from the Kurfürst in the early morning hours. He had gone home and was startled by its urgency. A short while later, he faced an atmosphere of suspicion. His Highness was with his private secretary, Freiherr von Moritz, who looked grave. The Kurfürst did not address Rodenstein. He did not even look at him.

Moritz asked him quite bluntly for information about the director of the court theater.

"Karl von Eberau? Her Highness suggested his appointment as theater director, and he attends court functions. I believe he has carried out his duties satisfactorily."

"What is his personal relationship with Her Highness?"

"Personal? What do you mean?" As he was her Master of Ceremony, it was appropriate that he should be consulted about those who served her, but this question was troubling. Rodenstein suspected that Karl Theodor knew of his own close "relationship" with Elizabeth Augusta.

"You may answer as specifically as you please," said Moritz coldly. His Highness drummed his fingers on the desk and stared at the wall.

Rodenstein knew Elisabeth Augusta was innocent of any affair with Eberau—so far—and he intended to warn her against the man. He said firmly, "Her Highness takes a lively interest in the theater. She may, from time to time consult with the director about the choice of plays and operas and about the performers. To the best of my knowledge, that is the extent of it."

It did nothing to dispel the frigid atmosphere. Rodenstein realized that Eberau—and by implication, Her Highness—were suspected of being somehow involved in the shooting.

Moritz eyed him thoughtfully for a moment, then pushed a piece of paper toward him. "Do these names mean anything to you?"

Rodenstein took up the paper. Someone had written "Cato - Spartacus - Minos - Ptolemy" across it and added a large question mark. He made a superhuman effort to remain calm and replaced the paper on the table. "Only as famous men among the ancients," he said in a reasonably steady voice and looked back at Moritz.

Moritz said nothing for several moments. Then he remarked, "It would be best if Her Highness avoided any connections that might be construed to be of a political nature. And you would be well advised to keep a close eye on her associates. I trust you take my meaning?"

It was a warning. Rodenstein bowed and wished he could accuse that villain Eberau and be rid of him once and for all.

The meeting ended in mutual stiff hostility. Rodenstein returned to his quarters and sent for Eberau.

Eberau had relaxed with a sigh of relief and a bottle of wine in one of the anterooms, when a lackey came to take him to the colonel. Muttering a curse under his breath, he straightened his shoulders and followed.

Rodenstein looked apoplectic, his face mottled and his double chin quivering. "What the devil have you been up to now, you cretin?" he ground out between clenched teeth after Eberau had closed the door and sat down near him.

Eberau said coldly, "I beg your pardon, sir, but I have no idea what you refer to. Having just assured the local authorities that I did not challenge that lieutenant to a duel over an actress, it would pain me to have to challenge you for calling me a cretin."

"Oh, give over," snarled Rodenstein. "Karl Theodor suspects you, me, and Her Highness of plotting something very nasty indeed. Surely even you comprehend the seriousness of that?" Rodenstein leaned closer and hissed, "I want the truth. Was it you who shot Brandt?"

Eberau said, "Of course not. How dare you, sir, when I have just said that I am innocent?"

"You, innocent?" The colonel gave a sharp bark of a laugh. "We both know better. I think you've finally gone mad. It's time we sever our relationship. You will stay away from me and from her. Let people think that I've taken umbrage at your tasteless flirtation."

Eberau was furious but took satisfaction from the knowledge that he was close to success with the lady. The great man was about to lose his place as favorite. He shrugged and looked bored. "As you wish."

Rodenstein's face mottled again. "You're very cool. I must warn you that you are in very hot water and may be arrested. My advice is to go away instantly. Go to Italy. Let it be known that you wish to see the antiquities and study the opera there."

Eberau raised a brow. "Are you serious?"

"Very serious. If you don't . . ." Rodenstein let his voice trail off.

Eberau almost laughed. So the fat bastard was jealous enough to try to frighten him away. "Aren't you a little presumptuous?"

Rodenstein got to his feet. "Good day to you."

Eberau did not bother to reply or to bow. He got up and left, slamming the door behind him.

His anger carried him outside where he saw preparations for the court's return to Mannheim. It reminded him of some small problems before he, too, could leave to pay assiduous court to Elizabeth Augusta.

There was the matter of his rifle in its hiding place. It was not safe to collect it and he decided to leave it behind.

The other dilemma was more complicated. The girl at his house must be got rid of quickly. Her condition made it unlikely that she would remember much, and Desirée could be bought off. It would cost him dearly, but he would soon have more wealth than he ever imagined. She was a very good liar—and so was he.

With the help of two of the inn's servants, they got Stiebel upstairs and into bed, where he regained his senses. Franz loosened his collar and offered to send for a glass of port.

Stiebel, his eyes closed, shook his head and clutched his chest.

"What is wrong, sir? Are you in pain?" Foolish question. Remorse struck like a sledgehammer. "Why did you need an apothecary?" Franz asked belatedly.

Stiebel compressed his lips and shook his head again. His wig had slipped. Franz took it off and looked for Stiebel's night cap. His hands were shaking. "I'll send for a doctor," he muttered.

Stiebel looked shrunken, like a child with an old man's head, or rather like a dying dwarf. "Just a rest," he breathed. "Don't fuss."

Franz ran for the doctor.

Downstairs, the innkeeper told him that Stiebel had collapsed the evening before and that they had sent for the apothecary.

Panic took hold of Franz. "Who's the best doctor in Schwetzingen? Run and get him! Hurry! I think my friend's dying." The innkeeper gaped, and Franz cursed, searched his pocket, and pressed a *taler* into the man's hand.

Upstairs, he undressed Stiebel as best he could, then sat beside him, looking at the drawn features, watching for every slightest breath. Stiebel seemed asleep, but Franz feared that such a sleep might pass imperceptibly into death, into the great void. He thought of praying, but God had turned his back on him long ago at Freiberg. That was almost a year ago now—a year in which he had found himself again because of Stiebel. If Stiebel died, he would be truly alone in the world.

There was a knock on the door. The innkeeper had returned in a surprisingly short time. The man with him was Dr. Mai, who nodded to a startled Franz and went past him to Stiebel, taking his pulse and asking questions, which Stiebel, awake again, answered in a weak voice. When the doctor turned to Franz, he looked grave.

"There is little I can do," he said in a low voice. "The night's excitement upset an already dangerously weak condition. Your friend is not a young man any longer. I'm told that both of you were involved in the shooting last night?" He eyed Franz's bloody hair.

"He saved my life. I think he must have run all the way." Franz looked away, ashamed of his tears. "And then they kept us all night, asking questions. Some foolish apothecary had given him a sleeping draft, but I didn't know. It's all my fault. What will I do?" The last almost sounded like a wail.

Mai looked confused. He came to inspect Franz's head. "That is just a superficial cut. Any vertigo?" he asked. "Or vomiting?"

"No, no. I'm not hurt. I only fell and cut my scalp a little. But what about my friend?"

"The constitution weakens with age. Much like a flame consuming the candle. There is little to be done except to have him rest. May I ask what happened?"

"Someone fired a gun in the palace gardens and killed one of the servants. My friend thinks the bullet was meant for me, but the police say it was a poacher. The Kurfürst's game preserve adjoins the garden just there." Franz looked at Stiebel, who was watching them from the bed. The mention of the candle reminded him of the old baron. He looked at Mai. "Are you still certain that the baron died of old age?" he asked.

Mai glanced at Stiebel. "We don't die of old age. It is some critical part of the body's engine that wears out."

"But you still have no suspicion that it might have been murder?" Franz persisted. "We were told that the poor old gentleman had suffered a bruised arm and had upset his glass. The door to his room gives onto the terrace and was unlocked."

Mai sighed. "Why would anyone murder Winkelhausen?"

"Perhaps because he suspected someone. He is said to have been very loyal to His Highness."

Mai stiffened. "If this is another attempt to blacken Her Highness's reputation in order to discredit her with her husband, you're addressing the wrong man. I am Her Highness's personal physician."

From the bed came the sound of a slight cough. Stiebel waved the doctor closer. "Not Her Highness," he said in a faint voice. "But someone near her . . . or who expects to be . . ."

Mai relaxed a little. "That would include me."

Stiebel's lip twitched. "We did consider it."

Mai sat down abruptly on Franz's chair. "I cannot believe it. This . . . shooting last night, do you think that was part of . . . some plot against the Kurfürst?"

Stiebel nodded. "We think so. But I'm very tired and know little. If you wish to serve Her Highness, speak to *Herr* Moritz." He closed his eyes.

The doctor rose. "I can hardly credit it," he said uncertainly, then turned to go. At the door, he paused. "He must rest at all costs. Any more activity or excitement will be certain death. I'll have the apothecary send some calming drafts. After that he's in God's hands."

# 20

# Matters of the Heart

*What is the life of man? Is it not to shift from side to side?—from sorrow to sorrow?—to button up one cause of vexation!—and unbutton another!*

Laurence Sterne, *Tristram Shandy*

Frau von Langsdorff poured out her grievances and sufferings to Jakob Seutter as the carriage rushed through the rain toward Schwetzingen.

"There I was, hardly alive, and Augusta left me! She didn't even tell me. The inn's maid brought the message with a bowl of pottage. Dreadful food—not that I could eat a morsel. I ask you, sir, is there anything more painful to a mother's heart than to find herself abandoned by her children? Without money in a strange place—fighting for her life?"

Seutter grunted. He was past caring about anything but Augusta's safety and no longer capable of even common courtesy to the woman he held responsible for what had happened.

He and Max had traveled without resting the whole way from Lindau, a feat that could only be accomplished by pouring gold into innumerable outstretched hands, paying extra for couriers to ride ahead between stages to have fresh horses and a new post-boy ready every 15 miles, paying heavy bribes to snatch away promised teams from other travelers, buying a new carriage rather than having his own repaired when an axle broke, and bribing local officials whenever they threatened to slow down his progress.

Max had proved useful in these transactions, though Seutter knew well that some of the gold found its way into Max's pockets. Seutter did not like Max. He had disliked him all along and finally, irritated past tolerance by Max's continuous claims of being devoted to serving him, countered that he must be burdened with a very bad conscience. This had the astonishing effect of a confession by Max that he had done things he was sorry for but had become a new man who hoped to atone for his mistakes. Seutter suspected that Max had attacked Franz and befriended the Langsdorff women for some evil purpose. But the fellow seemed at least sincere in his avowed devotion to Augusta and anger at her foolish mother.

The rumors that the women had been raped were laid to rest by the gendarmes in Heidelberg. Seutter's love for Augusta had made him imagine the worst even when his good sense told him that people had morbid or prurient imaginations.

When they found Frau von Langsdorff in Mannheim, her face was no longer swollen, but she was appallingly bruised and looked a fright. She had made such a nuisance of herself that the innkeeper had been about to show her the door. He complained bitterly until Seutter paid him an exorbitant sum to release her from debts she had incurred by ordering special delicacies and sending the inn's servants on errands.

In spite of her pitiful condition, their meeting was awkward. She was happy to see Max, calling him her hero and savior. To Seutter she said merely, "I must say, Herr Seutter, that you have done the Christian thing in coming to the rescue of a fellow citizen."

He ignored this and asked, "Where is your daughter?"

"Oh, don't speak to me about that girl! She's run off to Schwetzingen to be with her brother, leaving her poor mother at death's door."

"That's not like Augusta. When did she leave?"

When she told him, Seutter was too angry to speak more than a few words to her on the way to Schwetzingen.


The door to the sick girl's room was locked. Desirée put her ear to the key hole. Silence.

She knocked and called out, but there was no reply. This worried her, but she did not dare go for help. In the end, she gathered all the keys in the house and tried them, one by one, until the lock clicked open.

The lieutenant's little sister was curled up stark naked on the bed, and the room stank of vomit. God only knew what the devil had done to her. Desirée was sick to death of his perversions and cruel whippings for the empty promises of a good part. She had hoped to attract a wealthy man who would marry her, or at least keep her in luxury, but it no longer seemed worth the sacrifices. Besides, she doubted he would keep his word.

"*Cochon!*"

She spat, then bent over the girl. At least she was still breathing. Desirée shook her by the shoulder but got only a moan of protest. Then she saw the brown bottle and the empty glass on the bedside table.

A sniff told her what the bottle contained. He had given the girl laudanum to put her to sleep so he could have his way with her, and the girl had thrown it up all over him. Good for her! But that meant he would be back to finish what he had started, and then it would be all over with the poor thing. Girls like her took the loss of their virginity very hard.

Desirée sat down—carefully, for the devil had whipped her buttocks raw—and pondered what to do.

In the end pity for the girl overcame her self-interest. She gathered the clothes, and tried to wake her, but the girl muttered and pushed her hands away. Desirée spoke soothingly and persisted. She got stockings on her legs, and tugged the petticoat up to her waist.

Hardest were the shift and dress. For this Desirée had to raise her, and she kept slipping from her grasp.

Desirée fell to admonishing her in French. Her fear made her eloquent, and finally the girl opened her eyes and asked hoarsely, "What?"

"*Mademoiselle, écoutez! Il faut s'enfuir vite.*"

"Leave me alone."

"*Parbleu!*" Desirée shook her. "Zere is danger," she managed in German. "You and me—we run, escape. *Vous comprenez? Ah, mon Dieu, quelle bêtise!*"

The girl must have understood something for she let herself be dressed, but when Desirée had slipped the ugly shoes on her feet, she fell back on the bed. It took another struggle to get her up and walking. A nightmarish descent of the stairs followed. She kept sitting down. In the end Desirée pulled her the rest of the way by her feet.

At that point, Desirée considered the sick girl in desperation. She could not walk and, as she was taller and heavier than the petite Desirée, she could not be carried.

A decision was taken from her, for there was the sound of a key in the front door.


Franz sat beside Stiebel's bed and felt wretched. Where was the justice in this world? The person who had saved him from himself now lay near death's door because of him.

The light was dim in the room, and gusts of rain slashed at the window. Stiebel lay so pale and still in his bed, with his eyes closed and his breathing so shallow that it was imperceptible, and Franz wondered if he was dead. At one point, he flung himself across Stiebel's body, racked with grief, but Stiebel opened his eyes and asked, "Have you found your sister?"

Franz retreated to his chair, wiped away the tears, and smiled with relief. "No, sir. Not yet. I'll ask downstairs later."

Stiebel's pale face flushed. He glared. "Why aren't you out turning the town upside down for her? For God's sake, man, she's your sister."

Franz stammered, "Why, I . . . I thought to sit with you, sir."

Stiebel struggled upright, pressed a hand to his heart, and gasped, "I don't know you any more, Franz, and I don't like who you've become. You don't have a heart in your body. Leave me. I'm weary to death of you."

Franz got up. "What have I done? What would you have me do, sir?" he asked helplessly.

Stiebel fell back, exhausted by the outburst. "Search your heart. If you can find it."

When Eberau realized that the two women had been about to walk out of his house, he slammed the door behind him and locked it. "What the devil are you up to now?" he snarled at Desirée.

Desirée raised her chin. "*Elle est trés malade. Il y'a grand besoin d'un médecin.*"

"Oh no, you don't," he snapped, shoving her aside and sweeping up an unresisting Augusta in his arms to take her back upstairs. He managed two steps, but Desirée pulled him back, and he stumbled. Augusta slid from his arms as he tried to keep from falling. In a fury he turned on Desirée, who saw his face and ran. Augusta called out weakly for him to stop.

He did—in the kitchen, when common sense returned and told him that he was making things worse. By then, Desirée's nose poured blood from a vicious slap.

"Wash your face and keep your mouth shut," he told the girl more calmly. "I decide what will be done. If you obey me, this is yours." He pulled a purse from his coat and emptied it on the kitchen table. Desirée's eyes grew large when she saw how much gold there was. "And you get twice that much again in Mannheim, if all goes well. If you don't obey, then you get nothing and you'll never work again. So what is it going to be, my girl?"

Desirée counted the money, then nodded.

When he returned to the hall, he saw Augusta struggling to her feet. She looked at him fearfully. Why, oh why, did fate put such obstacles in his way?

"Forgive me, my dear," he said smoothly, "for frightening you, but I lost my temper when she caused me to drop you. Are you hurt?"

She shook her head. "I want to leave," she said. Her voice was hoarse and weak. "I don't know you, and I don't know this house."

He breathed a small sigh of relief. If she did not remember him, then all was not lost. "Don't be afraid. Desirée always makes a big outcry because she knows I'll pay extra when she does. French maids are born actresses." That was true enough, truer than this girl knew.

She stared at him uncertainly. "I want to leave. Please let me go."

He raised both hands in a gesture of defeat. "But of course, if you wish it. Only there's a freezing rain outside. It will be the death of you." He gestured at his wet cloak.

She shuddered and swayed a little on her feet.

"Come, I'll light the fire in the salon, and Desirée will heat some milk and honey for your throat. Meanwhile, I'll put the horses to the carriage. It's covered and will carry you back to the inn dryly and quickly."

He saw her weaken and was careful not to touch her but just to open the door to the salon. She walked in unsteadily and sat while he busied himself lighting a spill and holding it to the kindling in the small fireplace.


Outside their room, Stiebel's words rang in Franz's head.

*Leave my sight!*

*Search your heart!*

Had Stiebel been in his right mind? He was very sick. And now Franz was forbidden to care for him, no matter how much he longed to repay past kindness.

Perhaps Stiebel had fired him.

For long minutes, Franz looked at the closed door, wanting to go back, to kneel beside the bed and ask again how he had offended.

Stiebel had been strangely insistent about Augusta. Franz still did not believe that she was here, but in the end, he turned and went out into the rain to ask the grooms and stable boys who dealt with post coaches.

They told him a young woman had indeed got off the stage two days ago but she had been met by a gentleman with a carriage. Franz thanked them and started to leave.

That was when the youngest of the stable boys, a filthy urchin with a dripping nose, piped up, "It were that Baron Eberau what took her. I seen 'em."

Franz felt his heart stop. It could not be, must not be. Not that man! Not the one who had vented his rage on Desirée and who hated him enough to want to kill him. His voice strangely distant in his ears, he asked, "Where does he live?"

They told him, and he hurried back to their room. He was very quiet, but Stiebel was asleep, and Franz found his sword and left.

As he trudged through the rain to Eberau's house, his leg ached and the roadway was slippery with mud. Fear for Augusta—he no longer doubted that it was she—and hot fury filled his heart. He plodded on, memories crowding in of happier childhood years together and of Augusta caring for him tenderly after his attack. He was ashamed. He had thought only of himself and never of his sister's hardship.

The shame fueled his fury. Franz had allowed Eberau to mock him and manipulate him. He had accepted this because he was crippled, unfit, less of a man.

But Eberau had overreached himself when he took Augusta to avenge himself on her brother for taking his woman.

He would die for what he had done—and surely he had done it by now.

He slowed when he saw the house. Unlike Stiebel, he did not think it was empty. There was smoke coming from its chimney, and a carriage had left fresh tracks in the rain-soaked drive. He compressed his lips and put his hand on his sword.

He was near the house when a covered chaise came from a nearby farm and pulled up at the door. Franz ducked behind a large shrub.

The driver jumped down and tied the reins to a post. It was Eberau, great-coated but unmistakable. He took the steps in two strides and disappeared inside.

Franz emerged from cover and walked as quickly as he could to the house, climbing the steps more slowly because of his leg. Leaving his cane, he drew his sword, and opened the door on a small entrance hall.

Stairs to the upper floor faced him. To his left an open door led into a parlor. Eberau was there, bending over a woman on the settee. He turned his head. "What the hell—?"

The woman was Augusta. A very pale Augusta with frightened eyes.

Franz stumbled forward, raised his sword. "Leave her alone, you swine!"

Eberau straightened, perfectly in control again. "Why, Lieutenant! How convenient! I was about to drive your sister back to the inn. Do put that sword away."

Augusta struggled up. "Franz?" She seemed barely able to stand.

"I'm going to kill you for what you did to her," Franz said, lunging toward his enemy.

Augusta cried out, and Desirée appeared. She shouted, "*Non! Arrêtez. mon brave!*"

Impossible. Franz's gorge rose at the thought that this animal had spent his days and nights with both women, subjecting them to God knew what torment and degradation. Oh, if only he could move as well as Eberau, who was backing away, dodging Franz's blade, his hands raised beseechingly while he shouted something about being innocent.

Franz ignored it and concentrated on catching the other man so he could deal the fatal blow. He pushed forward, turning only on his good leg and using the other as little as possible until he had driven Eberau into a corner.

But before he could strike, Desirée flung herself at him, grasping his arm, and jerking him off balance. Flailing madly, he fell. Eberau slipped past with a grunted "*Merçi, ma petite,*" and fled.

Cursing Desirée, Franz stumbled to his feet, looking wildly about. Both girls now tried to restrain him and a struggle resulted in more delays. Finally, he pushed the

French girl away roughly and moved Augusta out of his way. Hobbling back out into the hallway, pursued by pleading females, he saw Eberau coming back down the stairs with a leather satchel in one hand and the naked blade of his sword in the other. Franz blocked his way at the bottom of the stairs.

The women cried out and fled, Augusta back into the parlor and Desirée through the front door, leaving it open behind her.

Eberau stopped on the stairs. He looked desperate. "Stand aside," he warned, "or you'll never walk again."

"You're not leaving alive," Franz replied with deadly calm.

There was the merest spark of uncertainty in the other man's eyes as he glanced past Franz through the open door. "Look, Langsdorff," he said, suddenly conciliatory, "you made a mistake. I found your sister lost and very ill and gave her shelter until you could be found."

Franz laughed bitterly. "If you think I believe that, you must be a fool besides a villain. Come down and fight.

Eberau warned again, "Don't make me kill you. I have witnesses that you forced this quarrel on me."

"I don't give a damn. You're a murderer, and this time you won't get away."

"You're mad."

"You killed Captain von Loe at Freiberg and his father a few days ago in his bed. You tried to kill me, and you intend to kill the Kurfürst. If you think you're safe, you didn't reckon with me. I don't care what happens to me as long as I kill you. Come on! You still owe me a duel."

There was a moment's silence. Then Eberau dropped the satchel and vaulted down the steps, his face contorted with rage, the point of his sword aimed at Franz's chest. Franz twisted aside, but the attack had been too sudden, and his bad knee buckled. He staggered and gasped with pain.

Before he could recover, Eberau's sword flashed toward his belly. Franz parried at the last moment and moved a step back. Eberau attacked again in an instant. They were so close in the confined space that their moves could not follow the rules of fencing. Each man was out to kill the other as quickly as possible. Eberau drove his blade forward and kicked at Franz's crippled knee. He missed the knee, and Franz parried, then lunged, and their swords locked. Eberau gave Franz a vicious kick in the stomach to separate the blades. Stumbling back against the wall, Franz could not catch his breath. He gagged and doubled over just as Eberau came again. At the last moment, he found a remnant of strength to push himself away from the wall and forward into the coming sword.

It was surely suicide, but he would not be skewered like some collector's butterfly or rare insect; he would die fighting like a man.

Perhaps because his knee put him off balance, the blade just missed him, and the force of Eberau's attack drove his sword deep into the doorjamb where it stuck fast.

Franz turned, still clutching the red hot pain in his belly with one hand. Eberau was pulling and twisting his weapon, and the blade broke near the hilt. He dropped what was left, and stood, waiting for the *coup de grace*.

Franz took a ragged breath and gathered his unwilling muscles. Some primal thrill caused him to stretch out the moment, to move in slowly and to put the tip of his blade to the soft underside of Eberau's chin—just close enough to cause a thin line of blood to appear.

Sweat beaded Eberau's face. Somewhere in the room beyond, Augusta sobbed.

Franz looked into his enemy's eyes and saw his fear. His triumph was complete. The monster was about to die. And Eberau no doubt saw his death in Franz's eyes, just as had all the Prussian soldiers.

The gloating words on Franz's lips died unspoken. Eberau's eyes had become those of the Prussian Captain on *Trois Croix*, and of the captain's faithful sergeant, of every man Franz had killed that day in close combat. That look in their eyes, the recognition of death as they looked into his own eyes, struck horror into his soul.

He let his blade drop and stepped back, sickened. "Go," he said, his voice hoarse, "go and be damned!"

Eberau blinked, then swallowed and ducked past Franz. Snatching up his satchel, he dashed out the door.

It poured steadily when Jakob Seutter arrived in Schwetzingen. He was the first out of the coach, leaving Augusta's mother to fend for herself while he splashed through the puddles to the inn and asked for Franz von Langsdorff. A servant told him that the lieutenant had just left but that his companion was sick in bed upstairs.

Stiebel's appearance shocked Seutter profoundly. He found him dozing, looking shockingly shrunken and senile without the customary wig. As anxious as Seutter was about Augusta, he tiptoed to the bedstead and asked softly, "My dear friend, are you awake?"

To his relief, Stiebel opened his eyes and looked instantly more animated. "Jakob! Of all that's wonderful! You find me sadly out of sorts, I'm afraid."

Indeed, his voice was weak and he did not seem to have the strength to raise himself. "You're sorely needed. The boy's gone to look for his sister, but . . . well, he's young." He took Jakob's hand, and pulled him down on the chair beside his bed. "You must find the young Augusta, poor girl. I fear she's tangled up in this infernal mystery of ours. A very unscrupulous man by the name of Eberau may have got hold of her." He told Jakob of the recent events and his suspicions, pausing frequently to gasp for breath. Eventually, he stopped in utter exhaustion.

Seutter, sickened by what he had learned, looked at the gray face on the pillow and at the gray rain outside the window. He did not think it was possible to feel sadder than he did just then. To Stiebel, he said with false cheer, "I shall take care of everything. You must rest as the doctor said and leave this to me. Augusta and I are betrothed. It was her wish." He paused. "At least that was our understanding in Lindau. In any case and always respecting her own wishes, her welfare is my charge."

Stiebel smiled very sweetly. "Bless me," he murmured, "what joyous news!" and fell asleep.

Seutter ran back downstairs, where he found that Max had helped Frau von Langsdorff out of the coach, leaving her ankle-deep in the mud. He was leading the tired horses off toward the stables.

"Max," Seutter called, "let the grooms take care of that. I need you."

"Just what I told him," wailed Frau von Langsdorff. "Really, I don't know what's come over Max. He used to be so accommodating, but here he leaves me standing outside in the rain and mire with not so much as an arm to lean on when I'm in delicate health." She sniffled and raised her skirt. "I shall need new shoes."

Seutter clapped on his hat and eyed her coldly. "Sorry, madam. Max and I must look for Augusta. She's not here. Pray, go inside and wait." She opened her mouth to protest. He ignored her and said, "Tell them to put the charges for rooms and stabling on my account."

Seutter had hoped that the confused tale about murder and mayhem was due to his old friend's illness. But when one of the grooms confirmed that Augusta's brother had gone to look for her at Baron Eberau's house, his heart sank.

He and Max started to walk, quickly soaked to the skin by the cold rain. Max was glum and said, "What if she's been taken away from here in that carriage?"

The thought demoralized Seutter. "No! Not that. She's here, I feel it. She must be. Look, you're younger. Run ahead."

Max departed at a trot, leaving Seutter a measure of privacy. If his girl had been carried off to some other town, why then the whole wide world might hide her forever from him. And if she was here, well then things were bad enough. He bowed his head, and the rain mingled with the first tears he had shed since the loss of his wife and child some fifteen years before.

As Max turned down the rutted private lane, he nearly collided with a very pretty young woman in a rain-soaked blue silk gown. She was wild-eyed and babbled at him in a foreign tongue. He kept shaking his head and she stamped her dainty foot and screamed at him. It was hopeless until he asked, "Augusta?" She nodded vigorously then and pointed over her shoulder, adding another stream of gibberish. Max started running.

The house looked unoccupied, its shutters closed, but a covered chaise with a pair of horses waited at the door. It was just the sort of house where a villain might hide away his angel—and just the sort of vehicle he would carry her away in. But Max would rescue her. As he ran, he imagined her eyes shining up at him and her arms wrapping themselves gratefully around his manly neck.

A man came from the house, tossed a travel case into the chaise, took the reins, and jumped in.

Franz stopped. Oho! What was Koehl doing here? Koehl, the hateful bastard who had ordered him to kill Augusta's brother?

The chaise started rolling.

"Wait!" shouted Max and started running again.

Koehl ignored him and whipped up the horses.

If Augusta was in the carriage and that bastard Koehl was taking her away, the only chance of saving her was to stop the chaise now.

As the vehicle flew toward him, Max did not jump clear but instead flung himself at the horse on the left and clung to its halter, yelling to Koehl to stop. Koehl, his face distorted with anger, used his whip. The horse reared, then both animals shied. Max was lifted off the ground and clung on for dear life as they careened down the lane and the frightened animal tried to shake him loose. Koehl bawled curses and snapped the whip at their backs and at Max. Max clutched the animal's neck with both arms and swung his legs toward the carriage pole. He meant to get enough purchase to climb on the animal's back. He had almost managed it and murmured Augusta's name to give himself courage when his wet hands slipped, and he fell under the flying hooves.

Seutter heard the sounds of shying horses and shouting and started to run. The chaise appeared from the lane at a furious pace, almost tipping over as the driver took the turn. Seutter jumped aside and rushed down the lane.

He saw the shuttered house ahead, its door open. And he saw the motionless figure lying across the muddy ruts left by the chaise. A woman in blue was bent over it. His heart leaped, but she was a stranger. The lifeless body belonged to Max.

He knelt and checked briefly the crushed skull and the twisted limbs, then got to his feet. "He's dead," he said heavily.

He heard a girl's voice calling "Jakob" and looked up. In the open doorway of the house stood Franz, leaning heavily against the jamb, but Seutter's eyes were on Augusta, who came toward him with faltering steps, her arms out-stretched.

When they were closer, he could see that she was ill, her eyes feverishly bright, and her voice weak. "Jakob," she said, "oh, Jakob. You came. Oh, you came!" There was a world of love in her words, and if she gave a small sob, he thought it was from joy. His heart melted. He opened his arms, and she tumbled into them, clutching him fiercely.

# 21

# What Price Happiness?

*. . . what a thing is the heart of man! . . . there would be far less suffering among mankind , if men—and God knows why they are made that way—did not use their imagination so assiduously to recall the memory of past sorrow, instead of bearing their present lot with equanimity.*

Johann Wolfgang von Goethe, *The Sorrows of Young Werther*

Franz knocked softly and entered when he heard a robust "Come."

Jakob Seutter sat at the small desk of his room, writing into a notebook.

"I wonder, sir," murmured Franz, shifting his weight awkwardly, "if I might trouble you for just a moment?"

Seutter got up and came, his hand outstretched. "My dear Franz, nothing could please me more. I have just finished with the sad business of Max's funeral. How fares Augusta today?"

They shook hands. "She's much improved, sir. We are greatly—no, immensely—in your debt. In every way." Franz stood, clenching and unclenching his hands and avoiding Seutter's eyes. "I've come to . . . to express our gratitude."

"Not at all." Seutter's voice had cooled a little. "I trust my friend Stiebel is also on the mend?"

Franz glanced at Seutter's face but saw nothing there beyond polite interest. "As to that, sir, I'd hoped you could tell me. I haven't . . . it seemed better not to . . . I haven't seen him since midday yesterday, sir."

"Bless my soul." Seutter's eyebrows shot up. "Well, I did speak to him last night to give him the good news about Augusta. He seemed quite strengthened by it."

"I'm very glad to hear it." A silence fell. Franz glanced helplessly around the room and shuffled his feet. His knee still ached abominably this morning, making it even harder to find the right words. "I . . . I . . . also c-came t-to—" He gulped down the stutter, and enunciated the words slowly and clearly. "I must apologize to you, sir, for what I said in Lindau. I spoke in haste, and I was quite wrong—I see that now and should have seen it long ago. It was inexcusable, of course, and Doktor Stiebel told me so, only I didn't listen and, like a fool, I denied my sister the right to make her wishes known." He gulped and shifted his weight, leaning on his cane more heavily before plunging on. "I've spoken to Augusta, both last night and again this morning, and

I'm persuaded that she knows her own mind. And so I came to say that I was wrong, sir, and that I'm truly sorry."

Seutter's face broke into a smile. "God love you, Franz." He put a large, warm hand on Franz's shoulder. "It's devilish hard to know what to do for others sometimes," he said. "I worry a good deal myself. There's the matter of poor Max, but never mind. In the end you did what you could for Augusta, and I honor you for that. As for the other, well, you thought I was too old for your sister, and so I am. But she will not have it so. Truth to tell, she makes me the happiest man alive, and I'll make it my life's work to love and care for her as she deserves." He cleared his throat, then gestured toward a chair. "But come, you mustn't stand there. Sit and rest your leg."

Franz did so gratefully and glanced at the window. It rained still quite heavily. The droplets trailing down the panes were like tears. Rain always made his knee much more painful. He thought of Augusta, who was feverish and uncomfortable but filled with a quiet happiness. He said, "Indeed, Augusta deserves much love and care. She's had little enough of it from her mother and me." He hung his head. "She's been good enough to forgive me."

Seutter beamed. "She's a generous girl, isn't she? I'm truly blessed that she should look with favor on an old, clumsy, common fellow like me." He gave a little shamefaced laugh. "What a fine day this is: my Augusta's mending, her brother tells me he'll give us his blessings, and with God's help my friend Stiebel will get better soon. We shall all travel home together. Oh, how I miss home!"

Sorrow settled over Franz like a suffocating black cloth. He, too, longed for his lake, but he would miss Stiebel even more. "As to that, sir, I shall stay here. Mama has borrowed money that must be paid back, and I had hopes of giving Augusta something for a dowry. I'm afraid the house in Fischergasse must be sold. I regret very much that we cannot . . . that is, my father would have wished a dowry . . . oh, the devil, sir . . . we're as poor as church mice, but you knew that. Only we're much poorer now."

Seutter shuffled through the papers on the desk and came up with one. "No need to sell the house. You may pay back the loan as you can, and it shall be Augusta's dowry."

Franz stared at the papers his mother had signed. "I don't understand. How did you come by these?"

Seutter chuckled. "I didn't like what the other fellow planned to do, so I bought the loan. I trust Stiebel pays you enough to save a little? There's no hurry, no hurry at all. And someday soon, when you're an advocate yourself, you may find this a very small burden indeed. I assure you, Augusta and I shall not press you, and the interest is exceeding low."

Franz said dully, "You're very kind, but Doktor Stiebel has dismissed me. I shall not be going home." He laid the loan papers back on the desk and stumbled to his feet. In a moment he would be blubbering like a child. Grasping his cane, he said quickly, "Thank you, sir, for your generosity and your affection for my sister," and made for the door.

Seutter came after him. "Wait, Franz—I may call you that, I hope, and you must call me Jakob. Surely you cannot think to leave my friend Stiebel. It would break his heart. I know he never meant to dismiss you."

Franz turned away his face and said thickly, "I dare not go to him. If I should upset him again, it might be his death."

"Well then, let me smooth the way, and I shall tell you when the time is right. Now take back the paper. I insist."

Eberau passed through Schwetzingen without stopping— a man pursued by furies. Fate had turned against him: the cripple had won, his sister was likely to lay charges against him, Max had found him and, if he had survived the fall under the carriage, he could implicate him in robbery and attempted murder.

But eventually his old bravado resurfaced from this crushing tide of retribution, and he considered his position more calmly. There was no proof of anything he had done, and so it would be their word against his. And Desirée would support him. She was paid heavily for her testimonial.

He reached his house in Mannheim exhausted, dismissed his servants, and fell into bed.

The very next morning brought good news, a double dose, in fact. The first letter was from the palace and confirmed his position as director of the court theater for another year with a raise in salary. The second was a note on thick cream-colored paper, sealed with the private seal of Elizabeth Augusta. It was short but in her own hand, and Eberau devoured the words:

"If he will come to the small eastern entrance on the garden side one hour past midnight, he will be met by my woman of the chamber. E.A."

Eberau kissed the note, not lustfully—though he gave a passing thought to his performance—but greedily, for it stood for titles, legitimate at last, and estates better than those of his father and equal to the hated Rodenstein's. And perhaps someday there might even be power.

Franz approached Stiebel's door fearfully. What if Seutter was wrong? What if Stiebel got angry again and the mere sight of Franz brought on a fatal fit?

He stood there for a while, stared at by a maid with an armful of linens, and then knocked softly.

"Who is it?" came Stiebel's voice. He sounded stronger, and Franz took courage.

"It's Franz, sir."

"Well, come in then."

Franz opened the door and peered toward the bed. Stiebel was sitting up. He was in his nightshirt and wore a night cap but looked more like himself, his eyes bright but unsmiling.

"I hope I see you better, sir," Franz offered.

"Come in and close the door. Where've you been all night?" Stiebel demanded. "I thought you'd fallen into more mischief."

"I . . . I slept outside the door, sir."

"You what?"

"You told me to go away."

"Humph." Stiebel frowned. "And since when do you do what I tell you?"

"By your leave, sir, I strive to do what you say. I . . . I thought you were angry."

Stiebel had the grace to blush. "And so I was. Have you made your peace with your sister?"

"Yes, sir, and also with Jakob Seutter."

"Good. Now help me into my clothes. I want to eat my breakfast like a Christian."

Eberau took great pains with his appearance on the night of his triumph. He ordered a bath to be got ready, had his manservant shave him twice, both his face and his head, so that no unseemly and uncomfortable stubble should remain, then selected his finest, lavender-scented and lace-trimmed shirt and his most flattering coat and breeches. Wearing his cocked hat and a caped cloak, he left for the palace shortly after midnight.

He was halfway down the street from his house, when it struck him that what he was about to do might hold some danger. True, he had skirted close to the abyss so many times that it seemed he had always been preserved by fate for some great purpose—the glorious future he was embarked on this night—but caution prevailed. He returned to his house to get a loaded pistol and shove it into the pocket of his coat. Then he set out again.

It was a dark, overcast, and chilly, but thoughts of the coming affair warmed his blood. He hoped his sexual powers would not fail him. The middle-aged and fat Elisabeth Augusta was quite a different proposition from the lithe young actresses and dancers he had fucked, but he had dined on oysters and sweetbreads and, if matters got too discouraging, he would close his eyes and imagine . . . what? . . . the cripple's little virginal sister beneath him.

He found the door easily, a small one used by servants only. No matter, his was a visit that required sacrifices. But it was not a lady-in-waiting or maidservant who stood there in the dark, but a man, who immediately murmured a warning not to speak. Eberau's hand felt for the pistol in his pocket. But the fellow had used his name and so he said nothing and followed him.

The darkness inside was dense, and his guide had only a shuttered lantern which cast a vague spot of light on floors and stairs. They climbed upward, traversed a number of small unlit rooms, then climbed again, all of it in silence. Eberau, who was familiar with the location of Elisabeth Augusta's apartments, was content that he was being taken there. Eventually, the doors his companion opened and closed for him became more ornate and the floors changed to inlaid parquet. When they entered a room that was lit with candles in sconces, he recognized it as Elisabeth Augusta's private study because he had reported to her here about the theater. She took an avid interest in the female performers because of her husband's past and current liaisons.

The candles flickered in the draft from the door and cast a warm glow over dusky rose silk draperies, gilded chairs, and a Savonnerie carpet adorned with wreaths of roses and blue ribbons. When Eberau turned to see who his guide had been, the other had already slipped from the room.

He stood alone for a minute or two and waited. Then he fixed his eyes on the double doors leading to the next room, which he took to be Elizabeth Augusta's bed chamber, or perhaps her private sitting room. He cleared his throat. When nothing happened, he took off his hat and cloak, laying both across a chair beside the doors. Then he knocked, very softly.

A female voice called, "Come."

He depressed the handle and opened the door into the bed chamber—and what a bed chamber! It was large enough to contain an ordinary man's house. A gilded and carved bed dominated it, its canopy and hangings of white silk with golden embroideries of birds, flowers, and butterflies. An embroidered scene of a shepherd and shepherdess hung at its head, and the cover was of deep blue velvet trimmed in gold. This was turned back invitingly to show white lace-trimmed linens covering the plumpest of pillows and featherbeds. Eberau swallowed hard: the bed of a sovereign was the stage to start his climb to power. He turned his head to look at the woman of his dreams.

Elisabeth Augusta was *en negligee*, seated at a small, inlaid desk with her back to him. Otherwise the room was empty, its drapes drawn and its several white and gilded doors closed.

Eberau closed the doors softly behind him. He took a few quick steps toward Elisabeth Augusta and flung himself at her feet. "I came, my goddess," he said, catching her left hand and kissing it. "I came on the wings of a hundred angels to pay homage to my Venus, my Aphrodite. I am yours to do with as you please, to live or to die at your feet."

She drew back her hand, too quickly he thought, but then he knew that she was a passionate woman.

"Eberau! What does he want?"

Surely a rhetorical question.

She rose and backed away, but in the direction of the bed. He jumped up eagerly and followed. It was a game she wanted, and he looked forward to it. Already he gauged the distance, the heaving bosom. "My beloved," he said and thought, *In a moment, my dear! Oh, how you shall enjoy this.*

She cried, "*Au secours!*"

He stopped and made shushing noises. She had a remarkably loud voice for a gently raised princess. No market woman could have outdone her. Was she calling her French maid? But perhaps the cry for help was part of the game. Yes, surely she had made certain they would be private and wanted him to play the ravisher. He leaped forward and seized Elizabeth Augusta around her ample middle. The impetus carried her back, and they fell across the bed with him on top of her. She struggled and cried out for help, pummeling him with her fists. He pulled apart her silken *negligee* and seized her heaving breasts with firm hands, laughing as she struggled. Reading Captain de Sade's tales would stand him in good stead in this case.

At that moment the doors burst open and people spilled in.

Eberau climbed off the half naked body of the Electress and backed away as he took in the incomprehensible arrival of several large, liveried lackeys. And that was not all, for here came His Highness, the Elector, himself, followed by Moritz.

He realized in an instant that this had been a trap, that he had been set up from the beginning. His hand plunged into his coat pocket and pulled out the pistol.

"Don't touch me!" he snarled at a brawny manservant who came toward him.

Behind him, Elisabeth Augusta, that lying strumpet, wailed accusations. He waved his pistol around the circle of men closing in on him. "Stay away. It's not true," he cried. "She sent for me. She invited me to her bed. What was I to do but obey? I'm her subject."

That was as far as he got. At least six of the lackeys jumped him. The pistol fired, shattering a large mirror. They threw him face down and tied his hands and feet with rope, and then they carried him away, bucking, shouting, and cursing. It took all six to subdue him, and they did not mind how they did it.

# Epilogue

I n time, Stiebel and Augusta were deemed sufficiently recovered for the strenuous homeward journey.

Frau von Langsdorff did not want to leave Mannheim. Seutter had given her generous funds for new clothes for herself and Augusta, and they had been shopping for fabrics and shoes and patterns for robes in the latest French fashion. For once, her interest shifted from herself to Augusta, soon be wed and in need of a trousseau fitting for the wife of a city councilman. Among her friends and neighbors, such splendor must reflect on the bride's mother.

Seutter was so happy that he sometimes felt dizzy. How beautiful his dearest girl was in her fine new clothes and new hairstyle! He was very conscious of his own figure beside hers and took some pains to make himself fashionable. And since the worries and exertions of the past days and weeks had taken his appetite away, his new appearance was a great improvement. Yet in his foolish, loving heart, he knew what he was and would remain: a middle-aged, plain-faced man with too

much belly and too little hair who did not deserve such
happiness.

Stiebel and Franz dealt gingerly with each other.
Franz felt a good deal of shame, and Stiebel was afraid
that his angry outburst had done irreparable harm to
Franz's trust.

Toward the end of their stay in Mannheim, they received a visit. Herr von Moritz, soberly dressed in
black to match a sober face, asked to speak to Stiebel
and Franz privately.

"I trust I see you recovered, sir?" Moritz said to
Stiebel. "I should have been greatly grieved to mourn
your demise along with the other troubles caused by
that unspeakable villain."

Stiebel thanked him and waited.

"As you may have heard—gossip travels on wings
hereabouts—it was thought best to have Eberau confined as a dangerous lunatic. His Highness is very conscious of his spouse's reputation. In truth, I attended
the man's arrest and can attest to his maniacal behavior."

"So all is safe now?" Stiebel asked.

"Oh, yes. He was responsible for all of it. When it
became clear that he posed a danger to the Elector and
herself, Her Highness bravely offered to assist in the
capture. Eberau is now in solitary confinement and will
never be released." He paused and smiled at Stiebel.
"You, sir, must be credited with alerting us to this
threat, and your help has been duly and gratefully noted. But we beg that you will both keep the details of the

unhappy creature's activities to yourself as they might be interpreted wrongly by enemies of the Kurpfalz. May I have your assurance?"

Stiebel and Franz gave it.

Moritz next reached inside his coat and brought forth a fine leather case. Opening it, he displayed a blue enameled cross of heavy gold, resting on a broad deep blue silk ribbon. This he presented to Stiebel. "His Highness wishes you to have this in recognition of your service to the country."

Stiebel's eyes grew large with pleasure. "Dear me, sir. I am speechless."

Moritz smiled. "A conventional expression of appreciation will do quite well."

"Oh, please convey my very humblest thanks to His Highness. Should I make my obeisance in person?"

"No. His Highness knows of your ill health and wishes you a safe journey."

Stiebel fell into a small trance peering at the order. "I hardly deserve . . . what a very handsome thing it is! The golden lion of the Kurpfalz."

"Yes. The order of merit. And well deserved. On the back are His Highness's insignia. Wear it in good health for many years." Moritz bowed and turned to Franz. "His Highness also wishes to express his regrets that you and your sister should have come to some harm from a member of his court." He took a folded paper from his coat and presented it to Franz. "This draft may be drawn on the Kurfürst's banker. Now, if you will allow me, I have some pressing business waiting. *Bon voyage*, gentlemen."

The day before their departure, Franz returned from a trip to Schwetzingen. He had been so secretive about this that Stiebel thought he had gone to see his little actress.

Franz brought back a large covered wicker basket which he carried into Stiebel's room with a look of smug pleasure.

Strange rustlings and soft clucking noises came from the wicker container, and Stiebel eyed it nervously. "What's this?"

"My gift to you, my dear sir. Go ahead, take a look."

Stiebel inspected the strange present. He undid the string that held down the lid and lifted it a little. Two beaked heads crowned with tufts of white feathers emerged from the gap and surveyed the room with bright eyes, chattering to each other.

"Oh, my!" Stiebel breathed. "Oh, my! What very beautiful chickens! Quite the prince and princess of fowls. How did you get them?"

"I persuaded the baron's nephew to part with these two. They're Dutch and quite rare. I thought you might like to raise a flock. A little family."

Stiebel brought out a large white handkerchief, dabbed at his eyes and blew his nose. Then he peered more closely. "Just look at those feathers on their heads—for all the world like plumes. Such regal splendor." He smiled at Franz. "Perhaps we shall have eggs with our breakfasts, Franz."

## About the Author

I. J. Parker was born in Germany. After a university career teaching English and Comparative Literature, she turned to writing. Her mysteries, set in eleventh century Japan, are partially the outcome of research into Asian literature. In 2001, she won the Shamus award for a short story, "Akitada's First Case." The Akitada mysteries have been published by St. Martin's Press, Penguin, and Severn House and are translated into twelve foreign languages. The HOLLOW REED is a two-volume family saga set in twelfth century Japan, THE SWORD MASTER a samurai novel, and THE LEFT-HANDED GOD is the first novel set in her native Germany. She lives and writes in Virginia Beach, Virginia.

Her web site is http://www.ijparker.com. You may contact her from there via e-mail.

Books may be ordered from Amazon and your favorite book store.

Also by I. J. Parker

The Akitada mysteries in chronological order:
*The Dragon Scroll*
*Rashomon Gate*
*Black Arrow*
*Island of Exiles*
*The Hell Screen*
*The Convict's Sword*
*The Masuda Affair*
*The Fires of the Gods*
*Death on an Autumn River*
*The Emperor's Woman*
*Death of a Doll Maker*

The collected stories
*Akitada and the Way of Justice*

The Historical Novels
*The Hollow Reed I: Dream of a Spring Night*
*The Hollow Reed II: Dust before the Wind*
*The Sword Master*
*The Left-Handed God*